I0452579

# DIVINE DISORDER

# THE UNMAKING OF EVERYTHING

### DIVINE DISORDER: BOOK ONE

*Stella Drexler*

An imprint of Diogenes Club Press

Worldly, Whimsical, and Weird Books

www.diogenesclubpress.com

Dallas, TX

Copyright © 2015 by Stella Drexler

All rights reserved. This book, its logos, symbols, images, and likenesses are copyrighted by Author name. No part of this work may be reproduced in any media or format without prior written consent of copyright holder except for limited selections intended for journalistic review.

DC Dreams, an imprint of Diogenes Club Press
8619 Reva St. Dallas, TX 74227
www.diogenesclubpress.com

The characters and events in this book are fictional. Any similarity to real persons, living or dead, is coincidental and not intended by the author.

ISBN: 9781622010301
Library of Congress Control Number: 2015942419

# CHAPTER ONE

*I*t was a sunny day in Aether City. The two men sitting across from each other at a table in a swank outdoor cafe eyed each other warily. They weren't, strictly speaking, especially uncomfortable with each other. On the contrary, they often rather enjoyed each other's company, though on this particular day they felt rather as though there was somewhere else they ought to be, something else they ought to be doing and someone else with whom they ought to be doing it. They were most accurately somewhat uneasy for, though hardly anyone ever paid either of them any attention most of the time, if their respective higher-ups were to discover the clandestine meeting, there would certainly be very severe consequences, which would likely result in neither one of them ever meeting with anyone else ever again, least of all each other.

A brilliant flash of light cast down from the heavens. It blinded the unwary passers-by. It inconvenienced the crisply attired waiters carrying platters of drinks and plates, many of whom stumbled and were subsequently compelled to apologize profusely as their trays crashed to the ground and splattered the angry customers with hot coffee and sandwiches.

A winged, naked man swooped down from the sky and plucked a portly, moustachioed man in a smart pinstriped suit directly off the street. The man barely had time to shriek and wave his arms in a frantic, futile attempt to escape before the angel shot back up into the sky, disappearing in a flare of glorious white, heavenly light.

The two men sitting across from each other at the table in the swank outdoor cafe watched silently. One of them, the dark-haired one in the charcoal and black-checked suit, sighed deeply. "That is the third one this week," said he. "What is your side playing at? I liked that guy."

The other man, the blonde one in the plain black suit lifted his shoulders. "Just think of it as a job well done. Have you been listening to a word I've been saying?"

"Yeah. Yes. Sure. World thrown out of balance and all that. The usual." The dark-haired man was called Darius. It wasn't really his name. His real name would have been impossible to pronounce by an ordinary human tongue, regardless of the infernal origin of said human tongue. Darius had seemed like a good name. It had been between Darius and Ludwig, but he felt more like a Darius. He simply didn't have a taste for powdered wigs.

The blonde man was called Ptolemy. At the time, it had seemed like a very strong and lyrical name, but he had since wished he'd given it a bit more thought. Once you made decisions like that, you had to stick with them. The higher-ups did not appreciate frivolity. His pale face was young and smooth and ethereally handsome, but it was scrunched now into an irritated scowl.

"No, not the usual!" said Ptolemy. "We are facing the potential unmaking of the world as we know it."

Darius did not look impressed. He sipped at the small, delicate coffee cup with his long, slender pinkie extended. The obscenely large diamond sparkling upon his finger caught his attention. He took a moment to admire it before replying. "Your kind is always so dramatic. Honestly, you'd think we don't have people to take care of things like this."

"We do. And this time it's us."

The dark-haired man was not paying attention. He was looking around the cafe, admiring a young, heavy-bottomed waitress leaning over a table of university students and giggling conspiratorially with the young men.

"Beg pardon?" he asked distractedly.

Ptolemy was disgusted. "Darius, for once, pay attention. That absolute fool Zebulon Tan has discovered a way to re-open the gateway to Hao."

"Tan? Never heard of him."

"That's because he's been one of ours!"

"What's he doing opening gates to Hao, then?"

Ptolemy sighed deeply. "He's misguided. He thinks the Haosul Cel can help him."

"Well, who's guiding him to that idea? Not my side. I can tell you that."

"Not all catastrophes are brought on by your side. Sometimes perfectly good people with perfectly good intentions can wreak far more havoc than any of your lot. There's nothing more terrifying than a well-intentioned human utterly convinced of his own righteousness."

"But what has any of this got to do with me? Aren't the Haosul Cel exactly the sort my kind wants coming through?"

Ptolemy slapped his hand down on the table in a fit of pique. "No! There is a reason they don't let their sort into our world. They are creatures of pure chaos. If they're allowed to run amok, they will turn this world into a wasteland. It will be the end of everything. Of us, of you, of all the rest of it. No more street cafes or garden parties or fancy dress or fine wine."

Darius gasped, appalled.

Ptolemy nodded in agreement. "No more mucking about on terra firma pretending to be a normal human. No more physical bodies. If we did survive, which we probably would not, we would be nothing more than shapeless bits of ether and dreams and disassociated thoughts."

Darius looked slightly uneasy, though he was as yet unconvinced of the immediacy of the danger. "This sort of thing just doesn't happen, Ptolemy. There are safeguards against it. The higher-ups won't allow it."

"Don't be a fool. This sort of thing is happening all the time. The world is constantly on the verge of utter devastation."

"Well, I've never heard about it."

"That's because we always stop it before it gets to that!"

"I didn't think that was your job. Doesn't your side usually just deal with the aftermath?"

Ptolemy sighed. "Usually. Occasionally our higher-ups feel it's necessary to involve ourselves before a seemingly innocuous event destroys the entire world."

"Well, do it then," Darius said, flicking his fingers.

The blonde man ground his teeth. "Obviously, if I could, I would. My side can't do anything about it."

"Why not?"

"Because Tan hasn't done anything wrong! You know the rules; his intentions are pure. It's outside our jurisdiction."

Darius was still unconvinced, and he preferred to avoid helping if he could. "Didn't they close off connections with Hao centuries ago? I didn't think anyone could open a gate. I thought the seal was unbreakable."

"It was supposed to be, but you know what it's like. With all those gods of ambiguity and narrow escapes, nothing stays hidden forever."

The dark-haired man scoffed. "But how did he even find out about them?

I mean, it isn't as if anyone is going about advertising the Haosul Cel are a peaceful, fun-loving bunch and let them out for a nice time. The higher-ups took measures to conceal them from the humans! Not to mention isn't opening a gate to Hao extremely difficult?"

"Sure. Of course it is. But it's not impossible. You just need the combination."

"But how did the human find it?" Darius demanded. "It's not exactly written in any manuscripts or--" He swept his serviette from his lap and waved it at the blonde man. "--on a cocktail napkin."

Ptolemy's eyes slid away. He looked extremely uncomfortable. "Actually...it is."

"What?" Darius spoke through clenched teeth.

"Well, not a cocktail napkin, as such. More of a...scrap bit of paper."

"And how did he find it?"

The blonde man's boyish features set in a grim expression. He slid a business card across the table with long, pale fingers. Darius snatched it up and read it with a slight frown. *Lucian. He Who Finds Things Long Forgotten. 6 Silverbranch Square.* He didn't frown often; it caused wrinkles, and he found the expenditure of energy required to smooth them back again could be applied in much more pleasurable and rewarding ways. This, however, was a time in which a frown was so necessary he would simply have to skip the manifestation of certain anatomical elements he'd planned for later that evening.

He cleared his throat delicately. "I see. It seems as though Lucian has forgotten to mention the bit about 'and Best Left Lost.'"

"Yes," Ptolemy replied dryly. "That little omission hadn't escaped my notice, either. I suspect its inclusion would be slightly bad for business. Are you going to do something about this or not?"

Darius leaned back to sip his espresso. His face flushed in embarrassment. "Well...but my side probably commissioned it. It sounds like exactly the sort of thing they'd want to happen."

"But you don't, Darius. Think of all the things you'll miss."

His voice needled, and a look of intense unhappiness crossed Darius' face. "You don't know the sorts of things my kind does to traitors."

Ptolemy wasn't impressed. "Probably very similar things to what mine does."

"It's this damnable duty. I mean, we exist to do a specific job. You go a little off the beaten path, maybe do a kind deed or help an old lady across the street, and you're sent off to burn in the fiery pits of hell for the rest of eternity. It's so arbitrary. There's no middle ground. You're either crusading for the triumph of evil over good or you're being introduced to hitherto undiscovered heights of misery and torment that just go on and on, and so much for second chances, I tell you—"

"Can we focus, please?"

"I am focussing! I am focussing on exactly how bad of an idea getting involved in this is."

Ptolemy rolled his eyes. "Can you, for once, think of something other than yourself?"

This was completely unfathomable to Darius. "It is intrinsically contrary to my nature to do so."

"All right then," Ptolemy snapped. "Are you prepared to give all of this up? Even if we do manage to survive somehow, there are no cappuccinos on the ethereal planes, no theatres, no upscale nightclubs, no silk suits, no ostentatious jewellery, no sensual massages..."

Darius sighed. "Yes, all right. I'll see what I can do. No promises."

"No women..."

"All right, all right! I know someone. But if my side hears about this, I'm finished."

"I can take care of your side. Stop worrying. I can give you some time in which no one will be watching. Use it wisely."

Darius stared at him. Finally, he closed his eyes and hitched a deep, long-suffering sigh. "Right. Fine. All right. If that's it, then."

"That's it."

"Terrific." Darius rose to his feet. He bent in a low, ironic bow to the blonde-haired man. Then he snapped his fingers and, with a small pop, he disappeared in a small puff of smoke.

Ptolemy waved his hand in front of his face and sighed. The smoke smelled faintly of sulphur.

\* \* \*

*Meanwhile, night falls in Penthos...*

A woman in a long, black dress stood alone beside a tombstone in a bleak graveyard. She had dressed for the occasion. She was very beautiful. She prided herself on her great beauty, though no one was there to see her tonight. She was not concerned with this. It was enough to know she was beautiful, and she would have company soon enough. She intended to make a good showing.

Her name was Imogen, but there were few left alive who knew it. There would be one less before the night was through.

The white stone grave seemed to glow in the pale moonlight. The words upon it shimmered.

*Mercy Song*

*Taken too soon, My Beloved*

*In Death may we be united again*

Imogen's lips curved into a malicious smile. She raised her arms to the sky. She spoke in a low, musical voice. The incantation was so ancient, so foreign, no one left in Pandia but the darkest and oldest of magicians even remembered it had ever existed at all. The words crescendoed into a high, intense, resonating note, and then they trailed away into the silence of the night. She lowered her hands. Then she waited.

Moments passed. There was silence. Even the birds didn't sing in this lonely, desolate place.

The grave seemed to sigh. It rumbled, quietly. Then it stopped.

Imogen waited. The barren ground beneath her feet lurched and roiled. She took a step back. The earth where she'd been standing split and a small, pale hand broke the surface. It clawed and clutched the dirt around the grave, and the body of a young woman rose slowly out of the ground.

She was only recently dead. Her thin, white silk dress was streaked with dirt. Her hair had once been brilliant copper and gold, but it looked dull now in the pale moonlight and matted with the earth from around her former resting place. She had been in the ground but days, and though her flesh was mottled and grey, the vestiges of her former beauty still remained upon her face. Her pale blue eyes were milky and hollow.

The dead girl stood perfectly still, like a puppet without strings that awaited its master's expert hand. There was no spirit within her. Imogen took a moment to admire her. She smiled, and then she raised her arms again. This time her cry was wild and forceful, and it did not fade away into the darkness. The chant went on and on as though it had taken over the enchantress' throat.

Slowly, a wispy, smoke-like figure shimmered into existence before the enchantress. It grew more and more opaque until its resemblance to the reanimated dead woman was striking. It looked different than the corpse. It looked younger and more alive, though it was only a spirit and Imogen could have struck a hand through the smoky substance, dissolving it into nothing more than wisps of icy cold air. The young woman's spirit looked terribly, heartbreakingly sad, as though mourning the utopia from which it had been so cruelly ripped.

Then the spirit's face twisted in an expression of absolute horror. It shivered. It flailed wildly and clawed at the air, fighting the inexorable pull that was suddenly sucking it toward the still lifeless body it had once inhabited. Mercy Song's spirit seemed to be screaming. Its mouth opened, but no sound escaped its translucent lips.

The body jolted suddenly as the spirit rushed back inside the rotting, ex-animate husk. The dead girl's eyes lit with a gruesome, abominable life that only the darkest, most horrible magic could bestow. She looked about the forsaken graveyard around her like a trapped, hunted animal. Her reanimated body quivered as though it was attempting to fight against the bonds holding it in this macabre half-life.

Imogen's laugh was soft at first, and then it intensified until it crashed and rolled over the barren landscape. Mercy Song flinched. She flailed wildly. Her body lurched and jerked, but it moved not a step. The brief flicker of hope that had crossed her waxen features snuffed out.

The enchantress smiled. "Now. In death shall you be reunited. And much sooner than he anticipated, I expect."

\* \* \*

*Meanwhile, in a place that is neither here nor there...*

A young, lanky, awkward-looking man in a black and white striped blazer and baggy, bright yellow pants stood outside the entrance to a seedy-looking bar. The old, wooden sign over the door read **The Dirty Damastes** in faded gold letters. It looked nothing like the sort of place one would expect to find any sort of god, except perhaps those who enjoyed hanging around lushes, criminals and other dodgy characters.

There was a wary expression on the young man's pale, freckled face. He did not approach any closer to the place. He tried to straighten the miniature top hat on his thick, curly mop of flaming red hair, but the hat slipped immediately, settling at a skew-whiff angle that might have looked jaunty on a less ungainly man. He sighed deeply. It had been a very disappointing day.

A woman glided to his side, pausing to peer up at the battered wooden sign. The young man turned to her, and his cheeks flushed. She was very tall and so beautiful, his breath caught in his throat. She looked to be ten years his elder or more. She had long, dark hair that tumbled in waves across her shoulders and down her back. Her black cloak billowed out behind her. He knew her instantly for what she was. She was, he was quite sure, just like him. Well, not exactly like him, he suspected. There was an air of mysterious confidence about her that unsettled him.

She smiled indulgently. "First time?"

He opened and closed his mouth, but no sound came out. "Oh, uh, yes, actually," he finally stammered. "It is."

She inclined her head. There was something patronizing in her smile, but he didn't mind. She was the most beautiful thing he had ever seen. It didn't matter he hadn't seen many things so far. He was sure she would outshine anything. "It's always a little overwhelming the first time. Why don't you join me?"

He blushed scarlet and shuffled his feet. "Thanks." He dug his hands into his capacious black and white striped blazer and drew a deck of brightly coloured cards from the large, bottomless pockets. He riffled the cards nervously. "Would you like to see a trick?"

"No."

She stepped forward and pushed open the door to the Dirty Damastes. The young man followed closely on her heels, watching the subtle sway of her hips in the tight red dress as the cloak shifted, revealing quick, exciting flashes of her body beneath. As the woman strode inside with her magnificent head held high, the eyes of every man in the room turned to her. She ignored them, walking towards a table in the back of the crowded, dusty bar.

As she passed, the men in her path clutched at their hearts as though the sensitive organs were causing them terrible pain. She didn't seem to notice them at all. The young man looked around nervously, shrinking back as the same eyes swivelled to him with hatred and jealousy. He avoided the venomous gazes and tried not to watch the woman's backside as he followed her; he suspected, though she was being rather kind to him, she would not appreciate his ogling eye.

She paused at a table in a curiously empty area of the bar. It appeared as though the patrons avoided the two men and one woman who sat hunched over their drinks, peering languidly around them with varying degrees of boredom. They didn't look like much, but the young man knew he didn't, either. They looked up at the woman as she approached and noticed the young man behind her. They lifted their eyebrows in interest.

"Who's your friend, Love?" The man who spoke was slender and nondescript. His hair was pale but not quite blonde, and his features were even though not quite handsome. He peered at the young man through eyes that were not exactly green and not quite blue. He possessed the sort of face which a person might easily forget, thought it was memorable enough to cause one some inconvenience in the recall, as a name on the tip of the tongue or a fleeting thought that was gone before it could be fully explored.

"Love?" the young man repeated.

She tossed her long, dark hair. "Of the Unrequited variety."

The woman sitting between the two men at the table leaned forward eagerly. She was a petite, ragged-looking person with choppy, uneven hair dyed a bright, electric blue, thick black makeup on her lips and on her eyes, and several piercings in her face. Her cheeks were flushed, and the young man suspected she'd been at the bottle rather a while. "Are you new?"

"What are you called?" asked the other man, a short, burly and outrageously hirsute man with curly, gnarly black hair on his head and face.

"Oh, uh, I—well, I'm not called anything," the young man admitted. "Not yet. I'm new, you see." His eyes followed Unrequited Love in disappointment as she slid into the seat next to the ordinary-looking man. She ignored them both utterly and lifted a hand to a waitress across the room. The young man in the striped blazer and miniature top hat sat beside the woman with blue hair.

"Well, what do you do?" the featureless man asked. He did not seem affected by the woman beside him, though she threw the cloak from her shoulders, revealing bare arms and a long, graceful neck that drew the eyes of nearly every other man in the bar.

"Uh, magic tricks. Well, not very well, actually. You could say I do Poorly Executed Magic Tricks." The young man's cheek flushed in embarrassment.

"What, like card tricks and optical illusions and such?" said the hirsute man.

11

"Um, yes. I can pull a coin out of your ear. Except I'd probably muck it up somehow and kerchiefs would come out your...erm. Well, I pulled a rabbit out of a hat once."

"That sounds nice," Unrequited Love said absently.

"It was dead."

"Phil," the blue-haired woman burst out suddenly. "We'll call you Phil. You look like a Phil."

The hirsute man scowled at her. "He doesn't either. Don't listen to her. You can't trust her judgement."

"Well, that's true," the blue-haired woman said with a thoughtful nod. "But it isn't my fault. I didn't choose to be Severe Errors in Judgement."

"No, but you would have," Unrequited Love replied scornfully.

Severe Errors in Judgement considered this a moment. She sighed. "Yes. Probably so."

The newly christened Poorly Executed Magic Tricks opened his mouth to speak, but he snapped it shut again. There were two men approaching their table on the empty side of the bar. One was short and plump and balding, and his suit looked expensive and well tailored. The other was tall and beanpole thin, and he wore plain black from head to foot.

Unrequited Love signed in resignation. "Oh, no. It's them."

The two new men reached the table. They were both smiling happily. Despite her remark, Unrequited Love beamed hugely at them. Poorly Executed Magic Tricks was new to the world, but even he could see it was a false smile. The two men did not seem to notice.

"Hey, guys!" the tall, thin man said. His hair was over-long. He required a haircut, though there was something in his air that suggested he had little interest in such mundane matters as his personal appearance, which was ghastly.

"Hi," the young man's first and only friends replied unenthusiastically.

"Can we have a seat?" the fat one asked keenly. His dark, beady eyes glinted with an almost manic intensity. "I really want a seat."

A silent, collective sigh passed across the table, but Severe Errors in Judgment grinned widely and gestured the two new arrivals cheerfully. "Sure. Yeah! 'Course you can."

The three others beside her at the table glared angrily at her. The short, fat man and the tall, thin man didn't seem to notice the ire of Unrequited Love and her companions. They sat down.

The moment they did, a series of strange events occurred.

A short, skinny man with a pimpled face hugged a beautiful blonde woman around the waist, dragging on the floor and clinging onto her as she attempted to shove him off and escape his unwanted attentions. His mouth twisted down into a hideous, desperate plea.

At the same time, a man in a crisp business suit sitting at the bar knocked over his drink and spilled it across the pile of very important looking papers in front of him.

Meanwhile, a large, drunken man with a shaved head and several faded, greying tattoos followed, hand in hand, a dubious-looking woman out of the bar. The unconvincing woman was thick and muscular, and her tight red dress bulged in rather the wrong places. She had a thick uni-brow and a dark five-o'clock shadow across her chin, cheeks and above her lip.

A small, hairy creature flew out from behind the bar, fangs bared and claws extended. It squealed maliciously as it leapt upon the face of an unsuspecting man awaiting his drink at the bar. The man stumbled back, flailing his arm.

"Aagh! Animal attack!" His scream was garbled and horribly wet.

"Where did that come from?" a waitress asked, staring in shock as the hairy creature abruptly tired of its victim and leapt down to the floor to scurry away. The man clutched at his face as ribbons of ruby red blood dripped through his fingers. The waitress patted his back ineffectually.

The hirsute man looked unconvincingly innocent.

A tall, lanky man in a purple suit posed before a group of very pretty women, attempting to perform a most impressive magic trick. He fumbled, and the cards flew from his clumsy fingers in every direction. The women laughed and turned back to each other, sipping their drinks and forgetting him utterly.

Poorly Executed Magic Tricks watched all of this with a look of concern, but his companions seemed not to have noticed.

The beanpole thin man was speaking to him. "So, you're new, are you?"

"Oh. Yes."

"What's your thing?" the fat man demanded. His eyes burned with some

13

intense, almost creepy need that caused Poorly Executed Magic Tricks some unease. "Can I see your cards? I really like your cards."

"Don't give him anything," Unrequited Love said austerely.

Poorly Executed Magic Tricks was confused. He looked back at the thin man. "I do magic tricks."

"Can we see one?" the fat man asked. "I really want to see one."

"Uh, maybe later." The young man blushed. "So what's it like being—um—well, being a god?"

"You get used to it," the featureless man told him in a weary sort of voice. He reached for his drink, and his fingers fumbled. The glass tipped and spilled its sticky, amber contents into Poorly Executed Magic Trick's lap.

Tricks, as he'd come to consider himself in the last few minutes, jumped to his feet, mopping at the spreading spot on his trousers with a cocktail napkin.

"Oh, sorry about that, my friend," the ordinary man said. He looked extremely embarrassed. "I can't exactly help it."

The young man sighed. "It's all right. It's only a Minor Inconvenience. Are you Clumsiness?"

The ordinary man's cheeks flushed. "No."

"Then what—? Oh."

"I wish I was Clumsiness," the fat man said as if to himself. "He's got a great temple. Worshippers days and night. They leave wine offerings all over the floor."

"Not on purpose," the thin man said scornfully.

"You have a temple," the hirsute man told the fat man in exasperation. "A big one. All ivory pillars and gold trim."

The fat man shook his head. His jowls quivered. "But I want *his* temple!"

"And you have an entire order of nuns to do your bidding," Minor Inconveniences added.

"But they're not very attractive nuns. Ill-Gotten Gains has loads of busty, blonde nuns. I want *his* nuns."

Tricks wasn't listening anymore. He was looking around the bar. Something very strange was happening. In fact, many strange things were happening.

A skinny man in a black top hat attempted to draw a bouquet of flowers from his sleeve and present it to the pretty black-haired woman at the bar. As he pulled it out, petals flew everywhere, and the skinny man looked down at his bunch of empty stems with an abashed expression. The black-haired woman rolled her eyes and turned away from him in distaste. Beside her, a large, muscular man in a tight tee shirt appeared, wrapping an arm around her waist. His dark eyes watched the failed performer with increasing irritation.

The performer held up a finger as he searched through his pockets. He seemed unable to discover that for which he was looking. He drew a kerchief from the capacious pocket on his hip. More kerchiefs followed until they pooled at his feet. He looked embarrassed, for this seemed not to be his intention. He scowled and shook the kerchiefs from his hand. They clung stubbornly to his fingers.

The black-haired woman's large, muscular boyfriend moved toward him with a forbidding expression. A look of panic crossed the skinny man's face. He began to back away, but the crowd suddenly thickened around him, and he was unable to make a hasty escape through the wall of people blocking his path. As if to ward off his large aggressor, the skinny man stuck his hands into his pockets, tossing whatever he could reach into the air between them: a deck of cards, which fluttered around them ineffectually, a rubber chicken, which squeaked and bounced off the large man's solid chest, and a wand that blossomed with bright, orange flowers.

The performer whipped off his black top hat. From inside the hat, a rabbit hopped out. It flew at the performer's surprised face, its teeth and fangs bared. The unfortunate performer screamed, flailing wildly as he attempted to pry the vicious rabbit from him. The muscular man paused and stared at him a moment in shock. Then he burst into laughter.

Tricks turned back to his companions, who appeared still oblivious to the spectacle around them. "Does this sort of thing always happen when we get together?" he asked.

"No," Unrequited Love replied testily. "Only when DC's here." She jerked her head towards the beanpole thin man.

Tricks glanced at him in confusion. "DC?"

"Direct Correlations."

"What, like Cause and Effect?"

Direct Correlations swelled in consternation. "No, not like Cause and Effect.

15

There's a difference. Just because there is a link between two things, it doesn't necessarily mean one causes the other, thank you very much, Unrequited Love."

She tossed her head dismissively. "Whatever. It's all the same to me. It still happens."

"Now, Adultery," the fat man said suddenly. "He has a great temple." He rubbed his hands together eagerly. "What I wouldn't give to get my hands on his temple."

The hirsute man turned back to Tricks. "It's not bad, being a god. You learn to live with it after a while. You sort of stop noticing what's happening around you."

Minor Inconveniences frowned. "You might."

The fat man leaned across the table towards the hirsute man. "Can I have a drink of your wine? I really want to try your wine."

"You have your own!"

"But I want yours!"

"Oh, will you please get Covetousness out of here before I directly correlate my fist to his face?" Unrequited Love snapped angrily.

Direct Correlations was highly offended. "Right. Fine. We're leaving, then. Sorry for the Minor Inconvenience."

Minor Inconvenience glared at him. "Oh, very cute. Very witty."

"We'll just see what Meekness and Low Self-Esteem are doing. They may not be the--" Direct Correlations made quotation marks in the air with his long, skinny fingers. "--'cool kids,' but at least they're not elitist jerks." He seized Covetousness by the collar and yanked him to his feet.

Covetousness did not want to go. He reached desperately towards the table, making grabbing motions in the air with his fingers as Direct Correlations dragged him away. "But I want this table!"

Unrequited Love snorted in disgust. "Those two. They always manage to ruin a perfectly good night."

"They aren't half as bad as Poorly Timed Evil Monologues, though," Minor Inconveniences put in, rolling his eyes. "That bastard will talk your ear off explaining in excruciating detail all the dastardly ways he plans to ruin your night. Never gets around to it, though, does he?"

Tricks frowned. "It's who's handing out these powers is what I want to know. I mean, God of Poorly Executed Magic Tricks? Honestly, who needs a god for that?"

"Even failed magicians need a patron god," Severe Errors in Judgment said reasonably. "It makes them feel as if there's some divine purpose behind the whole thing."

The hirsute man tugged on his wiry black beard. "It's the humans. It's like they need a patron god to tell them when to change their underpants."

"They have one," said Minor Inconveniences. "The God of Uncomfortably Soiled Underthings. He's a bastard."

"I mean, what sort of followers does the God of Poorly Executed Magic Tricks get?" Tricks asked. "It's an endless procession of amputated assistants and people who levitate on the heels of their feet and forget to tuck their thumb when they pretend to pull it off. It's all so depressing."

"Don't start having a go at your followers now," Severe Errors in Judgment warned, wagging a finger in the air. "They're the only thing keeping you from fading into non-existence."

"For once, Severe Errors in Judgment is right," the hirsute man said. "We're immortal and all that, sure, but that doesn't mean we can't snuff it if the humans forget about us."

"The followers aren't so bad, really," Unrequited Love told him. "As long as you don't communicate with them in an official capacity."

Tricks tried to avoid staring at her. "What do you mean?"

"Don't tell them who you are," Severe Errors in Judgment explained. "Trust me. I did that once. It did not go well."

"Sure, you might get a flashy temple or an order of nuns, but you'd be nothing better than a cult leader. It's an embarrassment to us all," Unrequited Love explained. "If people were meant to be aware of us, they would. We wouldn't go about living normal lives and keeping a low profile."

"It's plausible deniability," Minor Inconveniences continued. "I mean, if people knew gods were running about all over the place, they would expect miracles and divine solutions all the time. We'd never get any rest."

The hirsute man shook his head in exasperation. "Not to mention if you muck anything up. Humans expect infallibility from their gods."

"The quandary there is who created us," said Unrequited Love. "How can an imperfect race expect its creations to be flawless? It's just illogical if you ask me."

Severe Errors in Judgment sighed as she gestured the waitress for another drink. "They want to be able to relate to us is the problem. No one wants some supreme ruling god up there knowing everything and playing some convoluted game of cosmic Solitaire without anyone to make sure he isn't really just pulling one big, complicated joke on everyone. It's inherently contradictory to human sovereignty. They need to believe they don't need us because they are in control of their own destiny."

"And when they realise they are, it all falls apart from there," added the hirsute man.

"It's not wanting to take responsibility, I tell you," Minor Inconveniences said. "They want free will and control over their own cosmos, and when they muck it up and everything goes horribly wrong, they want someone else to blame."

"And who do they look at?" Unrequited Love demanded. "Us. That's who, and it's not like you can say 'Right, well, it's not my fault I was made this way. Whose fault is that, hm?' So, it's best just not to let them know we're here at all. Saves us all a lot of trouble."

Tricks sighed. "Right. Well, I expect a lot of my followers would be none too pleased to discover it's my fault they can't manage to get the handcuffs unlocked before they drown in a big tank of water."

The hirsute man shook his head. "It doesn't really work that way. I mean, we personify the thing, yeah, but we didn't create the thing. Quite the contrary. The thing created us, in a manner of speaking."

They were all silent a moment as Tricks considered this. The information was somewhat overwhelming this soon after his recent divine manifestation. It was always overwhelming at first. It wasn't easy discovering you'd just blinked into existence one day to personify the next big thing—or the next foolish, embarrassing thing.

"Are there any sorts of gods of pleasant things?" he asked. "It's just that I've noticed we all seem to be sort of...well, sort of crap gods, to be frank."

The other glanced at each other. They didn't seem to be offended by his remark.

"Yeah," Minor Inconveniences sighed. "We are."

Unrequited Love waved her hand. "They don't hang around this bar."

"Can you be promoted?" Tricks asked. "I mean, can you become the god of something better, if you're really good at your job? It's just that I don't want to have to be bad at something all the time."

"Can you be really good at being bad?" the hirsute man asked thoughtfully.

"'Course you can!" Severe Errors in Judgment replied positively.

"Anyway, it doesn't matter," Unrequited Love told him. "You're stuck with it. You don't get to pick something you like better. It's just the way it is. You'd better just get used to the idea."

Tricks was disappointed.

"Buck up. There is something we're all good at."

As though they'd been prompted, the gods cheerfully held up their glasses. "Drinking!" they said in unison.

They all drank, and then they drank some more. It was a dreary existence, theirs. You took what you could get. Tricks showed them a few of his tricks. They failed miserably, but the others laughed.

"I suppose you don't have to be good to make people happy."

Unrequited Love smiled. "People are much happier watching other people fail. Never underestimate your own charm."

Tricks smiled dreamily at her. "You're so nice. I love you."

She tossed her hair. "I don't love you back. You're simply too bad at magic."

Severe Errors in Judgment smiled across the table at the freckled young god. "I'll go out with you."

Tricks grinned and held up his glass. "To being a crap god!"

The others held up their glasses. "Here, here."

They didn't sound as enthusiastic as before.

# CHAPTER TWO

The sun was bright, but the dodgy-looking street in the centre of Hyperion City was gloomy, as though a dark cloud had singled it out and crouched overhead, waiting silently for the right moment to strike. The thoroughfare was eerily quiet, despite the number of people bustling along in their shabby work clothes. Most of the people in this part of the city were the decent, hard-working sort; they went about their business without bothering their neighbours or causing trouble. There were others, though, that looked rather sinister, lurking about in the darker corners as though they were looking for something unsavoury to do with their day. They didn't bother the respectable working people as they passed, however; their business was evidently more sophisticated than pickpocketing or swindling, and no one who passed by had much to steal, anyway.

Darius stood outside a clean, innocuous-looking pale brick building. No one spoke to him. They avoided his gaze as they passed as though he was one of the more sinister folks lurking about, but even the shiftiest, toughest-looking of the sinister lot dared not approach him. It was just as well; he had little time for such trifles at the moment. The world with all its theatres and sidewalk cafes and beautiful women and sensual massages was at stake, after all.

The sign on the door before him read Sho Sange and Associates. For Hire.

There was nothing to indicate what sort of business it was, but those who needed Sho Sange and his associates hardly required such fanfare. If one did not already understand the nature of his business, they likely did not need him or they more likely could not afford him.

Darius did, and he could. And though he might have liked to have done, he did not have the time to stand around outside the unadorned building listening to the thoughts and intentions of the dodgy characters lingering in the streets with cagey, watchful eyes. He yanked open the door with rather more force than was strictly necessary.

There were no windows in the large room. The walls were covered in clocks of all shapes and sizes, though none of them kept the same time. One of them, surely, at least told the correct time, though it was hard to say which, as the hands seemed to spin and bend and twist into odd shapes just as one looked at them, as though they were charmed to confuse their observer. Amulets and totems of strange creatures covered the remaining space and were scattered on the small tables and shelves spread randomly through the room.

The chairs were arranged in odd places around the room, far apart from each other, for it was generally assumed that these people's clients would be averse to conversing with each other, should they find themselves arriving in the same place at the same time. There was, however, hardly ever anyone sitting around and waiting in the room.

On the far west wall, a winding staircase led up to the second floor where, Darius understood, Sho and most of his associates lived. The team spent the majority of their time out of the office in the field or in the private workshops and offices concealed behind doors similarly adorned with the wily clocks and esoteric amulets. As such, there was no one attending the large, littered reception desk in the centre of the room. It did look as though someone might have been sitting there moments ago. A still steaming mug of some hot liquid nestled amidst papers which stuck about all over the place amongst numerous unidentifiable and likely inoperable gadgets and charms either broken or in their earliest stages of development.

The place bore a distinctly disreputable air, like the laboratory of a mad scientist or a depraved sorcerer's workroom; it was difficult to say which. Above the large, cluttered desk was an enormous brass bell pull. Darius stepped forward and yanked the bit of rope. Somewhere inside the large, high-walled building, the bell clanged urgently.

Darius waited. Nothing happened. He waited a bit longer. He tapped his foot impatiently.

He stepped back toward the desk to ring the bell again then paused with his hand beneath the rope. There was a scurrying noise in the room behind one of the curiously decorated doors. A young woman with thick, wavy caramel-coloured hair burst from it into the lobby. She was very compact, and she wore a long, red and white striped waistcoat over calfskin breeches and tall black boots with gaiters. Around her waist was a tool belt that looked stark, as though she had used the tools and failed to return them to their places afterwards.

Her dark eyes were lit with excitement, but when she saw Darius, she slouched with disappointment. She slumped into the spinning chair behind the desk. "Oh, it's you."

Darius lifted his eyebrows, but he did not make any response to this rude reception.

The young woman spun around and shouted over her shoulder. "Sho, it's for you!"

The man in the black and charcoal suit rolled his eyes in disgust. An unusually tall man in black appeared so silently around a corner, even Darius had scarcely heard him enter. The man was near to seven feet tall. He was slightly built, but he looked strong enough. It was hardly his physical prowess, though as rumour had it quite impressive, for which he was so highly sought in his particular profession. His snow white hair was combed neatly back. Though it was over-long, looking as though it required a trim, it stayed neatly out of his eyes, knowing better than to irritate the unforgiving man, lest it be removed completely from his person with prejudice.

Sho Sange was still a young man, and he carried himself with a subtle, mysterious confidence that seemed infused into his every move and gesture. He hardly looked up at his client as he strode into the room. He seemed only vaguely aware he'd been called and that there was anyone else in the room with him. He scowled down at the blood red parchment in his hands. The parchment was covered in a tight, spidery black scrawl.

"Who is it, Panya?" he asked without bothering to look for himself. The contents of his letter must have been troubling indeed; the expression in his gunmetal grey eyes was tempestuous.

Panya, the young woman who had greeted Darius with such grace and professionalism, shot her boss a reproachful look. Darius cleared his throat.

"It's your special friend," she announced proudly.

Sho did not look up from his letter. "Huh?"

Panya beamed at Darius. "It's the flash bastard in the expensive suits."

Now Sho's head snapped up. He tucked the letter into the pocket of his black jacket. "Oh, it's you."

Darius' mouth twisted wryly. "Such service, Sho. It is no wonder your lobby is so jam packed with clients." He gave Panya a pointed look, but she merely lifted her hand to shoot him an obscene gesture in response.

She spun round wildly in the chair then vaulted out of it, flipping several times in the air before landing smartly on her feet. "Yes, fine. I'll leave you two alone."

Sho watched her flit silently from the room. Then he turned back to Darius with an expression of weary resignation. "What is it, then? What can I do for you today, Darius?"

22

Darius puffed out his chest and tried to look very cool. "I need a very small, inconsequential favour."

The tall man lifted a dark eyebrow. Darius was unsure whether the young man had changed the colour of his hair or his eyebrows. He often wondered if he'd done either; Sho's people were unusual, indeed. The man in the dark suit often wondered if the dark line around Sho's eyes was natural or if he painted it on everyday to look more intimidating. Indeed, he looked quite intimidating, and a weaker, less infernal man might have actually quelled under his stormy gaze.

"By favour," said Sho wryly, "I assume you mean work that pays?"

Darius waved his hand dismissively in the air, as if this suggestion was highly insulting. "Yes, yes. For the usual fee, of course."

Sho crossed his arms over his chest. He realized as he watched the smaller, dark-haired man, that something was quite wrong. Darius was rarely so flustered as he appeared today, despite his attempts to look completely untroubled. It was not often that even a Darklord could gain the upper hand on one of Darius' sort. Sho smirked. He was going to deeply enjoy taking the piss. "What is it, then?"

"A small matter that needs...clearing up."

"By small matter, I assume you mean horrendously tricky task that will probably get one of my people killed and which you are too lazy to do on your own?"

Darius hitched a deep sigh. "Now, Sho, you are very uncharitable today. Have I ever sent you out on such an errand for selfish reasons?"

"Yes."

"Oh, all right, I would, and I have. But I assure you; this is not one of those times. This really is a small matter of...tremendous importance."

"Ah. One of those."

"Naturally I would simply take care of it myself, only...it's not exactly the sort of thing my, ah, employers would approve."

Sho eyed him a long moment. The dark-haired man in the dark suit wrung his hands. "I see. So we'll be working on behalf of the good guys this time? That's rather unexpected and morally gratifying."

"If you like."

"What is it, then?"

"Well, there's a bit of something...just a small matter, you understand, going on at the Gwydion Academy of Advanced Sorcery."

Sho strode to the desk Panya had recently vacated and sat down in the spinning chair. "Stop wasting my time with cryptic rubbish, Darius. I'm a busy man."

Darius scoffed. "Oh, yes, I can see. You're simply overrun with interested paying clients. Why, I had to fight my way through just to secure this thus far highly productive audience."

"Let's hear it, then."

Darius pulled up a chair across from Sho at the desk. His back was rigid, and he folded his hands in his lap. "Zebulon Tan, one of the professors at Gwydion, you see, is planning to open a gate to Hao."

"What the hell is Hao?"

"It's not important," Darius said impatiently. "What is important is that he is stopped. At all costs."

"Why?"

Darius ground his teeth. "Does it matter?"

"I am attempting to suss the actual urgency of the matter at hand."

"Fine. If he is successful, he will unmake the entire universe."

Sho considered this silently for a moment. Darius was not the sort to make wildly dramatic statements without at least some basis in truth. "All right. I now appreciate the urgency of the matter."

"I am so pleased. This is a matter of extreme delicacy, you understand." He hesitated. He squirmed uncomfortably in his seat. Sho had never seen the man squirm. It was rather unsettling. "It is something in which I most emphatically should not be involved."

"Ah. I see. Ptolemy put you up to it."

Darius shot him a glare. His dark eyes glowed red for a split second. "I don't want to hear that conniving bastard's name."

Sho grinned back at him. "So what is it exactly that you would like us to do?"

"Just stop him."

"Ptolemy?"

"No, not Ptolemy! Tan."

"How?"

"Well, I don't know! Tie him up. Lock him in a closet. Kill him if you have to."

"You know, that is not exactly what we are in the business of doing here."

"Think of something else, then! This is your job. If I knew what to do, I wouldn't have to hire you, would I?"

"All right. How exactly is Tan planning to open this gate?"

"He's gotten hold of a spell. One that was supposed to be very difficult to find."

"What's the spell? How did he get it?"

These questions were not, in Darius' estimation, productive. "Look, I don't hire you to ask a lot of questions. In fact, that you do not ask questions is the principal reason I work with you."

"All right. Do you know how far he has come in completing the spell, then?"

"No." Darius looked miserable.

"So you want my team to get inside the school and stop Tan from completing the spell which will open a gate to Hao which will, one way or another, unmake the entire universe, but you don't have any idea how far he's gotten or how to stop him short of killing him."

"Yes. That is it exactly. Very succinct."

Sho rose abruptly. "I can't do it."

Darius' carefully arranged face went instantly purple. He shot to his feet. "What?!"

The tall man seemed unaffected by the ire of the dark-haired man in the dark suit. "There is a matter to which I must attend in Scathach. My father's best friend, Darklord Spirit, has died. My father has requested my immediate return to the Darklands. I cannot refuse him at such a time."

"You're all I have!"

"I understand that."

"If Tan is successful, there will be no Darklands!"

Sho sighed. "Were that that were true."

"It seems to me you are, in fact, failing to grasp the urgency of the matter at hand. No sensual massages...no women..."

"That will do, Darius. There are several other members on my team. I cannot personally attend to the matter, but there are others who are fully capable of stopping one old man from unmaking the entire world."

Darius brightened. "I want Oni!"

Sho's expression was stern. "I told you. We aren't going to kill him."

The other man looked highly disappointed.

"I was going to ask Oni to accompany me to Scathach, but as you are a very... special client, I will concede to abandon the idea."

"Oh, gee. I am sincerely indebted. I'm quite reassured that the fate of the entire world, not to mention my long-standing weekly appointment with Enid, a very highly skilled masseuse, by the way, does in fact take preference to your personal comfort."

"I do like to give. It's one of my many admirable qualities."

Darius looked suddenly serious. His tone was urgent. "Sho, I need to know you're going to do this."

"Have I ever failed you?"

Darius sighed. "No."

"Good. Are we done?"

"Yes, we're done." The dark-haired man's handsome features puckered sourly.

"Great."

The two men, one very tall and very smug, the other smaller and rather more flash, walked towards the door as two men who, though they had reached a mutual understanding, was neither particularly pleased with the other. They paused, eyeing each other warily at the exit. Sho reached for the door handle, but he paused as the sound of brisk, smart footsteps echoed through the lobby.

The most recent arrival to this tense audience was a thin man of rather middling height in a brown plaid waistcoat and trousers. Atop his mousey brown hair was a tweed cap, which made him look pompous and silly but which he refused to remove, as he considered it to be quite cool and debonair. His age appeared to be somewhat in middle years, but his nature was such that it was difficult to determine precisely, and he would never, under any circumstances, give up the information voluntarily. There was not, it was suspected, a living person who actually possessed the knowledge, which was a source of much smugness on the part of the mousey man.

He squinted at Darius through round-rimmed glasses. He did not need them, but they added, in his estimation, a rather smart appeal to his lean, ordinary, even-featured face. He knew the man in the dark suit, and Darius knew him. They eyed each other somewhat suspiciously.

"Oh, it's you," the man in the tweed hat said wearily.

Darius drew himself up to his full height, which was still quite shorter than Sho, but which he was smugly aware was several inches taller than the man in the tweed hat. "Why does everyone keep saying that?" he demanded in exasperation.

The man in plaid narrowed his eyes behind his round glasses. "Why are you here?"

Darius lifted his chin defiantly. "I have a job for you."

The other man sighed. "Brilliant. Something dastardly and destructive, I shouldn't wonder. Sho, we really should be more selective about our clients."

Darius looked offended. "For your information, I am working for the other side this time."

"Oh, well, that's an interesting twist."

"Isn't it? Nearly as interesting as someone such as you working in a place like this."

"I'm sure I don't know what you mean," the man in the tweed hat replied stiffly.

"I'm sure you do." Darius spun away from him and nodded to Sho to pull open the door. At the last moment, he spun back to the man in the tweed cap. "Always a pleasure, Sho. Accid--"

"Simon!" the man in the tweed hat cut in angrily.

Darius smirked. "Right. Simon. Ta ta, then."

Sho closed the door behind him and glanced at Simon in interest. Simon's cheeks flushed scarlet. Sho did not bother to take the piss. He'd had enough sport with Darius, and his good humour had been thoroughly exhausted. "Gather the team in the conference room. We have a job."

*** *

The conference room had not been cleaned in some time. The round table around which Sho Sange and his associates sat was covered in half-empty bottles of liquor, stacks of scattered paper and weird, mysterious, and mostly broken gadgets Panya and Hyde had stashed there when their rooms had begun to resemble a mad scientist's rubbish pile. Most of the team sat with their feet up, mindless of the chaos and debris around them. Simon had meticulously cleared a space on the table, and he sat perfectly upright with his hands folded on the shining surface before him.

Sho was not sitting down. He stood at what he considered the head of the table in the tiny, windowless room, peering at them with his palms flattened on the surface of the table. Inches from his eerily long, slender fingers, was what looked like a glass pistol filled with some sort of swirling, electric blue liquid. He ignored it. Behind him, a man in a long, black military-style jacket with long, black and white hair dreadlocks leaned against the wall like a silent sentinel with his arms crossed over his broad chest. He looked humourless and very dangerous, despite the unlikelihood of anyone attacking his boss in a room with his closest friends and associates. The stern man was called Xen, and no one paid him any attention.

Panya spun in the chair between Oni and Simon. She looked bored. Across from her, Hyde, a small man with elfish features and short, curly hair who resembled Panya so closely, he could have been her brother but for his sometimes pointy and occasionally furry ears, stared vacantly into space.

Oni, a tall, callipygian woman with black hair that curled around her ears and fell into her beautiful, brazen face punctured a stack of papers which looked important with pointy, high-heeled black boots. She leaned back in her chair, sipping straight from one of the bottles she'd snatched from the table and smoking a cigarette on a long filter. Her wide-brimmed, feathered hat was drawn down roguishly over her eyes. She'd just come in from an assignment, and she still wore the short, ruffled skirt and leather corset in which she'd masqueraded as a saloon girl in one of the shadier taverns in the elf district.

Simon coughed pointedly and waved his hand in the air with an expression of extreme distaste and vexation. "Must you smoke that in here, Oni?"

Oni grinned. "What's the matter, Simon? Are you afraid it will kill you?"

He sighed wearily. "Is this another poorly thought out attempt on my life?"

Her expression was mischievous. "Sticks and stones haven't worked so far. I thought I'd try a new approach. A slow death by lung poisoning. You're frightened, aren't you?"

He scowled. "It's a disgusting habit. The smell is seeping into my skin."

"Enough, you two," Sho said wearily. "Oni, no smoking in the boardroom."

She dropped her feet to the floor and sat up sharply. "Since when?"

"Since now!"

"What's got your knickers in a bunch, boss?"

"Oni!"

Her mouth turned down into a pout. "Fine." She dropped the cigarette into an empty bottle of expensive, ogre-crafted scotch.

"Can we get on with it?" Sho snapped.

Panya sighed deeply. "Yes. Go on, please."

"We have a job."

She eyed him suspiciously. "A paying job?"

"Yes, of course a paying job, Panya! What do you think I'm running here, an outreach program?"

"It's from the flash bastard in the suit, isn't it?"

Oni's face illuminated. "Oh, do we get to do evil this time?"

"We aren't doing evil," said Sho irritably. "Darius is just the messenger this time."

Xen scowled. "Whose messenger?"

Sho half turned to him and shrugged. "The other side's. Darius was not pleased about it."

The man with the black and white hair looked amused. "I wonder how they managed to talk him into that."

"It had something to do with a weekly appointment with someone called Enid, from what I gathered."

Xen rolled his eyes. "What does he want us to do?"

Sho sat down in the chair in front of him. Xen remained standing behind him. "A professor at the Gwydion Academy of Advanced Sorcery has been working on a spell to open a gate to Hao."

"What the hell is Hao?"

Sho shrugged again. "No idea."

"Then how do you open a gate there?"

"How should I know?"

Simon's expression was horribly grim. "I know what Hao is. It's an alternative dimension, and it's very bad." Oni beamed at him, but he shook his head. "Not the sort of bad you like, Oni."

She sat back in her seat with a pout.

"See?" Sho said. "It's very bad. And Darius wants us to stop it from happening."

Xen frowned. "How?"

"How the hell should I know? I don't even know where it is."

"It isn't anywhere," Simon said. "Well, until some idiot professor opens a gate to it, anyway. Then it's there."

Panya still didn't look impressed. "You don't know how we're supposed to stop it?"

"I don't even know how he's doing it."

"Your leadership skills are leaving a little to be desired here, boss," Oni told him.

"Then you won't like this."

Oni gave him a suspicious look. "Won't like what?"

"I'm not going with you."

"What? What do you mean?"

Sho sighed. "I have to return to Scathach straight away. Lord Blood has ordered me home."

Panya stopped spinning indignantly. "Can he do that?"

"He's my Lord. And he's my father. Yes, he can do that."

Oni grinned excitedly. "Oh, can I go? Last time we were in the Darklands, I was almost crowned their queen."

Sho rolled his eyes. "That is not exactly what happened. I think you will find, upon reflection and looking past whatever fantasies you've built up in your head,

30

that you in fact were nearly executed for crimes against the state."

She shrugged. "Darklord tribunals are very misleading."

"Potential political fiascos aside, I'm afraid you can't go with me this time."

Oni looked hurt. "Why not?"

"Darius requested you specifically for this job."

Oni leaned across the table and shoved Hyde's shoulder. The young man looked only mildly interested in the proceedings. He hardly glanced at Oni. Instead, he watched Panya intently, but she seemed more interested in how many individual specks made up the ceiling tiles than the conversation at hand.

"It's because I'm so good," Oni told him.

"It's probably because you're so crazy, and demons like crazy," Hyde replied matter-of-factly.

"Darius isn't a demon, Hyde," Simon told him quietly.

"He's not a demon? I thought he was a demon."

"He's not a demon," Sho snapped.

"If you aren't coming with us, Sho," Xen said irritably, "who's running this operation, which is very likely going to fail?"

Sho didn't turn around. "You are, Xen."

"Oh, terrific."

Panya jerked her head towards Xen. "So what happens if the vigilante over there cocks up the whole thing and this professor actually succeeds?"

"Panya, are you still mad the Lumina took away your magic shoes?"

She was suddenly enraged. "I could walk on walls in those things!"

Sho sighed in a long-suffering sort of way. Simon cut across whatever Xen had opened his mouth to say. "The entire world is destroyed," said he.

They all looked at Simon, sobering instantly.

"What?" Xen asked tersely.

Simon pushed his glasses up his nose primly. "If the professor succeeds in opening a gate to Hao, the entire world will be unmade."

Sho smiled. "Right, then." He stood and strode towards the door. "Good luck. Try not to cock it up. See you all when I get back."

\* \* \*

The Gwydion Academy of Advanced Sorcery was a looming, white stone building in the centre of Hyperion City's bustling magical district. A thick iron fence surrounded the beautiful green, flowering courtyard around the campus on three sides. On the west side of the campus was a huge, blue lake that sparkled like a sapphire in the brilliant morning sun. Even at this early hour, the courtyard was filled with students and professors studying for exams or practising their arts.

Arcs of lightning zigzagged between the flowering trees. Balls of fire flew between the students as they tossed them back and forth like juggling pins. Tiny dark clouds swirled over groups of people, pouring rain over their books and soaking their clothes as they shrieked and raced out of the downpour. Terrific, intense gusts of winds nearly knocked over a couple of elderly professors as they passed from one building to the other.

Oni grinned through the metal bars of the front gate beside Simon and Xen. She laughed raucously as an old wizard in flowing, sea green robes walked directly into the path of one of the fireballs and ignited. He screamed and flailed wildly until a young man raced over to him, lifting his hands to shoot a powerful stream of water from his fingertips. The old wizard smoked and smouldered and shouted at the fire witches, who looked extremely sheepish.

The Academy's newest professors looked rather like three people who hadn't the least idea what professors should in fact look like. Oni's scarlet skirt was cut up to her thighs, revealing criss-cross stockings and tall, lace up boots. It trailed on the ground behind her in the back, and Simon had to step aside to avoid tripping upon it. Her coat was belted with a wide swath of leather that laced up to her ribs. Even Simon had difficulty resisting the urge to drop his gaze to her ample bosom, which spilled over the top of the ruffled white shirt she wore beneath her coat.

As was his custom, Xen wore black leather from head to toe. His jacket buttoned up to his jaw with large, brass buttons. His boots were studded with bronze. His long, dreadlocked hair fell down his back, and he looked so alarming, the students who caught sight of him through the doors of the gate jumped and turned to hurry the other way.

Simon, on the other hand, looked as boring and conservative as ever in his plaid suit and tweed hair. A pipe stuck out of the corner of his mouth, though he wouldn't dream of smoking it; he abhorred the habit, but he thought it made him look more like a proper professor. He was practically vibrating with excitement.

He had always thought he would make a very good professor.

"It's very big," Oni said, looking up at the Academy with large, glittering dark eyes. She cocked her head to the side to study the domed roofs and panoramic windows on the upper floors. "It's made of an awful lot of glass. I wonder how good their insurance is."

Xen glanced doubtfully at Simon. "How did you actually manage to get us jobs here, Simon?"

"Oh, yes, me especially," Oni added. "I'm not employable anywhere."

Simon looked mightily pleased with himself. "Sho didn't hire me for nothing. I do have my uses, after all."

"You mean you have your friends."

He blushed slightly. "Well, I may have had a little help from a friend."

"You mean the God of Convenient Plot Devices?"

"Convenient," Xen added.

"Yes. Just so."

Oni grinned. "You think Panya and Hyde mind being left behind while we gleefully debase the credulous youth and take the piss out of the educational system?"

Simon waved his hand. "Surely not. Someone has to man the office. I hardly think it requires five people to stop one feeble old man from performing a complex and probably unworkable spell, besides."

"Enough exposition," Xen ordered irritably. "Let's get on with it."

"You know, you're very bad tempered these days, Xen," Oni told him reproachfully. "You used to be very funny."

"Him?" Simon said. "Funny?"

"It's funny when he gets all freaked out on bad juju and throws things about the room," Oni said brightly.

"That isn't funny," Simon replied. "That's dreadful."

"Leave off, you two," Xen snapped. "I'm not in the mood."

"Aw," Oni said, grinning. "Are you missing the boss already?"

"I'll have you know I can function just fine without Sho."

"Sure, unless you get too angry or depressed or become displeased with the weather and get the bad juju rage," Simon said.

"I don't have bad juju rage! I'm fine!"

Oni considered this. "Except you'd probably be in some dark wizard loony bin somewhere if not for Sho." She drew an enormous syringe from somewhere under the short, voluminous skirt and brandished it in front of his eyes. "If you do get the juju rage, I've got this. It would put down a tremendously large mammal or a circus animal of moderate size."

Xen glared at her.

"This is fun, but leave him alone, Oni," Simon told her. "He's fine." He leaned toward her and spoke behind his hand. "And we don't need him getting the juju rage this early into the affair."

Xen didn't hear the last bit. He looked gratified. "Thanks, Simon."

Simon smiled and stepped towards the gate with his hand raised. As he did, a mechanical crossbow poorly concealed under a pile of leaves sprang up and fired an arrow straight through his chest, tearing a hole through his new suit. The arrow lodged there, between his ribs.

He spun on Oni with an irritated expression. She stopped snickering, disappointed. "Damn. I was sure that would work."

"Oh, that's nice, Oni. That's really very mature. You've completely ruined my suit!"

"Good. You look like a creepy librarian who tries to lure schoolboys into the quiet room with old adventure novels and locked-door mysteries."

"I look nothing of the sort! I deeply resent that!"

Xen sighed. "This is just going to be great. I'm just really looking forward to this. Can we get on, please?"

\* \* \*

The Beginning Incantations classroom was a large, circular room with high walls and a domed, glass ceiling that glittered brilliantly in the late afternoon sun. In the evenings, the stars twinkled over the students seated along the walls in tiered mahogany benches. Now the students waited patiently for their professor to appear. When he did, it was with a dramatic air. His coattails flapped as he trounced into the room carrying an enormous blue leather-bound book.

He glided cheerfully toward the centre of the room and swept his tweed hat from his mousey brown hair, tossing it aside with a flourish. He hoisted the book onto the lectern in front of him. He opened it slowly, paging meticulously through it until he found his place. He pushed his glasses up his nose and lifted his head to look up at his class. They stared back at him expectantly, pens poised over their parchments.

He cleared his throat. "Welcome to Beginning Incantations. I am Professor... well, you can call me Simon. Can anyone tell me the proper incantation to transmute spirit into matter?"

The students glanced around at each other nervously, whispering amongst themselves as if they couldn't understand why he would ask such a question.

"Anyone?" Simon peered around at the young, aspiring incanters through his round glasses. His brow furrowed in irritation. "I know this is a beginning class, but haven't you been studying on your own? Do you know nothing of basic advanced incanting?"

A young girl with a long, dark plait down her back sitting in the front of the class rose with her hand lifted into the air. "Sir, we are all first years students," she told him in a wavering voice. "We haven't learned how to work with spirit yet. We were learning to move pencils from one side of the desk to the other."

As she spoke, something strange happened. The buttons of her white, ruffled blouse suddenly popped open, exposing her ivory pale bosom to the class. She did not seem to notice the sun shimmer on her bare skin or the gentle breeze in the air.

Her classmates giggled and pointed.

Simon blushed crimson. "Uh, miss...."

The young girl looked down and gasped in shock. She slapped her arms across her chest to cover herself. Her cheeks blazed, and she fumbled to re-do her buttons.

Simon looked as terribly embarrassed as she. He held up his hands to silence his students' giggles, but to little avail. "Well...well, can you all tell me how far you've gotten in the text?"

The girl in the front row directly across from him rose to her feet. She was petite and very conservative looking in a plain black dress that fell to her knees. Her long, blonde hair fell in a straight sheet down her back. She was not especially pretty, but she looked intelligent, and she looked quite put out by her classmates' behaviour. "Sir, I have read the book cover to cover. There is nothing in there about transmuting spirit into matter. However, on page 875, the

35

author states that the proper incantation for turning spirit towards matter, in the manner of using it to manipulate matter is--"

A brusque breeze swirled through the classroom and lifted her skirt. She was not wearing underpants. She gasped and cut off, covering her bare bottom with her hands.

The boy directly behind her burst into startled laughter. "Emi! Good lord! You're starkers under that awful dress!"

Emi covered her blushing face with her hands. Simon sighed. Things were not going as planned.

"Let's move on, shall we?" he said wearily. "Why don't we just start on page 1?"

\* \* \*

Oni's classroom was similar to Simon's. The students sat in a circle around her in tiered seats up to the domed ceiling. This afternoon, the sun's rays cast down across their faces, bathing them all in a golden light. Oni swept in with a flourish, her skirt train dragging on the floor behind her. She grinned wickedly around at the young, innocent faces staring back at her. They were blissfully unaware that the woman now charged with influencing their eager, pliable minds had no qualifications whatsoever.

Some of the students looked expectantly at her as though she might offer some wisdom or insight into the esoteric world of magic. Some of the boys goggled at her. A few of the girls looked scandalised. It was everything for which Oni could have possibly hoped.

There was havoc to be wrought. This assignment was turning out to be the best ever.

"Hello, class. Who wants to learn about...magic?" As she spoke, she swept the wide-brimmed hat off her head and yanked out a fat, white clockwork rabbit with big, glittering red eyes that whirred and popped and ticked as its windup limbs whirled and spun erratically.

Suddenly, the mechanical rabbit exploded in a shower of sparks. Oni cackled maniacally.

A very pretty young girl with long, chestnut brown hair stood. She was fresh-faced and dewy-eyed, and Oni had to resist the urge to rush to her and pinch her pink petal cheeks. Simon had expressly forbid her from fondling the students, even if it just involved a little pinch and squeal over their extreme cuteness.

36

"Uh, Miss...Oni? I thought this was a Beginning Love Charms class?"

Oni stared at her in shock. "Love Charms? Really?" She laughed quite indecorously for several moments, clutching her stomach and flapping her arms in the air. The students stared back at her in confusion. "Me? That's brilliant."

"So, um, are we going to learn about love charms?"

Oni's teeth glinted in the sunlight cast from above. "Oh. Yes. Sure. Why not?"

She yanked the big, black satchel from her shoulder and dumped an enormous pile of little brass balls with spikes, incendiary devices, explosives, gears, copper wires, bits of clockwork, miniature directed energy pistols and a variety of taxidermy animals on the lectern in front of her.

"But first," she said, grinning hugely, "who wants to have some fun?"

\* \* \*

Xen stormed out of his classroom, slamming the door behind him. The brass plaque on the wall read, **Professor Xen. Talismans and Amulets**. The corridors in the Gwydion Academy of Advanced Sorcery all looked the same. The walls were sparkling white stone, and there were so many closed doors, he would have been unable to find his own room without the nameplate.

He spun towards his office several doors down and promptly crashed into a young woman carrying a huge stack of books. The books tumbled to the floor around her feet. Xen reached out to steady her. She was more than a head shorter than him. She looked up at him with large, limpid blue eyes. Her long, golden blonde hair was mussed around her pretty, heart-shaped face. Xen stared down at her, and he felt a strange flutter in his chest.

"Sorry, sorry," said Xen, bending down to help her pick up the books.

The young woman smiled, piling the books back into her arms. "It's all right."

For a moment, they peered at each other. The air around them felt charged and alive with electricity.

Then Xen spoke, and the moment passed. "I'm Xen."

"Sora Bale. You're new here?"

"Yes, I just started." He gestured towards the nameplate behind him. "In Talismans and Amulets."

Sora smiled. She had a beautiful smile. It seemed to light up her small, innocent face. "You must be filling in for Professor Omari."

"Uh...yes." Fleetingly, he decided not to bother wondering what had happened to the previous professor.

"It's such a shame what happened to him...such an irony that he was put into a coma by his own faulty serenity amulet." She turned abruptly and started down the hall away from him.

Ah, so that was it, not that he particularly cared, but he could see the humour, despite his dour expression. "Ironic. And convenient, as well."

Sora paused and turned back to him. "What?"

Xen, still carrying most of her books, fell into step beside her. "Nothing." For several moments, they did not say anything. Then he asked, "Are you a student? I haven't seen you in any of my classes."

She laughed. "Don't be fooled by my childlike exterior. I am a badass sorceress."

This sounded extremely silly coming from her. Her voice was like a soft, musical bell. Xen lifted a sceptical eyebrow. "Really."

Now she looked slightly embarrassed. "Well, not really. I'm an assistant professor. I work in the Runes department with Professor Tan."

Xen paused for a split second. "Zebulon Tan?"

"That's right." Her smile took on a peculiarly dreamy quality. "You've heard of him?"

"I may have."

"He's the head of the Runes department." There was something uncomfortably reverent in her eyes when she spoke of her professor. "He's the best Runic Sorcerer at Gwydion. Probably all of Hyperion City."

"Why not all of Pandia? You seem to be quite an admirer of his."

She didn't seem to notice the dry tone of his voice. "Oh, yes. He was my professor when I was a student. He inspired me to teach. He does such great work."

"I see."

Sora stopped abruptly and spun to face him with a chilly expression.

"Why did you stop?" Xen asked in surprise. "Did I say something wrong?"

She laughed again. It was such a sweet, musical sound, Xen felt an odd sort of shiver down his spine. "No. This is my classroom. Thanks for carrying my books."

"Yeah. Sure. No problem."

"See you around school maybe."

"Yes. You will."

She smiled at him. "Could you get the door?"

"Oh—yes. Of course." He piled the books in his hands onto the several she already carried. Her face disappeared behind the enormous stack. He pulled open the door, and she hurried inside.

"Goodbye, Professor Xen." He could barely hear her behind the books.

"Goodbye, Sora."

With that, she hooked a foot around the door and pulled it shut. He stared at the gnarled wooden door for several seconds.

Zebulon Tan's assistant. Now that was convenient, indeed.

He didn't hear Oni creeping towards him with exaggerated stealth.

Oni cupped her hands around her mouth and leaned towards him.

"Whatcha doin'?!"

Xen did not startle. He turned his head to her with an expression of deepest apathy. He frowned. "Nothing."

She took a moment to eye him suspiciously. "Why do you look all weird?"

"What do you mean 'weird'?"

"You look weird. You're all googly-eyed."

He took offence to this. "I'm not googly-eyed."

"Yes, you are."

"Whatever." He fell into step with her, and they strolled side by side through the white stone halls of door after door. "How was class?"

"Did you know I'm teaching Love Charms?"

Xen snickered. "You?"

She lifted her chin. "I'll have you know, I am very loveable."

"You?"

"Yes. Hey, do you want one?"

"What? A love charm?" he demanded incredulously. "What do I need with a love charm?"

"Dunno. You're the one with the googly eyes."

"I do not have googly eyes!"

"If you say so."

"Do you even know magic?" He sounded sulky.

"No. Do you think that's going to be a problem?"

"I'm sure you'll find your way around it."

"Hey, I wonder how Simon's doing."

Xen rolled his eyes. "I'm sure he's doing fine. He loves the idea of moulding students into boring little bookworms like himself."

Oni thought about this for a moment. "What do reckon he's excruciatingly embarrassed by now?"

Xen smirked. "I would love to see into that classroom." He raised his hands in surrender as Oni wagged a warning finger at him. "Except I'm a teacher, and that would be inappropriate."

"Inappropriate? I was thinking it would be more fun to set him loose in the common room after hours and see what sort of things pop up." She grinned. "Or out."

\* \* \*

The school cafeteria was noisy and crowded. The ceiling in this room was the same as that of the classrooms, and the night sky twinkled above them. Xen, Oni and Simon sat at a table amidst the other professors and students. No one seemed inclined to approach the trio. Many of the students goggled openly at them, as though they were somehow more outlandish and frightening in appearance than the many dwarves, elves, shape-shifters, elementals, reptilians, and other various monsters that constituted much of the staff.

None of them minded. They weren't interested in making friends at the moment. Even Simon shovelled his dinner into his mouth like a man who hadn't eaten in several days. The food at the Academy was much better than anything Panya or Hyde might have cooked. At least the cooks hadn't added any sort of strange herbal concoctions, exotic plants, creepy creatures, dubious potions or–as was often the case when Oni happened to wander into the kitchen unattended–poison.

Simon pushed his empty plate away and leaned back with a satisfied noise. "So," he said with the air of a man who is attempting delicacy. "Does anyone have any idea how we're going to accomplish this farce of an assignment?"

They met each other's eyes with miserable, guilty expressions.

"No," Xen admitted.

"Xen, so far your leadership is not that which I would have expected from someone with years of experience tracking down dark magic," Simon told him prissily.

"We just got here," Xen replied defensively. "Nothing's even happened yet. We'll think of something."

"We could just tie him up and lock him in a closet until this whole thing blows over," Oni suggested.

"I don't think that will do a lot of good. I'm fairly sure the best sorcerer in the city can suss a way out of a closet."

"Who says he's the best?" Simon asked somewhat grimly.

"His assistant, Sora Bale."

"His assistant?"

"Yes. I met her earlier."

Simon stared at him. "It didn't occur to you that Tan's assistant might be useful to us?"

"What do you mean?" His eyes narrowed dangerously.

"If we're going to get close to Zebulon Tan and stop him from unmaking the entire world, don't you think his assistant might be able to help in some way?"

Xen blinked at him in surprise. "I hadn't thought of her that way."

"You were thinking about her some other way?"

"No." He looked suddenly embarrassed. "I wasn't thinking about her at all."

"Ohh!" Oni said in sudden realisation. "She's the one giving you the googly eyes."

"She gave you googly eyes?" Simon asked interestedly.

"She didn't do the googly eyes," Oni explained. "She caused the googly eyes."

"Ohh."

"Don't 'ohh' like that," Xen ordered. "It's rubbish."

"Sure it is," said Oni positively. "Anyway, this is great news, Xen. You can get close to his assistant...I know you want to..."

"I don't know what you're talking about."

"Stop playing coy and just get on with it," Simon said impatiently. "We haven't got unlimited time here. As a matter of fact, we have no idea how much time we actually have. The fall—" He cut off and cleared his throat delicately. "Darius really didn't have any idea?"

"No. In fact, he didn't give us much. Just enough to get us into this mess."

"Then we have to get it from your girl," Oni put in.

"She isn't my girl."

"Stop being so difficult and just see what you can find out from her."

Xen sighed. "Fine."

"Terrific."

For a moment, they peered around at each other.

"So..." Simon said, lacing his fingers across his chest. "Has anyone actually seen Zebulon Tan yet?"

\* \* \*

*At nearly precisely the same moment...*

Zebulon Tan's tower workshop was the largest at the Academy. Its domed ceiling was darkened, for he was jealous of his work. Bookshelves lined every wall, so stuffed full of books and grimoires, hardly an inch of wall showed through. Tables were littered with amulets, wands, gemstones and various gadgets scattered in seemingly random patterns around the large room. In the centre of the room was a podium surrounded by a circle of stones and jagged cut crystal. A large, ancient book lay open upon its surface. It was from this podium that the sorcerer performed his most important spells.

Zebulon Tan was not before it now.

Sora Bale bent over a scuffed study table in the corner of the room, pouring over an enormous book. On the table around her, several other large books were stacked so high she could hardly see Zebulon as he entered the room. He rounded the table to lay a hand upon her shoulder.

"What are you doing here, my dear?" He was an elderly man, but he did not look his age. His long, wavy hair and flowing beard were still dark, steel grey. There were lines around his bright, brilliant blue eyes and around his mouth, but his ruddy features were hearty and practically glowed with virility. His expression was kindly. "Shouldn't you be downstairs enjoying dinner?"

Sora smiled up at him. There was weariness around her eyes, but they were alight with excitement. "Soon. I am almost finished with the volume. I am confident I'll find the fifth rune tonight."

Zebulon patted her on the shoulder. "You're working too hard, Sora. Go. Get something to eat. I'll finish up here."

"Now who's working too hard?"

"It is my cross to bear, young lady. Not yours. Go on."

She hesitated, but she finally nodded. She stuck a silver bookmark between the pages of the book and gently closed the cover. She kissed him on the cheek as she rose. "Okay. I'm going. See you tomorrow. Don't stay up too late."

He smiled and waved her off. "Good night, Sora."

He watched her go. When the door closed behind her, he yanked the text she'd abandoned towards him and flipped open the cover. He leaned down, his eyes scanning the pages ravenously. Time passed. The domed ceiling above darkened and swirled with his mood. The grandfather clock hidden behind a stack of books in the corner ticked loudly. It chimed once. And then it chimed twice.

He reached the end of the book. Despite Sora's confidence, the fifth rune wasn't there. He slammed the cover shut. "Damn!"

He shoved the book off the table. It shattered the small, glass bottles of glowing liquids on the floor beside the table. He didn't bother to clear up the mess. He dropped his head in his hands and shot abruptly to his feet.

Something had happened to him as the time had slipped away. His virile body was stooped and his limbs felt stiff. His heart raced in fear, and he rushed as quickly as he could towards the mirror in his sleeping chambers. He'd shrivelled. The muscles in his arms and legs were weak, and the skin hung limply from his brittle, twisted bones. His dark steely hair looked white, thin and grizzled. His features had lost their ruddiness, and his pale face was etched with deep, criss-crossed wrinkles. The blaze of his brilliant blue eyes had extinguished. They were watery and pale and bloodshot.

He took a deep breath that rattled in his chest. "I'm running out of time."

\* \* \*

*Meanwhile, in another part of the Academy...*

Xen prowled the white stone and glass ceilinged hallways. He couldn't sleep, especially in a place where every movement and sound echoing through the ancient building and every star twinkling overhead in his sleeping quarters was like a nail pounded through his brain. His senses screamed. His nerves felt like a million tiny needles. He never slept much, not since he had touched the artefact, but it was so much worse here. All the magic in the place raked across his hyper-charged flesh.

He felt like a caged animal. The sooner he could get out of this place, the better.

And he was lost. All the doors in all the corridors looked the same. He cursed under his breath. He spun around to re-trace his steps, but he couldn't tell if he'd been in the halls before or if he had taken another wrong turn. He stopped abruptly and looked up at the sky. He didn't know much about the stars, but maybe if he could find just one, he could judge his position.

Suddenly, someone collided with him.

She was so small, she barely staggered him, but she bounced off him as though he were made of rubber.

Chuckling, Xen caught her shoulders. Sora Bale's blue eyes were large, and her cheeks coloured slightly. "Oh, hello, Professor Xen," she said breathlessly. "I am so sorry."

He grinned at her. "It seems only fair. Are you all right?"

She seemed to realise he was still gripping her arms. She took a delicate step back and smiled up at him shyly. "Yes. Quite. But I am...rather embarrassed."

"There is no need for embarrassment. I am certain it was entirely my fault."

Sora's face was pink. "What are you doing out so late, Professor?"

"I...do not sleep well in strange places."

"I see. Well, I hope, for your health, it will not seem strange for long."

He was quiet a moment, peering up into the glittering night sky through the glass above. He did not reply to this. When he looked back at her, his dark eyes were expressionless. "What about you, Professor?"

She glanced away shyly. "You don't have to call me Professor. Just Sora is all right. I am not a real professor yet, besides. I'm just an assistant."

He lifted his eyebrows. "From what I hear, you teach most of Professor Tan's classes."

There was a hint of defensiveness in her tone. "Zebulon is very busy with his work. He's taught me enough to follow his lesson plans. I simply facilitate."

Xen considered her seriously for a moment. "I am sure you do not give yourself enough credit." There was embarrassment in her smile, and he returned it almost involuntarily. "So where are you off to so late? Are you on a secret mission from your truant boss?"

Sora laughed. "I've been researching runic texts all night. I missed dinner. I'm hoping the kitchen can scrape something up for me."

"May I join you?"

She scuffed her foot on the marble floor. "Yes. All right. I would like that."

The kitchen was the only room Xen had seen so far with stone ceilings, and he sighed in relief. It wasn't right to have the stars so close, looking down upon your every move. He preferred to be left alone. He felt more relaxed as he sat across from Sora at the old, scuffed wood table in the centre of the room, surrounded by copper pots and pans and fire pits. The staff had already done for the night, but they hadn't seemed surprised to see Sora there so late, and they had grudgingly prepared her a plate.

Xen sipped a mug of coffee and watched her eat. He felt more cheerful in this quiet, stone room. The bleak grey walls kept out the warring magical resonances that swirled and collided with each other around the campus. Sora looked tired, and he wondered exactly what she'd been doing with her evening. Nevertheless, she was cheerful, and there was still a brightness to her eyes that suggested whatever her task, it had been successful or promised success in the future.

She blushed under his scrutiny, dabbing self-consciously at her mouth as though she feared there might be an errant crumb on her lips.

"Did you always want to be a professor?" Xen asked her abruptly.

Sora considered this a moment. "No. Not really. I didn't really want to be anything. I grew up in Aether City, you see. When I was very little, my parents died."

"I'm sorry."

She waved her hand as though the wound had long healed. "Thank you. In the orphanage, I tested high on aptitude tests and was sent to boarding school on a scholarship. While at school, my professors detected a talent for magic, and so the headmaster sent me to magical secondary school. To pay for my expenses, I took a post as an assistant to the professors, mostly grading papers and running errands." She smiled fondly. "Zebulon must have seen something in me. He offered me a post as his personal assistant when I graduated. I have known ever since that it is what I am meant to do."

"Give your life to his work?"

This caused her to frown. "It isn't like that."

"I didn't mean to offend you."

"Zebulon is the greatest wizard in the city. Probably all of Pandia. He is teaching me what I need to know to be a great sorceress."

Xen looked slightly sheepish. "Sorry. I didn't mean to suggest--"

She waved her hand dismissively, but she still looked nettled. "It's all right. People don't understand, but they haven't worked for him. They don't know what he knows. Each day I learn more and each thing I learn, I realise how much I still need to learn."

"Is that what you want?"

"What do you mean?"

"Do you want to dedicate your life to magic?"

She lifted her shoulders delicately. "I have never known anything else, aside from primary school." Her eyes slid away, and there was something so deeply, profoundly sad in them, Xen's heart fluttered reluctantly. "And it is nothing to which I would wish to go back."

They sipped their coffee in silence.

"What of you, Xen? You're here, same as me."

He leaned back in his seat and crossed his arms over his chest. "Yes. I suppose I am."

"Why? Did you always want to be a professor?"

He laughed. "No. I didn't."

"Then why?"

"What do you mean 'why'? I'm here to teach."

"Are you really?"

He leaned forward now. There was curiosity in his dark eyes. "Why do you think I'm here?"

She smiled. "I don't know. Tell me."

"I did."

"All right. If you say so." She looked disappointed.

He looked at her seriously. "I'm looking for someone."

"Someone? Who?"

He shrugged. "Maybe you."

"Me?"

"Sure. Why not you? Or maybe myself. Could be myself."

Her pretty, heart-shaped face looked slightly confused. "Do you think you will find yourself here?"

"Maybe. I already found you."

Her cheeks flushed. "You are very charming."

"Yes, I am."

"But not as good at evading my questions as you think. I told you my story. Fair is fair. Tell me how you ended up here. You must be very good at magic if you're already a professor."

"It's easier than you think, actually, if you know the right people."

She gave him a pointed look.

He sighed. "You're not going to let this go, are you?"

"No." When he didn't say anything to this, she reached across the table towards him. For a moment, his instinct was to jerk away, but he didn't move. Her fingers were warm and soft, and there was something so tender in her touch it was as though his nerves stilled and quieted for the first time since he'd touched the artefact. She smiled at him, and his heart thumped in his chest. "Is it so bad?"

He frowned and drew his hand from hers. "It could be."

"I won't judge you."

"I find that hard to believe."

"All right, you don't have to tell me." She pushed her empty plate away from her and stood abruptly. Her smile was gentle, but there was something a little icy in her brilliant blue eyes. "I have an early morning. Good night, Professor Xen."

He sighed deeply. He did not rise to see her out. "Good night."

\* \* \*

Simon's private bathroom was small and attached to an equally small bedchamber. He didn't mind the size. He appreciated the quiet quaintness of the room. It was different than his room at home. There weren't booby-traps or shape shifters hiding under his bed to pop out and frighten him. There weren't broken pieces of clockwork, wire, glass, amulets, gadgets or deadly artefacts stashed under his covers or in his drawers or wherever he was mostly likely to come upon them unaware. There were books and a crackling fire and a sense of deep, solitary peace.

He hummed a happy little tune as he prepared for bed. He brushed his teeth. He put on pyjamas patterned with little books and eyeglasses that felt like silk against his skin. When he finished in the bathroom, he turned down the brown flannel sheets of the large, four-poster bed in the sleeping chamber. He climbed under the covers and placed his glasses on the nightstand beside him. He turned down the lantern to a low glow and snuggled comfortably back against the soft, down pillows.

He blinked a few times in surprise as he focussed on the strange brass pattern above his head. It took him several moments to realise it wasn't a part of the ceiling. It was some sort of clockwork contraption, an array of gears and cogs and pulleys. It resembled a sort of large press with long, sharp spikes pointed directly down at him.

There was no time to roll away, for, by the time he sussed the nature of the contraption, he heard the horrifying sound of the chains that anchored the clockwork to the ceiling dropping with sickening speed.

And then the spikes were moving closer and closer until the single point of the spike directly above his face was the only thing he could see.

\* \* \*

"Oni!"

She snickered wickedly, crouched in the corridor outside Simon's door.

48

Simon threw open the door in a huff. His patterned pyjamas were perforated with large, jagged holes. His hair was mussed, but he'd remembered to place his round-rimmed glasses back on his face. It was purple with rage. He was otherwise completely unharmed.

Oni straightened, sighing in disappointment.

"Bloody hell, you homicidal hooligan!" Simon raged. "That really hurt!"

She rolled her eyes. "Oh, quit whining. You're fine."

"That is not the point! This has got to stop! Don't you have anything better to do than concoct elaborate death scenarios?"

She looked at him as though he'd said something very foolish. "Yes. Of course. Much better things."

"Then do them!"

Xen rounded a corner with an expression of intense irritation. When he spotted them, he relaxed. He looked between them. Then he lifted a disdainful eyebrow at Simon. "Nice pyjamas."

Simon drew himself up indignantly. "I'll have you know, they were my favourite pair!"

"Uh, huh." He kept walking. Oni fell into step beside him. He half turned his head toward her. "Do you have any idea where my room is?"

"I am not done!" Simon shouted after them.

Oni stopped and turned back to him. "I know! If you were, I wouldn't be plotting how to smuggle a venomous flying viper into your britches!" When she turned back to Xen, he was already rounding the corner. "Xen. Hey, Xen! Wait up."

He paused and waited for her to catch him up. His expression was surly. "Oni, what have you been doing?"

"Murderin'."

"Unsuccessfully, by the sound of Simon's continuing complaints."

"Ah, well. Next time. Why do you look so dark and broody?"

"I don't."

"It must be a girl."

"Oni..."

"I take it you said something stupid and insensitive and ruined everything and have taken us one step closer to the end of the world?"

"Yes. Probably."

"Ah, well. There's always tomorrow." For a moment, a thoughtful expression crossed her face. "I wonder what Sho's doing while we're cocking this all up."

# CHAPTER THREEE

*Meanwhile, in Scathach...It is night. It is always night.*

Lord Blood's study was the sort of place one might expect to find a deranged old man with a black bird on his shoulder, sipping brandy from a little crystal snifter, reciting dreary poetry or accusing people of murder. Or possibly inviting his guests to be poisoned. Mostly probably the poisoning part. The drapes were blood red. The walls hung with fine, expensive artwork with images of men, women, children and twisted creatures with elegant gaping wounds or dark landscapes of the Darklands' crimson sand beaches.

It was not as gloomy as one would expect, despite the macabre art and the gloomy atmosphere, for Luca Sange, Darklord Blood, was not a bad sort of man. He was merely one of his kind: a Darklord, whose tastes ran to that of his race—morbid and grim. Lord Blood was, in fact, a rather good-natured sort of man. He could even be rather cheeky when he was in the right sort of mood, and he was often the life of the Darklord parties and balls, which were frequent and usually quite boisterous.

Tonight, however, Lord Blood was sitting morosely in his armchair. Upon the table at his elbow was a decanter half-full of deep red liquid. He wasn't sipping the liquid from the small snifter in his hand. It tilted ominously close to spilling across the steel grey carpets; he had long since forgotten he held it. His chin was sunk into his chest. He looked weary and sad.

Sho watched him silently for several moments. His father, whom he had once resembled so closely, they had often been mistaken for each other, now looked much, much older. Lord Blood did not notice him. He seemed sunk into some fit of despair. Sho did not wish to disturb his father's grief, but his own desire to be done with the entire affair was stronger still.

"Father."

Lord Blood jerked in his chair. The liquid sloshed around a bit in the glass, but it did not spill over. When he looked up at his son, there was no expression on his pale, lined but still exquisitely handsome features. "Sho," he said in a voice so toneless it sent a chill down his son's spine. "You came."

Sho's expression was likewise stony, but his tone was surly. "I didn't have much of a choice, did I? Your summons was quite inarguable."

His father gave him a wry smile. "I see you still haven't forgiven me for... well, whatever it is I'm supposed to have done. Raise you, educate you, prepare you for the greatest honour of the Darklordship, which you still refuse to acknowledge."

"I never asked for any of it!" Sho growled angrily. "I just want to live the life I choose for myself. I want to be free."

Blood held up his hand wearily. "I did not call you here to fight or discuss you abjuring your birth right. I apologize for the nature of my summons, but I was certain you would not come otherwise. Despite our differences, I could not bear to face this time without my only son at my side."

Sho relaxed. He sighed deeply and hung his head. "I'm sorry, Father, for your loss."

His father nodded. He poured a snifter of the red liquid from the table beside him and held it out to his son. He gestured Sho to sit in the steel grey leather armchair beside him.

For a long moment, they eyed each other silently.

"What happened?" Sho asked finally. "Lord Spirit was quite well when I last saw him."

Blood shook his head. "No one seems to have any idea. It was completely unexpected. The medics from Malady's keep have no answers as to why it happened. His heart simply stopped in his sleep four nights ago. He never awoke." He sighed. "Spirit was not a young man, but he was robust. No one can explain why he might pass in such a way."

There was another grim silence between them.

"Is there any reason to suspect something untoward happened to him?" asked Sho after several long moments.

His father's brow furrowed. "What do you mean 'untoward'?"

"Well, it is rather unusual for a Darklord to die so long before his time, especially under such mysterious circumstances. Has anyone asked any questions?"

"This is Scathach, Sho," said Blood stiffly. "Not your perverted world of criminals and mad science and manufactured sorcerers. The sort of thing you are suggesting does not happen here."

"How can you be so sure? Why is it so impossible to believe? Just because it hasn't happened in your lifetime doesn't mean it never has before or couldn't now."

Anger glittered in Blood's eyes. "There are ways to prevent such things. There are fail safes."

"Fail safes? You mean the pre-cogs? They are losing their touch. They've been breeding out their powers for centuries. When was the last time they predicted anything more substantial than a slight shift in the normal weather patterns?"

"They have had no need to do so. The Darklands are as protected as ever they were. It is only our people here. There are no outsiders who would wish us harm." He glared at his son. "Not since you brought one here." He looked around suddenly, as if he expected someone to leap out from among the drear décor. "She isn't here, is she? We still have not fully recovered from the last time."

Sho rolled his eyes. "Oni apologized for that."

"Wrath's hounds are still too frightened to leave their cages. It's quite inconvenient when we've a mind to hunt."

His son ignored this. "She's not here. She is otherwise occupied."

Blood's lip curled. "On one of your cabalistic and evidently exceedingly important assignments, I shouldn't wonder."

Sho pressed his lips together angrily, but he did not reply to this.

"You have not completely disregarded our customs in this, at least," his father went on. "This is not a time for outsiders to be among us, regardless of your apparent attachment to them. It is a time to mourn our brother. Decay would have my head if that woman created another taxidermy tableaux on his land, however ignorant of our customs and well-intentioned she claims to be."

"Father, why are you so determined to disbelieve one of our own people might be responsible for Spirit's death? He was your best friend. Don't you care at all to find out how he died?"

"Sho." Blood's voice was low with warning. "Malady's people have already concluded the matter of Spirit's death. There is nothing left but for his brothers to send him off into the next world."

"You are being very closed-minded about this--"

Blood slammed his snifter down on the table at his elbow. "I'll not have you speak of our people that way, Sho, not at such a terrible time as this. Before you left, you would never have said such a thing. You would never have even considered it. We have lived in peace among us for centuries. We do not harm each other. It is our binding law and no one would dare break it."

"Things change, Father. The world is not so black and white as you seem to think. People do unspeakable things to each other all the time without regard for law or consequence. People have desires that run contrary to the law and customs of their people, even if you do not."

"You clearly speak for yourself. You have spent too much time outside. Our people would do nothing like you are suggesting. We have no such compulsions. I cannot say the same for you."

Sho lifted his chin. "I am merely suggesting that someone ought to investigate. We are the masters of the darkest of elements. Is it so difficult to think that power might corrupt?"

The colour drained from Blood's face. "You sound like those who fear and rally against us in the cities and provinces outside the Darklands. Have they so corrupted your thinking already? Is that really how you see your people after all this time away? Have you taken up against us, as well?"

Sho sighed and scrubbed a hand across this cheek. "No. I am sorry, Father. I should have said no such thing. I know quite well the prejudice we face among outsiders who do not understand us. Nevertheless--"

"That is enough, Sho." Now his father's voice was low and weary. "I'll not hear more of this. I have no stomach for the argument now. We will never see eye to eye on this matter, as so many others."

His son pressed his lips together in a tight line, but his father was not wrong about this.

"Will you be staying a while?" asked Lord Blood into the tense silence.

Sho sighed. "Until after the funeral."

"And then?"

"And then...I hope there will still be a world in which to form plans."

\* \* \*

*Meanwhile, elsewhere...it is a very dark night...*

The immense white stone mansion loomed dark and gloomy in the depth of night, casting a wide shadow across the dying courtyard that surrounded it. It looked as though it was in mourning. The trees were black and bare, and the grass had turned to brittle brown. It had once been beautiful and luxurious. The courtyard had been green, and flowers had bloomed in colours so magnificent, they had been the inspiration of artists and landscapers across the verdant countryside of Penthos.

A tall, iron fence encircled the mansion. An engraving upon the gate read Argus Moon. It was locked, and sharp, jagged pieces of glass lined the top of the fence. Imogen did not intend to climb the fence. She had other means to enter. She strode to the gate and motioned the unfortunate creature to her.

Mercy Song's reanimated corpse struggled against the magic binding her to the necromancer. She tried to stop herself, but her body moved against her will, propelling her forward towards the home of Argus Moon. When her body reached the gate, it stopped.

And then Imogen spoke under her breath, and Mercy Song felt a horrible, wrenching sensation in her gut as her soul separated from her body once more. Death had been nothing to this agony. She did not remember the nature of her death, but she remembered the sweet, gentle sensation of release as her spirit abandoned the body and drifted up, away, into a serenity that had been stolen from her when she had been forced back in to the rotting shell of her former self.

Her body crumpled uselessly to the ground. Mercy floated above it, and if she could have made a sound, it would have been a chilling, anguished scream. Though her spirit was free of the desecrated corpse, it was bound still to the sorceress. She was still capable of fear, and it seized her now, though when Imogen lifted her hand to point towards the mansion, she was compelled to move. She shook her head vigorously, but her refusal was to no avail.

Imogen smiled as she watched Mercy's spirit float through the gates, towards the home of the lover who still mourned her death.

\* \* \*

Argus Moon slept alone in a grand, four-poster bed. His sleep was troubled. His dreams swirled with horrible visions of finding his love dead upon the floor of the room he had hoped they would soon share; memories of the terrible fury in the dark eyes of the woman he had scorned; and he saw himself, lying dead in his own bed, bloodied and broken with dead eyes still filled with the shock and horror of his death.

He awoke with a start. He could see only vague impressions of shapes in the thick darkness. The air felt suddenly charged and dangerous. It carried upon it the faintest impression of a whisper. It might only have been the wind, but his heart raced and pounded.

Suddenly, a spectre appeared, floating in the air above his bed. He goggled at her in shock. He knew her. Of course he knew her, for she had been his greatest love, the face he saw when he awoke and when he fell asleep and all the time in between. He could see the shadow of the canopy through her glimmering body now. He could have swept his hand through her. She could not be real.

Her face was so heartbreakingly sad that his chest ached. "Mercy?" His voice was a choked sob.

Then he saw the knife in her hand. It was long and thin and it glinted in the faint glow of her spectral body. It was not transparent or phantasmal. It was real.

"Mercy?" he whispered again.

Her voice was a ghostly whisper. He might only have imagined it. She might not have made any sound at all. "Argus, my dearest love, I am sorry."

\* \* \*

The pile of books moving toward him was so tall Xen could barely make out Sora's head over the top of them as she hurried along the winding path through the green, flowering courtyard between the main building and the enormous sparkling white stone and brass, domed-ceiling library. He wondered that she could see around the tomes at all, but she had likely spent hours along the route. Her feet, in high-heeled, lace-up black boots, travelled over the marble path as though they knew it by heart.

He'd been looking for her, and now that he found her, he paused on the pathway several metres in front of her to wait. She seemed to sense there was someone in her well-trodden path. She stopped and peered around the side of the stack of books. "Xen?"

The movement unbalanced the books, and they started to topple sideways. Sora swayed frantically, attempting to steady them, but they were determined to fall. Xen rushed forward to catch them before they hit the ground. They looked very old. The covers had practically crumbled away, and the pages were brittle.

"Can I help you carry some of these?" he asked, trying not to laugh.

She sighed in relief. "Thank you."

"What are these for?" he asked as he fell into step beside her.

"Zebulon needs them for his research."

"What research?"

She glanced at him. She looked uncertain. "Are you trying to charm me for information about Zebulon?"

He smiled. "No. That's not why I'm trying to charm you."

Her expression softened. She laughed. "We're researching Runes."

"For what? Class?"

"No. Actually, I don't know."

"What do you mean you don't know?"

"He hasn't told me what they're for."

He lifted his eyebrows. "Really?"

"Is that so odd?"

"A bit."

She shrugged, and the books swayed precariously. "It's his way."

"All right. As you say."

They were silent a moment as they approached the steps outside the main building. He muttered something under his breath, and the door swung slowly open to permit them inside. Sora glanced at him, surprised. "I thought your speciality was Talismans and Amulets. I didn't know you were an incanter, as well."

He considered how to respond to this. "I have dabbled in a number of disciplines."

She sighed. "I see."

He hurried after her into the building. "Sora."

She turned back to him with an expression of exasperation. "Yes?"

"I was part of the Lumina."

"What?" Her eyes widened in surprise.

"The Lumina," he repeated. "Have you heard of it?"

There was wariness in her eyes. "I've heard of it."

"Do you know what it is?"

"A vigilante group, so I've heard."

"In a way. It's an order of wizards whose purpose is to seek out and destroy dark magic."

"All right. Are you trying to tell me you've come to seek out dark magic? At the Academy?"

He chuckled wryly. "No. The Lumina sacked me years ago."

Her eyebrows rose. "Why?"

"For using dark magic, of course."

"Ah. Yes. I can see how that may run contrary to their mission statement. What sort of dark magic?"

"I was sent to Nostiluca to recover a necromantic artefact that purportedly imbued the bearer with great powers."

"At a price, I shouldn't wonder."

"Oh, yes. There was a price."

"You found the artefact."

"Yes. I found it."

"Did it work?"

He smiled. "Yes, it worked."

"And you used it."

"I did."

"Why?"

"I couldn't help myself."

She didn't look convinced. "Really?"

"I wanted the power," he admitted.

"So much that it was worth turning against your order?"

"The artefact's draw was very strong."

She thought about this for a long moment. He waited. "Was it worth it?" she asked finally.

"I don't know yet."

Sora paused in the middle of another featureless corridor. Xen didn't even know what wing they were in. "Does that mean you're strung out on evil?"

He smiled. "Not anymore."

She looked slightly disappointed by this. "That still doesn't really explain why you're here."

"No? I thought it was a grand overture. You know, opening up. Sharing a little piece of myself with you."

He sounded so completely serious that she had to smile. "I suppose it was. That is, if it was a genuine gesture and not some clever distraction."

"It was genuine. I am perfectly sincere. Was it everything you'd hoped?"

She thought about it. "No, but it's a good start. Don't think I've failed to notice you've still evading my direct questions."

"I'm not sure exactly why I'm here. Maybe it's for you."

She rolled her eyes. "You said that already."

"Did I? Then it must be true."

"I doubt that very much."

"Why not? It's as good a reason as any, I think. Better than most."

They had reached her classroom door before Xen even realised it had been their destination. She tilted her head towards the door. "I have a class."

"Oh." He piled her books back on top of the smaller stack she carried. "See you after class?"

She peered around the side of the books. This time, Xen reached out to steady them for her. She smiled. "Yeah. Okay."

\* \* \*

*Meanwhile, at Sho Sange & Associates, it is a very dull day, indeed...*

Panya hunched over the reception desk. She adjusted the long, telescopic pince-nez strapped to her forehead. Her small, pink tongue stuck out from the corner of her mouth. She twisted a screwdriver into what appeared to be nothing more than a tiny brass ball with suction cups covering its surface. It was much more than that; she hoped, anyway. If she could just get the proportions right, the tiny brass ball would blow a Panya-shaped hole in any wall or window at which she threw it.

She cranked the screwdriver, and the brass ball suddenly broke apart. A spring shot out, bouncing off her pince-nez. She jumped back in surprise. The spring flew around the room for a few moments, rebounding off the clocks and amulets. Panya watched it irritably.

Finally, it shattered the glass of a clock with six hands and no face and dropped uselessly to the floor.

"Damn!" she complained loudly. "I wish Oni was here. She'd know how to rig this thing to blow up when someone gave it a stern glance."

She threw her hands up in the air and leaned so far back in the chair, her head nearly touched the ground.

"I'm so bored!"

She leapt off the stool and flipped several times in the air before landing gently on her feet with her hands in the air. It had been many years since she'd left her home city of Komodia, the city of pleasure and spectacle in the very heart of Pandia, but she still remembered growing up the child of circus performers and funambulists. She was still quite remarkably gifted in the circus arts, but she had long since given up performance.

Now her skills were often put to more profitable and, occasionally, slightly less legal ventures.

When she didn't have a wall to scale or a wicked magician's home to slip into unnoticed, it was a very nice way to relax. The lobby was large and cluttered with breakables. It was a perfect place to practice her flips, somersaults, tumbles and contortions. If she didn't break anything, she was having a very good day. If she did, well, Simon's reaction was just as much fun.

Hyde paused on the stairs in mid-descent, watching the wild tumbling and contortions in the lobby with bemusement. Then a wide smile stretched his mouth, and he bounded down the stairs, leaping into the air. He landed on the hardwood floor in a smooth somersault. His body shifted and changed, rolling up like a pill bug until he resembled a large bouncy ball with wide, flat eyes and an enormous, stretched grin.

Panya squealed in delight and leapt upon the ball, rolling around on it and flipping in the air as she tried to balance on Hyde's rubbery, bouncy surface. She laughed and whooped and twirled, and then she jumped up, flipping gracefully through the air to land neatly on her feet. She held up her hands again, as though hearing the echo of an audience's applause in her head. She bowed low.

Then she stopped. She turned to face the human bouncy-ball. "You know, it's really weird when you do things like that. You look like a big rubbery bug."

60

The bouncy-ball unfolded once more into Hyde's elfish shape. He blushed. "I thought it was fun."

She sighed dramatically. "I'm bored."

"Me, too."

Suddenly, Panya's deceptively innocent pixie features lit up deviously. "You think you could change into something that walks on walls?"

He grinned, holding up his hands, which now resembled large, flesh-coloured suction cups. "Sure! Why?"

Panya rubbed her hands together gleefully. "No reason...It's just there's this really pretty, expensive ruby on the top floor of the Centre for Invaluable and Irreplaceable Trinkets I've been wanting to get a look at...up close...at night...when the security guard is looking the other way." She nudged him encouragingly. She grinned at him. "Are you up for an adventure?"

Hyde nodded with a devious smile that rivalled her own. "Will I get to wear the circus costume again?"

"Oh, yes."

\* \* \*

*An awkward interlude...*

Simon strolled cheerfully through the courtyard towards the library, which his fellow professors had promised housed the finest, rarest, most advanced and terribly expensive books of magic in all of Pandia. He hummed a little tune to himself. A young student passed him on the marble path, and Simon tipped his tweed hat to him.

The young man smiled a little bemusedly. Then he stumbled as his belt expectedly broke and his pants dropped to his ankles, tripping him. He sprawled face-forward upon the pathway, his bare bottom exposed to the other students lounging around the courtyard, who shrieked and giggled.

Simon didn't notice. He was in no mood for such things.

"Good morning, Professor Aliana," he greeted the Advanced Potions professor as he met her in the lane.

She inclined her head, but she did not pause to share a friendly greeting. In fact, she seemed eager to be far from him as quickly as possible. The gentle breeze suddenly swirled up, lifting her long, pearly grey sorceress robes. She gasped and clamped her hands over her skirts, but it was already too late.

"Well, hello, Professor," a boy in the fourth year Incanting class said, leering at her.

She flushed scarlet and ran the other way.

Simon ignored this. The library was only a few metres away, and he wasn't going to let anything disturb his cheerful mood.

"Hello, Professor Simon," a girl from his Beginning Incantations class said a little warily as he reached the large, brass doors of the Academy library. She was coming out with a stack of books, which he was pleased to see bore titles like **Ridiculously Advanced Incantations for the Struggling Wizard** and **Do Not Try This at Home: Incantations for Those Who Simply Hate to Wait.**

"Oh, hello, Maude. How are you today?" He smiled broadly at her.

There was a soft, tearing noise, and Maude's eyes widened. "I have to go," she said quickly. She clutched her books to her chest and rushed away, but not before Simon caught a glimpse of bare skin.

He sighed, but the sheer number of books on shelves of shining brass and copper stole his breath and distracted him from the flush that threatened to spread across his face. He clasped his hands together in delight. He hadn't seen so many books since he'd been in the company of Unreadable Gibberish, and these books weren't even complete rubbish.

The librarian sitting in the large, gilded circular desk in the centre of the room grimaced when she saw him. "Just—help yourself," she said and jumped quickly to her feet to escape between the bookshelves.

She tripped on her floor length skirt, and it tore down the centre, exposing her thigh-high stockings and skimpy underthings. She gasped and tried to clutch the skirt around her.

Simon sighed. "I think I'll just take a couple of these and go back to my room."

\* \* \*

The sun shone brilliantly over the cafeteria. Xen watched Sora eating across their small table in the centre of the bustling room. She paused with her fork midway to her mouth and smiled at him. Surrounding them were students, professors and a strange man with a mop of curly red hair wearing a top hat and a mis-matched striped suit that clumsily riffled a deck of cards for a group of bored, unimpressed women. Xen and Sora didn't notice any them. They didn't notice Oni sitting with three of the younger male professors, giggling and flirting outrageously. They didn't notice as Simon passed three elderly sorceresses, whose robes fell victim to a sudden gust of wind.

Xen returned her smile. Something inside his chest fluttered a little. He regretted that he was about to ruin the moment. "You know, I still haven't seen your Professor Tan around the school."

She nodded. "He spends most of his time in his workshop these days."

"What about classes?"

"I teach them nearly all the time lately."

"The Academy doesn't mind?"

"It is the way of things here. Zebulon is a very well-respected wizard. It's his prerogative to delegate as he pleases."

"But he's getting quite old, isn't he? Perhaps he isn't as fit as he once was."

Sora looked offended. She scowled at him. "He's fine. He simply has more important work to be getting on with than worrying about the day to day responsibilities to which he trusts me to attend."

"Like the spell he won't tell you about?"

Her voice was tight. "We just became friends. Do you really want to nettle me again so soon?"

He peered at her intently for several moments. "No. I would rather be your friend."

She glanced away shyly. A faint pink blush coloured her cheeks. "So would I. Zebulon will tell me what we're working on when the time is right."

"Does he do this often?"

"Yes. Well, sometimes."

"It doesn't bother you?"

She lifted her shoulders. "He does great work, and I am confident that my contribution is worthwhile. He'll reveal his plan to me when it is time for me to know." She sighed as she met his doubtful gaze. "Can you please just let it go?"

His brow furrowed. "Yeah. Sure. Just be careful, all right?"

She smiled. "Of course. I'm always careful." She lifted a forkful of her dinner to her lips then paused with a bemused expression. "Why would I need to be careful? I'm perfectly safe here. Zebulon would never cause me harm, if that's what you're implying."

"I'm not implying anything."

"Good."

He smiled at her, and his dark eyes crinkled at the corners. He saw her expression soften almost instantly. "How long has it been since you've been off the campus and out on the town?"

"Well...I'm sure I've been..." She hesitated.

"You don't remember?"

She laughed. "It has been a very long time. I have everything I need here. Why would I need to leave?"

"To have a little fun. Unwind. Go on a bender."

"A bender?"

"Well, maybe not a bender. But there are other things to do in the city."

"Like what?"

He thought about it. He lifted an eyebrow. "Care to find out?"

"With you?"

"Unless you feel you can navigate the hostile streets of Hyperion City without the accompaniment of a particular salty and uniquely qualified guide."

She laughed. "Are you asking me on a date, Xen?"

"Do you intend to say yes?"

Sora looked thoughtful. "Perhaps we could have dinner first."

He gestured around them. "We're having dinner now."

"Then perhaps something a bit more private."

Xen lifted an eyebrow. He waited until she glanced up to meet his gaze. "I can arrange that. Meet me later tonight."

\* \* \*

The cafeteria was empty but for the two young professors, who sat in a dark corner beneath the glittering stars. They sat close, talking in soft murmurs with their heads together. Sometimes, they stopped speaking and just gazed soulfully at each other. Something was happening between them. Even across the shadowy cafeteria, Zebulon Tan could see it. Even an old, sickly, dying man recognised the twinkle in their eyes from across a room.

He watched them with blank eyes and tight lips.

The man with the long, black and white hair reached a tentative hand across the table and touched Sora's fingers. She looked a little surprised, and then she slid her hand closer. He wrapped his fingers around hers and tugged her closer to him. She leaned against his side, resting her head against the crook of his arm. Xen leaned down to press his lips to the crown of her blonde head.

Zebulon could see the faint pink blush spread across her cheeks. They were very sweet.

This was an unexpected development.

Zebulon spun and walked away.

\* \* \*

*On a gloomy day in Penthos...*

The clouds hung low and dark over the lonely cemetery. It looked as though it was about to rain. There were only a few people standing around the fresh grave, and they were not speaking. They huddled together under a large, black umbrella. Their expressions were solemn. No one shed a tear, for the man had not been living at all when he'd been alive, not since he'd lost his reason for it.

The small, grey stone marker read Argus Moon. So that he may join his love in death, as in life.

Argus Moon was buried beside his love. Mercy Song's grave was barren, and the earth was cracked. It looked strange, as though someone had recently torn apart the earth and piled it back in place with little regard for its dignity.

Imogen stood on the edge of the cemetery beside a bare, spindly black tree. Her cold, beautiful face stretched in a humourless smile. Beside her, Mercy Song sobbed silent, spectral tears. Imogen glanced at her. She laughed. She laughed until the sound echoed across the barren fields.

The mourners did not look around. Perhaps they were afraid, or perhaps they already knew what they would find.

Imogen stopped laughing abruptly. "Oh, Argus. May you, indeed."

\* \* \*

*Meanwhile, in Scathach, the night is filled with sorrow...*

The sand on Lord Decay's beach was colourless, desolate grey. Skulls and bones crunched under the guests' feet as they stood around the shallow hole in which Lord Spirit lay entombed in a crystal coffin. He was part of Decay's domain now, silent and still, where his body would decay beside his ancestors forever. The Darklords and Ladies of Scathach stood around the shallow grave in black mourning dress. The ladies wore black veils over their faces.

No one cried, for Spirit would not be lost forever. His body would remain, as it was meant to, on Decay's lonely beach, but his soul would return to its home, where it belonged, with the spirits over which he had once ruled. Sho stood beside his father and mother, staring down at the old, lined face of the man he had known his entire life. Spirit was pale, for he had been pale in life. His skin was thin and translucent. He had been a good-natured man, but his expression was now morose. It was as though Decay had smoothed his face for his burial.

Sho had heard he had died with an expression of rapt horror.

The ascended Darklord Spirit stood over his father's grave. There was no expression on his face, which was pale and uncannily like his father's. He was older than Sho but only by a few years. He did not look as though he mourned his father, but perhaps he understood more about death than the others. His father would be with him again. He would be with him forever.

Sho watched him. Spirit knelt beside his father's grave. The brass plate on the sand above his head read, **Darklord Spirit. And he will rise to live eternally in Spirit.** The young Lord waved his hand over the coffin. Something spectral shimmered into existence. It was a rose or it was the spirit of a rose. He laid it upon the glass. He stood.

"Darklord Spirit, it is time," announced Decay, a man so elderly and emaciated, he appeared already to have begun his own decay. "He must be reaped."

Spirit's mouth twisted into the tiniest grimace, and then it was gone. He inclined his head. He had not reaped before, but it was tradition for the newest Spirit's first reap to be that of the one who came before. He lifted his chin. He bent back down beside his father's grave. For a moment, he hesitated.

Sho glanced at his father. There was no grief upon Blood's features, but his dark eyes were sad. Though they did not see eye to eye, Sho wondered if he could ever reap his father, even if it was his inherited birth right.

He did not even want the birth right he had, and it did not include spending eternity with his dead father's ghost.

The Darklords and Ladies watched silently. Darklord Spirit leaned over his father's grave. He lifted his hands above the body. He did not speak, for the reaping required no incantation. It required only the inherent powers of the current Lord of Spirit.

From inside the coffin, a pale, spectral light seemed to swirl around the late Darklord's body. Then the faintest shimmer, the faintest impression of a body floated up, out of the glass. Spirit held out his hands, beckoning the spectre as though to draw it to him.

The spectre hesitated a moment, apparently reluctant to be drawn to the young Darklord.

Then it moved, flowing towards him, seeping into him through his long, deathly pale fingertips. Darklord Spirit stood motionless until the last wisps of what resembled pale, shimmering smoke disappeared into him, absorbed into his body, into his essence.

And then it was over. The last Darklord Spirit would live on forever in the spirit of the new.

Darklord Blood took a hitching breath. Beside him, Darklady Blood wrapped an arm around her oldest, dearest friend, Darklady Spirit, but the widow seemed not to need the comfort. She smiled sadly as she watched her son ascend to his birth right. It was as it should be. It was as it always was.

Darklord Spirit passed, and he lived forever eternal in his son and every son that came after, for the reaping of the last Darklord Spirit imbued the new with all the spirits they had ever possessed.

Sho felt a strange tremor in his stomach. He sighed deeply. He glanced at Lord Blood.

Hesitantly, he lifted a hand and laid it upon his father's shoulder.

\* \* \*

Sora bent over a table in Zebulon's workshop. She pushed her small, square reading spectacles up as they slipped down her nose. At the table nearby, Zebulon poured over his text with a rapt expression, like a man possessed. His bright blue eyes practically burned.

His attention did not last. After several long moments, he glanced up at his young assistant. His voice startled her, for he rarely interrupted their research. "I've noticed you've been spending time with the new Talismans and Amulets professor, Sora."

She looked up at him. His expression was kindly, and she responded with a smile. "Yes. I have been."

"What's he like?"

Her eyes slid away, and a dreamy expression overtook her pretty, heart-shaped face. "I'm not sure yet. He could possibly be a dark wizard."

Zebulon raised his eyebrows. "A dark wizard, Sora?"

"I'm sorry." She smiled sheepishly. "I seem to have drifted off for a moment. He ran afoul of dark magic, but it is all behind him now."

"Are you sure?"

She considered this seriously. "I'm sure he wants it to be. Sometimes that's enough."

Zebulon was not truly interested in whether or not the new professor was a dark wizard. It mattered little. "It is interesting that he and his strange friends have suddenly shown up now."

She blinked at him in surprise. "Why?"

"What do you mean?"

"Why now specifically? It would not be interesting another time?"

He shrugged. His eyes twinkled with humour he did not feel. "I'm sure it would interesting at any time, from what I have gathered about them. I have heard many rumours of the tomfoolery to which they get up."

Now Sora laughed. "As have I. This school has never been so enjoyable."

He shook his head at her in disapproval. "I may not leave this laboratory often, but I still receive news. I have heard the woman—Oni—has taken up with Professor Wilder. And Professor Lang. And Professor Wardyworth."

His assistant laughed again. Her cheeks flushed with her unusual high spirits.

He held up a warning finger. "It is a dangerous thing to take up with one's co-workers."

"Is that a warning, Professor?"

"Not for you, my dear. I am sure you will make the right choices." His expression was serious, however. "The man they are with, the librarian—"

"Professor Simon? I do not think he is a librarian. In fact, I hear librarians turn tail and flee when he is within sight."

He ignored this. "What do you know about him?"

68

Sora was nonplussed. "Nothing." Her cheeks turned pink. "Except that girls seem to lose their shirts rather a lot around him."

"Is that a euphemism of some sort?"

She giggled. "Uh, no, actually."

Zebulon nodded and bent back over his book. He could feel Sora's eyes on him. Just as she turned her attention back to her own text, he lifted his head. "What do you really know about this man?"

"Simon?" Sora asked, confused.

"No. Xen."

She shook her head. "Not much. He's quite talented at Talismans and Amulets, but I suspect it isn't the only disciple he has mastered. He doesn't say much about his past if he can help it."

"How can you be sure that you can trust him?"

Sora's eyes were far away. "It is only a feeling I have. I don't know for sure, not yet. He's very mysterious. He can be quite reticent at times. I wonder that what he does tell me is even the whole truth." She seemed to sense that this unsettled her mentor, for she smiled reassuringly. "It is the way he makes me feel, Zebulon. I know his intentions are good, even if I don't understand everything about him yet."

"What has he told you about himself?"

She hesitated, and he feared she might not confide this in him. He held his breath. "I know that he was a member of the Lumina before he came here," she admitted at length.

Zebulon frowned thoughtfully. "Was he?"

"Many years ago. He was sacked."

"For what?"

"For using dark magic, as I understand it."

"But then, is he dangerous?"

"I think he could be, if he wanted to be. But I don't think he's a danger to me. He is too...careful with me. It's as though he's afraid I might break if he is too ungentle." Her cheeks flushed, and she ducked her head in embarrassment. "Not that—well, he is a perfect gentleman. He's made no untoward advances."

"Just be mindful, my dear. It is never wise to lose your head over someone you scarcely know, especially a man with such questionable credentials as he and his companions seem to possess."

"I have not lost my head," protested she, looking hurt. "I can take care of myself with Xen."

He reached across the table to stroke a gentle hand down her cheek. "I trust you, dear Sora. Of course I know you can. You are a child no longer. I only wish for you to remain on your guard. I don't want anything to happen to you. Not ever. You will forgive my overprotectiveness?"

She smiled up at him. "Of course, Zebulon, but I am perfectly all right with Xen. What can happen to me here, besides? With you here, it's the safest place in the world."

# Chapter Four

*T*he bobby frowned at the young man and woman cuffed to the two rickety wooden chairs in his lobby. They peered back at him sheepishly.

"So," he said, propping his hands up on his hips in disapproval. "You two broke into the Centre for Invaluable and Irreplaceable Trinkets to steal this ruby."

The young man opened his mouth to reply. The young woman beside him nudged him roughly, and he snapped it shut again. They stared up at him with eerily identical wide, unconvincingly innocent eyes.

"But what I don't understand..." The bobby pinched the bridge of his nose in exasperation. "What I don't understand is those outfits. Honestly, what is with the outfits?"

Hyde grinned hugely. "These are our circus costumes!" He slipped his hands out of the cuffs and lifted his arms to display the shiny silver bodysuit with small, metallic green checks.

Panya and the bobby stared at him incredulously. Hyde sat down hastily and slipped back into the cuffs with blushing abashment.

"Your circus costumes," the bobby repeated. He looked between them. Panya's circus costume was gleaming hot pink and black. "And you thought... you would be more discreet dressed like this?"

Panya lifted her chin defiantly. "He likes the circus costumes. It was the only way to get him to help."

Hyde looked at her with a wounded expression. "I would have helped without the costumes."

The bobby held up his hand. "Okay, that's enough. You two just sit here quietly. This just...this is going to make one hell of a story at the next force picnic." He jabbed a finger towards Hyde. "And you—you stay put. I don't want any more nonsense."

Hyde nodded shamefacedly.

When the bobby had gone, Panya scooted her chair towards the front desk, but she could not reach the brilliant, glittering red ruby the bobby had stashed there until the curator for the Centre of Invaluable and Irreplaceable Trinkets arrived to reclaim it. She sighed in frustration. Then she looked at Hyde eagerly. "Hey, can you get out of those cuffs again and grab the ruby?"

Hyde frowned at her. "The policeman told me not to do that again."

"So? Are you going to listen to a silly bobby, or do you want riches and bragging rights beyond your wildest dreams?"

"I don't think that is what I would get. The bobby told me no, and I would have to leave you behind. You would get in trouble." He looked disappointed. "Adventuring is not as rewarding as you would have had me believe."

She scowled. "None of this would have happened if your suction cups were strong enough to hold us both up on the wall!"

"I am sorry. I did not account for gravity on the way down."

Hyde's expression was deeply hurt, but Panya ignored this ruthlessly. "I was so close. I just wanted to touch it."

"You did touch it," he reminded her. "That is the problem."

"I wanted to hold it forever!"

"Well, I am sorry. How was I to know the clock was actually an alarm?"

"It wasn't!" she snapped. "It was the window you broke with your stupid hammer feet that set off the alarm."

"I am sorry! Being an adventurer is hard and not as much fun as you let on!"

"We were having fun."

"This isn't fun."

She sighed. "Well, at least I'm not bored anymore."

The bobby strode back into the room. He eyed them suspiciously. "Is there someone you can call?"

Hyde and Panya looked at each other sadly. Oni and Xen were off at the wizard school somewhere, and they didn't have time to bail them out of jail yet again. Simon, of course, would radiate such disapproval it was never worth calling him at all, even if he would come, which he always did. Then, at the same time, the two wildly unsuccessful criminals lit up.

"Yes!"

\* \* \*

*Meanwhile, on a bleak night in Scathach...*

Sho paced to the window in his bedroom high up in the tower of the ancestral Blood Keep. The room was exactly as he'd left it. His parents still refused to give up hope that he would return home any day to reclaim his birth right. The enormous, four-poster bed was draped in scarlet brocades. Even the heavy drapes were deep red, and the carpets gleamed like wet blood. He sighed. He didn't mind the décor; it wasn't the mind-boggling disorder of his office lobby, but it was luxurious and comfortable. He tried to ignore the feeling that the room, despite its luxuries, was a tower prison and he its captive prince.

The funeral had passed days ago, but Sho could not yet escape his homeland. His father insisted he remain in the Darklands until after the new Lord Spirit's ceremony in a few days time, during which the new Darklord would be welcomed by his dark brethren and ascend to his lordship. There was no real necessity for his continuing presence, but Darklord Blood would not have his son out gallivanting around Hyperion City whilst his people observed their most ancient rites in honour of his closest friend, the late Darklord Spirit.

Sho was not anticipating the ceremony with any enthusiasm. He had not heard that the Darklady Nailah would return to Scathach for the ball. In fact, his mother had not once mentioned the girl to whom his parents expected him to be married, but he suspected his parents would spring her on him when he was at his most unguarded and vulnerable. They seemed quite determined that he would accept the pesky young woman, regardless of his life-long aversion to her. He could, not, however much he might desire to do, buck the ancient traditions of his people. He would attend the ceremony, and he would...consider Lady Nailah.

His father's determination to force his son into the mould of the next Darklord Blood was little distraction from his mourning. He did not express his sorrow over the loss of his closest, dearest friend. On the contrary, he was often silent and cold, prowling the expansive halls of the Blood Keep as though he expected his friend to manifest in his spectral form. If Lord Spirit remained in the Darklands, he did not appear to be able to visit those he had left behind. Or perhaps he knew it was kinder to stay away, that it would only prolong his friend's misery should he suddenly appear, only a shade of the man he had once been.

Sho couldn't wait to get out of Scathach. His irritation with his father aside, he was not comfortable with watching the once powerful Darklord so weakened by his grief. He wanted nothing more than to get away as quickly as possible. There was nothing here for him in the Darklands. There hadn't been for some time.

There was only his father's sadness and his mother's gentle persistence that he approach the Lady Nailah with the utmost haste.

He sighed and dropped back onto the bed without bothering to remove his pointed leather boots. He picked up the thick, red silk-covered book on the nightstand beside him. He couldn't focus on the words, though it had been his favourite story since he'd been a child. He was not a child any longer, and the fantastic story of elves, nymphs and warriors could not hold his interest.

When the small, crystal orb in his pocket started to chime, he moaned in relief. He fumbled the orb out of his pocket. It blinked red and chimed again. He pressed a tiny dimple in the smooth, glossy surface. "Sho Sange." He tried to contain the excitement in his voice.

The voice that issued from the orb sounded tinny and far away. "Mr Sange, this is Constable Corley of the Hyperion City Constabulary."

Sho groaned.

"I have two individuals in custody who claim they work for you."

He pinched the bridge of his nose. "Which ones?" Sho worked with insane, reckless people with little regard for the safety of anyone and even less regard for the legal system. This wasn't the first call of this sort he had received.

"A Miss Panya and Mr Hyde."

Sho sighed. Evidently, he should not have left the two alone in the office. "What did they do?"

"They were caught attempting to remove a very precious ruby from the Centre for Invaluable and Irreplaceable Trinkets."

Sho snorted. "Why doesn't that surprise me? Are they to be charged?"

The constable hesitated. "They offered...considerable financial compensation for their indiscretion, but someone will need to come...claim them."

Sho cursed under his breath. "I cannot. I am in Scathach."

"Well, if someone does not come to get them, we will have to process them."

"No, no. I will send someone. Just...give me a little time."

"Time is running out, Mr Sange. Please be expedient."

The orb went silent, and its glow extinguished. It was little more than a crystal ball. He held it out on the palm of his hand and muttered under his breath. The orb glowed red once more, and after several moments, a clipped voice answered the call.

"Is it done?" Darius demanded.

Sho sighed. "No."

"Then why are you calling me? I'm with Enid. This had better be important."

He squeezed his eyes shut. "It is important. I need a favour."

Darius huffed irritably. "Now?"

"Yes, now."

"But Enid--"

"Get another appointment. I'll pay for it. Do you want to stop the unmaking of the world or not?"

Darius growled low in his infernal throat. "Fine. What is it, then?"

\* \* \*

Zebulon Tan stood before the mirror amidst the disarray of his sleeping chambers. He had not bothered to clean the room in some time, and he could not afford to allow one of the maids to discover his secret. He'd learned to live with the spreading mess and the creeping, insidious stink of filth that had overtaken his chambers. It was of nothing to him.

He etched a rune in the air. The effort it took to transform from the withered old man to the vital, virile sorcerer was almost staggering. As his body straightened and thickened, he leaned against the wall, gasping. His knees trembled. Finally, he stood upright and snatched up the clear crystal orb lying on a pile of robes covered in glowing red and blue stains. He muttered over it.

A red glow swirled in the centre of the orb. After several moments, a gruff, gravelly voice issued from somewhere within its swirling depths. "Yeah?"

"It's Tan."

"Tan." He sounded almost amused. "I thought you were done for."

"I'm not done for!" Zebulon snapped.

"All right, all right. Well what do you want now, then? Another god? Another finder of lost things? Another long lost spell?"

Zebulon scowled. "I want information."

"Ah. I see. And what sort of information is it this time? The key to a lost civilisation that will somehow cure all the ills of mankind?"

"I do not appreciate your sarcasm. You will do what I pay you to do. I do not require your cheeky commentary or subtle disparagements."

The voice on the other end of the orb was silent for a moment. When he replied, his voice sounded more subdued. "What information, sir?"

"I want to know who the people at my school are."

There was another pause, as though the gravelly-sounding man was attempting to curtail his cheeky tongue. "Are you speaking of any particular people?"

"Very particular people."

"Well, who are they?"

"They call themselves Xen, Oni and Simon."

"You got any last names?"

"No."

"Never heard of them."

Zebulon ground his teeth. "Then find someone who has. I want to know everything there is to know about them. Now."

There was an almost inaudible sigh. "I will do everything within my power. You may rest assured, my power is quite considerable."

"Let us hope that it does not fail you this time, then, or there will be consequences." Without awaiting a response, Zebulon tucked the orb into the folds of his capacious robe. He started towards the door, but he paused and turned back to the mirror. His disguise remained, and he appeared the powerful man he had once been. He strode purposefully from his chamber towards his workroom. He would solve this little problem, with or without assistance. He was more than up to the challenge of handling three mysterious strangers, particularly such incredibly ridiculous ones as Xen, Oni and Simon.

He still had powers and tricks even his illness couldn't rob from him.

\* \* \*

Darius strode swiftly into the bobby station. His hair was slightly mussed, but he hadn't bothered to set it right. He was annoyed. He'd travelled the aether from Aether City to Hyperion, and he hated such a hasty journey without even a moment to prepare, let alone he'd lost his weekly appointment with Enid, who refused to give him another client's spot, despite her claim that he was in fact quite a favourite of hers.

The lobby was quiet. A lone bobby manned the front desk. He rose when Darius entered. He eyed the man in the shiny dark suit and the mussed hair with a suspicious eye. He didn't seem to decide in Darius' favour.

Darius was not in the mood. "Where are they?"

The bobby did not have to ask of whom he was speaking. He jerked his head. "Through here."

Darius followed the bobby through the lobby into a small holding area. He lifted an eyebrow at Panya and Hyde, who sat side by side on a bench in the holding cell, handcuffed together in their shiny circus costumes. He sighed. "Oh, this is just brilliant. What did you do this time?"

Hyde grinned at him. "Hi, Mr D!"

Panya was not as happy to see him. She scowled. "Where's Sho?"

Darius rolled his eyes. "He's a bit busy at the moment."

"Why did he send you?"

"Who else would he send?" Darius sounded impatient now. "My options were to pull your less criminally inclined associates off my extremely important case or come myself."

"Less criminally inclined?" asked Hyde in confusion. "We have less criminally inclined associates? Since when?"

Darius growled. "Do you want out of here or not?"

"With you?" Panya sounded sceptical.

"You come with me or you stay in the cell."

She sighed. "All right, all right."

Darius tilted his head at the bobby, who slid open the holding cell door to release the prisoners. The bobby gave Darius a stern look. "I trust you will keep them from any further indiscretion?"

Darius eyed the thieves. "Not me. I'll see to it that Ptolemy will deal with them next time."

His words were not directed at the bobby. Panya gasped, and her pale, heart-shaped face went pink. "You wouldn't."

"It's not up to me. It's up to him. You know how well I like greed, but

Ptolemy...well. He has his own way of dealing with those sorts of things."

Panya glared at him. "You're bluffing."

He shrugged. "If you say so." Without waiting for them, he spun smartly on his heel and strode towards the exit. Hyde hurried to catch him up. At the door, Darius paused to call to Panya over his shoulder. "Are you coming?"

Hyde spun to Panya. A large grin stretched across his face. He held his hand to her. She sighed in exasperation, but she took another look at the stern bobby and high-tailed it out the door.

Darius gave her a sidelong scowl. "I'm docking your pay on this job for this, you know."

Panya's shoulders slumped. "Of course you are."

Hyde looked crestfallen. "You can't just do a nice thing?"

Darius snorted. "It is intrinsically contrary to my nature to do so. Anyway, have you seen what they do to my kind when we do nice things? It's horrifying."

\* \* \*

Zebulon cursed and shoved the heavy tome from the table before him. He dropped his head into his hands. He was so close. It had seemed easy in the beginning. The first few runes had appeared as though he was meant to find them, but the last were more elusive. He'd searched day and night, but they remained stubbornly out of his reach.

A soft knock sounded on the door, and Sora opened it, poking her head in before he had a chance to bid her enter. He spun towards her. "What?"

Sora recoiled in surprise at the harshness of his tone. "Zebulon?"

He sighed and strode forward to gesture her inside. "I am sorry, Sora. I should not have snapped at you. I have much on my mind."

"Can I help you?"

She looked so perfectly concerned for him that his heart sank a little over his brutish greeting. "You are helping already, my dear. It is just...these runes."

Her smile was tentative. "I understand."

"I would never mean to snap at you, my dear. Not you." He took a deep breath to calm his anxious nerves. "What is it?"

"It is time for class, Zebulon. Are you coming today?"

He waved his hand dismissively. "No, no. I have much work to do. Would you mind terribly?" She smiled, and he knew she was pleased, for she enjoyed taking his classes. Affection for the young, bright and ambitious girl surged in his chest, and he felt his mouth stretching to return her smile. "You will take them for me?"

"Of course."

"You are becoming quite adept, Sora. You will be replacing me in no time. Of that, I have no doubt."

"I don't want to replace you."

"The student always becomes the teacher eventually, and it will soon be your time. You are almost ready. You have proven yourself well."

Her cheeks coloured under his praise. "Thank you, Zebulon."

A warning bell chimed through the corridors. Sora smiled. "I must get to class."

"I know you will do well on your own."

She smiled at him and waved as she hurried from his tower workshop. As the door closed behind her, his face sagged from the effort of holding the smile. It was almost painful. He started as the orb hidden in the folds of his robes chimed. He fumbled it out frantically. "Tan."

"It's me," the gravelly voice told him in a voice that sounded unhappy.

"Well? What did you find out?"

The man on the other end of the call sighed. "Nothing."

"Nothing? What do you mean nothing?"

"Nothing."

"How can you have found nothing?"

"I'm sorry, Tan. It's as though they don't exist."

Anger flared in Zebulon's chest. "They exist! They are here, so they must exist!

"I found nothing."

"Then those aren't their real names!"

"They likely are not. I'm not entirely certain how you expect me to find anything out if you don't even know their names."

"That is your job!"

"Maybe someone has worked very hard to conceal them."

Zebulon took several calming breaths before he could speak again. "Fine. Call me if you find anything else." He did not wait for a response. He tossed the orb across the room. It crashed against a bookshelf, and several heavy tomes tumbled to the ground. He ignored them. He pushed his hands through his steel grey hair. It looked luxuriant, but it felt thin and brittle beneath his fingers. He cursed to himself. "Damn! Who the hell are they, then?"

He strode towards the centre of the room and flipped impatiently through the opened book upon the podium. "I will just have to take care of you myself, my little meddlers."

\* \* \*

Headmaster Whip's office was rather small. A large trophy case housing various diplomas, medals, ribbons and awards took up nearly half the room, glittering as though the tall, thin, austere-looking man spent most of his day polishing the glass and ensuring not a speck of dust had invaded the pristine showcase. He looked quite as though at that moment he'd rather be attending his vitrine than dealing with the situation unfolding in his office.

He peered around in deepest disappointment at the five professors crowded into the confined room. Three of them had formerly been some of his most steadfast and sensible employees, but now they looked as though they'd moments before engaged in a terrible brawl, which they had been. They, at least, seemed aware that this was rather inappropriate behaviour for such esteemed professors. They avoided his eyes shamefacedly. Bruises, lacerations and curious footprints stood out, livid and garish, on their faces. Oni and Simon, the new professors of whom he knew little but had heard an awful lot, looked only marginally sheepish. Neither of them had a scratch on them.

Whip gritted his teeth. "Will someone please explain to me what happened here?"

All three of his once steadfast professors began speaking at once.

"I had a date with Oni!" Professor Wilder said.

"I thought I was the only one," added Professor Lang.

"She is my sweetie! She only loves me," Professor Wardyworth insisted.

"She's my honey-bunny!"

"I'm her true love!"

"He stole my girlfriend!"

Whip sighed deeply and held up his hands for silence. "That is enough." He turned to the woman in question. "Oni?"

She lifted her shoulders. She did not look especially troubled by the proceedings. She sat back in her chair with an expression of utmost amusement. "Well, I didn't expect them all to find out about each other."

"This is a very small school!"

"Meh."

Whip pinched the bridge of his nose in exasperation. "And Simon, how did you get involved in all of this?"

Simon's cheeks coloured. "I was trying to break up the fight, but..."

"You pulled off Oni's shirt instead?"

"Not me!" Simon exclaimed, horrified. "It was Professor Wardyworth."

"And it did break up the fight," Professor Wilder said reasonably.

Oni thrust out her chest proudly. "They are rather show-stopping, aren't they?"

Whip frowned at Simon. "You pulled off her shirt to break up the fight."

"I told you! It wasn't me. It was Professor Wardyworth. It was an accident!"

Whip frowned imperiously at him. "There seems to be a lot of accidental nudity around you, Professor Simon."

Simon slumped in his chair, blushing scarlet. Oni turned a suspicious gaze upon him. He avoided her eyes pointedly.

Professors Wilder, Lang and Wardyworth smirked at each other.

"Look, you people can't be going around pulling off people's shirts and–" Whip looked at Oni sternly. "Well, whatever it is you are doing with your fellow professors. You are a sexual harassment lawsuit waiting to happen!"

Oni looked proud, but Simon appeared deeply embarrassed by this.

"This has got to stop," Whip added. He jabbed a warning fingers towards his staunch and shamefaced professors. "And you three! You know the rules at this school. Keep it in your pants!"

Professors Wilder, Lang and Wardyworth had the grace to look chagrined. "Yes, sir."

Oni stared contemplatively at Simon. He hummed awkwardly and looked away.

Whip rose. "That is all. Now, all of you just get out."

\* \* \*

*Meanwhile, in Scathach, things are growing tense...*

The silence in the dining room was heavy and awkward. Forks and spoons scraped the fine red china plates. Lord Blood picked morosely at his dinner, but he'd hardly eaten a bite. Despite the bad blood between her husband and son, though, Lady Blood's expression was cheerful. She'd missed her son terribly when he'd gone off to Hyperion City, and she was pleased to see him home once more.

She opened her mouth to speak, and Sho braced himself. He'd known the moment was coming. The funeral in Decay's domain had only silenced her for a brief time, long enough for her to feel as though she'd allowed her husband enough time to grieve his dear friend. He knew exactly what his mother would say.

"Sho..."

The time had certainly come. Her tone was delicate, but there was something indefinably provoking about it.

"You may have noticed that Lady Nailah has not been in attendance since you arrived."

"How could I miss it? When she is, she's perpetually underfoot. I've welcomed the reprieve." This was true. The Lady Nailah had been markedly absent from the Blood Keep, but Sho had not wished to jinx the stroke of fortune by bringing it up. He remembered the awkward adolescent daughter of Lord and Lady Shadow. She'd spent most of her days in the Keep, trailing behind him and constantly pestering him for attention.

"Oh, Sho," his mother scolded. "Don't be so cold. Nailah is a lovely young woman."

"She's a nuisance."

"She is nothing of the sort," Lord Blood snapped. "She is a Darklady. She is worthy of respect."

Sho curled his lip. "She is a vexatious child."

"Lady Nailah has gone to Hyperion City," Lady Blood cut in.

Sho turned his head to look at her in surprise. "I beg your pardon? Nailah is in the city?"

"She is indeed. She has been since the Autumn Equinox. She is attending the University of Elemental Conjuration."

"I would have expected her to attempt to contact me. She has always been unabashedly bothersome. I did not realise she would be so merciful in a different environment."

His mother frowned. She lifted her chin imperiously. "It is your duty to contact her."

"What? Why?"

"You are a Lord."

"I am not a Lord!"

She ignored this. "It would not be proper for a lady to contact you. It is beneath her."

Sho lifted his eyebrows. "Since when is such a thing beneath Nailah?"

"You will not speak ill of a lady of such high breeding," Lord Blood put in angrily.

Sho did not wish to upset him, for his father's constitution was still delicate. They had not revisited their argument from his first evening home, but it still hung unspoken in the air around them. "I apologise, Father."

His mother's expression was stern. "You will go see her."

"What?"

"It is your duty, as I stated. She is your intended."

"Lady Nailah is not my intended. Not intended by me, anyway."

"Whether you intend or not, your father and I, as well as Lord and Lady Shadow do intend, and you will not disappoint us or shame our family by ignoring her. It would be the absolute height of rudeness."

Sho sighed, for he knew she was right. "I know, Mother." Despite his acquiescence, anger roiled in his belly. He was not a child any longer, and he did not appreciate being treated as such. When he'd left home for Hyperion City, he had shunned his people and the rules by which they were governed. He did not intend to abide by them now. "Nevertheless, I still have no intention of marrying the girl. I will chose who I marry; that is, if I marry."

His father stiffened angrily. "When you finally come to your senses, Nailah will make a fine Lady Blood. You will not fail in your duty to your family and your people."

Sho bristled, but he did not argue with this. It was of little use. "All right. I will see her."

His mother smiled, and there was something smug and knowing in her eyes that chafed at Sho's nerves. He ignored it. "Wonderful." She leaned across the table to grip his hand warmly. "Now, tell me of the city, Sho. I have not been there since I was such a young girl. Does it still move so quickly there?"

"Indeed, it is much faster paced."

Blood lifted an eyebrow as though the idea was quite distasteful. "How so?"

"They have steam cars."

His father snorted at this cheek. Lady Blood frowned between them. "And how is your business, Sho? I understand you are quite busy much of the time."

Sho sighed. He did not really wish to reveal the nature of his work in Hyperion, for even his grandest, noblest of deeds would be little comfort to the family he'd abjured. Not that his father would ever view any of his or his associates' deeds as noble or grand or even marginally acceptable.

"Yes," said he carefully. "We are highly sought after."

Blood curled his lip. "I imagine your time is well spent carousing with that hooligan woman, chasing down rogue elves and recovering stolen mood-altering potions from drunken necromancers."

Sho bridled. "I'll have you know, Father, our work is most often more serious than that."

"Really. How so? You employ a former circus performer as a thief, a mad woman from Labraid, a dark wizard who was sacked by the Lumina and—well, Heavens knows what the other two are."

His eyes narrowed at his father. "They are the best in our field."

"If they are the best in the business, perhaps you are in the wrong business."

"Darling," Lady Blood said quietly.

They both ignored her. Sho glared at his father. "For your information, Father, we are currently in the process of stopping the complete unmaking of the world."

There was a moment of complete silence in which Sho realised he should not have risen to his father's chivvying. He felt much like a young man again, an adolescent furious at the constraints and demands of his birth right when he wanted nothing more than to live the life he chose wherever he chose to live it. Worse still, there remained an unwelcome compulsion to prove himself to his father. He gritted his teeth and clenched his hands together under the table.

Then Lord Blood burst into quiet laughter. "The complete unmaking of the world? And how, exactly, is this to come about?"

Sho stiffened. His resolve to remain calm shattered under that mocking laugh. "A wizard is attempting to open a gate to Hao."

His father closed his mouth, but mirth still twinkled in his eyes. "Hao? I'm afraid I know nothing about it."

"I am sure there is quite a lot about which you know nothing."

"Sho," his mother warned softly.

This did not offend Lord Blood. On the contrary, he smiled. "No, please. Enlighten me, son. How is this Hao to unmake the world, and how, exactly, do you intend to stop it?"

Sho sighed. "Hao is a chaos dimension. Its creatures, if unleashed on our world, will bring such wide-spread chaos, the world as we know it will be consumed."

"That does sound dreadful, indeed." There was still a hint of humour in his voice. "And how will you stop this from happening?"

Sho hesitated. "Due to the circumstances here in Scathach...I have left the matter in the hands of my team."

Blood smiled. "I see. Well, for the sake of all of us, let us hope you are not as integral to their success as you would have us believe."

\* \* \*

*Still meanwhile, after some wicked machinations...*

The accoutrements of dark magic surrounded Zebulon Tan as he stood at the podium in his workroom. Bones, skulls, eyes in jars and flaps of dried, husky skin, knives, vials of bubbling blood and simmering cauldrons encircled his workspace. They were little more than show. The old wizard needed none of these props to perform his wicked machinations, but there was something to be said about tradition. They still possessed power, the items that those weaker than him had charged with their darkest energy.

He drew upon their power, for his knees trembled, and his bones shook so violently, they rattled his teeth. He felt the guise of his virility stripped away. The strength and power was fading from his body with a rapidity that terrified him. He didn't let it distract him.

He lifted his hands. He drew the swirling black energy into himself. His body jerked. His eyes turned from pale, watery blue to deep, Stygian black. His mouth formed the ancient words, though he hardly knew what he was saying. The meaning behind them, however, was clear. His fury, and his loathing infused every senseless syllable.

His voice built into a passionate crescendo until the words became little more than a feral howl that shook the tower and crashed in murderous waves across the campus...

\* \* \*

*Presently...*

Oni squirmed in her rickety wooden chair. "Ooh. I think I felt a little tingle."

Simon peered down at his plate in distaste. "It must be the fish." He prodded the tray of colourless food with his fork. "No wonder the cafeteria's so empty tonight."

Xen frowned. "No. It isn't the fish. I felt it, too." His skin crawled as though a thousand bugs were teeming just under the thin layer of flesh. There was too much magic in the place. He waved his hand and muttered quietly under his breath.

Oni jolted again as the energy rebounded off Xen's invisible protective bubble. They could almost see the dark tendrils of magic as they bounced off the boundary. Then she relaxed. "That's much better. Someone must have blown one of the laboratories or something."

"I hate this place," Xen muttered. "There's too much magic."

Simon pushed his glasses back up his nose in annoyance. "Well, whose fault is that, eh? We've been here days, and we've learned nothing. You haven't gotten us any closer to Tan, and all Oni is doing is carousing with our fellow professors and getting us all into embarrassing situations and subjected to well-earned stern

86

talkings-to."

"I am working on it!"

Oni rolled her eyes. "Oh, please. You're just sitting around making moon eyes at that girl and holding her hand in the dark."

Xen looked horrified. He hadn't realised Oni had seen him with Sora the other night. "I am doing more than that!" he snapped. "I am talking her out into the city this weekend. Maybe once she's gotten some distance from Tan and the school, she'll be a bit more talkative."

"Let's be honest," Simon said in exasperation. "This isn't information gathering. It's wooing. You like her."

"Wooing never hurt anybody," Oni added.

"We have to be more proactive! We cannot keep on like this. We're getting nowhere, and every moment he gets closer. You've made it into Sora's life. Now you need to take it to the next level. If you're going to spend time with her, it needs to be productive. Do not forget why we are all here in the first place."

Xen looked almost offended by this suggestion. "She won't be happy if she finds out what we're doing."

"This isn't about her! We appreciate that you have finally discovered that there is a tender side to your nature, but, Xen, do you even understand how dangerous Tan is and what he could do to the world if he is successful?"

Xen sighed. He held up his hand. "Okay. Okay. I get it."

"No! You don't. I don't think you do or you would be thinking about the spell and how to stop it, not how you're going to get a leg over!"

"I am not thinking of getting my leg over! It's not like that." His eyes slid away, and two faint patches of red coloured his cheeks.

Oni eyed him suspiciously. "You really do fancy her. For real."

"I do not."

"It's all over your shifty face."

Xen glared at her. Simon huffed irritably. "Fine. Fancy her. Whatever. Just get her on our side and figure out what we're dealing with here so we can do something about it. If she's helping him research the spell, find out what it is and how far they've come."

Xen scowled at him. "Okay, okay."

"Don't get distracted. Don't forget what we're doing here. This isn't a joke."

"Everything is a joke," Oni put in positively.

"Not when the entire world is at stake, Oni, and if you could come up with some usefulness for yourself, that would be really terrific."

She lifted a finger to point accusingly at him. "Oh, and what about you?"

"I am trying to keep everything together!"

"Everything together? What about that girl's shirt as we walked in here?"

Simon pinched the bridge of his nose. Oni grinned smugly at him. "Can we please just focus?" he asked plaintively.

"Sure. Right. We are focussed," Xen said, scowling. "Get information about the spell. Don't get distracted."

"Don't get a leg over," Oni added.

"Oni!"

"What?"

\* \* \*

The Hedone District of Hyperion City was lively and noisy with laughter, singing, and the perpetual shrieks of delight that punctuated the tinny hurdy-gurdy music pouring out onto the streets from the many pubs and piano halls. Though it was not Komodia, Pandia's city of lights, laughter and all the pleasures man or beast could seek, Hedone was a mecca of delights, amusements and diversions for Hyperion's various castes and classes.

Sora Bale had never been to Hedone, and she gripped Xen's hand, uncertain whether to be frightened by the spectacles in the streets or delighted by the sheer brio of the scene. A man in a red and green checked bodysuit leapt into their path, contorting and gesticulating wildly towards a shining red and white striped building that looked more like a circus tent than a solid structure, though it had been around even longer than the Hedone District. The district, in fact, seemed almost to have been built around the tent until it resembled a massive circus grounds, complete with tumbling and leaping funambulists, large animals bearing beautiful men and women, and brightly coloured clowns who gambolled through the streets with outrageous makeup and almost frightening leers.

Xen felt Sora move closer to him, unsure how to react to the pantomime unfolding before them. He wrapped an arm around her waist. "How do you feel about the circus?"

She smiled up at him. "I've never seen the circus."

"I believe now is your chance." He bowed cheerfully to the mime and guided Sora into the enormous circus tent.

The show was already in progress. Funambulists tumbled around a large ring, leaping and flying through the air over each other while trapeze artists swung from chains and ropes on the ceiling. Sora exclaimed in delight at the colourful acrobats, barely noticing as Xen guided her into a seat around the large, noisy ring. A procession of lions, tigers, elephants, enormous horses and more exotic beasts in bright arrayment marched in a slow circle around the arena whilst the guests shrieked in excitement or fear.

Sora pointed towards the aerialists twirling in bizarre, graceful contortions. "Oh, Xen, aren't they wonderful?"

He smiled. "They're all right. Panya is much better."

She turned to him in surprise. "Panya?"

"She's from Komodia. She grew up performing."

"In the circus?"

"Yes. She was a funambulist. She's most impressive."

"Where does she perform now?"

He laughed. "She does not. She left the circus life and moved onto petty crime and larceny."

Sora looked utterly appalled.

Xen winked at her. "She doesn't do that anymore, either." He paused, considering this. "Most of the time, anyway, as long as she's kept otherwise occupied."

She was silent a moment, but her eyes did not gleam as they followed the performers like they had moments before. "There is so much about you I do not know. I know nothing of your life before you came to Gwydion." She sighed wistfully. "My life can be summed up completely by my work and my time at the Academy."

"That does not sound so bad, Sora."

She laughed. "Come now. Can you imagine a life of such mundanity? I've hardly experienced anything in this world. I've been content with that until..."

He lifted an eyebrow when she did not continue. "Until what?"

She smiled. "Until I met you. There is a whole world out there that I'd never considered before." She was silent a moment as she watched a large white tiger parade past them, draped in electric blue blankets. The tiger roared and clawed at the dirty ground beneath his paws. Sora turned back to Xen. "I never felt like I was missing anything before."

"And now?"

She contemplated this. "No. I do not feel as though I am missing anything. I feel as though...there are possibilities."

She did not say anything more for several moments. A woman with long, curly yellow hair walked unsteadily across a tight rope above their heads. Unexpectedly, she turned a cartwheel in the centre of the rope and hung there, suspended with her legs in the air. Then she flipped over several times and landed gracefully on her feet.

"So how did you meet Panya?" Sora asked suddenly amidst the applause.

Xen did not answer immediately. He was uncertain how to answer the question without revealing the true nature of his work, but Sora's eyes were shining with such innocence, such curiosity, he could not find the heart to lie. "When I left the Lumina, I was in a bad way. I was hopped up on dark magic, and I had lost my life's work. I was confused and angry. I did a lot of things...I should not have done."

Sora smiled wanly. "I am not certain I want to know those things."

"No. You do not. And I am not sure I would want you to know. In my defence, I did not know what I was doing. The artefact's magic was very powerful."

She considered this a long moment. "I am sure you regret what you have done."

"Every moment. I crossed the countryside from Aether City where the Lumina were headquartered to Hyperion. I left devastation in my wake. My own people were hunting me."

"The Lumina?"

"Of course. I was everything they despised. Not only did they sack me, they realised I was too dangerous to be set loose after touching the artefact, and they were hunting me down to kill me. I met some of them in the city. My power was strong—stronger than any of theirs—but they were prepared. They had me cornered. Someone...well, my friend--"

"Panya?"

He smiled. "No, not Panya. Sho. He found us, and he stepped in to help me fight them off. He thought they were muggers or something. When the fight was over, he realised there was something wrong with me. He took me in, and he... well, he sort of put me through a dark magic detox. He saved my life."

"So you're not...the dark magic is gone?"

"No. Not completely. It's always there, under the surface. If I...if I don't restrain my emotions, I could lose control and go into a rage." He smiled at her wary expression. "I'm very careful not to allow that to happen."

She lifted an eyebrow. "What has this to do with Panya?"

He smiled. "Sho ran into her much the same way. He has a way of...pulling people out of the darker places." His eyes twinkled. "Which is ironic."

"Why?"

"Sho is from Scathach. He is a Darklord."

She blinked in surprise. "A Darklord? Your best friend is a Darklord?"

"Yes. He's heir to Blood."

Sora shivered involuntarily. "Are they really...are they the way people say?"

"You mean evil?" Xen laughed. "No. They're not evil. They're just people. They just come from...somewhere else."

"And they have power over the darkest forces."

"Most people do not understand them. Sho is different from the others. He doesn't want to be a Darklord. Well, he wants to be a Darklord, but he doesn't want to actually lord over anything. He just wants to be free. To live the life he chooses."

She sighed deeply. "So you have a friend who is a Darklord, another who was a thief. You used to be Lumina..."

"Yes."

"And what about your other friends? The ones you came with? Oni and Simon? They are...very strange."

He laughed out loud. "Yes. They are."

"Are they some...is there some story about them, too? Did Simon used to be some kind of backstreet smut peddler or something?"

Xen lifted an eyebrow at her. "A smut peddler?"

"Not because...not because I know anything about that. It's just that there seems to be a lot of accidental nudity around him."

"Yes. There is." He grinned at her. "No. I don't think he used to be anything like that. I don't know much about him, really. I don't even know where he's from. He just sort of...came along."

"But you knew him before you came here."

"Yes, but Sho never told me how they met. He's always just...been around."

"And Oni?"

He shook his head. "She's...not the sort of person you get to know. Whatever's going on in her head...it's best not to know, I think. She's from Labraid."

"Labraid?" Sora shivered again. "I hear it is a dangerous city."

"It can be. Most members of polite society don't go there unless they're looking for someone specific."

"You mean the guilds of assassins and thieves."

Xen ignored this. "Oni can be unpredictable. I don't know how she came to Hyperion or what she did in Labraid. She and Sho won't talk about how they know each other, but there seems to be...well, sometimes I wonder if there is something more between them."

"They're in love?" Sora frowned thoughtfully.

Xen shook his head. "No. I don't think so. Maybe."

She looked offended. "Then why would she behave the way she does?"

He shrugged. "She has always behaved as she likes."

"It doesn't bother Sho?"

"No."

"Then they must not be in love."

He did not seem concerned with this. "If Sho doesn't tell me, I don't want to know."

"But how did you all come to be at Gwydion at the same time? Why are you here?"

Xen did not reply to this right away.

Sora gave him an arch look. "I may look like a child, Xen. I may seem innocent, but I am not stupid. I know there is something going on. There is some reason you are here. I want to know it." The expression in her large, blue eyes was piercing. "I think it involves me."

"Not you. Not you, exactly."

She gave him a knowing look. "Zebulon."

He sighed. "Sora...can we talk about it later? We're having such a nice time. I could tell you about my parents. My childhood and my days at the Lumina monastery."

She shook her head. Her eyes gleamed with determination. "No. I don't want to spend any more time getting to know you if you aren't really going to be honest. Who are you people really?"

"I am who I told you I am, Sora. There's just...something I left out."

"Such as?"

He hesitated. He didn't like the way her eyes seemed so distant now, so guarded, as though an invisible barrier was rising between them. He reached for her hand, but she pulled it away. His heart sank in his chest.

"Tell me, Xen. What's really going on? Who are you people?"

He sighed and lowered his head. His long, black and white dreadlocks fell into his face. He felt Sora stiffen beside him. Finally, he looked up at her. "I work for Sho."

"Okay. What does he do?"

"He runs a...a firm that specialises in solving problems."

"Solving problems? What kinds of problems?"

"Whatever it is we're hired to do at the time."

"You're...what? Mercenaries? Private detectives?"

"A little of both, I suppose."

"So you're not really a professor."

"I am right now."

"How could you possibly get a job as a professor? How could any of you? From what I hear, Oni doesn't even know magic."

He smiled at this. "Well, she is effective when it comes to love."

Sora gazed at him coldly.

"Okay, I'm sorry."

"So what problem are you here to solve? What has it got to do with Zebulon?"

He did not reply to this.

"Let's hear it, Xen. I know you aren't who you say you are."

"I am exactly who I say I am! I never lied about that."

"But you left something out, and I want to know what it is."

He stared at her for a long moment. He wanted to reach for her, but her body was rigid and untrusting. He did not touch her. "Let me buy you a drink."

Her eyes narrowed. Finally, she said slowly, "Okay."

She did not speak to him as they stepped back out into the boisterous streets. She did not exclaim in delight over the scenes around them, and she did not reach for his hand. She followed him so coldly and so silently she was like a different person. It would likely not get better after their audience, but the time had finally come. He could keep the truth from her no longer, not if he wanted a chance to hold onto her. He hoped for the best.

The tavern upon which they stumbled was called the Dirty Damastes. It was a dodgy-looking building, and the old wooden sign hanging over the door looked so old and rotted, it might plummet from its hinges at any moment. Sora did not protest the seedy accommodations. She was silent as she followed him inside.

The bar was noisy and crowded, even at this early afternoon hour. Xen led Sora past a table of men and women, laughing at a vaguely familiar man with a mop of curly red hair attempting to pull a rabbit from the battered top hat he'd swept from his head. He was disappointed when, instead, he drew a live chicken from the hat, which squawked and shrieked as it tried to peck at the young man's eyes. Xen and Sora ignored them and slid into a quiet booth in the corner.

Sora stared at him, but he did not speak until a waitress brought them two pints of ale. The waitress smiled at Xen, but Sora glared at her so fiercely, she scurried away before he'd even had the chance to tip her. When she swivelled the glare to Xen, he sighed and lowered his eyes to the frothy head of his drink. "It's about Tan."

She did not seem surprised by this. "What about him?"

"The spell he's been working on, the one you've been helping him research... the one he hasn't told you much about—What exactly do you know about it?"

94

"Nothing! I told you!"

He lifted his eyes to peer seriously at her. "I do."

"What do you mean?"

"I know what he's doing."

"But how? What is it?"

"Let's say there are people who are concerned about what the spell will do when it's completed."

"I don't understand, Xen. What is the spell? What could Zebulon be doing that could be cause for concern? He's a good wizard, not..." She gave him a cold look. "He hasn't touched any dark artefacts. He's not a Darklord. He's a good man."

Her words stung. "Not everything is as simple and black and white as that, Sora. There is much in the world that you don't understand."

Her eyes flared in anger. "Then make me understand."

He sighed. A beautiful woman with long, dark hair passed by their table, drawing Xen's eye. She paused in front of them, turning to give them both a long, mournful expression. "I'm really very sorry," she told them sincerely.

They blinked at her in surprise, but she did not wait for them to reply. She glided away, and as she went, the heads of the men around them turned to watch her progress towards the bar. Xen looked at Sora in bemusement. She did not seem impressed or distracted by this odd interruption. She gave him an expectant look.

"Your master's intentions are not necessarily bad, Sora. But what he is doing is very dangerous. The results will be very, very bad. If he completes the spell..." He paused, pushing his hands through his long hair.

"But what is it? What is the spell?"

"We're...not entirely sure. We need you to help us find that out."

Her eyes narrowed suspiciously. "What do you mean?"

"Sora, I need to know exactly what he has you doing and how close he is to completing that spell. It is absolutely imperative that we find out."

Her eyes flared, and her cheeks flushed in anger. "All of this...you've just been using me to find out about the spell?"

"No!"

She scowled at him.

"Well, yes. I have a bit, but Sora, it wasn't--"

"I can't believe this." She was not as fragile as she looked. The expression in her eyes was thunderous, and he braced himself for her wrath. "Of course. I should have known a dark wizard—a Lumina vigilante—would be a liar."

"I am not a liar! I never lied. Everything I have said is true, Sora. I swear to you."

"But you didn't tell me everything. You didn't tell me the most important thing. It's still lying."

"I couldn't...I couldn't tell you. Not right away. I needed you to trust me first."

"Well, I don't!"

"Sora, please listen. It's important. You have no idea how important. How I feel about you—it has nothing to do with Tan. I didn't do all this—I didn't get to know you or bring you here because I wanted to use you. I did it because I wanted to."

Sora did not look convinced, despite the desperation in his tone. "Just tell me what will happen if the spell is completed. It was important enough to...well, for you to feel you had to admit the truth. It must be important. So, go on. Tell me."

He sighed and swiped a hand across his face. "If Tan completes the spell, he will unmake the entire universe."

She stared at him in silence. The man with the curly red hair shrieked as the chicken, which he'd thought safely returned to the depths of his magical hat, leapt out and began pecking at his ears and neck.

"He will unmake the entire universe?" Sora repeated slowly. There was doubt in her voice.

"The spell you are helping him research will open a gate to Hao."

"I don't know what that is."

"Neither do I, really, except that it is an alternative dimension. A chaos dimension. It was closed centuries ago by the gods to keep its creatures out of our world. If it is opened, the creatures will overrun our world and destroy it."

Sora shook her head. "Why would Zebulon do that? It doesn't make any sense. He wouldn't. I know him. He doesn't want to destroy anything."

"Sora, you must trust me." He reached across the table and clutched her hand. He felt her resist, but he did not allow her to pull away from him. "I don't know why he's doing it, but he is."

She scowled. "How do you even know? He's a good wizard. He wouldn't do that! You must be wrong."

"I'm not wrong. Our client…" He sighed. "He does not make mistakes like that."

Her eyes narrowed. "Who is your client?"

"It doesn't matter. He's just…someone who is concerned with maintaining the balance of the world, and this spell will throw it off. It is happening. It doesn't matter why."

"But…" Her voice was weary now. "But I know him. He's a good wizard. And if he knew what would happen…"

"Do you really know him?"

"Yes! I do. But I don't know you." She jumped to her feet so suddenly he barely caught her up at the door.

"Sora!"

She glared at him. "If I'm going to trust anyone, it's not going to be you." She spun away from him and marched towards the door.

"Sora--"

"Just leave me alone!"

He cursed, but he did not chase her as she strode out the door, back onto the streets of the Hedone District. He pressed his hand to his forehead. "That did not go according to plan."

The beautiful woman with long, dark hair paused beside him. She sighed. "You really shouldn't have brought her here. This isn't the place for her or you. There are far too many direct correlations."

# CHAPTER FIVE

"What?" Simon shouted, sitting up so suddenly, he upset the collection of amulets, talismans and stacks of term papers teetering on Xen's desk. "You just told her?"

Xen did not bother to straighten the disarray of his desk. Most of the things belonged to Omari, the former Talismans and Amulets professor, and he had little vested interest in its safekeeping. He pressed the heels of his hands to his eyes. His long, black and white dreadlocks swung as he looked up at Simon and Oni, who sat staring at him incredulously from across the clutter. "Well, yes. What did you expect me to do?"

"Use a little finesse at least!"

"I was very suave!"

Oni rolled her eyes. "I doubt that very much."

"What?"

"Well, you're hardly a smooth talker at the best of times, and you don't even know what you're doing right now. You've completely lost your mind, obviously, over this girl."

"What are you talking about? I am very charming when I want to be."

"Just not this time, eh?"

He scowled at her.

"But did you at least learn anything?" Simon demanded.

Xen opened and shut his mouth. He dropped his head back into his hands. "No."

"Oh, that's just terrific. So you learned nothing new, and now you've completely alienated the only person from whom we had the slightest chance of learning what we need to know. This is all going just great. Sho made the right decision putting you in charge, that's for sure."

"Hey, back off, Simon," Oni scolded. "Can't you see he's lovesick?"

Xen lifted his head to glare at her. "I will fix it, okay?"

98

"You'd better fix it," Simon told him sternly.

"What are you going to do?" asked Oni. "Do you need one of my love charms?"

"I don't need a love charm! Stop acting like you're an expert in love all of a sudden because you got stuck with this stupid job! You don't even know how to make a love charm! You don't even know the most basic magic!"

She shrugged indifferently. "I don't really need love charms, anyway."

"That is obvious!" Simon snapped. "How are we supposed to get anything done under these circumstances?"

They all avoided each other's eyes miserably.

"This is not going according to plan, then," Oni guessed.

They both glared at her. "It would have been good if we'd actually formed some kind of plan," Xen remarked. "Instead of assuming it was going to be easy."

"Can't we just break into his workshop or something?" Simon asked. "At least we could see what he's been up to or...well, stick him somewhere."

Oni lifted her eyebrows. "Stick him somewhere? What do you mean 'stick him somewhere?' You mean like...in a crevice?"

"Oh, for heaven's sake, do you have to make everything sound so inappropriate? I mean stick him in some...alternate dimension or something. For safekeeping. Until this all blows over."

They looked at him in surprise. "Can you do that?" Xen asked.

He sighed. "No. Not actually, but I am sure I know someone who can."

"D'you mean like stick him in a crack?"

"Oni!"

"Anyway, it doesn't matter. I already tried that."

"What? What do you mean you tried it?" Xen demanded.

"Well, you didn't seem to be getting anywhere with the totty, so I--"

"Sora is not a totty!"

Oni waved her hand dismissively. "I tried to get inside his room, but he's got protections like crazy. Even my incendiary devices couldn't get through."

They stared at her.

"You used incendiary devices?" Simon growled.

"Well, how else was I supposed to get in? I don't know any magic."

The men sighed and pinched the bridges of their noses in perfect unison.

"They didn't even go off. They just fell on the floor...impotent." Her mouth turned down in a disappointed pout. "Anyway, Xen, you're going to have to make up with that girl because there's no other way in."

Xen sighed. "If I had known how this case would turn out, I would have turned it down."

"Oh, please. Even if we could tell Darius no—which we can't because you know what Sho said would happen if we did—you wouldn't tell Sho no. If not for him--"

"Yeah, yeah. I know. I would be in some dark wizard loony bin. You don't have to keep reminding me. I get it." He surged irritably to his feet. "I'll see what I can do, okay?"

\* \* \*

Xen knew his way around the identical corridors by now. He could count the turns and doors, but instead he used his senses, following the timbre and texture of the magic towards Sora's room. It was tucked back in the student's dormitories, for she did not yet have her own office, and the erratic layers of the students' clumsy magic thrummed in his blood. He could feel her there, in her room. Her magic was subtle, almost delicate, and it felt so familiar to him, so close, that his chest suddenly ached.

He hesitated outside her door. Things were not going well. Whatever he thought he was starting to feel for Sora didn't matter. He had to make things right with her, at any cost. She was their only chance of getting close to Tan, and they had to get close to Tan. They had to stop the spell.

As ridiculous and irreverent their efforts, Xen knew more about the world than he let on. He knew more than Sho, whose experience consisted of the Darklands and playing mercenary for fallen angels and other motley creatures with deep pockets. The Lumina had known the truth. It wasn't good versus evil, not even in the Order where their sole purpose was to wipe out dark magic.

The Lumina could battle the forces of darkness, but only to the extent that they never won the battle. All things must remain equal. The Lumina was temperance, not justice; balance, not perfection. It was the way of the world, and if Tan were allowed to complete his spell, the resulting chaos would overrun the delicate order and send the world into a tailspin.

There was more at stake than the others realised, and he was cocking it up big time.

He leaned his forehead against Sora's door and sighed. He had to make it right. He rapped lightly on the door. "Sora?"

She did not reply, but he could feel her inside, just behind the door, and he knew she could hear him.

He knocked again, more loudly. "Sora!"

\* \* \*

She ignored him, turning back to the book in front of her as though it might drown his words out. "Dark magic. It's not dark magic. He wouldn't. He's wrong. Xen is wrong."

"Sora, please, let me in."

She pressed her lips together and turned the page.

He sighed. "Sora, I'm sorry. Please let me in. I need to explain."

She glared at him through he door. "Go away!"

"I didn't mean to hurt you. I didn't mean to trick you. That's not what I was doing. That's not why I got close to you. Sora, I need your help! Please."

She slammed the book shut and threw herself down on the bed. She covered her head with the pillow, but she could still hear him.

He cursed. "Sora!" He pounded roughly on the door. "Please!"

Sora threw the pillow across the room. Her stomach roiled. She'd trusted him, and he'd tricked her. He'd been using her all along to get to Zebulon. She couldn't trust a word he said. Zebulon was right about him. She should have been on her guard. She'd been foolish to let him so close.

"Just think about it, Sora. We need you. It's the only way we're going to be able to stop this, and we have to stop it. You have to know how important it is."

She rose and paced to the door. She knew he hadn't walked away. She could feel him through the door, as she could always feel him when he was near. She did not know if it was the dark energy swirling around his aura or if there was something inside her that yearned for him so desperately, it recognised him whenever he was near, drawing her inexorably towards him. She lifted a hand and pressed her palm to the door.

Suddenly, she wanted to pull it open. She wanted to forgive him, to help him with his mission, regardless of the consequences. But Zebulon...she could not betray her master, no matter how she felt about Xen. She knew Zebulon. He was a good man, a good teacher and friend, and he would never become involved with anything evil.

Xen was wrong.

"Sora, you have to change you mind! You have to help us. Even if he doesn't know what's going to happen, it is still going to happen. You can't change that by insisting he's a good man! It doesn't matter how good he is. He can still destroy the world!"

She scowled and stepped back from the door as though it had burned her. "Just go away, Xen. Go! I don't want to talk to you."

"Sora-"

"No! Go away. I don't want to see you again."

She didn't want to hear his reply. She turned away from the door and pressed her hands over her ears.

&ast; &ast; &ast;

*Meanwhile, at Sho Sange and Associates...*

Hyde watched Panya with a dreamy expression as she paced back and forth across the lobby, muttering to herself. She paused at the desk to check the building blueprint over and over, though she surely had memorised it by now. "We won't mess it up this time. We just need to plan it better."

She paused and pushed her hands through her curly hair so it stuck out around her head. Hyde smiled and leaned his chin on his hand.

"Hyde, are you listening to me?"

He straightened abruptly. "Yes."

She resumed her pacing as though there had been no interruption. "We could get in from the top." She looked at him. "Do you think we could get an airship? No. No, of course we can't." Her face lit up. "Hey! Can you turn into an airship?"

The dreamy expression on his face faded. He sighed. "No. Not one that could carry you."

102

"What? Why not? Are you saying I'm fat?"

He looked shocked. "No. Why would I say that? You aren't fat."

She narrowed her eyes at him as though she didn't quite believe him. "How come you can't carry me?"

Hyde lifted his shoulders. "If I change shape, I still maintain the same mass. If I got bigger, I would be too light to support your weight."

She sighed. "Damn." She resumed pacing.

Hyde smiled as he watched her.

She stopped abruptly and looked at him. "Hey, if we could knock out the security guard, you could shape-shift into him--"

Hyde sighed deeply. "Is that all you see in me?"

She spun to him in surprise. "What?"

He rose and rounded the desk to face her. His body shimmered, and he shifted suddenly, growing over a foot. His hair turned white, and his skin was ivory pale.

Panya shrieked at the image of Sho standing before her. "What did you do that for?"

Sho's normally cold and expressionless face fell in disappointment. "I thought you would like me better if I looked like him."

She looked appalled. "Well, I don't!"

Hyde shifted again, and this time Xen stood in front of Panya with a most un-Xen-like hopefulness on his face. "How about now?"

"No! You look all...crazy-eyed like you're going to snap any second or something." She watched in horror as Xen's face slowly shifted to Simon's. "Ew!" she shouted, and the change stopped so suddenly she was staring, alarmed, at a tall man with Simon's glasses over Xen's crazy eyes, and his tweed cap over long, black and white dreadlocks. His features were crooked and confused. Panya shuddered.

She sighed in relief as Hyde shifted back into himself. She eyed him thoughtfully. "How about Oni? Can you do Oni?"

He grinned. "Yeah!" In seconds, his body filled out into Oni's voluptuous shape. He struck a pose to show off one of Oni's more revealing red dresses, which barely served to cover her more interesting bits.

Panya lifted her eyebrows. "That's pretty good."

"I can't do the explosions." His voice was smoky and low, just like Oni's, but the edge of playful mania was absent. He would have to work on it.

She slumped in disappointment. "Damn." She waved her hand. "Go back." For the first time, she studied his usual form. He looked slightly embarrassed under her gaze. He twisted his caramel-coloured curls in his hand. His large, dark eyes slid away. "What do you really look like?"

"Huh?"

"You don't look like this, do you? I mean, you kinda...you look like me right now."

He looked surprised by this. "What? I do?"

"Yeah. A little." She cocked her head. "So what do you really look like?"

"I don't know what I really look like. I'm a shape shifter. I don't look like anything."

"You look like something. Everyone looks like something."

He thought about it. "I don't really know. I started changing as soon as I was born. I never had a chance to get a fix on it."

"Oh." She looked disappointed. "Is this how you always look, then?"

"No. Just when I'm here."

"Well, what else can you look like?"

He smiled brightly. "There are a few forms I use sometimes."

"Let's see, then."

"Okay." The air around him shimmered, and orange fur sprouted from his face, chest and arms. There was still a human quality in his eyes, but his features flattened and widened until he resembled a large, ginger cat on two legs.

Panya made a face. "No."

The ginger cat shifted into a large, grey wolf-man.

"Ew. No. I don't like dogs."

The air shimmered again, and he looked almost human again, but he was tall and slim with translucent pale skin and pointed ears beneath spiky red hair.

Panya considered him for a long moment. "No. Not that one."

Suddenly, the elf became a tall, dark and handsome human man with strong

104

features and high cheekbones. His eyes smouldered at Panya. She turned pink. She stared at him silently for several seconds. The tall, dark and handsome man ruffled the back of his hair nervously. "What? You don't like it?"

"It's...ah..." Panya fanned a hand in front of her face. "It's okay."

Hyde sighed. "People always act weird when I look like this."

"Oh. Yeah...I can see why."

Hyde shifted back into the form in which she usually saw him. He lifted his shoulders sheepishly.

Panya sighed in disappointment. "Yeah. I guess you'd better stick with that one."

"Okay."

She frowned thoughtfully. "Are you really a boy or a girl?"

He shrugged. "I don't know."

"Oh. So, uh...So...you think you can..." She scuffed her foot on the marble floor. "Can I see that form again? The, uh, the tall one?"

"Okay." The tall, dark and handsome man smiled bemusedly at her.

Panya smiled dreamily back at him.

"Panya?"

She shook herself. "Huh? What? Oh. So...about that security guard."

Abruptly, the handsome man shrank back into Hyde. His mouth turned down sadly. "Maybe we should just do what Darius said."

"Darius? Since when did we start listening to Darius?"

"You know what he would do if we got in trouble again."

She scoffed. "Yeah, yeah." But she didn't argue. Her lower lip stuck out in a pout. "Okay, fine. We'll just stay here and be bored."

Hyde grinned. "Hey. Want to see me do Darius?"

A sly look came into her eyes. "If you did, do you think we could make it work for us?"

"Panya..."

"Okay, okay. No Darius." Her cheeks flushed. She fluttered her eyelashes. "How about the tall one again?"

Sora wasn't concentrating on the book in front of her. She'd read the same passage several times, and she couldn't remember a single word of it. She sighed deeply. The tower workshop was quiet. The clock hidden amongst the books on Zebulon's shelves seemed to be ticking at half speed.

She started as the door burst open. Zebulon looked at her in surprise. "You're here early."

Her smile was wan. "Yes."

"I thought you would be at breakfast with your new...friend this morning."

Sora looked up at him in surprise. "New friend?"

He smiled. "I heard you went out into town with Professor Xen on your day off yesterday."

She hesitated. "Yes." She gave him a wavering smile.

Zebulon noticed her lack of enthusiasm. "But what's wrong, dear?"

She studied him a moment. She opened her mouth to speak, but the proper words did not come. She did not even know what they were. "Nothing's wrong."

He gave her a kindly smile and sat beside her at the battered library table. "Sora, I have known you many years. You seem unhappy. Did you and Professor Xen have a row?"

She sighed. "It isn't Xen."

He lifted an eyebrow. "Then what is it? What could possibly be troubling you so?"

For a moment, she did not say anything. She took a deep breath to steel her courage. "This spell we're working on..."

Zebulon stiffened. "What?"

"It's just...the spell, all the work we have done for it...what is it for?"

He didn't say anything for a moment. He seemed caught out. Then he narrowed his eyes. "It's research, dear. As I explained."

"Yes, but for what?"

He frowned. "Has Xen been saying something to you?"

"It is not Xen. It is all this secrecy, Zebulon."

"Do you not trust me?"

"Of course! Of course I do."

"Then why this sudden interest in my work?"

"I thought it was our work. I have always been interested. I trust you very much. It's just...we've been working so hard, and it seems to mean so much to you. I only wished to know why."

He sighed. "I knew this day would come. When you'd finally had enough of my eccentricities and demanded answers." He smiled. "You are a brilliant, inquisitive girl. It is why I chose you as my apprentice." He laid an affectionate hand on her shoulder. "Sora, we are working on a spell to stop death."

Astonished, Sora said nothing for several moments. "Stop death?"

He inclined his head. "Yes. Well, not to stop it; that would be impossible. But to prolong life. To cure disease and decay."

"But that...that, too, is impossible, Zebulon, is it not?"

"Perhaps many would think me mad. And so I did not share with you the nature of my work."

"The runes, then?"

"I intend to try a number of combinations that I believe will restore youth and health."

She considered this a long moment. Something inside her relaxed, for it was as it should be. She should never have doubted his intentions. "That is truly your intention?"

"My dear, I am an old man. My time will soon come. I hope only to suspend it."

She laid a hand on his. "Oh, but you are still vital and so robust."

He smiled indulgently. "Ah, but I will not always be. And there are others who would desire to put off their natural time. It would be a great gift to mankind."

"But does it not go against the natural order? Is it not contrary to nature and thus dark magic?"

"My dear, magic is contrary to nature. By its own nature, the world is unnatural. It is a supernatural place. Can we not, then, use it to our advantage?"

"But I am uncertain it is right to attempt to deflect death."

"Not deflect, dear, no. To simply put it off for a time."

She thought about this. She smiled hesitantly. "Do you think it will work?"

He smiled. "I can only theorise, my dear, but I am confident that I will find the right combination."

She was silent for a long moment. Finally, she looked up at him with a troubled expression in her eyes. "I must think on this a bit."

"Of course. You must know I could never put you in the way of harm."

But she could not shake Xen's words, his urgent warnings, for she knew he earnestly believed what he said. Xen was not a foolish man. On the contrary, he seemed quite competent, and...Well, if anyone knew dark magic, it was he. "But...has this spell something to do with Hao?"

Zebulon blinked in astonishment. "Hao? What have you heard of Hao?"

"I know nothing of it. I have only heard the name."

"Hao is merely a legend, my dear."

"A legend? I did not know..."

"Do not mention it again." She had never heard him sound so stern.

She stared at him in surprise. "I don't understand, Zebulon. Are you trying to open a gate to Hao?"

"A gate? To Hao?" He laughed. "My dear, what is this nonsense? Why would you think such a thing? It is that man, isn't it?"

"No." Her voice sounded high-pitched, even to her own ears. "Xen has nothing to do with my concerns."

He smiled and patted her arm. "I assure you, Sora, Hao is only a legend. It isn't real. It's nothing to do with me or our spell."

She frowned thoughtfully. Could it be true? Was Xen wrong? Surely he had knowledge of the world that she did not, but Zebulon had never lied to her before. Perhaps...perhaps there was merely a misunderstanding. Perhaps Xen simply did not understand the nature of Zebulon's work.

Zebulon's brilliant blue eyes seemed to pierce straight through her thoughts. "Your friend is clearly mistaken, Sora. There has been, I think, some kind of misunderstanding."

He had a way of stealing her thoughts, and she had always found it comforting. His gaze was so serious and so sincere, she could not argue. She smiled. "Yes.

Of course. I am sorry I accused you, Zebulon. It was foolish of me."

He laughed. "Not at all, dear. It is never foolish to be inquisitive. You have every right to question your mentor. If you did not, I would be certain you would never take my place as master." He squeezed her shoulder. "Worry not, my dear. I promise you I would never do anything to harm you or anyone else."

"Oh!" She shook her head earnestly. "Of course I know that, Zebulon. Of course you would never." She smiled and patted his hand warmly. "I trust you."

\* \* \*

Zebulon Tan strode purposefully down the dodgy, rubbish-littered street. His expression was so fierce and his step so determined, even the pickpockets and street-hawkers did not approach him. The building for which he was searching was old and crumbling. A large display window enticed shoppers with old, battered books and broken magical paraphernalia. Zebulon passed the showcase without glancing inside and darted into the alley.

The office door was unmarked, but he knew it well. He pressed an eager palm to the scuffed wood. When he did, letters appeared in shining gold script. Lucian. He Who Finds Things Long Forgotten. Zebulon did not bother to knock. He twisted the knob and burst inside. His eyes burned with anger.

A small, squat man with watery green eyes and thin, wispy blonde hair occupied the single chair before Lucian's desk, which was cluttered with an assortment of broken watches, beaten old rag dolls, rusty medals and other long lost and best forgotten debris. Lucian's client clutched an old teddy bear with empty eye sockets. Zebulon could practically see the fleas leaping off the thing and biting the elated man.

Lucian smiled indulgently at the client and glanced up at Zebulon with a chilly expression. He was a pallid man. His features were smooth and ageless, and his hair was long and pale. The irises of his eyes were almost colourless so the pupils looked huge and black. He gestured the client out with a shooing motion.

The client was not put out by this dismissal. He bent in a bow. "Thank you. Thank you so much." He spun away, cuddling the bear to his cheek. "Oh, Mr Pippin, I missed you so, so much."

Zebulon did not sit down in the chair the man had just vacated. He narrowed his eyes at Lucian.

"Zebulon." Lucian's voice was low and silky. "Please sit."

"No."

Lucian lifted a colourless eyebrow. "What is it, Zebulon?"

"How did they find out?"

"I am sorry, but you will have to be more specific."

"Someone found out about the spell."

"Zebulon, you are talking nonsense."

"It is not nonsense! You said no one would find out what I'm doing. How did these people learn about it?"

"What people?"

"Oni. Xen. Simon. Who did you tell?"

"I did not tell anyone."

"Then how do they know?"

"How could I possibly know that, Zebulon? Who are they?"

"I don't know! But they know about our plans."

"How can you be sure they know?"

Zebulon sighed irritably. "My assistant. They've gotten to her."

Lucian held up his hands in a calming gesture. "All right. Slow down. I don't know how they found out. But..."

When he hesitated, Zebulon snapped, "But what?"

"Well, I'm not all powerful, you know. There are those more powerful than me. It's all checks and balances. There is always something you can't overcome, something that can negate you. Well, me. Something that can negate me. My kind."

Zebulon growled in fury. He threw up his hands and sketched a rune into the air.

Nothing happened.

Lucian rolled his eyes. "I'm a god, you know. You can't harm me. I'm very insulted, and I think you should leave now." He sighed in disappointment. "I thought we were friends."

Zebulon threw himself into the chair in front of the desk. "But how do I get rid of them?"

"That is not my speciality, as you know. I have already done you a favour and

110

now you must decide whether or not to take your chosen course."

"You set me on this course!"

"I did as you asked. I did not advise as to the wisdom of your path."

"It is too late now. There is nothing else."

"Then you are on your own." Lucian flicked his fingers at him. "We are done. You go now."

\* \* \*

*Meanwhile at Gwydion Academy of Advanced Sorcery...*

The cafeteria was empty this late in the afternoon. Xen sipped the hot, bitter coffee. It burned his throat as it went down. He scowled into the chipped black mug. Things were going very badly. Despite his machinations, he still hadn't managed to figure out a way to get past Tan's door. When he'd taken the assignment, it had seemed straight forward enough, but they could do little when their target remained constantly under lock and key in his tower with more protections than the city officials.

There was only one way in, but he couldn't do it. If he accessed the black magic that simmered and swirled beneath the surface, there would be no way back. He might never return from another rage, and he would find himself locked up or put down by his own people—or Sho would be left to pick up the pieces of his best friend. He had promised Xen long ago that he would never let the Lumina take him. He had promised to take him out before he ever had the chance to hurt anyone again.

His black magic might be the only way. It would be better to die at his best friends' hands than allow the entire world to spin out of balance.

He sighed deeply and pushed his hands through his hair. He never wanted to go back, but there might not be any other choice. He could solve the problem easily enough. In seconds, even. But it would be the end of him and whoever stepped into his path. Dread hung over him like a dark cloud. He could feel the magic now, as though it sensed his thoughts. If he allowed it, it would take over his entire body, fog his senses and cloud his mind until he was filled with a surge of black rage that nearly blinded him.

The magic would control his every move. He would lose himself completely. The powerful surge of need to consume would fill his every thought. He could still feel the blackness now on the edge of his vision, bearing down on the corners of his mind. He could feel it starting to swell up inside him as his thoughts turned dark and despairing. He could feel the desperation when he thought of Sora, his only chance to make it out of this with his sanity intact.

He closed his eyes and took a deep breath. He had to push the thoughts away. He could not allow the darkness to overwhelm him. He had to calm down. Calm down.

"Xen?"

His eyes snapped open. He leapt out of his seat to face her. "Sora."

She looked away awkwardly. She took a step back as he reached for her. He sighed and dropped his hands dejectedly at his side. She scuffed her foot on the marble floor. "I...I spoke to Zebulon."

"What?"

He took a step closer to her. "You told him what I said?"

Her long, blonde hair flew around her face as she shook her head. "No. No, I didn't. I asked him what we are working on. Why we're doing this research."

Xen frowned. "What did he tell you?"

"He said we are working on a spell to prolong life." When Xen continued to frown, she rushed on. "He knows nothing of opening a gate to Hao. He said Hao is only a legend."

He gripped her shoulders. "Then he is lying!"

Her expression was hurt. "He wouldn't lie. Not to me."

"Sora, it's true. I'm sorry. But I am not wrong. He did lie to you."

"No! It isn't—it's just a misunderstanding. I don't know who told you or why or who you're really working for, but they're wrong."

"Sora, they aren't wrong!" Pity for the hopeful expression in her eyes roiled in his gut. Hoping wouldn't make the problem go away. "You must understand this!"

"No! He wouldn't. He wouldn't lie to me. He looked me in the eye, and he promised he was not doing anything of the sort. I know him." She took a step back. "But I don't know you. And I don't know who you are working for."

"I told you! I work for Sho."

"But I don't know who you are. I don't know what you are."

"Sora, I explained this. We're an agency that solves problems."

112

"But for whom? Who sent you here to spy on Zebulon?"

He frowned. "I am not here to spy. I'm here to stop him."

"There is nothing to stop."

"Please, you have to listen to me. Our employer, he is...someone who knows...things. There is a delicate balance in this world, and there are people whose job it is to maintain it."

She blinked in bemusement. "Balance?"

"You have no idea how vital it is to maintain balance in this world. With everything that happens, all the conflicting forces, balance is kept, but this thing...this thing Tan is planning to do will destroy everything."

She did not look convinced. "You expect me to believe that? Who is being secretive and untrustworthy now, Xen?"

"That is not my intention. I have seen much of this world, and you have seen none." She looked offended, and he sighed. "That is not what I meant. I just meant that you have not experienced the depth of evil and grace I have seen. There are creatures and forces out there...Sora, you have to believe me. You have to. If you don't...I am lost. Everything is lost."

She took a hitching breath. "I just don't know what to believe, Xen."

"Please, Sora. This is serious. I am trying to save us all. I am here to stop something terrible from happening, not destroy something good or hurt you or anyone else."

"Zebulon wouldn't do anything terrible!"

"No, maybe he would not. Not on purpose. But what he's doing will result in disaster."

Her eyes lowered as she thought about this. When she looked back up at him, there was uncertainty in her eyes. "But why? Why would he do it?"

He shook his head. "I don't know why. Only he knows. But he is doing it. And you can help stop it."

"I can't help you go against him, Xen. He is my mentor. And my friend."

"Sora, he may not know the consequences of his actions!"

She shook her head violently. "I trust him."

"It isn't about trust. It is about stopping him from making a mistake that could destroy the world." He caught her shoulders and drew her closer to him. His eyes burned into hers.

She pushed him away. "I can't help you, Xen. I'm sorry."

"Sora--" He reached for her, but she was quicker. She backed away from him and fled. He started after her, but the rush of students coming down from their afternoon classes blocked his path.

When he reached the corridor into which she had escaped, she was already gone.

\* \* \*

Xen paced rapidly from one side of his tiny office to the other. Simon sat primly behind his desk with his hands folded in front of him. Across from Simon, Oni leaned back in her chair with her high-heeled boots propped up on the messy surface. Simon cleared his throat. "So what now? You've cocked it up royally and now our only lead is completely resolved to work against us."

"I know. I know!"

"I thought you were going to fix it. It appears all you've done is make it worse."

"Simon, I know!"

"Simon, back off," Oni ordered in a low voice. "You know what could happen if you push him too far." When Xen turned his scowl upon her, she lifted her chin defiantly. There was no venom in her voice when she continued, "So what the hell are we going to do? Just sit here and let him finish his spell? Just insinuating doubt into her mind isn't going to get us anywhere fast enough. We have to actually do something."

Xen stared at her a long moment. His expression was so serious, even Oni sat up straight. "There is a way."

"What way?" she asked suspiciously.

His mouth tightened grimly. "I can break his protection."

"What?" Simon demanded incredulously. "What do you mean?"

Oni shot to her feet. Her brazen features were more serious than they'd ever seen them. Her eyes blazed. "No. Xen, no. That is not the way."

Simon stared at Oni as though he'd never seen her before. "What are you two talking about?"

Oni looked at him. "I might make jokes about it, but it isn't actually funny."

114

She turned back to Xen. "You cannot use black magic."

Simon lifted his eyebrows in interest. "Would that work?"

"Simon, no!"

"Well, what else are we going to do?" Xen demanded. "We don't have any other magic powerful enough to break him open."

Oni lifted a hand to point at Simon. "Don't you know anyone or have any friends who can help with this?"

He frowned. "My...friends are not obliged to help with this. In truth, they cannot stop him. Darius came to us for a reason. We are the only hope there is." He looked at Xen. "What is the consequence of you...you know, breaking out the bad juju?"

Xen sighed. He pinched the bridge of his nose. "It's...not good."

Oni glared at him. "You're not going to do it. It doesn't matter."

"Oni..."

She looked at Simon sternly. "I've seen it. It's not good. It's really, really bad. If he goes back under, he might not ever come out. It will take him over completely. And if he does, Sho..." She sighed and swiped a hand across her face. "Sho will put him down if the Lumina doesn't get to him first."

The colour drained from Simon's face. "So it's...not the ideal option."

"It's not an option."

Xen lifted his eyebrows. "I didn't know you cared, Oni."

She rolled her eyes. "I care about Sho. I know what it would to do to him to have to do that."

He snorted. "Right."

She turned her head away to hide her face from him. When she spoke, her voice was soft. "You can't do it."

"There might not be any other choice. We're not getting anywhere, and you know it. We're running out of time. If we don't figure out a way to stop it, we're going to have to do something drastic. It would be better to sacrifice me than to let everything be unmade. There is a reason Sho put me in charge of this debacle. There is a reason he keeps me around. If all else fails, there is always this. And there is a slight chance Sho can pull me back. He did it before."

"But it was horrible," Oni told him hoarsely. "Do you even remember? Sho's power comes from blood. Blood, Xen. You almost died last time. You might not be able to survive it again."

"It's a chance I might have to take."

She shook her head. For a moment, she paced silently up and down the floor. "There's still Sora."

"No, Oni. She's refused."

"But she fancies you. I can see it in her eyes. She fancies you, and you said she is refusing to help us because she doesn't believe that Tan would intentionally perform a spell like this. We have to convince her. We have to make her see what he really is. She won't just let him do it, will she? She won't help him when she knows what could really happen if he completes the spell."

"No. She wouldn't do that. She won't help him if she realises we're telling the truth."

"So we have to find a way to convince her."

"Oni, I have tried. Twice."

"Try again! Try harder! At least convince her that he doesn't know what the consequences are, as long as she believes what could happen if she helps him. We aren't going to let you do it."

"Oni, you know--"

"Yes, I know! I know it's serious. I know. I don't act like I take anything seriously, but I know how serious this is. But you aren't sacrificing yourself unless there isn't any other way. So you try. You find that girl, and you get her to trust you."

Xen grumbled under his breath.

She lifted an imperious finger to point at the door. "Go!"

\* \* \*

Sora was thinking of Xen. She hadn't stopped thinking about Xen from the moment she met him outside his classroom several days ago. He said such things. He had such a way of looking at her. But she didn't really know him. She knew that now. Much less did she trust him. He had been using her when he'd said those things and looked at her in that way that sent her stomach fluttering as though a dozen winged serpents had crept inside while she'd been too distracted to notice. She couldn't be sure there was not some other, more sinister ulterior motive to his words or his arrival at Gwydion.

She was young, and she was naïve, but she was not an utter fool.

She couldn't possibly trust him.

But Zebulon...he'd been acting so strange, so passionate and secretive about this mysterious work, even before Xen and his strange friends had arrived. Had he become so embroiled in his determination, so blinded by his ambitions that he would lose sight of himself and cross this terrible line?

She didn't know. She thought she knew him well, but perhaps it had been foolish all along to think so.

If Xen was right, if Zebulon's spell did have such dreadful consequences, surely she must do something to stop it. She could not simply sit back and watch Zebulon make an awful mistake. She was, at least, certain it was a mistake for Zebulon would never intend such a thing.

And if she did help Xen...if it was true, and she helped him stop the terrible spell, would he just be gone? Would she ever see him again? Had he meant the things he said when he'd confessed how he felt about her?

It could all be an elaborate plan to win her affection so she could help them destroy her mentor. Zebulon had enemies, surely. Could one of them have set Xen and his mysterious Sho on her master's tail?

She pressed the heels of her hands to her eyes. There was too much to think about. There were too many questions, and she felt as though she was the only one without the answers. She had to know. She had no reason to think Xen was lying, but she did have reason to believe Zebulon hadn't been as open and honest as she'd come to expect from him. Until Xen, she'd never thought to ask questions.

She had to at least consider the possibility that Zebulon might not be who she thought he was for his behaviour of late had been most secretive, though not entirely unusual. He might be up to no good. She realised now there was much about him she did not know, much about their work that he kept from her and for which he demanded unquestioning obedience.

She didn't know how she would find out, but she could not live with all these questions in her mind. They were close, and he had always been willing to talk things over with her. Should now be any different? In the past, however, she had rarely found occasion to demand answers of him. She'd followed him so blindly. She knew not how he would respond to her such sudden misgivings.

She had to go see him. He had encouraged her to be inquisitive. What could it hurt to find out exactly what he planned with this spell, in an instructional capacity, of course? Surely he would not now condemn her for her lingering doubts and fears. He would assure her that she was being silly, that it was nothing more than a misunderstanding. Perhaps he could even explain his intentions to Xen, and then it would all be over, and they could go back to their normal lives.

A normal life without Xen.

She sighed deeply. She wasn't sure she wanted that. In fact, she was sure she didn't. She hadn't even known she could feel such things until she had met him.

She lifted her chin and steeled her resolve. At the very least, perhaps she could learn how close her mentor had come to completing the spell. She would know then how much time she had to choose a side, if choosing sides she must do. She hoped it was a misunderstanding. She did not want Xen to be right. She did not want Zebulon to be involved in magic that would destroy the world, intentionally or not. Most confusingly, she did not want Xen to be wrong, either or worse, a liar.

She sighed as she left her chambers for Zebulon's tower. She almost wished Xen had never come into her life. Everything had become so complicated since he'd arrived. But then she could not imagine going back to the way things had been. Boring...routine...lonely. She couldn't imagine going back to before she had felt any spark of passion for something other than her work. She did not want to forget the breathless, fluttering sensation she felt in her chest whenever she sensed Xen was near.

She needed to know the truth. She needed to know who to trust before there was no turning back.

She didn't meet Xen in the hallway on her way to the tower. Part of her was relieved. The other part, the larger, weaker part of her, ached to see him so badly, it was like physical pain in her chest. She heard footsteps behind her on the stairs, and her heart skipped a beat. She stopped abruptly and spun to face the bemused student returning to his dormitory from a late dinner. He looked back at her in surprise.

She smiled wanly at the young man. He nodded to her.

Zebulon's door was closed. She tapped lightly on the door and opened it, poking her head inside the room. "Zebulon?" Her voice was soft and hesitant.

He sat hunched over a book at one of the research tables. She stepped quietly inside. Her mentor looked up at her, startled. She gasped in shock at the sight of him. He did not look himself at all. In fact, his robust, vital features were sagging and withered. His hair was thin and grizzled. He looked as though he had aged so many years in mere hours. He looked so...so feeble.

His watery eyes widened in surprise. "What are you doing here?" he growled. His voice sounded reedy and high-pitched. He threw his hands up to cover his face.

"I–"

"Get out!"

"But–"

"Go! Leave me!"

"But what are you—"

"Get out!" The force of his voice reverberated through the room. The walls began to shake. Glass bottles shattered, and books tumbled from the shelves.

Sora ducked as a book flew at her head. She turned and fled from the room, slamming the door behind her. She could hear Zebulon still shrieking at her from behind the door. She leaned against the wall to take a hitching breath and swiped a tear from her eye.

Then she turned and ran as fast as she could back to her room.

Something was very wrong. Something was very wrong with Zebulon. It had something to do with this spell. It must do. He looked so different, so deteriorated. Was his work taking so much from him? What was happening to him?

She intended to find out exactly what was going on.

She slammed the door to her room. Her heart thumped. She pushed aside the essays and term papers on her desk. There. Zebulon's runes.

There were seven of them. She had not asked what any of them were meant to do. Her task had been merely to discover their formation. She had not bothered to ask further questions, for her trust of her mentor had been unconditional. Obviously, she'd been extremely foolish.

They had discovered five of the runes, and she had copied them down like a good little apprentice. Now, she looked at them. She really looked, and the picture that unfolded inexorably before her eyes was chilling.

Heka: a rune to represent sickness, pain and suffering.

Hu: the force of will and determination.

119

Yaya: representing the spirit, the essence of pure magic and the willingness to give of oneself all that is in their power.

Thrall: the rune of bondage, restraint and subjugation.

Janus: the opening of a passage or gate that has been forcibly closed.

Her breath caught in her throat. Gate. Something wasn't as it seemed.

She did not know the other runes, for they still eluded her and her mentor despite their endless searching. Agni and Nun. She knew nothing of them. She wondered if Zebulon knew their meanings, if he had known all of their meanings from the very beginning, if he had been using her all along to further his terrible ends.

Where had he gotten the spell? Had he theorised the combination of runes, as he'd said? It was possible he had been telling the truth when he suggested they would prolong life, but...Gate. Opening of a gate. What did he really intend to do?

Her insides turned to ice. She had to know. No matter the cost, she would find out what was really going on here.

"Oh, Zebulon," she breathed. "What have you done?"

# CHAPTER SIX

Sora's steps faltered as she neared Zebulon's tower. She was uncertain if her habitual morning visit would be welcomed this particular morning, but neglecting her duties would do little to bring her closer to solving the mystery of the spell and Xen's dire warnings. Her heart thumped nervously, and she wished she could see Xen. He might be part of the problem, and seeing him might only confuse her already uncertain thoughts, but he had been someone she could talk to.

She'd never realised, until this very moment, that she had never had anyone but Zebulon. She had no friends, no close acquaintances or confidants. She had never before felt a need for any such companionship. Now, she was alone. She certainly could not share her fears of the man with the man himself.

She hesitated outside Zebulon's door. She took a deep breath. Her knees shook.

As she lifted her hand to knock lightly on the door, it opened abruptly from the inside. She nearly tumbled headlong into the room. Zebulon stood before his podium, and his eyes lit up when he saw her. He did not look the decrepit, withered man of the night before. On the contrary, she had not seen him so robust in many months. He smiled at her as though nothing in the world could make him happier than the sight of her at that moment.

He rushed to her, catching up her hands in his own. "My dear, I am so sorry. I was not myself last night. I shouldn't have shouted."

She blinked up at him in surprise. "No, I am sorry. I didn't mean to frighten you."

He smiled. "It was not you, my dear."

She eyed him carefully. "Are you all right, Zebulon? You looked so different last night."

"I am merely quite fatigued. We have done all this work and have seen little reward. It is greatly tiring me."

That did not sound quite right. "I see."

"Can you forgive me?"

She smiled. She could not remain angry with him, if angry she had been. "Yes.

Of course. I should not have entered so abruptly."

"It is your workspace, too. Of course it is your right. Is it all forgotten, then? Are we still friends?"

She laughed. "Of course."

His smile was radiant. "I am very pleased."

Sora did not feel quite as pleased, but there was little more to be said on the matter. "We should get started on our work. There is still much to be done if we are to accomplish your great goal."

"Yes." His eyes gleamed. "There is but two runes left."

This was somewhat troubling, but she did not say so. "Indeed. Shall we, then?"

They did not speak as they bent over their crumbling tomes. Sora could not concentrate on the words and formations before her. She looked up at her mentor. His eyes burned as they scanned the pages for the runes. For a moment, she studied him narrowly. He did not seem to notice her scrutiny.

"Zebulon..."

He looked up, startled. "My dear?" There was no impatience in his voice, but that passion still flamed in his eyes.

"This spell..."

Now his eyes narrowed. He seemed to realise it and blinked away the cold suspicion so she could not be sure she'd seen it at all. He lifted his eyebrows expectantly.

"All you all right, Zebulon?"

"I am not sure what you mean."

"It's just that...this spell for prolonging life..."

He laughed. "Dear, are you insinuating I wish to prolong my own life?"

"I was simply wondering if...there might be something wrong."

"Of course not. It is a service. A service to those around us."

"Yes, of course. I'm sorry."

"Are you beginning to doubt me, Sora?" His voice was light. "Are those people getting into your head?"

"No, no. It has nothing to do with them. I have severed my connection with Xen. I am merely...concerned for you."

"I am perfectly well. There is nothing wrong with me."

The clock chimed, startling them both.

"You must go," he said brusquely. "Classes will be starting."

Sora sighed. "Yes, of course. I will see you after classes, then."

Zebulon smiled as she slipped from the room. As the door closed behind her, the smile faded into a dark scowl. He rose abruptly to his feet and followed her silently from the room.

\* \* \*

The ridiculous woman didn't notice him as he slipped into the Love Charms classroom. The students stared at her in open-mouthed incredulity. She gestured towards the life-sized stitch-up doll propped up on the desk before her. "Now, class, it is extremely important to first determine the extent of the damage you wish to inflict upon your subject. There is nothing wrong with going overboard. If you didn't want to do some damage, you wouldn't bother making the doll in the first place."

Oni grinned hugely at them and withdrew an enormous pin, which resembled a shining brass cattle prod. She thrust it enthusiastically into the doll's belly. The doll's large, black button eyes looked mournful, but the crudely stitched mouth still smiled grotesquely. She turned to face the class and lifted an arm to gesture towards the doll with a flourish, as though she expected a round of applause.

The class stared at her. Her smile faded slightly. "Any questions?"

A short, fat young man rose to his feet. "Professor Oni, I tried that Love Charm you told us about last week, the one with the broken glass and pointy things, and it didn't work. The girl I asked to go out with me just laughed."

Oni lifted an eyebrow. "Well, of course it didn't work. Love Charms don't work if you are terribly unattractive and couldn't possibly get a date on your own."

A young woman with puffy cheeks and mousey brown pigtails raised her hand. "Professor Oni, isn't that sort of the whole point of Love Charms?"

She stared at them in confusion. "Is it?"

Zebulon snorted. This was whom they had sent to stop him, whoever they were? Surely the crusade had not been of this woman's making. She was an utter fool. An absurd pawn. She did not concern him. The librarian was scarcely any more impressive. In his classroom, Zebulon observed nothing more threatening than a series of pompous posturing, confused students and bursting blouses.

It was Xen who worried him. He was not a particularly good teacher, for he was not a particularly patient man, but he knew his stuff. The protection amulet upon which his students were practising was powerful. The man himself practically vibrated with the dark magic that surrounded him. His aura swirled and spiked and shot out around him like a twisted shadow.

Zebulon didn't like to think what might happen if the man lost control of the only barely contained black magic. Behind the back of the young girl in front of him, Zebulon sketched a rune in the air. Xen's head snapped up, and he frowned slightly, but it was the only indication he'd felt Zebulon's spell at all. He certainly didn't keel over, gasping for breath, as he was meant to do. He did not even seem troubled by the rush of magic. If he knew the nature of the spell, there was nothing in his dark eyes to indicate it.

There was something of distraction in his eyes, however. Sora had said she'd severed ties with the man. Could it be he was actually upset about it? Was Xen's interest in his young assistant actually genuine? Most interesting, indeed. If the young man was lovelorn, perhaps he was not so great a threat as Zebulon had suspected. Perhaps he was as foolish as the other two, after all.

He couldn't stop now. It was too late. He didn't have any other choice. If these were the people with whom he had to contend, he was confident he was up to the challenge.

The tinkling bell chimed through the school, signalling the end of class. Xen did not wait for his students to leave before he spun abruptly from the room. Zebulon hurried to follow him. His step was swift and purposeful.

And then Xen's feet faltered as Sora rounded a corner. For a moment, they stared at each other, and then Sora ducked her head behind the stack of books and hurried the other way. She did not notice her master at all, disguised as he was, and she might not have noticed him had he looked himself. Her blue eyes shone with hurt.

Zebulon smiled. Things were looking rather in his favour. He still had his closest ally, and his enemies, whatever knowledge they might have possessed, were complete idiots.

\* \* \*

*Meanwhile, in the Dirty Damastes, something is amiss...*

Tricks approached the table in the back of the bar where his friends sat, as ever, drinking beer and looking rather dissatisfied with the world. He looked around uncomfortably as he slipped into the seat next to Unrequited Love, who tossed her hair as though she hardly noticed he'd arrived. He spoke quietly. "Is DC here tonight?"

Minor Inconveniences shook his head. "No. He must have business elsewhere this evening."

Tricks sighed in relief. Unrequited Love lifted an eyebrow. "Who's your friend, Tricks?"

"Oh. I beg your pardon. I'd nearly forgotten you," Tricks told the rather homely young man, who hovered awkwardly in front of the table as though awaiting an invitation to join the party.

"Not at all," the young man said, scuffing his toe on the grungy wood floor.

Tricks looked at his friends, who stared back at him expectantly. "Ah, this is... um. Erm."

"Well?" Severe Errors in Judgment demanded rudely.

The young man blushed. "This is...Well, I usually call him A.S.S.," Tricks explained.

"Ass?" Unrequited Love asked, shocked.

"No! Not Ass!" the young man replied with obvious embarrassment. "A.S.S."

They all stared at him. No one seemed to know what to say. They glanced at each other and then away awkwardly.

"Well," said the hirsute man in a tight voice. "This has become a rather Awkward Social Situation."

A.S.S. sighed. "Yes."

"Oh," Minor Inconveniences said, nodding sympathetically.

"You can just call me Ace," Awkward Social Situations said dejectedly. "I think that would be better for everyone."

"Oh, but I like A.S.S.," Severe Errors in Judgment told him enthusiastically.

Unrequited Love scowled at her, and she snapped her mouth shut. Tricks looked around at his friends. They looked grimmer than usual this evening, and if DC wasn't around, it probably wasn't A.S.S.'s fault. "What's the matter?"

His four friends glanced at each other. "Something feels off," said the hirsute man.

"Off? What sort of off?"

"I keep forgetting you're new," Minor Inconveniences said.

"There is a delicate balance in this world, you know," Unrequited Love told him.

Tricks frowned and glanced at A.S.S., who shrugged. "What do you mean?"

"I mean everything must be balanced. Everything must have it's opposite. We all do. I have True Love," she explained. "Minor Inconveniences has Outrageous Fortune."

"I have Excellent Choices," Severe Errors in Judgment added.

"You probably have Spectacularly Successful Magic Tricks or something," the hirsute man put in.

"It's all a balance," Severe Errors in Judgment said. "It's what we're here to do. Maintain it. No one really knows what could happen if it's thrown off."

"But it has been suggested it would be very, very bad," Unrequited Love added. "It would be the end of everything."

"The end of everything?" Tricks asked, horrified.

"Yes. And there is something off. Something in the air. Something is happening."

"But what is it?"

Minor Inconveniences shrugged. "No idea."

"Just something bad," the hirsute man told him.

"Can't we do anything about it?" Tricks had only been around for a short time, and it had been very disappointing thus far, but he wasn't really ready for it to be over just yet, not before he even had a chance to understand the nature of his own existence.

Unrequited Love snorted. "What will you do? Riffle your cards at it?"

He frowned at her. "That is very unkind."

"Well, there's not much any of us can do, is there? We all have our specialities."

"Besides, we can't interfere," Severe Errors in Judgement explained. "Humans have their own free will. They are responsible for themselves. We have to let them make their own choices."

"Unfortunately, that means we are at their mercy," A.S.S. put in. He sighed. "And they are often so foolish."

Unrequited Love scowled. "And it doesn't help that Poorly Laid Plans is out there, helping them muck things up."

"And Dreadful Unforeseen Consequences," Minor Inconveniences added.

They all shook their heads in disgust. "Whatever is out there, whatever is happening out there, it could be the end of everything," A.S.S. said.

"And the only hope of stopping it is another human," Severe Errors in Judgment finished. "And that is overly optimistic."

Tricks sighed deeply. "Just when I was starting to get used to the idea of being a god."

"Well, at least you are a crappy god," she told him brightly. "It's not like you're a god of anything good. I mean, you don't even have you own temple."

He frowned at her. "Thanks for reminding me."

At the same moment, they all looked accusingly at A.S.S. He blushed. "Well, this is awkward, isn't it?"

\* \* \*

*Meanwhile, in Aether City, people are crossing to the other side of the street...*

Ptolemy and Darius didn't even notice as the bustling crowd along the busy thoroughfare parted as they passed, as though they sensed straying too near the two men would be a very poor idea indeed. It was a sparkling sunny day. The white stone streets glittered, and the sun's cheerful rays glinted off the glass and metal buildings that rose up into the sky. Overhead, gleaming white aerostats floated serenely by, and dazzling cars zipped past, filling the streets with warm puffs of steam.

Ptolemy was not in good temper. Darius was in slightly better humour; his dark eyes bore into the back of the head of a man several paces ahead of them. The man was young and his step was light. He seemed a cheerful, carefree sort of man, but his gait slowed as Darius worked upon him. The young man paused as a pretty young woman in a maid's uniform hurried past. His head turned to admire her ample backside.

Ptolemy snapped his fingers. The man burst into flames.

Darius glared at Ptolemy. "I was working on that one!"

"Well, you did a very fine job of it."

"I wasn't finished! He was just barely considering--"

"It's not important!" Ptolemy snapped. "What, exactly, have you done to stop what Tan is doing?"

"I told you! I put my best people on it."

"Your best people? The people who have done absolutely nothing to even slow his progress? Do you have any idea how far he's come?"

Darius gave him an insolent look. "No. Do you?"

Ptolemy scowled. "I did not anticipate his tenacity. He's far enough that if we don't stop him soon, it will be too late."

"Well, what do you want me to do about it? I am doing my best!"

"Your best? Your best is hiring that...firm?"

"Yes! I will have you know, they are typically extremely reliable and effective."

"Now is not the time to be atypical! This is serious, Darius. They have to succeed."

"I know that! I may appear to be oblivious to the consequences, but I do appreciate the severity of the situation."

"So what are you going to do about it? If he is allowed to complete the spell--"

Darius stiffened. "You could offer a bit of assistance, you know. I have offered what I can to get you started."

"You know my hands are tied!"

"You can't even offer a bit of information? It would be helpful if you could at least give us a time frame to work with."

Ptolemy sighed. "If I did, it would trouble you."

"Trouble me?"

"We are talking a matter of days, Darius. And there is nothing I can do to stop it. I am relying on you! And your people."

Darius paled. "A matter of days?"

"Yes, and it is becoming increasingly harder to keep my higher-ups from noticing we're involved."

"Damn it, Ptolemy! You could have said."

"Well, what good would it have done?"

"It might have instilled a greater sense of urgency in my people."

"Is not the unmaking of everything urgent enough?"

Darius considered this carefully. "I'm not so sure with these people. Half of them are likely looking forward to it."

Ptolemy shot him an annoyed looked. "Then find someone else! This is serious."

"There is no one else. They are the best."

"If they are the best...then things are grim indeed."

Darius looked highly offended. "I chose the right people. They can do this. They just need...I just need to further impress upon them the urgency of the situation."

"Good, then. See that you do. If not, all of this--"

"I know, I know! Balance thrown off, unmaking of everything, end of the world. No more street cafes or steam cars or sensual massages. I got it."

"Good." With that, Ptolemy suddenly lifted off into the air and disappeared in a flash of brilliant light from above.

Darius grumbled unhappily. Then he snapped his fingers, and Aether City disappeared in the blink of an eye. He sighed as he peered out at the bubbling blood red sea in Darklord Blood's domain. He hated this place. It was so dark and grim, even for someone so infernal as he. Not to mention, the red sand never seemed to wash out of his finely tailored suits, and he managed to keep tracking it into his house for weeks afterward, no matter how often he brushed out the soles of his shoes.

He looked up at the dark stone Blood Keep and sighed deeply. A light burned steadily in the barred windows on the ground floor. He strode swiftly up the glittering red stairs and lifted the iron doorknocker. He let it drop heavily against the door with more force than was strictly necessary. It felt good to make such a commotion in this dreary, desolate place.

The young maid who answered the door was not as Darius would have expected. She was young and pretty with long, blonde hair. She smiled sweetly at him. "Oh. Hello, sir." Darius leered at her and was rewarded with the slight flush across her cheeks. "Can I help you?"

"I am here to see Sho."

"Ah. I see." She looked uncomfortable, but she lifted her chin. "I am afraid Master Blood is dining with his mother and father."

"It is extremely urgent that I speak to him. I cannot wait another moment."

She hesitated. "I am forbidden from interrupting their meal, sir."

Darius sighed in frustration. "I have no time for this." He snapped his fingers.

The young maid sunk to the floor in a dead faint. Darius stepped over her. At the last minute, he turned and propped her carefully up against the wall. Then he remembered himself and pushed her back down onto the floor. It wouldn't do to get careless at a time like this. He was in enough trouble if anyone found out what he was up to; there was no sense making it worse by showing the girl such a kindness.

He marched into the dining room. The Blood family sat silently at a large, gleaming redwood table, sipping crimson wine. He sensed tension in the room as they all turned to look at him in surprise. The Lord and Lady of the house did not look pleased to see him. Sho, on the other hand, sagged in relief. He'd come at the right time, evidently.

"Darius," Sho said, half rising to his feet. "What are you doing here?"

Darklord Blood turned to his son, mortally offended. "Sho, what is that... creature doing in my dining room?"

Darius drew himself up to his full height. "That is quite rich coming from the Lord of Blood," he said snappishly.

Blood shot to his feet angrily. "I do not accept your kind in my home."

Darius narrowed his eyes. "Father," Sho said. "Darius is a friend."

"A friend? You are friends with that infernal thing?"

Sho scowled at his father. "I will not be spoken to like that," Darius said. He lifted a hand, which burned with such darkness it seemed to swallow all the light in the room.

Sho stepped into his path. "Darius, forgive my father his ignorance. He is set and old-fashioned in his ways. I assume you came to speak with me."

Darius took a deep breath, but the darkness around him faded into light. "Yes. It is a matter of grave urgency."

Sho turned to his parents and bowed. "Mother, Father, I apologise. I must speak with Darius at once."

Blood rapped his knuckles on the table before him. "I forbid you to leave this table."

Sho snorted. He ignored his father and spun on his heel, gesturing Darius to follow him out of the room.

"I expected a much more jovial welcome from your kind," Darius remarked as he followed him out into the gloomy, red-walled entrance hall. "Considering your dark natures."

Sho sighed. "Father is...having a troubled time at the moment. In truth, I am somewhat relieved to have been interrupted. I do not think I could have taken yet another meal in which my parents insist on hounding me about the Lady Nailah."

"Hm?" Darius asked, looking around the room distractedly. It was rather garish.

"Lady Nailah. Daughter of Darklord Shadow. She is my intended."

Darius' head snapped to him. "Your intended?" For a moment, he looked completely caught out. "You're engaged?"

Sho pushed a hand through his snow-white hair. "It is my father's doing. I haven't even seen the girl--"

"But what about Oni?"

Sho looked surprised by this. "What about Oni?"

Darius shook his head. "Never mind. It is not important. Sho! We are running out of time."

He'd been so caught up in the Darklands' politics and society, he'd nearly forgotten. "I beg your pardon?"

"Tan! The spell! The Haosul Cel! The unmaking of everything, remember? Tan has nearly reached completion of the spell."

"Ah. Yes. I had almost forgotten about that."

"What?! Sho, this is the potential unmaking of the entire world. You'd forgotten?"

"Well, things have been quite...tense around here."

"Sho, this is serious. Extremely serious. The most serious thing I have ever brought to you, and your people are mucking it up!"

Sho lifted his hands, abashed. "All right, all right. What is happening?"

"Ptolemy says it is only a matter of days before the wizard solves the combination and completes the spell."

"Days!" Sho's expression was almost pleased. "Ah. So I see. So, it would be necessary for me to leave the Darklands at once and address the problem myself."

"It would be, yes," Darius replied through gritted teeth. "That would be quite helpful of you."

"I just have to explain to my father--" Sho cut off. He sighed. Then he shook his head. "I cannot do it."

"What? Have I not impressed upon you the urgency of the matter?"

"You have done, Darius, but I cannot leave my people at a time like this. I am forbidden. The law of my people--"

"Damn your laws! This is serious, Sho!"

"Do you think I don't know that? But I cannot abandon my duty."

"This is absurd. If you don't do something, the entire world will end!"

Sho sighed. "I need to discuss the situation with Lord Blood. I will need to impress upon him the urgency of the matter."

Darius stroked his chin thoughtfully. "Maybe I should speak to him. Tell him about Enid..."

"No! No. I will speak with him."

Darius sighed deeply. "Sho..."

Sho had never seen him look so serious and so drawn. He nodded. "I realise it's serious, Darius. I will do what I can."

"Right. Good, then. See that you do."

\* \* \*

*Meanwhile, time gets even shorter...*

Zebulon's eyes widened. He whooped jubilantly. He'd found it. It was here. Finally.

**Agni.** The sixth rune.

Zebulon's insides turned cold as his eyes scanned the page.

A rune to represent an offering; the sacrifice of a most precious possession.

He shot to his feet and strode swiftly into his sleeping chamber. His horror-stricken reflection stared back at him from the mirror on the wall. His entire body clenched in pain. He doubled over, clutching at his middle. He groaned.

**An offering.** All right, then. **Sacrifice.**

He had nothing left to lose anymore but his life, and that was already slipping away.

\* \* \*

When Sora arrived at the tower, Zebulon was awaiting her with a gleam in his eyes she had not seen in many days. He rushed to greet her, sweeping her into a jubilant bear hug. She laughed as she pulled back to look up at him. "What's happened, Zebulon?"

He spun her around, laughing. "I have discovered it. The sixth rune. Agni."

"I am so pleased!" Her stomach roiled uneasily, but she did not let her smile waver. "There is only one left, then."

He released her and spun towards the bookshelves. "Indeed. Only one, and we are closing in." He pulled several books off the shelf and dropped them on the table. His eyes flamed with passion. "We cannot stop now."

Sora smiled and joined him at the table. She drew to her the first book her fingers encountered and opened it. Despite Zebulon's excitement, however, she could not concentrate. After several moments, she looked up at him. Her stomach clenched, but she steeled her resolve. "Zebulon..."

His head snapped up. His eyes burned like two tiny blue flames. "Have you found it?"

She shook her head. "Zebulon, I must speak with you. This spell..."

Anger flared on his face. "More concerns, Sora? More questions about my integrity?" He thumped a hand on the table. "I have no time for such things! I am so close!"

She stared at him in shock. "Zebulon, we have been friends for many years."

His expression softened slightly. "Yes, my dear. We have been friends for many years. And you are my apprentice. Can you not help me now and trust I am doing the right thing?"

"I can trust that, Zebulon. I can trust that your intentions are pure. I know you so well, and I know you would never do anything to harm me or anyone else. But will you not listen to me this once?"

He sighed and lowered his head. "I will listen to you, Sora. I owe you as much. You have been most faithful and steadfast."

"I am faithful still!" she said earnestly.

He relented. "Your loyalty has never been in question. I will hear your concerns, my dear."

She took a deep breath to steady her nerves. "These runes...I have looked at them."

His eyes narrowed, but he did not interrupt her.

"They are..." She gathered her courage, for she must hear his explanation before she drew such terrible conclusions about her oldest friend. "It seems as though perhaps it is...it is a spell to open a gate."

He scowled. "I have already told you! It is a spell for prolonging life!"

"Oh, I do believe that is true, Zebulon. I do! It seems as though it is. It is just...Janus. It is the rune to open a gate, is it not?"

His eyes burned with fury. "You went behind my back?"

"I simply attempted to understand the nature of the work we are doing! You said I was encouraged to be inquisitive."

"I expected you to trust me! How can I trust you if you do not trust me?"

"It is not a matter of trust!"

"Xen...I knew it was he who has turned you against me."

The cold expression on his face frightened her. "I am not against you, Zebulon. I am your faithful friend and your assistant. It is just that I believe Xen believes the spell...it is quite dangerous."

He shot abruptly to his feet and paced angrily across the floor.

"Please hear me, Zebulon. Please listen. For the sake of our friendship."

He stopped and turned his fiery gaze on her. "I want you to leave. You have lost your loyalty for that man. You are no longer on my side!"

"I am! I promise I am, but Xen says this spell—it will be the end of everything."

He blinked in surprise. "That is ridiculous."

"If this gate is opened, it could mean the unmaking of the entire world."

He laughed humourlessly. "What foolishness is this?"

"I know it is not your intention, but if you complete this spell, it could mean--"

He lifted his hand to point at the door. "I want you to leave!"

She stared at him with a stricken expression.

"I no longer require your assistance. Go!"

"Zebulon, please, I do not wish to go against you. I wish to help you, but I must make you understand--"

"It is you who do not understand! This work is important, and you could not begin to comprehend it."

Tears streamed down her cheeks at the harshness of his tone. "Please, Zebulon--"

"Go!" His voice was a roar, and his anger shook the entire room. Bottles fell and shattered upon the floor. Books tumbled from the shelves. The man himself seemed to swell and grow larger. Magic swirled around him in an almost tangible storm. "GO!"

Sora bolted for the door. Her tears blurred her vision, but she felt the rush of his magic propel her out into the hall. She spun back to plead with him, but the door slammed in her face. She pounded on it. "Zebulon!" She sketched a rune in the air, but it only sent her skittering backwards with the force of his instant protections.

She picked herself up off the floor, sobbing miserably. "Xen." She turned and fled down the hall. She needed to talk to Xen right away. He was the only one who could help her.

\* \* \*

*Meanwhile, in Scathach, things are just as bad...*

"I will not allow you to leave here before the ceremony!" Lord Blood was in a towering temper. "You are required to attend. It is the law."

"I can leave with your permission," Sho reminded him, trying to keep his voice steady. "Father, this is important. My work--"

"Your work?!" The wine in Blood's goblet sloshed over the side as he shot up from his leather wing-backed chair. The red stain seemed to disappear into the study's steel grey carpet. "Running around playing mercenary for fallen angels is hardly a job! I will not allow you to shirk your responsibilities this time. You are meant to be here."

"Father, if the wizard is allowed to complete the spell, it will be the end of everything."

Blood rolled his eyes. "Don't be so dramatic."

"It is not dramatic. It is the truth! This is serious, Father. I swear to you. I will come back when it is completed. We will discuss my future then."

His father waved an impatient hand. "Lies. You have never been willing to consider your duty. Do you truly expect me to believe you will now?" Blood laid the wine glass upon the small table beside his chair with a force that should have shattered it. He pushed his hands through his stark white hair and scowled at his son. "You will stay here. You will fulfil your duty as the future Lord Blood. I am tired of you behaving like a rebellious child! You will do as you are told for once in your life!"

Sho's eyes blazed in anger, and he stepped towards his father. His body stiffened suddenly. Magic thrilled through his blood, but it was not his own. He realised what his father had done. He'd not done it, even when Sho had been a small, insolent child. Fury coursed through him, and he fought against his father's hold upon him. He was not powerful enough to break his father's blood binding.

"You will go to your room," Blood told him in a low voice. "We will discuss this later."

Sho resisted his father's machinations, but he was powerless against the man's control. As though he was nothing more than a puppet, he marched up to his bedroom and shut the door. He could move freely through the room, but when he tried to reach for the doorknob, his hand froze. Pain coursed through him as he tried to fight the blood binding. He cursed loudly and spun to throw himself down on the bed.

The quiet orb on his nightstand suddenly glowed and chimed insistently. Sho jumped to answer it. "Yeah?"

"Sho."

She sounded different, but he was so relieved to hear from her, he hardly noticed. "Oni. God, I miss you."

"What's wrong with you?"

136

He sighed deeply. "Darius came to see me. Things are…"

"Dire. I know. This isn't going well at all."

"Lord Blood will not allow me to leave the Darklands."

"Since when has that ever stopped you?"

"You don't understand, Oni." His voice was low and grim. "He can control me."

"I've never heard of you letting anyone control you."

"I mean he can control my blood. He can force me. And he has done."

"Sho!" She sounded horrified.

"I will find a way to break it."

"You have to, Sho. Xen…"

She didn't say anything more. He frowned. "What about him?"

"We haven't gotten any closer to Zebulon Tan. We can't even get into his workshop. Our only lead…she's a dead end. Xen thinks the only way to stop what's happening is…well, to go back to the dark side."

Sho shot to his feet. "No! Oni, you can't let him do that! You know what will happen if he does."

"I know! I am trying to talk him out of it."

"Even if you have to do something drastic, Oni, you have to stop him."

She scoffed. "When have I ever shied away from drastic measures?"

"You have to stop him at any cost. If he goes back, I might not be able to pull him back. And even if I can…he might not survive it this time."

"I know that! I am doing what I can to stop him, but Sho…"

"Oni, whatever it takes. Stop him."

She sighed deeply.

"Please, Oni. Do this for me."

"I will, Sho. But only for you. It's not because I care what happens to him or anything. I want to make that clear."

He snorted. "Thanks a lot, Oni."

The orb's glow extinguished. Sho tossed it onto the bed and paced across the floor. He practically jumped at the light, tentative knock on the door. He glared at the door, but he did not turn to open it.

"Leave me alone!" he growled. "I am through arguing with you! What more can you do?"

"Sho?" his mother called.

He sighed and strode to pull open the door. His hand could not grip the handle. He gritted his teeth against the pain. "Come in, Mother."

The door opened slowly, as though she was afraid he might slam it shut. When he didn't, she stepped into the room and peered silently up at him for several moments. Her pale, still beautiful face was sad. "You have grown so much."

He scowled at her. "So?"

"You are the very age your father was when we were married."

Sho spun his back to her. "Is there a point to this, Mother?"

She did not sound angry. "Yes, there is. I know you are angry, Sho. I know your father is angry. You are our only son, and he doesn't understand why you cannot accept your birth right. He does not understand why you do not wish to be Lord."

"I never wished for it!" He crossed his arms insolently over his chest. "I just want to be free. I want to live my life."

She laid a gentle hand upon his shoulder. "I know. Your father and I wished that when you went to Hyperion City you would sow your wild oats and realise that you desire your destiny, but it has not happened."

He scowled. "No. It has not."

"And I suspect you will be very unhappy if you are forced to live a life you did not choose for yourself."

Sho glanced over his shoulder at her.

"You are my son, and I love you very much. Your father may desire your acquiescence, but I only wish for your happiness. Tell me what is troubling you."

He turned to his mother in surprise. She looked perfectly sincere. He sighed deeply, and his shoulders slumped. He felt much like a child again, but it hardly mattered now. "A wizard at one of the academies in Hyperion is planning to perform a spell which, if successful, will unmake the entire universe. We have been given the job of stopping him."

"I beg your pardon?" She sounded amused.

He glared at her. "It is not a joke, Mother. In the Darklands, we cannot appreciate that which is out there in the world, and it often falls on my people to assist in such matters."

She nodded thoughtfully. "All right. I do not understand completely how it could be, but I appreciate your belief in the seriousness of the thing. So this spell, if your wizard completes it, will unmake the world."

"Yes."

"And your people—your team—they cannot stop this?"

"They can. There is a way. But I will lose a close friend. He would sacrifice himself to stop this. I cannot let that happen, and I am the only one who can stop him."

She lifted her chin. "Then we must convince your father to let you go."

He blinked in surprise. "Mother?"

"Well, Sho, I may be a Darklady and have spent my entire life in Scathach and seen very little of the world, but I am aware there is more out there than what our people know. If what you say is true, if it is as serious as you say, you cannot allow it to happen."

Sho did not allow his hopes to rise. "Mother, he has bound my blood."

Her eyes widened. "He has done what?" She did not wait for him to reply. She spun abruptly on her heel and marched towards the door.

"Where are you going?"

When she turned to him, there was a steely glint in her eyes that he had never seen before. "I am going to speak to your father. This has gone quite far enough."

# CHAPTER SEVEN

*M*eanwhile, *in Hyperion City where all the trouble is happening...*

Sora rapped anxiously on Xen's door. "Xen? Please, it's Sora." There was no response. She leaned her forehead against the door and took a deep breath to steady her nerves. She could not feel him inside the room. He wasn't there. She spun away. Simon's office was in the Incanting wing, and she hurried towards it. If Xen wasn't with him, he might know where he was now; they were so often together, and now she knew why it was so.

Simon's room was empty. She could feel a strange energy lingering in the air around the room, but there was no one inside. She hesitated. She didn't want to go to Oni's room. She didn't know the woman well—in fact, she'd never spoken to Oni, but something about her frightened Sora. She would have to cope; things were becoming quite serious, and there was little time for cowardice.

There was no response when she knocked on Oni's door, but Sora was certain they were inside. She could feel Xen's dark, intense aura just beyond the door. She opened her mouth to call his name, but she snapped it shut again as Simon threw open the door, peering out into the hall.

"Oh! Professor Simon."

He blinked at her owlishly. "Oh. Hello. Are you looking for Xen?"

"Yes. I...I need to talk to him."

"He's inside. I'll get him."

"Thank you." Her heart thumped. From somewhere in the corridor, a breeze swirled up, lifting her skirt so it billowed around her waist. She gasped and clapped her hands over her bottom. Her cheeks flamed. "Goodness! I am so embarrassed."

Simon blushed. "It's quite all right. It happens all the time."

He turned to call to Xen, but the man was already behind him. Xen brushed past the sheepish professor and caught Sora's shoulders. Her eyes filled as she looked up at him. He drew her into his arms. "Sora, what's wrong? What happened?"

Simon faded back into the room as Xen pulled Sora inside. She took a

140

hitching breath. "Zebulon," she said in a wavering voice. "Xen, you were right. About everything."

"Did something happen? Did he do anything to you?"

"No! Well, he—he went sort of crazy."

"Are you hurt?"

"No, no. He didn't hurt me."

Xen leaned back to look closely at her face. He pressed a hand to her cheek. "Tell me what happened, Sora."

His voice was low and soothing, and she sighed deeply. It was all right. Xen would help. "I decided to...see if maybe you were right. I wanted to know what Zebulon and I have really been working on. So I researched the meanings of the runes he'd sent me to find. They are...they seem to be what you said they were. I think he really is opening a gate. I confronted him. He accused me of going against him, but I was only trying to get him to understand what you said could happen if he went through with it."

Xen nodded. "Come sit down, Sora."

"Oni and Simon are in there." She peered over his shoulder at the closed door through which Simon had disappeared.

"Yes. They are my friends."

"But I...I just want to talk to you."

He smiled. "All right. Let's go to my room."

"No," she said, startling him. "Let's go to mine."

He lifted his eyebrows.

She rolled her eyes at him. "Don't get any ideas. I have my papers there."

"Ah. Right, then."

Sora's room was a scattered mess of books and lacy, frilly feminine things, which she kicked hastily under the bed as they entered. She glanced over her shoulder at him, blushing, but he looked pointedly away, hiding his smile behind his hand. She riffled through the stack of scrap parchment paper on her desk and handed him a pile so scribbled upon, he could hardly read the words.

He had not expected she would be so disorganised.

"I don't know exactly what he's doing," she explained. "And I don't know why he's doing it, but I think you're right. This is the spell." She pointed to the hastily scribbled list of names. "There are seven runes. We have found six."

"Six?" He sucked in a sharp breath and pushed his hands anxiously through his hair. "This is not good."

"It has taken many months to find these runes. We have been working on it for some time."

Xen shook his head. "We should have stopped it before it got this far."

"Xen, what do we do?"

He sighed. His expression was grim. Her stomach sank. "Can you stall him? Can you keep him from finding the last rune?"

She dropped her head and sniffled softly. "He's dismissed me. He said he no longer requires my assistance."

Xen cursed softly under his breath.

"He has locked me out of his workshop. I do not think...I do not think he will accept me back this time. He does not wish to be stopped. I tried to make him understand the consequences of his actions, but I do not think he cares. Truly, it is as though...as though he's gone mad. I want to help but...I don't think I can do anything. I am sorry."

Xen wrapped his arms around her tightly. "It's all right. We have another way, Sora. We will sort this out."

She tried to pull away, but he did not release her. "What other way?" she asked into his chest. "You aren't going to hurt him, are you?"

"No. He isn't the one who is going to be hurt."

Now she lifted her head to look at him. "What do you mean?" When he didn't reply, she said, "Xen? What do you mean? What's the way? Tell me."

He did not meet her gaze. "It isn't important. It will work, and it will stop all of this. That is what's important."

"Is it you?" She frowned. "Xen? Are you going to do something insane?"

He leaned his forehead against hers. "I am going to try not to."

"Do you promise?"

"Yes." He drew away from her. "You have helped, Sora." He held up the scraps of parchment. "We have the spell. We might be able to do something with it."

142

She was not convinced. "What is the plan if you cannot?"

He looked away, but she stepped forward and pressed her palms to his cheeks, moving his head back to face her. Her eyes were stern. He sighed. "You're right. Tan is one of the best sorcerers in Hyperion. But he is not more powerful than me. Not when I..."

Her eyes widened. "When you go...when you go into the bad juju rage?"

He chuckled wryly. "Something like that. When I tap into the black magic."

"But...but you said you...you said there was no coming back from it."

He caught her wrists and thrust her gently away from him. "There isn't. At least...not a very good chance of it."

"Xen, no!"

He frowned. "Don't you understand, Sora? This is the end of the world. It might sound dramatic, but that is exactly what is happening here. If I don't do this, everyone dies. Everyone. It won't matter that I didn't go back to the dark side because nothing will matter. Everything will be over."

There was dread in her eyes. "Please, Xen...we have to find another way. I know him. I know Zebulon, and I know the spell. Well, I know the order of the runes, anyway. We can find a way. We have to try."

Xen sighed. "Sora..."

"No! I'm not...I'm not willing to lose you."

He smiled now and wrapped an arm around her waist to draw her against him. He lowered his head to press his lips against hers. She caught her breath, but he pulled away before she could return the kiss.

"I don't want to be lost. But this is serious. I will do what I have to do." He stepped back and tugged on her hand. "Come on. We have to tell Oni and Simon about what you know. They might have some idea what to do." He paused and gave her a grim look. "If we're very lucky."

\* \* \*

Zebulon tossed a book across the room where it shattered against a display case housing a collection of potion bottles and amulets. The glowing liquids spread across the floor in a smoking swirl of colour. "Damn! Damn damn! Where is it?"

It would be difficult to find the seventh and final rune without Sora. She had been his most useful ally, and now she was likely running to Xen and his friends, spilling everything about his plans. No matter. He would not let them stop him. He had to complete the spell. He had to save his life.

He loved Sora deeply. She was his closest friend, and he'd always considered her as dear as his own child. She had been with him from the very beginning of this quest, though she had not known it. She had given him the comfort he needed even when she did not know she provided it. He did not wish to go on alone, without her.

But he could not go on at all if he did not complete the spell.

He stopped smashing up the instruments and bottles in his workshop. His orb chimed softly from under a pile of torn pages and broken glass. It glowed brightly, casting prisms across the battered wooden floor. Zebulon scooped it up impatiently and swiped a hand across its surface.

"Yes?"

He must have sounded utterly mad, completely desperate. A gravelly voice on the other end of the orb chuckled. "I have some information you might like to hear."

Zebulon scowled. "What is it? Have you found them?"

"I found them."

His rage suddenly subsided, and a feeling of mad elation fluttered in his chest. "You found them?"

"That is what I do."

"Well? Who are they?"

"I'm going to need a bit more to go on."

"What do you mean?"

"I mean money-wise."

"You little swindler! Tell me what I need to know."

"It's going to cost you."

"It will cost your life if you don't tell me now! You think I cannot reach you from here?"

The gravelly voice chuckled again. "I have protection. You're not going to touch me."

The rage surged up in his belly again. He sketched a rune forcefully into the air.

There was a choking noise on the other end of the orb.

"Not from me," Zebulon growled. "You have no protection from me! I made sure of that. Tell me what I want to know!"

The man with the gravelly voice gasped for breath. "Okay. Okay. No need to be so testy."

"I am testy. I am very testy. And I am going to get testier. Tell me who they are!"

"It took a lot of persuasion." The man on the other end of the orb still sounded hoarse. "Most people don't know anything about them, but the ones that do don't want to talk about it."

"I'm waiting."

"Your guys work for Sho Sange."

"Am I supposed to know who that is?"

"It would probably be to your benefit. He's the son of Darklord Blood."

"Darklord Blood? He's a Darklord?"

"That's right."

"What's he doing out of Scathach?"

"Running himself a mercenary business, from the sound of it," the gravelly-voiced man replied. "They specialise in unusual cases. Things other people can't do. Like taking care of you, I expect."

"A Darklord," Zebulon mused grimly. "And the others?"

"Just a motley bunch of mercenaries. An ex-Lumina, a circus performer turned thief and few others I don't know much about."

"What about the woman?"

"No one knows anything about her. Apparently she's good with explosives. That's about it. She's got no history. At least, not by that name."

"And Simon?"

"No. Nothing. No history, either. I'm not sure where he came from. No one knows much about him or what purpose he serves on the team. He doesn't seem to do much at all. The others...well, they could be anybody. Contractors, maybe.

It's never the same guy twice."

Zebulon frowned thoughtfully. "Interesting."

"Hey, listen, boss, I'm not one to give advice, and I don't care much what happens to you because you're a horrible old bastard who keeps trying to kill me, but if these guys are out to get you, you might think about getting out of their way."

The horrible old bastard scoffed. "I hardly think a Darklordling and an ex-Lumina will be much good against me. I am well up to the challenge."

"If you say so. I'm just giving you a little tip. Just something I picked up on the street."

"Well, I hardly think I need your tip."

"Okay, then. Don't forget—you owe me, Tan. Don't be calling me again unless you plan to pay for my services."

Tan growled and tossed the orb across the room. It fell lightless to the floor amidst the rubble he'd created. "Darklord Blood," he muttered, kicking aside the debris as he paced the room. "So that's whose out to get to me."

He dropped into an old, rickety wooden chair and lowered his head. He needed to think about this. He knew of the Darklords, for they were well known across Pandia for their mastery of the dark elements. He would be powerless against the master of blood in a face-to-face encounter. There was...quite a lot one could do with blood. His stomach churned as he considered the possibilities. Sho Sange could draw it, drain it...he could use it to control him, and all would be lost.

He shot to his feet and rummaged through the detritus of his workshop until the found the book for which he was looking. He propped it on his podium and paged through it frantically. Sho Sange might not be in the school; in fact, he was certain the man had sent the foolish emissaries in his stead, but there was no telling what he had taught Xen or the other two.

Ah. There it was. He muttered under his breath. His heart thumped. He scooped up the long, thin-bladed dagger from the detritus and marched to the door. It would take more than a few runes to keep out the Lord of Blood. He dug deep with the knife as he carved the symbols along the doorframe. In a swift motion, he slashed the knife across his palm. He hardly felt the pain as his blood dripped onto the floor, the only part of his dying, miserable body that was still thrumming and thriving inside him.

He smeared his hand across the etchings, splattering the crude symbols with his blood. Then he stepped back.

The door shimmered as the protective barrier spread through the room. He sighed in relief. He would be safe from Darklord Blood, at least in his sanctuary. It would not solve his immediate problem, though. The Lumina and the two wild cards, Oni and Simon, were still dogging him. Though they'd clearly accomplished nothing, it did not mean they were not lying in wait for a moment of weakness.

Sora was probably with them now, revealing all his secrets. The unfaithful, ungrateful whelp. His temper flared. She'd been nothing before he had scooped her out of her miserable, lonely orphan life. He'd taught her everything she knew, and now she had joined his enemies against him to keep him from saving his own life. Fury swelled up in his chest. She had betrayed him in the very worst possible way, and he would never forgive her.

He could not force her to stay away from Xen and his people, but he could stop her from revealing his intimate secrets. He could stop her from ruining him and everything for which he had worked so hard. He could stop her from stealing his one chance at life.

There was only one way. He must take her from them. He must take revenge for her dreadful deceit.

He spun on his heel and strode back to his podium. He did not need the pages of the book to remember the series of runes he sketched in the air or the incantations that he muttered under his breath in the ancient language of the darkest magic.

\* \* \*

*Subsequently, Oni's room is a dangerous place to be...*

The air rippled. Sora cried out suddenly, doubling over in pain. Xen flew across the room in seconds, scattering the scraps of parchment upon which Sora had scribbled Tan's spell. "Sora! What's going on?"

She leaned against him, but she did not speak, for it seemed as though her mouth had sealed shut. She looked at him with huge, frightened eyes. Oni and Simon hurried to them. Oni fluttered around them as though she might spot the culprit skulking around the room.

"What's happening?" Xen growled.

Simon's head swivelled around the room as though he was scenting something in the air. "It's Tan," he said grimly. "He's doing something to her."

Oni scowled and glanced around as though she might catch him lurking in the corner. "What is he doing?"

Simon shook his head. "I don't know. Sora?"

She gasped for breath, but none seemed forthcoming. Her face was startling white. Xen gripped her shoulders, but there was nothing he could do to stop what was happening. "Simon, help her!"

"You're the dark sorcerer! You do something!"

"No!" Sora's voice was little more than a gasp.

"She's right. Xen can't use dark magic," Oni said, scowling. "Do anything else."

Sora seemed unable to say anything more, but she nodded vehemently.

Simon sighed deeply. "Oh, fine." He hesitated for a split second then he snapped his fingers.

The air shimmered, and then they felt the collision of the magical energies in the air. Sora clutched her throat, but her breath was returning. The colour returned slowly to her face. She sagged in Xen's arms, but she was breathing almost normally.

Oni lifted her eyebrows at Simon. "Oh, that was impressive. What did you do?"

Simon looked uncomfortable. "I just put a protection around her. One that... well, one that she might regret having later."

"What do you mean?"

"What did you do to her, Simon?" Xen asked in a low voice.

"She's...well, I sort of made her...well immune to magic."

"Immune to magic?"

Sora's mouth opened in horror. "Do you mean you took my magic away?"

Simon blushed. "Well, it was either that or let you die."

"But...but I..." She looked up at Xen. "But I would rather be dead! What do I have without magic?"

"Calm down, Sora," Simon ordered. "It is not as bad as it sounds. Yes, the magic you had is...well, it's gone, but you can get it back. You just have to...start over from scratch. Even the most non-magical people can learn it."

Tears sprang into her eyes. "But my job--"

"Sora, this is more serious than your job. I am sure you can still teach."

"Yes," Oni said bracingly. "I don't know any magic, and I am the best teacher in the school. All my students say so."

They ignored her and didn't bother to point out her students were likely too terrified of her to say anything else.

Xen helped Sora into a chair. She seemed almost to crumple over herself, covering her face with her hands. "My magic. My entire life."

Xen wrapped an arm around her shoulders. Oni stepped forward and swung her fist at Simon's jaw. It connected with a sickening cracking sound. Simon cursed angrily, rubbing his chin. "What did you do that for?"

"You took away her magic?"

"It was the only way! She was going to die otherwise."

"You couldn't do something else? Throw yourself in the path of the curse or something?"

"It would not have done any good. It would have just bounced right off me." He jabbed a finger towards Oni. "You are the one who said no dark magic! What else was I supposed to do?" He drew himself up, lifting his chin in defiance. "Besides, it's not the end of the world. That's the other spell we're trying to stop."

Sora sobbed quietly into Xen's shoulder. "It's all right, Sora," he said in a low, soothing voice. "He saved your life. I would rather you had no magic than were dead." She took a hitching breath, and she nodded, though the tears still streamed from her eyes. Xen wiped them away and kissed the top of her head.

Simon and Oni stared at him. He ignored them.

The sudden rap on the door startled them all. They stared around at each other in surprise. "Who is that?" Xen demanded, rising to stand in front of Sora protectively.

Oni shrugged. "Could be one of my boyfriends, I guess." She did not sound convinced, and her jaw tightened grimly. She crept slowly towards the door, pressing a finger to her lips as though the caller might turn away if they suspected the room was empty.

The door burst open. Sho smirked at them.

"Sho!"

Sora peered around Xen in interest. "Sho?"

Oni vaulted into Sho's arms, wrapping her long legs around his waist. He caught her as naturally as though she did this everyday. "I am so happy to see you! Everything is rubbish!"

"So I've heard." He set her down and pushed her gently aside to face Xen. His expression was stern. "Darius came to me. He said I needed to get myself over here. Apparently, everything is falling apart."

This didn't seem to greatly bother them. He was right, and they were so relieved to see him, he could insult them all night long if he felt like it.

"We are handling it," Xen protested with only half-hearted sullenness.

Oni spun to him with angry eyes. "You were going to use dark magic! You were going to give up everything."

Sho crossed his arms over his chest. "You know you can't do that, Xen."

Xen sighed and glanced over his shoulder at Sora. Sho peered around him in interest and met Sora's eyes. They stared at each other silently.

Simon rolled his eyes. "Sho, this is Sora Bale. She was Zebulon Tan's assistant. Until tonight, I understand."

"Hello," Sora greeted, lifting a hand to wave at Sho. "I have heard a lot about you."

He scrutinised her another long moment with a strange expression on his face. "What's been done to you?"

"It was Tan," Simon explained quickly. "He attacked her."

"And Simon took her magic away to stop it," Oni added.

Sho frowned. "It was the only way?"

"Well, you weren't here!" Simon snapped. "It would have been helpful if you had arrived ten minutes ago. "

Sho took a deep breath and closed his eyes. "It's still here. In the air."

"My magic?" Sora asked.

"Yes."

"You can feel it?"

"In my blood." He opened his eyes and strode towards her.

She recoiled involuntarily. She had not known any Darklords in person before, but she had heard much about them, and Sho was an intimidating man. His thickly lashed, gunmetal grey eyes were piercing, as though he could see into her skin, straight through to her blood. He was also rather a large man, quite larger even than Xen. His expression was stern, but he did not seem to mean her any harm. On the contrary, he looked more interested in what Simon had done.

"Can you get it back?" she whispered.

He paused and shook his head. "No. I'm sorry." She lowered her head, and Xen wrapped his fingers around hers. Sho gave his friend an incredulous look, but he did not remark upon this strange behaviour. "Darius said we are running out of time. It is only a matter of days before the spell is to be completed."

"Days!" Simon exclaimed.

"Yes. Days. We have to do something now."

"We can't get to Tan," Oni told him sulkily.

Sho did not look amused. "Has it occurred to you to simply bind him?"

"Of course it has," Simon snapped. "It is impossible to get to him. He never leaves his room and has protections even Oni's explosives can't break."

Sho rolled his eyes and gestured towards Sora. "But we have his assistant on our side. Can't she get into the room? She sees him, doesn't she?"

Sora sighed. "I only just came over," she explained. "I was sacked. I can't get in, either."

"He tried to curse her," Xen added. "He might have been trying to keep her from helping us."

"Well, that is troubling." Sho lowered his tall, spindly frame into the chair behind Oni's desk. "So what have we got, then? Anything?"

"We've got the spell," Oni said brightly.

He sat up straighter. "Why didn't you say so? Give it to me."

Xen gathered the scraps he'd scattered and handed them to Sho, who looked them over as though he didn't notice the scribbled penmanship or the disorganised arrangement. "Seven runes." He looked up at Sora. "I assume it is in order? It must be the combination. What do the sixth and seventh runes mean?"

Sora sighed and shook her head. "I don't know. He gave me only the names and I had to find them. It was only then I learned the meanings."

"These are all of them?"

"Yes. When I looked at them, I knew it was true what Xen had said. I was sure these runes would open a gate."

Sho nodded. "But we do not know the meanings of the other two. That is troubling, indeed. You're certain he's found the sixth rune?"

"Yes. He told me, but I did not get the opportunity to see it for myself or discover its meaning."

Sho sighed. "Okay. I will see if I can get into his workshop."

Sora looked sceptical. "Zebulon is the greatest sorcerer in Hyperion City."

Sho chuckled. "Well, I am a Darklord." He eyed her a moment. "I may require your assistance. If I can understand the way his magic works, it is possible I can undo his protections."

She hesitated. Her eyes darted towards Xen as though he might possess the answers to her uncertainty.

"I do not intend to hurt him unless it is absolutely necessary, Sora." Sho's voice was curiously reassuring.

"But I don't think I need to remind you that he did, in fact, try to kill you about ten minutes ago," Simon told her primly. "I had to take away your magic to stop it."

She sighed. "All right. I will help you."

"Right." Sho rose to his feet and tucked the scraps of spell parchment in the pocket of his black jacket.

"What are you doing here, anyway, Sho?" Simon asked. "Shouldn't you be home getting groomed to be the next Darklord Blood?"

"Yes." Sho's tone was arctic. "I am supposed to be at the ceremony binding the new Darklord Spirit. Father forbade me to leave. In fact, he bound my blood."

Simon gasped, horrified. "He bound your blood? Isn't that...isn't it...?"

"Like taking me prisoner. Yes. He was angry."

"Can you bind blood?" Sora asked.

He looked down at her. "I have complete power over blood. If I wanted, I could make you do cartwheels and backflips in the air."

She recoiled from him.

"But that wouldn't be polite," he told her lightly. "We only just met."

She smiled. He was scary, but he wasn't what she had expected. He actually seemed a little nice.

"How did you get here, then?" Xen demanded.

Sho sighed. "After I spoke with Oni--"

Xen shot her an angry look. "You called him?"

"Well..."

"You didn't think I could handle it?"

She propped her hands on her hips and scowled at him. "Well, no. I didn't. You were about to go back under."

"I am not a child, Oni. I didn't need Daddy coming home to solve our problems." Sho lifted his eyebrows at him, and Xen sighed. "All right. Maybe I did."

"I take offence to being called 'Daddy,'" Sho said.

Oni smirked. "Unless it's by me."

He frowned at her. "Oni."

Sora looked around at them in bemusement. "What exactly do you think you people can do?"

They all looked at her with identical smug smiles. "You would be surprised by what we can do," Xen told her.

"I'm still stuck on Scathach," Simon said. "How did you get out of the ceremony?"

Sho waved his hand dismissively, but he looked slightly embarrassed. "Just let it go, all right?"

"Sho," Xen said pointedly.

He sighed. "Fine. Mother intervened."

They all snickered. "You had to have your mother stand up for you?"

Sho scowled at them. "That's enough. I won't listen to you all disparage me. We have work to do. I am here, and it doesn't matter how I got here." He strode towards the door and gestured them to follow. "Are you coming or not? Let's have a look at this Zebulon Tan."

\* \* \*

*Meanwhile, on a dark night in Scathach...*

Darklord and Lady Blood stood together in the grand ballroom of the Spirit Keep. Around them, the Darklords and Ladies murmured quietly together. It was a party, of course, but few of the guests seemed interested in celebrating, despite the typically quite enjoyable occasion of a Darklord ascension. The soft, mournful music playing in the background of the soft chatter did little to lift the mood of the evening.

The Spirit Keep was quite unlike the Blood Keep. It was dazzlingly beautiful, but it looked almost as though it was made of glass. The walls and drapes were pearly grey, and the marble beneath their feet shimmered like the spectres that drifted across Spirit's domain on their way beyond. The Darklords and Ladies, clothed in the colours of their elements, stood out starkly against the almost colourless room.

Blood and his Lady were the most startling of the Darklords, in their brilliant scarlet raiment. No one seemed to notice, for it was as it should be. The Blood family had always been quite a standout in the Darklands. They bred well, and Lady Blood was certain Lady Nailah, the beautiful daughter of Shadow, would make a most excellent addition to their gene pool. She did not mention this tonight, for Nailah was not in attendance this evening, which only sufficed to fuel Lord Blood's already simmering temper. He was offended that any Darklord offspring should wish to avoid such a ceremony, for he considered it a most inflexible duty.

He did not actually enjoy the ceremonies himself, and Lady Blood knew he would have skived off at the least possible opportunity, was he not so bound by his unshakable sense of duty. Lady Blood sipped her champagne and glanced at her husband.

His brow furrowed. "Sho should be here," he said in a low voice. He looked around them as though to see if anyone had heard, for his wife knew he was most ashamed of the failure of his son to appear at this most important function. It was, she knew, a great stain upon the family honour.

"I know you want him to be you, dear, but he isn't," she told him gently.

He did not scowl or reveal his displeasure upon his face, but she knew the angry glint in his dark grey eyes quite well by now. "You should not have intervened. You had no business."

She turned equally fiery eyes and equally stony face upon him. "He is our son; not just yours. You know him as well as I do. You know he will not submit if you force him."

"It should not be a matter of submission. He should want to take up his birth right. He should not desire a life gallivanting around the city for fallen angels."

"Perhaps he should not, my darling, but he does. And we must accept it."

"Accept it? Should we just allow our line to die out? Allow another family to take over the Blood Keep?"

She smiled and patted his arm. "Dear, Sho will come home eventually. He knows his duty, and I suspect he even embraces it. He is still young, and he is still sowing his wild oats."

"He is consorting with some—some woman from Labraid when he should be courting his betrothed."

Lady Blood laughed. "Oh, Luca, what do you expect? Nailah is…challenging."

"Challenging? She is a lady of Shadow. A perfect example of a Darklady, and she is his intended wife! If he continues this way, she won't have him when he finally decides to accept his duty."

His wife laughed again. "Of course she will have him. She's been following on his heels for years. It's no wonder he is opposed to her; she does live up to her name." At his look of confusion, she grinned. "Lady Shadow."

Her husband did not look amused.

"Anyway, it is all he remembers. A young, awkward girl, always underfoot."

"She is nothing of the sort."

"Now she is not, and I am sure when he meets her again, he will see it, as well." She smiled. "Just give him a chance to live his life. Allow him to make his own decisions. If you fight him—if you bind his blood and try to force him to be something he is not, you will lose him completely. It is only a matter of time. Sho is a good man, and he knows his duty." She squeezed her husband's arm. "He will come back to us."

Lord Blood did not look convinced, but he did not try to argue this. His attention was caught by the sudden shift in the atmosphere. He sighed. "It is time. I must welcome the new Spirit."

His wife smiled sadly and trailed behind him to join the Darkladies as they looked upon their husbands and fathers, who lined up before the young Spirit behind Decay, the eldest of the Darklords and therefore the honorary leader of their people. Behind Decay was Wrath, a stout man with thick muscles and wild, unruly hair. He looked angry this evening, but then, he always looked angry, especially when he'd had a bit to drink. Night was a dark-skinned man with dark eyes and a mournful expression, for he had been close, as well, with the late Lord Spirit. Lord Dreams was not a commonplace-looking man, for his face seemed to change and shift with the mood, forming features that made little sense most of the time. Lord Malady was tall and formidable with shortly cropped hair and intelligent eyes.

Blood stood before his friend Shadow, and there was deep sadness on his face, for once Spirit had stood between them, and they had been the dearest of friends since they had been young men. The Lords Suffering and Bondage were the same age, for their mothers had been dear friends and had conspired to birth the children on the same day. They rarely spoke to each other, despite their mothers' connection, and they did not seem to mind which of them stood ahead of the line. They were quite disagreeable company most of the time, for they were both quite dreary and dull. Debauchery leered around at the assemblage, but no one seemed bothered by his behaviour. It was as it should be, and he was quite the charmer, not to mention a riot at parties most of the time. He had been the youngest of the Lords, hardly older than Sho.

That was, until Spirit ascended and would take his place at the end of the procession.

The Lords took their turns greeting the new Spirit in a language so ancient, even Decay had forgotten it. The meaning behind the words, however, was well remembered. They completed the ceremony that bound the new Lord to his element, that would bind Spirit to his domain and welcome him among the other Darklords. As the men took it in turns to speak the long, melodic phrases to their newest brother, Lady Blood joined her dear friend, Lady Spirit, whose eyes shone with the mingled grief of losing her husband and joy at seeing her son finally ascend.

Then Lady Blood felt something strange in the air around her. It was not the magic of the ritual commencing before them on the stage. It was something else. Something strange and sad. She looked around her, and was startled to see a sort of shimmering spectre floating in the air around them. They were, of course, in the domain of the Lord of Spirit, and so there were many ghosts and spirits among them, but they were meant to be reaped, to be sent out on the shore where they could move peacefully on to the next world. It was what Lord Spirit did for his people. It was his duty.

There should not have been a spirit lingering in the grand ballroom, overseeing the ceremony.

She looked around, but she could not get a fix on the spectre. She could not spot it with a direct gaze, and the glimpses she caught from the corner of her eye did little to reveal the spirit's identity. There was, however, such a feeling of rage and resentment and betrayal emanating from the manifestation that she wondered it did not fill the room or the faces of the Lords and Ladies around her.

Her birth family was Night, and so she possessed no useful powers to comprehend the spectre. She could sense it as it moved around the room, floating over the heads of the party. It moved now across the hall, lingering beside her husband and Shadow. She watched her husband's face. Lord Blood's brow furrowed slightly, but he did not turn to the spectre as though he understood it was there. Nevertheless, he seemed to sense the sensation of its presence. If he did notice something amiss, he did not dwell upon it. He turned his attention back to Lord Decay, for the eldest Darklord was speaking again, murmuring the ancient closing of the oldest of rituals.

Lady Blood watched the rippling air as the spectre moved now to hover behind the new Lord Spirit. The young man's face did not change, but she was certain he knew it was there. He must, for he was the lord of all spirits in this domain and otherwise. He must sense it. His even, expressionless features did not even twitch in recognition.

She looked around, but it did not seem as if anyone else sensed the spirit. She squinted her eyes at the thing. *Who are you?* She pushed the thought from her mind, towards the angry spectre. She did not expect it would reply. *What are you doing here?* She wondered if it could hear her at all.

And then, as though the air had whispered it in her ear, she heard a low, almost inaudible sound. *Don't trust him.*

She blinked in surprise, but the air had returned to normal. The spectre was gone. She looked around in confusion, and she wondered if it had ever been there at all. Perhaps she'd simply been so bored with the ceremony she'd seen so many times that she had manifested the spectre herself for her own private entertainment.

She didn't think so. She looked back her husband. His face was neutral. He, as the others, bowed in unison to the new Lord Spirit. Spirit's mouth turned up in the slightest of smiles, and he took his place behind Lord Debauchery. Lady Blood frowned. *Don't trust whom?*

# CHAPTER EIGHT

*Meanwhile, Sho tries to salvage the mess at Gwydion Academy of Advanced Sorcery...*

Sora trailed Xen and Sho, trying to keep up with their long strides and feeling like a small child. The two men talked to each other in quiet, earnest voices, but she wasn't listening. Her magic was gone. Xen refused to allow her to accompany Sho to Zebulon's chamber alone in case her former mentor made another attempt upon her life. She didn't remind him that, without her magic, she was perfectly safe. She didn't want to talk about it.

Sho glanced over his shoulder at her. "You are certain you cannot get him to take you back?"

She shook her head, ducking to swipe a stray tear from her cheek. "No. He has made up his mind, I am sure. He sacked me, and then he tried to kill me."

"I am not certain he would have killed you," Xen said thoughtfully. "I think he just intended to stop you from helping us."

"Nevertheless, I do not think he would accept me back in earnest. He would recognise the ruse. And I do not think...I do not think I am up to such subterfuge, even if he would accept me."

Sho sighed. "All right. We will have to take other measures, then." They did not speak until they reached the stairs that led to Zebulon's tower. Sho stopped abruptly. "The barrier is here. I can't go any further. Sora?"

She slipped past them, but she could pass no further than they. She shook her head. "He has expanded his protections, and I am apparently not on the guest list."

"Do you know the protective runes he uses?" Sho asked.

"I know the runes he used before, but he...This barrier is new, and I suspect he has taken measures against my deconstructing it." She turned back to the men. "I am afraid I can be of little help to you now."

"You have been of much help already," Xen told her gently.

Sora smiled gratefully at him. Sho shot him an amused glance. Xen ignored him. "Well, then," Sho said. "Back up, please. I need to concentrate, and this could get a little messy." He unbuttoned the cuff of his right sleeve and rolled it up. He paused in the act and looked at Sora. "I don't suppose you have any of his blood?"

"What?"

He rolled his eyes. "I have blood magic. I need blood. Mine or the subject's. Preferably the subject's."

Sora stared at him. "No. I'm sorry. I don't keep that sort of thing lying around. I hadn't anticipated I would ever be asked for it."

"No one is ever prepared. You would be quite surprised by how rarely one possesses the blood of their subject."

"I don't know that I would."

"It's not that difficult to obtain, you know."

Xen waved his hand impatiently. "Can we move on?"

"Right." Sho pushed his sleeve up his arm and held out his palm. With his other hand, he ran a finger across the flesh, and a shallow wound opened. Blood dripped from his hand onto the stone stairs, staining them scarlet.

Sora watched in fascination, for she had never seen anything like it. Sho muttered under his breath, and the blood in his hand bubbled and swirled as though it possessed life of its own. "What are you going to do?" she asked.

Sho ignored her. "He's going to use his blood to break the barrier," Xen answered for him.

"How?"

Xen did not reply. Sho pushed the palm of his hand out, splattering his blood against the invisible barrier.

"Oh. And then what?"

"We storm in," Sho said through clenched teeth. He seemed to be expending much energy, for his skin was paler than usual.

The blood turned black and slid down the barrier, pooling on the floor at their feet.

Xen and Sho stared at it. "Does that mean it worked?" Sora asked doubtfully.

They looked up at her.

"No," Sho said slowly. "It means he has protection against blood magic."

"Oh."

"Well," Xen said. "That is too bad."

"I am impressed," Sho remarked. "He is better than I thought."

Xen frowned. "This is troubling, isn't it?"

"It is...pretty worrying, yes, considering breaking the barrier, barging in and binding his blood was my only plan." He lifted his eyebrows. "Got any back-up ideas?"

"Yes. The one."

"I am not sure your black magic will be able to breech that barrier if my blood magic couldn't."

Xen scoffed. "Don't think I don't know what you're doing. Of course it will. You know it will."

Sho sighed, pushing his hand through his hair. "Xen, you know we cannot go down that road again."

"What if you bind my blood? You could be in control of the power."

"I can't bind you when you're in that state. I did try. We both know it didn't work. I had to..." He cut off, scowling.

"What did you have to do?" Sora asked in a quiet voice. Blood. He needed blood.

Sho and Xen exchanged a glance. "I had to drain his blood," Sho replied grimly. "Until he nearly died. He barely made it out alive."

Sora looked up at Xen. "Is that the only way to cure it?"

He met her gaze. "Yes. That or let it burn out, but by then I will have done so much damage, there would be no point in coming back. And my body probably would not survive it."

She shook her head vehemently. "Then you can't do it."

Xen sighed. "Sora, we thought this would work. We thought Sho could do something. Even he can't find a way inside. I might be our only choice."

"Xen..."

"We will try everything else first. I don't want to do it. There is too much to lose."

Sho cleared his throat. They seemed to have forgotten he was there. They looked at him in surprise. "We should get some rest. We'll need it if we're going to figure out a backup plan."

Xen frowned. "What if Tan tries to attack her again?"

Sho shrugged. "She's immune."

"What if he...what if he tries to attack her physically?"

"That would be very convenient."

"What?"

"I'm still here, you know. I can hear you talking about me."

They ignored her. "Well, he would have to leave his tower to go after her," Sho said. "I would be able to get near enough to bind his blood."

Xen scowled at him. "We are not using her as bait."

Sho sighed. "All right, all right. If we must, Oni can watch over her."

Sora was not entirely comfortable with this idea. Xen seemed to suspect as much. "She seems insane, but she's decent. She will keep you safe."

She shrugged. "All right. I suppose if someone is planning to attack me, I would like her on my side. As long as she doesn't get it into her head to do the attacking."

"Oh, she almost never attacks innocent people without provocation anymore," Sho told her positively.

"Right."

Oni jumped up as they returned to Simon's office. She looked excited. "Did you do it? Is he bound?"

Sho sighed. "No. I cannot breech his protections."

"What?" She huffed indignantly. "You can't? He's serious, isn't he?"

"He wants to complete this spell, all right."

They all turned to Sora. "Any idea why?" Simon asked.

She shook her head. "I don't know. He said something about prolonging life, but I believed it was a lie. Perhaps...there was some element of truth." She thought about it. "When I went into his workshop, I saw...he looked different."

Simon lifted his eyebrows and pushed his glasses further up his nose. "Different?"

162

"He always looks so healthy. So vital. He is an old man, but he always seemed in great health. But...the other night, he looked so old. So frail. When I saw him, he exploded. He shouted at me to get out. When I saw him in the morning, he claimed he was simply tired, but he had looked so different."

They all thought about this a moment. "Perhaps there is something wrong with him," Simon suggested. "Perhaps he is ill."

"Zebulon?" Sora said. "No. Surely he would have told me if he was ill." They all looked at her doubtfully. She blushed. "Right. Perhaps not. Things are not... as I believed them to be at all."

"If there is something wrong with him, if he is ill," Simon said, "it is all the more reason for him to continue his course."

"I have never known him to be selfish," Sora said, looking sad. "But I believe he knows or at least suspects the consequences of this spell."

"People are rarely rational when their lives are at stake."

A grim silence fell in the room. Sho broke it. He turned to Oni. "We want you to watch over Sora tonight."

Oni blinked in surprise. "What? I don't get to play?"

"What are you going to do?" Simon demanded tersely. "Throw more bombs at his door? It's useless."

Her lower lip stuck out in a pout. "I need to speak to Xen," Sho told her. "There is nothing more for us to do tonight but lick our wounds and recalculate our plan."

Sora did not look pleased about being dismissed so easily, but she did not argue. Oni sighed. "Fine. I will babysit while you boys talk about us behind our backs."

"We aren't talking about you. Don't be so conceited."

She grinned and hopped down from her perch beside him on Simon's desk. She caught Sora's arm on her way, dragging her towards the door. "Come on. Let's go get drunk and talk about them behind their backs."

Sora's expression was wary, but she smiled at Xen on her way out. He did not look happy about the circumstances, but he lifted a hand in a wave. "Call us if anything happens," he ordered. "We will be right there."

Sora opened her mouth to respond, but Oni yanked her out into the hall and slammed the door.

Xen turned to Sho. "So, what is the new plan, then?"

Sho pinched the bridge of his nose. "I don't know."

"You don't know?"

"Well, we have the spell, at least."

"Not the entire spell. We do not know what the last two runes represent."

"It doesn't matter. It's just a combination. You etch the runes and the gate is opened."

"It might matter," Simon put in.

"Well, we don't have the luxury of finding out what they mean at the moment. It is close to completion," Xen said.

"Yes," Sho sighed. "It is. So we need to figure out what to do when it's done."

Xen scowled. "That is the new plan, then? Let him open the gate and try to close it back again when he does? We can't even get into the place."

Sho thought about this. "I think we can overcome that."

"How?"

"There are one or two...people who have ways of getting around locked doors."

Simon groaned. "Sho, he is complete bastard." Sho looked at him sternly. He sighed. "All right, all right. I'm going. But I make no promises. You know they can't interfere directly. They can just give a little push in the right direction."

Simon and Sho did this sort of thing all the time. Xen did not ask any questions as Simon rose from his leather wing-backed chair and strode out of the room with an irritable hitch to his shoulders. He didn't know where Simon was going or where he ever went after he and Sho had conversations like this. Sho would tell him if he needed to know.

When Simon was gone, Xen lifted his eyebrows. "Out of curiosity, are you ever going to tell me what he's all about?"

Sho glanced towards the door through which Simon had disappeared. "Simon?"

"Yes, Simon. Who else?"

Sho considered this a moment, then shook his head. "I think if you don't figure it out on your own, it is best you do not know."

164

Xen rolled his eyes. He rarely got anything else out of Sho when the Darklord was feeling particularly reticent.

"So this girl..." Sho said abruptly.

"You want to talk about girls?"

Sho laughed. "No. Not really. It's not exactly my nature to gossip. But I can see there is something going on between you and Sora."

"I hardly know her." Xen did not meet Sho's doubtful gaze.

"I don't really care what you do with your time, Xen, but this is serious. We are going to try, but..."

"I know. There is still a chance we're going to have to face the fact that I might be our only chance at stopping him."

"Yes." Sho did not look pleased about this. "We will try everything."

"You know I don't want to go back down that path, Sho. But if it means stopping the unmaking of everything, I will do what I have to do." He sighed. "You can't tell her."

"No. If she knows, she will likely try to stop it and get in the way. She does seem to care for you." He smirked. "I don't know why."

"I'll have you know, I have a sensitive side."

Sho snorted. "Whatever. I don't want to know about things like that."

"So, what do we do now?"

"I'm going to talk to someone I know."

Xen rolled his eyes. There were a lot of secret contacts with whom Sho met and about whom he did not talk. Xen didn't really mind terribly much; he was happy following orders and acting as Sho's muscle. Obviously, he had no business leading the pack; he never had done before. Even with the Lumina, he had been little more than a foot soldier.

"I think we can find a counter-spell," Sho said thoughtfully. "If we get lucky, we can find a spell that will negate it completely."

"What about the spell in reverse?"

"No. That only works with incantations. Runes, once etched, can't be un-etched. I doubt defacing them will have any effect on this particular spell."

"Magic is very complicated," Xen remarked.

"Yes. Which is why you just touched a dark artefact to learn it."

Xen snorted. "I know magic. I am a very popular Talismans and Amulets professor, you know. I have been told I am quite gifted."

"Yes, but that's because, even without the dark magic, you still frighten children."

Xen laughed. "Whatever." He narrowed his eyes thoughtfully at his friend. "You know, I suppose I don't feel so inadequate as a leader. You don't seem to have any better ideas."

Sho's laugh was wry. "Well, I do have one or two more resources." He sighed and dropped into Simon's wing-backed chair. "I'll talk to my contact tomorrow." He pinched the bridge of his nose, but he did not say anything more.

Xen suspected something more than the spell was troubling him. "Do you want to talk about it?"

"Nailah is in Hyperion City."

"Really."

"Apparently, she wants to study magic outside of Scathach and...see the world."

"She wants to hunt you down?"

Sho sighed in annoyance. "Probably. It's likely."

"What are you going to do?"

He flicked his fingers irritably. "My duty. I am obliged to go to her and offer my service."

"Your service?" Xen smirked.

"You know what I mean. She is, after all, my betrothed. It would be the height of bad manners to spurn her."

"But you did not choose her."

"I am not afforded the luxury of that sort of choice."

"What about Oni? What's she going to say about it?"

Sho lifted an eyebrow at him. "I thought we didn't talk about that sort of thing."

Xen shrugged. "Right. Don't ask; don't tell. But I can see there is something between you two. We all know it. Does she know about Nailah?"

166

The Darklord hesitated. "She knows. She has always known. It has just never been...anything more than an intellectual inevitability. Now that Nailah's here... well, it doesn't matter. It's nothing, anyway. I do not intend to marry the girl."

"Which girl?"

Sho glared at him. "I do not intend to marry anyone. Not yet, anyway. I will have to marry when I return to Scathach. Until then..."

Xen grinned. "Until then."

Sho scowled. "Let's just get on with the job, all right? I'm not comfortable with this touchy-feely ooey-gooey sensitive thing you've got going on right now."

"What? What the hell are you talking about? Sensitive. I'm not sensitive."

"Right," Sho replied solemnly. "No. Definitely not."

\* \* \*

*Meanwhile, girls will be girls...*

Oni's pyjamas had tiny sticks of dynamite embroidered upon them. She popped the cork on a bottle of wine with her teeth and poured Sora a glass. She was giddy. It was strange to see Oni giddy, for she was not the sort of woman upon whom one would ever expect to attach such a label with any sincerity. "Sooooo...." Oni said, grinning hugely.

Sora sighed. She'd never had a sleepover before. She'd never had a friend who was a girl. She suspected Oni hadn't, either, and she was overcompensating.

"Let's have girl talk."

"What exactly is girl talk?" Sora asked nervously.

"I don't know. I think it's about boys and hair and fingernails, maybe."

"You talk about hair and fingernails?"

Oni thought about this. "No. Not typically."

"Do you have any girl friends?"

"No. Well, I have Panya. She's a girl. And my friend. I think."

"So she isn't your girl friend?"

"Ew, no! She's in love with Hyde."

"Who's Hyde?"

"He's a shape-shifter."

"Panya's in love with him?"

"Well, I think so. Ohh...or maybe he's in love with her. I don't really remember. I get them confused. They look the same."

Sora stared at her. "They look the same?"

"Well, Hyde can look however he wants, so he looks like Panya."

Sora wasn't sure why this would be. She didn't ask. "What do you talk about with Panya?"

Oni grinned. "Explosives. I'm really good at those. Oh! And breaking into places. Panya's good at that."

Once again, Sora did not know how to reply to this.

Oni gestured enthusiastically. "Drink!" She looked mightily pleased as Sora sipped the red wine. "Want me to braid your hair?"

"Do you know how to braid hair?" Oni nodded happily, and Sora sighed. "All right."

Oni hopped off the bed and moved around to stand behind her. Her fingers were clumsy, and she tugged a bit more forcefully than necessary on Sora's long, blonde hair. Sora did not complain. She wasn't certain how volatile the woman really was.

"Oni, is Xen really..." Sora's voice trailed off.

"Is he really an insane dark wizard?" Oni guessed.

"Yes."

"Well, I've seen him in a rage. If he goes back into one, he will be."

"It's serious, then."

"Yes. It's all serious."

"Then why don't you act like it's serious?"

Oni shrugged. "There's no sense in letting it get in the way of a good time."

"So if he does go back..."

"Back to the dark side?"

"Yes. What will it be like?"

"It will be horrible. His eyes turn black and his face goes white, and his
168

muscles bulge out, and he goes all berserker all over anything in his path." She paused in her work and sighed dreamily. "Actually, it was kind of sexy."

Sora turned her head towards her in shock. "Oni!"

"What?" She tugged the braid to reposition Sora's head. "It was. Xen is... well, he's quite fit, isn't he?"

Sora frowned. "You like him?"

"I like lots of people." She tugged on the braid again. "Don't worry. I'm not trying to steal him away. He wouldn't have me, anyway. I think he rather fancies you."

Sora smiled. "I think he does, too." She was silent a moment. Now that they'd gotten started, girl talk was a little fun. "Are you and Sho...?"

Oni laughed. She dropped the braid down Sora's back and leapt back onto the bed to face her. She grinned at Sora, but she didn't reply.

"If you love Sho, how can you be with all those other men?"

She laughed again. Her dark, almond shaped eyes gleamed. "It's fun."

"Is that all that matters?"

"Yes. To me. Not to you." She wiggled her eyebrows suggestively. "So, have you ever...you know? With Tan?"

Sora gasped in shock. "What? That is just...just disgusting!"

Oni rolled her eyes. "Oh, lighten up. I was only teasing you." Her face lit up. "Hey, can I paint your fingernails?"

"What?"

"I've never gotten to paint fingernails before. Can I paint your fingernails?"

Sora sighed. "Sure."

Oni leapt off the bed once more and disappeared into the closet for several moments. When she returned, she held up a large can of varnish and a huge paintbrush.      She gave Sora a gleeful grin.

"Oni, no."

"Aw." She slumped in disappointment.

"If we can't find another way to stop Zebulon, I'm going to lose Xen, aren't I?"

This sobered Oni. She set down the paint can and brush. "We all are. But none of us want that. Sho will find a way. And Simon..." She paused, frowning. "I'm not exactly sure what he is, but he knows people. If anyone can find someone who can help us, it's him."

\* \* \*

*Meanwhile, at the Dirty Damastes, Unrequited Love gets an unwelcome surprise...*

Unrequited Love was unhappy to see Simon standing outside the entrance to the Dirty Damastes with a look of dread upon his face.

"Oh, god, it's you," she said.

He lifted an eyebrow. "Which god?"

She ignored him. "We've got enough problems." He sighed dreamily as she stalked irritably past him to the door. He reached for it, but she did not wait for him to open it for her. She strode inside. He trailed after her, trying to ignore the ensuing chaos they left in their wake.

A woman leaned over the bar, smiling dreamily at the publican, who seemed not to even notice she was there. She held up an arm to attract his attention, and her halter top suddenly sprang open. Seconds passed before she noticed the cool air on her bosom and a look of horror crossed her face. She spun and raced towards the bathroom. Several men hurried after her, but the publican never even turned his head.

A squirrel ran across the bar towards a man in a stool at the end. He stepped back to avoid it as it leapt towards his face, but he tripped as his belt snapped and his pants fell to his ankles. He flailed his arms and screeched as he fell backwards, trying to fend off the angry squirrel on his chest.

Simon sighed and kept walking. Unrequited Love dropped into her usual table beside Tricks and glared at him. Severe Errors in Judgment, though, leaned forward eagerly and waved. "Hey! Haven't seen you in a while!"

"Uh, Errors," Unrequited Love warned.

It was too late. Her buttons suddenly popped, and her blouse sprang open. She blushed and crossed her arms over her chest. "Oh. Right."

Unrequited Love shook her head in annoyance. Tricks stared at Errors in shock.

"Oh, uh, oh. Maybe...would you like to...Lets go out sometime!" A.S.S.

170

blurted loudly, startling them all.

Severe Errors in Judgment lifted her chin. "No, thanks."

They all turned to her in shock.

Unrequited Love sighed and gestured towards Simon. "This is--"

Simon cleared his throat delicately and straightened his glasses. "Simon."

"Simon?"

Unrequited Love rolled her eyes. "He prefers to be called by his...human name. Anyway, what are you doing here, Simon? I thought you hated this place. It is rather...dodgy for your tastes."

Simon blushed. "I'm looking for Holes."

Tricks lifted his eyebrows. "Holes?"

Simon's cheeks flushed a darker scarlet.

Unrequited Love pursed her crimson lips. "What do you need him for?"

"I just...need him. Is he about?"

"Yes, probably. He's usually about. He was sitting with Mockery and Potentially Violent Scuffles earlier. He should still be around, ruining people's nights and their subsequent lives. He should come with a warning."

Simon laughed weakly. "I think we all should, don't you?"

She frowned at him. "You, especially."

He sighed. "Well. Thank you." He spun and promptly tripped on a chair. He flailed his arms to catch himself, but only managed to grip the collar of a young woman's shirt at the table nearby. It tore in his hands. He goggled at her exposed bosom as he fell forward, landing at her feet.

"What the hell, man?"

Simon looked up in dread at the large, thickly-muscled man standing above him. "Are you trying to cop a feel on my girlfriend?"

"No! No! It was an accident!" Simon exclaimed.

"It was an accident," the man mocked in an exaggeratedly prissy tone. "I ought to pop you one." He glared for several seconds at Simon, who rose to his feet and brushed off his tweed jacket.

The young women reached up to catch her boyfriend's arm. "It's all right,

Tom."

He looked at her. "Are you all right, babe?"

She slipped a jacket on over her torn shirt. "I'm all right. It's just a Minor Inconvenience. It was an accident."

Tom glared at Simon, but he turned away. Simon straightened his lapels with a scowl. "I hate this place."

He found Holes sitting at a table with several other men Simon recognised with no little dread. "Simon," Direct Correlations greeted politely. They were not close.

Simon nodded to him. Low Self Esteem and Meekness, two of the ugliest men Simon had ever seen, hid their faces behind their hair. "Hello," Meekness said meekly. Low Self Esteem just glared at him through a curtain of greasy black hair.

Simon lifted an unenthusiastic hand to wave at them. "Hi, Simon!" Covetousness said eagerly. "What are you doing here? I want to know what you're doing here. I didn't know you needed glasses. Those are nice glasses. Can I see those glasses?"

"No!"

The short, fat man sitting beside Meekness shot abruptly to his feet and rushed at Simon. Simon reared back, but the fat man threw his arms around him in a very intrusive embrace. Simon shoved him away. "Good god, man! What are you doing?"

"Sorry." The fat man blushed. "I was compelled."

"You ought to get a handle on that."

"I'd like to," he replied sadly.

"Compulsion, sit down," Low Self Esteem snapped. "No one wants you to touch them. No one wants any of us to touch them."

They all lowered their heads sadly.

"I hate this place," Simon muttered. He turned towards the tall, thin, rat-faced man with spiky blonde hair sitting beside Direct Correlations. "Can I speak to you a moment?"

The spiky-haired man lifted his eyebrows. An amused look crossed his face. "You came to talk to me? You? I thought you were above all this. I thought you were trying to be...well, something you aren't."

Simon scowled at him. "I am not trying to be anything, Holes. I am just trying to live my life without...well, without perpetual humiliation."

Direct Correlations laughed bitterly. He waved a hand. "I would like that, too. I wish she would stop hanging around here."

"That's rich, coming from you."

Direct Correlations swelled indignantly. "What is that supposed to mean?"

"I think you know." He turned back to Holes. He was dreading what was surely to come, but there was little choice.

Holes smiled and rose to his feet. He gestured grandly towards a table in the corner. "Step into my office."

"I would rather not."

"Oh, don't be such a prude. It's not like it's an issue here. Well..." He smirked. "It might be, with you here, I suppose."

Simon glared at him.

"So what do you want?"

"I need a favour."

"Oh, really?" Holes' face lit up deviously. "A favour? From me? And what do I get in return?"

Simon sighed. "I will...I will owe you one?"

"Owe me one." Holes thought about this. "How about one solid here and now?"

"One...solid?"

"Yeah. You do me a solid. Tonight."

Simon pinched the bridge of his nose. "End of the world. The potential unmaking of everything. Chaos and disorder. World thrown out of balance." He stopped muttering to himself and looked up at Holes. "All right. And what 'solid' would that be?"

Holes grinned and pointed across the room. "You see that couple over there?" Simon followed his finger to the homely young woman hanging on the arm of a tall, muscular man. He pushed the homely women off and leered at the shapely waitress as she passed.

Simon sighed. "No."

Holes lifted his eyebrows.

"All right, all right! What do you want me to do?"

"Well, just...give him a little something to attract his attention. You know, so I can work my magic."

"Oh, that is disgusting!"

"What?"

"I don't even want to think about what that means."

"I don't think you have to think too hard about it. Anyway, do it, will you? Then I'll do you a solid."

"That is just...a whole new disgusting meaning to the word."

"How badly do you need this favour?"

"Really, really badly."

"Right, then. Just do it. Go on. Add a little...spice, will you?"

Simon sighed, but he squared his shoulders and strode towards the couple. He had to make it good with Unrequited Love and DC in the room. He walked past the woman and flicked his fingers. He couldn't remember the last time he'd used his powers on purpose. In fact, he tried to avoid it as often as possible. This was humiliating.

*End of the world. Sho's counting on me.*

The man turned to push the woman off him, but his hand slipped right down her shirt. His eyes widened as his palm closed over her breast. She smiled at him. He jerked his head towards the door, and she nodded eagerly. She grinned over at Holes, and he gave her a thumbs-up. Simon flushed with shame as he returned to Holes' side.

"Stylish and elegant," Holes said proudly, clapping him on the shoulder. "So, what can I do for you? You need a Small Hole One Wishes Had Been Detected at the Time?"

"Yes, but not for—well, not for that."

Holes rolled his eyes. "Obviously. What do you need?"

"I need to get into a room. It's heavily protected by charms."

Holes thought about this. "So you need a hole in a ward, eh?"

"Yes."

"That is not exactly what I do, you know."

"Yes, I know. What you do is disgusting. Do you think you can make it happen?"

He nodded. "Yeah. Sure. I think so. But I might need to get close to the problem."

Simon groaned.

"Where is it?"

"Hyperion City."

"Nice. I do a pretty roaring trade there. I suppose I could take a little vacation. Where am I going?"

"Gwydion Academy."

Holes lifted his eyebrows. "I see. You're still working with that Darklord, then?"

"Yes. I'm still working with him."

"What do you do that for? You could make a great living here or anywhere, really."

"Like you do?"

"Sure. If you're going to have powers, you might as well get used to them."

"And profit from them?"

"Sure. There's no rule against it."

"It's immoral!"

Holes shrugged. "It's not immoral to make a living, is it? We still have to keep going on this miserable earth, whether we want to or not. No getting out of it."

"I am not going to exploit my ability for money."

"Well, suit yourself. But if you ever decide to make a little dough, I think we could make great partners."

Simon's lip curled in disgust.

"Think about it, anyway."

"I will do no such thing." He glanced around with distaste. "I have to go. I would prefer not to ply my trade here, of all places."

"What are you talking about? This place is the best!"

"It's a total crap-hole, Holes."

Holes laughed.

"You owe me one. Don't forget. Be ready when I call."

"Yeah, yeah." Holes lifted a hand to wave at him. "See ya, Nudie!"

Simon spun towards him in horror. "It's Simon!"

\* \* \*

*Meanwhile, night darkens in Penthos...*

Penthos would pay for the pain it had caused her. Imogen peered down at the little houses and cottages in the valley below. Mercy and Argus stood motionless beside her, side by side. Their eyes were dead, and their tongues lolled from their rotting mouths. Their faces were not capable of emotion, but their spirits howled silently inside their re-animated corpses. They shared their anguish, and they shared this grotesque half-life, but they could only appreciate their mutual suffering.

Imogen seemed to understand this. She laughed. "You are together now. In death as in life. Aren't you happy? Isn't this what you wanted? You wanted to be together forever." Her cold, dark eyes narrowed upon Argus. "You spurned me for her, but I did not hold a grudge. No. I have given you what you wanted. Now you will give me what I want."

She turned back to peer down at the village below. It was dark. The night was deep, and the lights had been extinguished in the tiny cottages hours ago. A gentle breeze blew her long, dark hair back from her face. Her lips twisted into a cold smile. She lifted her hand towards the village. When she spoke, her voice was low and commanding. It issued from somewhere deep inside her chest. It rumbled over the hills and down into the valley.

"Go. Take my revenge upon the people who turned their backs on me." She glanced at Argus and Mercy. She sensed their horror as powerfully as if they spoke it aloud. "Take my revenge upon the people who loved you."

Mercy and Argus turned their stiff, crumbling necks to peer at each other. They were horrors, monsters, and inside they were screaming. Imogen waved her hand, and then they clutched in their rotting, claw-like hands two long, shining blades. They tried to resist the force that propelled them forward, but Imogen's power was irresistible.

The sorceress threw out her arms, and the corpses shambled forward. Then the magic took control of them, and they raced down the hill, into the valley with their knives raised ominously above their heads like berserkers. Imogen watched them streak down into the village, into the houses below. Her low, cold laugh grew louder and louder until it seemed to roll and crash across the hills and over the miserable village below that would become a gruesome graveyard before the night was through.

Then the screams began.

# CHAPTER NINE

Sho wasn't paying attention to where he was walking. He frowned down at the scrap of scarlet parchment in his hand. He grunted in surprise as he collided with a large, blue-skinned man who glared and grumbled at him. Sho held up his hands in supplication, but the blue-skinned man pushed angrily past him.

Sho sighed and tucked the parchment into his pocket. He hadn't the time to worry about Lady Nailah at the moment. The world was about to be unmade, and he was apparently the only one who could stop it. He quickened his step. The streets sparkled in this part of town, and men and women in beautiful, luxurious clothes strolled carelessly past, pausing to peer into the glass shop windows or take their tea at one of the street cafes along the thoroughfare.

He veered into an alley between a shining, metallic stone building and a quaint, white brick hat shop. In seconds, the opulent, wealthy part of Hyperion City fell away, and old, crumbling tenement buildings surrounded him on either side. This was a noisy part of the city. Women shouted at each other from across the alleys below as they hung their washing on thick ropes strung from building to building. Children raced up and down the rusty, creaking metal fire escapes, shrieking with glee. Vagrants huddled in piles of debris. No one paid them any attention.

As Sho past, the vagrants rolled in on themselves and disappeared under the rubbish and grubby moth-eaten blankets to escape him. They did not even ask him for loose change, though he might have given it. No one ever asked a Darklord for loose change. He stepped over the vagrants. He lifted a hand to trail across the crumbling brick of the wall next to him.

There it was.

He stopped and turned towards the wall. It seemed to be nothing more interesting than the same featureless brick, but he could feel the magic that charged the stones here. He pressed his palm to the wall and muttered an incantation under his breath. No door appeared. Instead the wall shimmered, and Sho stepped through it.

The room in which he stood was small and cluttered, appointed equally with large, aged armchairs with the stuffing half out of the drab, faded upholstery and small tables stained with moisture rings. It looked much like the sitting room of an old scholar. Books lined the walls and were stacked up on the floor beside the armchairs. In the centre of the room was a small, rickety wooden table. It was battered and scuffed. A large, cracked crystal ball glowed a low, dull blue upon a metal claw on the table top.

There did not seem to be anyone in the room with him. Sho cleared his throat. The atmosphere around him suddenly shifted and shimmered. Then a little bald wizened man stepped out of thin air. He dropped his head back to smile toothlessly up at Sho. "Sho Sange." His voice was reedy. His watery eyes glittered with some emotion that Sho could not recognise. "I didn't expect to see you back here since you attempted to kill me the last time I saw you."

"I did not attempt to kill you, Ipwick."

Ipwick cackled. "I must have gotten confused by your slashing my throat."

Sho rolled his eyes. "I did nothing of the sort. You were in the throes of an astral attack. I required your blood to save you."

"It was not an astral attack. I was merely communicating on a separate plane, which required me to...die a little."

"Then you won't mind that I had to bleed you. I was merely attempting to negate your near death with..."

"Near death?"

"You healed quite nicely."

Ipwick smiled. "No thanks to you." He swept aside the long, faded blue robe, which pooled at his feet as though it had been made for a much taller man, and sat at the table in front of his crystal ball. He gestured Sho to join him and waited until the Darklord had lowered himself into the short, rickety chair before asking, "What is it that I can do for you today, Blood?"

Sho pressed his lips together in annoyance, but he did not complain about the nickname; it would only encourage the old man. He drew a slip of parchment from his pocket and smoothed it upon the table top. He pushed it across the table with one long, pale finger. Ipwick snatched it up and studied it for several moments with furrowed brows.

"Ah. I see." His pale, watery eyes looked cold as they snapped up to meet Sho's. "And what, precisely, do you want me to do with this?"

"Do you know what it is?"

"I have been around a very long time, Sho. I know what this is. Where did you get it?"

"A sorcerer at Gwydion."

Ipwick barked with humourless laughter. "Are they teaching them to unmake the world now?"

"So you do know what it is."

"I said I did. And I know the consequences of it."

"They are not teaching them anything of the sort. This sorcerer got hold of it on his own."

"How?"

Sho's lip curled. "How else? Lucian."

"That old busy-body. He found this?"

"That's what he does."

"It was probably best left lost."

"That's the idea."

Ipwick raised his eyebrows expectantly. "So what do you want?"

Sho leaned back in his seat and eyed the old wizard a moment. "It is becoming increasingly likely this sorcerer will compete the spell."

"So you have failed to find a way to stop him." Ipwick looked amused.

Sho scowled at him. Ipwick always seemed to know far too much. "If you want to put it that way, sure. He is a powerful sorcerer, and his protections are quite impressive."

"You can't get through, eh? You had intended to rush in and bind his blood?"

"It had crossed my mind. I had hoped to approach the subject a bit more gently than that."

"So, you need a counter-spell for this." He helped up the parchment between two thin, bony fingers.

"Yes."

"It will cost you."

"Fine."

"A lot."

"I get it."

"I will have to think what I would like in return."

"Fine. Then can I have the spell?" He held out his hand.

Ipwick scoffed. "Do you think I have the counter to something like this in my junk drawer? I will have to spend a little time working it out."

Sho slapped a palm onto the table top. The crystal ball jumped on its claw. "I don't have time!"

Ipwick was not impressed. "I have other clients, you know."

"And none of them will matter if we allow him to successfully complete this spell. I do not think I need to impress upon you that it will mean the unmaking of the entire world, Ip."

The old wizard rolled his eyes. "Always so dramatic." When Sho narrowed his eyes at him, Ipwick held up his hands. "All right, all right. I will make it a priority."

"We have no time, Ip. Hours. Maybe days at most."

Ipwick nodded. "I will have it by the end of the day."

"Thank you."

"And I will expect payment on delivery."

Sho braced himself. "What do you want?"

The old man had never really needed to think about it; he'd been waiting for years. "Blood."

"What?"

Ipwick smiled his toothless smile. "Your blood."

Sho hesitated. "Ip, I don't think you know what you're asking."

"Yes, I do. My clients want magic. That's why they come to me. The more powerful, the better. And your blood is...powerful."

Sho scowled and shook his head slowly.

Ipwick held up a bony finger. "It's that or the unmaking of everything. What's a little blood?"

"All right." Sho's voice was tight with anger. He knew Ipwick had been waiting a long time to trap him into this. "I'll do it."

"Excellent. Now go. I have work to do."

Sho rose to his feet. He stared down at Ipwick in anger, but there was little he could do. He had no one else. He turned and stepped into the wall through which he had come. When he turned back to look at it, there was nothing more there but a crumbling brick wall.

\* \* \*

A series of loud bangs sounded from the centre of the room. The students jumped in surprise, covering their heads. Fireworks exploded above them, showering them with colourful sparks in the shape of hundreds of tiny hearts. Oni cackled maniacally, throwing her hands above her head. Some of the students laughed, but most of them merely looked relieved when the end of class bell chimed through the classroom.

Sho strode into the room. Oni composed herself and waved at her students as they filed out of the class. Some of the girls slowed to eye Sho more thoroughly and flutter their eyelashes at him on their way out. He did not return their smiles. He stared at them coldly. It did not seem to deflect their attention in the least. Teenagers.

"See?" Oni said, grinning at him. "Look how effective I am. These girls are practically falling at your feet."

Sho snorted. "I don't think it's the love charms, Oni."

She rolled her eyes. "You are so conceited." He laughed and perched on the edge of her desk. Her expression turned suddenly serious. "Did you get the counter-spell?"

"No."

She exhaled heavily.

"Ipwick is working on it. He's asked for…he's asked for my blood as payment."

Her eyes widened. "But you…you can't give him that."

"What other option do we have? If we don't stop this spell, it will be the end of everything."

"But if we do, some crackpot wizard is going to have a vial of your blood. What do you think he's going to do with it? He could destroy the world himself."

"I don't think that's what he wants it for."

She scowled. "You can't do it, Sho."

"I have to. There isn't any other choice. We have to stop this spell, Oni. It isn't a joke. We can't approach it like we approach everything else. We're going to have to take this seriously."

Oni sighed. "I hate taking things seriously."

"You think it's better to let Xen go back to the dark side than me give up a little blood?"

"It's more than that, Sho. You know it is. He could do worse with your blood than Tan can do with the Haosul Cel."

Sho shook his head. "I don't think he will. I think he just wants…wants it to boost the power of his own spells."

Oni did not look convinced. "This is dangerous."

"It's a risk we have to take."

"But he could control you."

"No. He couldn't."

"Are you sure? I thought you could control people with your blood. Can't he use yours to make a spell to do the same?"

"No. Not mine. He might be able to use it to create a spell to bind blood, but not my blood."

"How can you be sure?"

He caught her hand and drew her closer to him. "Because, Oni. My powers are more than my blood. I can protect myself."

"But he can bind others."

"Yes. He probably could work out how to do that. If it is the reason he wants it."

She scowled. "When you go back to him, I'm going with you."

"I don't think that's a good idea."

She looked highly affronted. "Why not?"

"You do remember last time? I don't think he'll even let you in the door if he doesn't already have magical protections against you."

"He won't have a choice. If he tries anything, I want to be there to stop him."

He smiled. "You're trying to protect me?"

"Someone has to, besides some mad dark wizard who could fly into a bad juju rage at any moment. He's not good for that."

Sho ran a finger along her knuckles. "I appreciate your concern, but what do you think you can do against him? He's one of the most powerful elementals in Hyperion."

She shrugged. "Elementals are still nothing to explosives and directed energy weapons."

He rolled his eyes. "Fine. You can come, but don't be ridiculous."

"When am I ever ridiculous?"

He gave her a pointed look. "We need that spell. I will give him what he wants."

Oni nibbled her lower lip. "Sho, all kidding aside—"

"Are you even capable of that?"

"Shut it. I don't like this. It's dangerous."

"This whole situation is dangerous, and I think this is the least of our concerns."

"Maybe we should not have taken this job."

"You know there was no choice. I can't say no to Darius."

She sighed. "Just...think about what could happen."

"I have thought about it. I have to take the risk. I can't let Xen do it."

Oni was not pleased by this, but she didn't argue. "Do you think Simon will be able to get into the room?"

He grinned. "Oh, he'll get in. So we need to have something to use when we get in there. And there's only one way to get it."

"Okay. Fine. But when this is all over, I say we go back to the slimy little bastard and take your blood back."

Sho smiled. "All right. We'll give it a try." His expression changed suddenly. He tugged on her hand to draw her against him. "Oni, I need to talk to you."

She draped her arms around his neck. "I don't like that tone. It implies we're actually going to have a serious conversation."

"We are."

184

"I don't like serious conversations."

"I know, but we need to have this one."

She sighed in exasperation. "Fine. But can I pretend not to listen?"

He smiled. "If you must."

She stepped away from him and kicked the chair out from behind the desk. She threw herself into it and propped her feet up on the desk. Ignoring him completely, she scooped up the small, smooth brass ball from where it sat on top of a stack student essays which she had failed to even realise had been turned in, let alone graded. She tossed the ball up into the air and caught it again.

Sho stared at her incredulously. "Is that a bomb?"

She caught the ball and held it, looking at him as though he'd announced he intended to marry Simon and run off to Komodia to join the circus. "A bomb? You think I would throw a bomb up in the air?"

"Yes."

"Not near my face, I wouldn't! It isn't a bomb." She lifted her chin. "It's an incendiary device."

He rolled his eyes.

"Do you mind?"

Sho waved his hand. "As you were." He watched her balance the ball on the end of her nose. "While I was in Scathach, my parents..." He sighed and pushed his hands through his hair. "Lady Nailah is here."

Oni sat up suddenly, dropping her feet to the floor. "She's here? Where?" She whipped her head around keenly.

"Not here. Not at the school. She's in Hyperion City."

"Oh. Okay." She shrugged. "So?"

"Oni, you understand..."

"She's your betrothed."

"Well, yes."

She shrugged again. "Okay."

He scowled. "Oni...we can't..."

She looked at him with such a bland expression he could not tell what she could possibly be thinking. "Are you going to find her and marry her?"

"What? No! Not—I don't want to marry her. It's just my duty to offer her my service."

She cackled. "Your service? Which service?"

"Not—not like that! I mean, it is my duty to offer to assist her in any way I can. Our families have been closely bound for many centuries. Even if I can put it off indefinitely, I will have to reconcile myself to my fate eventually. And that fate…" He sighed.

"It includes Nailah."

He ran a hand through his hair again. "As much as I wish it didn't."

"How do you know?"

He looked at her in surprise. "What?"

"How do you know you wish you didn't?"

He laughed. "Trust me, Oni. I know."

"Well, when was the last time you saw her?"

Sho stared at her a moment in confusion. "Are you trying to help?"

She glared. "No! I don't help. That's not what I do. I cause destruction and damage and turmoil. I do not help."

"Okay." He ducked his head to hide his smile. "It's been many years since I've seen her. She was just a child." He curled his lip in disgust. "A child that follows me around and forces me to look at her dresses and pesters me about how many kids we're going to have when we get married."

Oni laughed and jabbed a finger at him. "It sounds terrible. Sho, the lord of his castle with a wife and little Shos running around in their nappies."

He couldn't hide his reluctant smile. "That is not exactly my picture of a perfect life, Oni."

"It doesn't matter. I'm sure you'll get used to it after a few decades of hard drinking. Anyway, why do you need to tell me?"

"You know why."

"Well, what do I care?"

"Oni…" He could see the slight glint in her dark, almond-shaped eyes, and he did not believe she didn't care for a single moment. He rose and stood over her.

She looked away. "It's not like...well, anyway. That's nice. Thanks for telling me." Her voice was perfectly even.

Sho reached down and yanked her out of the chair. "Oni." He gripped her chin in his hands and turned her to face him. He knew there was a chance she would strike out at him—he never knew what Oni would do--but he didn't care. "I don't love Nailah. I don't even like her."

Oni shrugged and stepped out of his arms. "I don't care, Sho. Go on and do what you have to do."

He scowled. "Things are not going to change between us."

She laughed aloud. "I know."

He stared at her, uncertain what to make of her reaction.

"Is that it?" she asked lightly.

"Yes."

"So when do I get to meet her?"

"Nailah?" Sho was shocked.

"Yes, Nailah. Who else are you planning to run back to Scathach with and get married?"

He rolled his eyes. "You're angry."

"I'm not angry. I said I don't care."

"Yes, you did say that."

"So what do we do now?"

He drew her back into his arms. She looked up at him with an unreadable expression in her dark eyes. He gripped her chin in his hands so she could not pull away again and leaned down to press his lips to hers. For a moment, she stood rigid in his arms then she wrapped her arms around his neck and kissed him back enthusiastically. He lifted her up and sat her down on the desk, fumbling for his belt.

Oni pressed a palm to his chest and leaned back abruptly. "What about Nailah?"

Sho shrugged. "I haven't seen her in ten years. I don't think she'll notice another few days."

Oni smiled and pulled his face back to hers. "Let me show you some of my love charms. They are really impressive."

"I'm sure they are."

She reached down to help him with his belt. "Not that I need them."

\* \* \*

"I haven't seen Ipwick in ages," Oni remarked as she strode beside Sho through the sparkling city streets.

"That's because he's forbidden you from ever going near him again."

She laughed. "He's hardly even alive. He's probably forgotten by now."

"I wouldn't count on it, but I think he wants what we have enough to put up with you for a few minutes."

She caught his hand, surprising him. "Sho, are you sure you want to go through with this? We could try something else. You said Simon could get us inside the room. Can't you just go in and bind his blood?"

"Oni, I honestly don't think it's going to be that easy. I couldn't get inside the room with my blood. He seems to have some sort of protection against me. I don't think I'll be able to bind him. We need to have something to counter that spell."

"Well, what about Sora? Couldn't she try to get back in his good graces?"

"I doubt it. It sounds as though the rift between them is too great. Besides which, there isn't much she can do. She has no magic anymore. All she can do is keep us apprised of the status of the spell. We will be able to accomplish nothing before he has completed it."

"I thought we were going to stop him."

"I have come to the troubling conclusion that the only way to do that is to kill him."

"So?"

"So none of us can get close to him, and we aren't in the business of assassination, Oni. I've thought it over. I think the best way to stop all this is to let him complete the spell, then counter it with one of our own. We can shut the gate before any damage can be done."

She sighed. "It sounds stupid and dangerous. If what Darius said is right, we might not be able to close it at all. It might be too much for us."

"It won't be."

"How do you know?"

"Because, Oni, we still have a Plan B."

"Yeah. Xen. Right. Perfect." She scowled. "This is the worst job ever. The next time Darius comes into the office, I think we should all get together and throw firebombs and explosives at him."

Sho laughed. "That's not a bad idea, actually. I wouldn't mind getting in on that."

"You could just bleed on him."

"That will only make him cross."

"But it would be satisfying."

They were still smiling when they reached Ipwick's hidden door. Sho pressed his palm to the ancient brick and muttered the incantation. The wall shimmered, but before he could step through it, Oni shoved him aside and leapt into the small sitting room with her arms outstretched.

"Hellooooooooooo, Ipwick!"

The wizened little wizard was sitting at the rickety table in front of his crystal ball. He shot to his feet with a speed of which his tiny, feeble body could scarcely be capable. He pushed his hand out towards her, curling it into a sort of horrible, shrivelled claw. Oni felt the energy hit her square in the chest.

She flew backwards into Sho with a force that staggered him. He caught her, laughing. "I see he hasn't forgotten the last time you were here, after all."

Ipwick glared angrily at them. "Why did you bring that maniacal woman here?"

Oni straightened and moved towards him, but Sho kept hold of her shoulder, drawing her back against him. "I'm here to make sure you don't try anything sneaky," she told him sternly.

"Sneaky? That's offensive." Ipwick drew himself up indignantly. "When have I ever been sneaky?"

They both stared at him incredulously.

He smiled toothlessly and flapped his hand at them.

"Do you have the spell?" Sho demanded.

"Yes. I have it." He cackled gleefully. "But you aren't going to like it."

Sho frowned. "Why?"

Ipwick snapped his fingers and another chair slid across the room, settling around the centre table. He gestured his guests to sit.

Oni dropped into the chair and reached immediately for the crystal ball. "Ooohhh..."

Ipwick smacked her hand. "You've already cracked it, you mad woman. Leave off."

She pushed her lower lip out in a pout.

"Ip, why won't I like it?" Sho demanded.

The old wizard grinned. He held up a small slip of parchment between his two fingers. Sho reached for it, but he pulled it away. It disappeared in a puff of smoke. "No no no. Not until you give me what I want in return."

"I want to see it first."

"I think not. But I will tell you about it."

Sho narrowed his eyes dangerously.

"Let's just say..." Ipwick's eyes twinkled. "It involves a sacrifice."

Oni and Sho sat up straight.

"The best spells always do," Ipwick reminded them. "Did you really think you would get out of this without one?"

They looked at each other grimly. "What sort of sacrifice?" Sho asked.

Ipwick cackled. "Not one either of you can offer. Or any of the rest of your people, I expect. Except perhaps the freaky little shape shifter. I haven't figured out that one yet–"

"Ipwick..." Sho's dark eyes glinted warningly.

Ipwick sighed. It was fun to play with them, but it wasn't wise to anger a Darklord. "Take all the fun out of it, why don't you?"

"Just spit it out, old man," Oni ordered.

"If you want to close the gate, you will have to offer the sacrifice of a pure, innocent soul."

They blinked. "Are you sure?"

"Of course I'm sure," he snapped. "I am the one who created the spell."

190

Sho sighed, pinching the bridge of his nose. "This could be...problematic."

"Oh, it's quite bad," Oni agreed. "A pure, innocent soul? Where are we going to find one of those, Ip?"

"That is not my problem. Do you want the spell or not?"

"Yes. We want it," Sho replied. "We will figure it out when we get there."

Ipwick opened his hand, and a small, crystal vial appeared on his palm. "Then give me what I want."

"Sho..." Oni said in a low voice.

He ignored her. He drew a finger across his wrist, opening a wound. He tipped his hand, allowing the blood to drip into the bottle. When the flow stopped, Ipwick stoppered the vial, holding it up to his eyes. The scarlet liquid inside shimmered and swirled, moving as though it were alive. Ipwick grinned and squealed in delight, hugging the vial to his chest. He held out the parchment.

Sho snatched it from his fingers and smoothed it out on the table to look it over.

Ipwick spun his back to them, muttering in an ancient language. He uncorked the vial of blood and waved his hand over the lip. He turned back to Sho, peering at him expectantly. His eyes burned with a manic, eager glee.

Sho crossed his arms over his chest and leaned back in his chair with a reproachful look.

Ipwick's face fell.

"If you expected to be able to bind my blood, you are going to be disappointed. It's mine. It doesn't work that way."

Ipwick sighed in disappointment and threw himself back into his chair.

Sho read through the spell swiftly. Suddenly, he sucked air through his teeth as though he was in pain. He snatched up the parchment and handed it to Oni. She looked down at it without comprehension. She handed it back.

"I don't know why you gave that to me. I don't know why you think I would understand it."

His mouth turned up slightly. He rose to his full height and stared down at Ipwick. "I think that's all then."

Ipwick looked sulky. "Yes, that's all." He crossed his arms over his chest and looked away. He flicked his fingers at them from under his arm. "Just go."

Sho offered Oni a hand and led her back out through the shimmering wall. Oni glared at him as they stepped back out into the dilapidated alley. "How the hell are we supposed to find a pure and innocent soul? Are there even any left in the world?" She stopped suddenly, struck with an idea. "Hey. Do you think we could use one of the students?"

Sho shook his head at her. "I don't think that's strictly allowed."

"It's not?" She looked genuinely surprised. "I thought that's where you got pure, innocent souls."

He rolled his eyes. "I should not have sent you out on this job, Oni. You have no business around children."

She scoffed. "I have no business in polite society." She hugged his arm and fluttered her eyelashes up at him. "That's why I have to hang around you and the rest of our socially unacceptable team."

\* \* \*

Sora tapped hesitantly on Simon's office door. Xen threw it open so abruptly, she reared back in surprise. He reached out into the corridor and yanked her inside. "Where have you been?"

She smiled. "Grading papers. I still have to take Zebulon's classes. I wasn't sure what would happen when he sacked me, but apparently he still hasn't come out of his room, and I couldn't just leave his classes unattended."

"So he could be up there working the spell right now," Simon said.

Sho shook his head. "No. I think we will know when he's done it." None of them looked particularly convinced by this, but none of them argued with him. He glanced at Simon. "Did you speak to him?"

Simon sighed. "I spoke to him."

"Well? Did he agree to help?"

His cheeks flushed. "He agreed, but I had to...give him payment."

"Ew!" Oni squealed.

"Not like that! I had to give him a fair trade for his services."

Sho smirked. "I see."

"What did you give him?" Oni demanded.

Simon's eyes shifted away in embarrassment. "Nothing."

"Who are you talking about?" Sora asked, staring between them bemusedly.

"A friend of Simon's." Oni rolled his eyes. "He has a lot of friends. They all have peculiar...abilities."

Sora nodded, but she did not feel any more enlightened than before. "So he can get us inside Zebulon's rooms?"

"He can...make a hole," Simon said.

Oni snorted with laughter.

"In his ward!"

"The problem is when we get inside," Sho added.

The smile faded instantly from Oni's face.

"What do you mean?" Sora asked. "Didn't you find a spell to counter Zebulon's?"

"Yes. We did."

"But that is good, isn't it?"

Their expressions were grim. "It should be, but..."

Xen shook his head at them from behind her back.

Oni ignored him. "It involves a sacrifice."

Sora paled. "What kind of sacrifice?"

"The usual."

"I don't know what that means. I am not familiar with that sort of magic."

"The sacrifice of a pure, innocent soul," Simon explained miserably.

"Oh. So what are we going to do?" Her voice was barely a whisper.

Xen sighed. "It's all right. It sounds horrible, but it will be all right."

"How can it be all right?"

"Well, it won't have to be any of us," Oni told her positively. "We don't have pure innocent souls." She sounded unnecessarily proud of this.

Sora looked at her in bemusement. "But someone has to die."

"Not necessarily," Simon said thoughtfully. "We might just have to sacrifice their soul."

A shiver thrilled down Sora's spine. "That doesn't sound any better."

"On a positive note, it can't be you."

"Why?"

"Because you're immune to magic. We won't be able to extract your soul to sacrifice." Simon smiled bracingly at her, and Xen sighed almost inaudibly in relief.

This, however, did not seem that reassuring to Sora. They might not be able to extract her soul from her body, but they could still use her soul; they just had to take her body with it.

Oni waved her hand dismissively. "We can find an animal or something."

"That sounds horrible," Sora said, appalled.

"We don't have a lot of choice," Sho told her. "These sorts of spells are serious. They require serious magic. Blood is the most powerful of all."

Sora eyed him nervously. His power came from blood, and she could feel it radiating from him even though she had no magic of her own anymore. "Can't you just...get inside with your friend and bind his blood like you planned?" Her voice sounded weak.

Sho's expression was blank. "I don't think it will work. His protection prevented my blood from having any effect."

"How can he have done that?"

"I don't know how, but he must have learned who I am. He was prepared for me."

The others hadn't seriously thought about this before, but the atmosphere in the room grew gloomier still.

"Are you sure about being unable to bind his blood?" Simon asked.

"No. But if I take the chance and fail, we will blow our only chance. We'll only get one. We have to make it good. We have to be ready with the counter-spell."

"So we just wait until he completes the spell and try to...what?" Sora demanded, frowning. "Bring in a donkey or something to kill in his workshop?"

"Oh, no," Oni said vehemently. "Those dirty bastards. There's not a pure, innocent soul among them."

This was not helpful.

"I will have to think about it," Sho replied. "Xen, Simon and I will try to figure out how to work this spell without losing anyone."

"That seems to leave too much to chance."

Xen shrugged. "That is typically how we operate. It works most of the time."

"But how will we know when he's completed the spell?"

"Well, we'll be thrust into utter chaos and destruction," Simon replied.

"Won't it be too late by then?"

"Oh, yes, obviously."

She frowned. "This is not going to work, is it? We're going to need to know when to be ready with that counter-spell. We can't wait until it's too late. We need to already be inside when it happens."

Xen knew where she was headed. "Sora, no."

"Well, why not, Xen? It's worth a try. You said yourself this is serious. If we're willing to sacrifice someone's life over it, I can do this small thing."

"He tried to kill you." His dark eyes glinted angrily.

"He is not himself. In fact, I think he's gone quite mad. But I am safe now from his magic. I can convince him to take me back as his assistant."

Sho frowned. "You said yourself you're sure he won't take you."

"He might not, but surely he knows something stopped his spell on me last night. He knows I'm still taking his classes. He might at least be curious to find out how. In any case, he and I have been friends for a long time. I know him well. I think I can find a way to convince him to take me back."

"Do you think you will be able to keep up the deception?" Simon asked interestedly.

"If I have to, I think I can. And I do have to if we're going to get this sorted out. I made a mistake when I confronted him about the spell. I should have come to you first. I would already be inside. We all know I need to be inside. I helped get this thing rolling. I have to help fix it now."

"What if he won't take you?" Xen demanded. "What if something happens?"

They all turned to look at Simon in the same moment; Sora only looked because everyone else had. She didn't know for what they were actually looking.

A look of horror crossed Simon's face. "Oh, no. No no no. I am not going back to that place."

"What are you talking about?" Sora asked.

"I can't keep doing this, Sho," he said, ignoring her question. "You know that isn't the way it works. They can only interfere on the smallest of levels. Just minor nudges in the right direction. We're already sticking out neck out here with Holes. You can't use them exclusively to solve your problem. If you could, Darius would have sent someone instead of hiring us."

Sho sighed. "I can do it," Xen said firmly.

"No!" Sho snapped.

"We all know I am probably going to need to access the artefact's magic in order to be able to perform the kind of spell that will counter Tan's spell."

"No, you won't. We'll make sure of it. We agreed we would try something else. You're our last resort. We haven't exhausted other options yet."

"I must try to speak with Zebulon," Sora insisted. "If it doesn't work, we can explore alternatives then."

Simon sighed. "I feel as though this job is about to go horribly wrong."

"It probably is," Oni agreed in a conversational tone. "So, if the Haosul Cel really do make it into our world, do we live or it is really lights out?"

Simon shook his head. "It will unmake the world as we know it. I don't know exactly what will happen."

Oni thought about this. "So it could actually be a good thing? It could make things more interesting, eh?"

"No! That is not what would happen. If any of us did survive, we would likely be turned into some sort of monsters."

She lifted an eyebrow. This sounded rather cool.

"Not the kind of monsters you like, Oni. It's bad. No good will come of it, not even by your estimation."

She sighed. "Okay. Okay."

Sora looked around at them all. Sho's team spent a lot of time nattering amongst themselves. It did not seem very productive. "So, we'll try to get inside without anyone having to go crazy and hope we'll be able to close the gate in time. Are we done?"

Xen's brow furrowed. "Sora—"

"I'll be fine. I'm immune to magic, right? He can't hurt me."

Oni lifted an eyebrow. "You aren't immune to knives. Or bombs or guns or

196

anything."

Sora rolled her eyes. "I don't think that's how Zebulon operates, even if he has gone mad. I will be all right."

"Sora, if it looks like it's getting dangerous—"

She cut him off again. She didn't have time for this. "I'll get out. I'll run screaming through the halls." He scowled. "Xen, I'm fine. It will be fine. Please, do not worry about me."

He stepped forward and gripped her arms. "Just be careful. Hang in there. We're going to sort this out."

She smiled wanly. "But it will never, ever be the same. Even if we stop him, nothing is going to be the way it used to be."

He sighed. "I don't want you to be alone tonight."

His friends pretended they weren't listening. Sora coloured slightly. "I will be okay."

"Nevertheless, I want to know you're safe."

"Fine. I'll stay with Oni again tonight."

"Yay!" Oni put in happily. "I learned how to make love charms for real today. A student told me all about them. We could practice together."

They all looked at her incredulously. "Sure," Sora said.

Xen nodded. "Good." He walked her to the door.

"But tell her I don't want her to braid my hair again," she whispered. "When I woke up this morning, it took half an hour to detangle it."

He laughed. "I'll tell her."

She turned from the room, but he caught her in the corridor. "Sora—" She turned back to him, bracing herself for another warning, but he wrapped an arm around her waist, drawing her up against him. His dark eyes glinted intensely, and then he bent down to press his mouth against hers. His lips were hot and urgent, and she sighed dreamily. She enjoyed it while it lasted. Quite a lot, actually.

When she pulled away from him, she smiled, and then she felt a pang of guilt shoot through her belly. "I will see you soon," she told him, pressing a hand against his cheek.

"Okay." He leaned down to lay a kiss on her forehead. "Be careful."

She waved and spun away from him, her step slightly more hurried than was strictly necessary.

Xen opened the door and peered back into the room. His friends wore identical expressions of amusement. He glared at them. "What?"

# CHAPTER TEN

Sora's step did not falter as she strode determinedly through the corridors towards Zebulon's tower. She paused as she reached the invisible barrier on the stairs. She wasn't certain how she would overcome the barrier, but she was determined to try. If nothing else, she could scream his name until he was forced to open the door or lose his mind—though, she thought, he likely already had done.

When she stepped up on to the stair, however, there was no resistance. Immune to magic, she remembered. Perhaps she could get through his protections. No, that should not have been. Surely his protections precluded entry by any non-magical person as well as his enemies. Had he then simply relaxed? She doubted that very much. Zebulon was not the sort to be lulled into a false sense of security, though that was, she reminded herself with a tremulous feeling, precisely what she intended to do.

Well, no matter. There was little other choice, and there was little sense wasting time dwelling upon her good fortune. She did not hesitate further but stepped up to the door. She took a deep breath to steady her nerves and lifted her fist to rap smartly on the door. "Zebulon?"

There was no response from inside the room.

"Zebulon, please open the door. I'm not here to fight with you. I just want to talk."

Silence answered her.

"Zebulon, I want to come back. I want to help you. Please!"

Still nothing.

"I know you would never do anything to hurt anyone. I am sorry I accused you. I'm sorry I wasn't loyal to you. I was wrong about Xen. He doesn't know you like I do. I'm sure there's been some sort of misunderstanding! Please let me come back and work for you again."

She knew she sounded like a shamefaced child. It was precisely how she intended to sound.

"Zebulon? Please! I'm still your friend. I want to help you."

There was still no sound from behind the door. Sora sighed deeply. She hadn't expected it to be easy. She only half expected it to work. She waited, turning to slide down to sit against his door. Nothing happened. She could not have forced her way through the door had she still possessed her magic. She had nothing but her resolve to stop this thing, no matter the cost, without Xen losing himself to the blackness of a dark artefact's terrible magic.

She sighed and dropped her head back against the door. She would sleep there if she had to. She would curl up right outside the door until he had to come out to eat or simply starve to death before he ever completed the spell. She had no intention of leaving.

She did not know how much time passed. Her thoughts raced, and her body trembled with dread. She had helped this along. She had done most of the work, in fact. If this was going to happen, she was as responsible for it as Zebulon. She wasn't going to let Xen or anyone else sacrifice themselves for something she had set into motion. She had to get inside that room.

The evening deepened into night. And then, something happened.

"Are you still there?"

Sora shot to her feet. "Yes. I'm not leaving until you agree to talk to me."

The door opened an infinitesimal crack. "What do you want?"

"I want to apologise. I miss you, Zebulon! I don't want to quarrel anymore."

The desperation in her voice must have touched him. He pulled open the door, though he blocked her entrance with this body. He looked tired, but there was such vitality in his face and his eyes that she wondered again how he could have looked so withered before. His eyes narrowed suspiciously. He still did not trust her.

"You look so tired," she told him. "Have you been sleeping? Have you remembered to eat?"

Her concern was sincere, for she loved him still, despite the horror of his chosen course. His mouth turned up slightly in a smile. "You do worry too much about me, dear."

"As well I should! Someone must. You would allow yourself to simply waste away in here if someone wasn't looking out for you. When was the last time you ate something?"

He thought about this. "I don't remember."

She laughed. "Let me get you something."

Zebulon smiled. "Perhaps...perhaps I could eat something."

"I'll go down to the kitchen."

He shook his head. "No, I will get something later. There is no need."

"You always say that, but you never do it. You look quite peaky. Let me get you something, all right? A peace offering."

He laughed. "Then I expect there will be extra chocolate and no tomatoes."

She grinned. "As you wish. I'll be right back." She turned and hurried down the stairs. She sensed he believed she was sincere, though she could not be sure with him. She had thought she knew him so well, but much had happened to disabuse her of this notion.

She could only bank on how well Zebulon thought he knew her, and she knew he had always underestimated her. She had even underestimated herself.

The kitchens were not empty, despite the lateness of the hour. The three cooks, dressed in quaint, grey maid's uniforms greeted her cheerfully. Yelena, the eldest of the women strode forward to embrace her warmly. She had long, dark hair streaked with grey, but she was still pretty, and her huge, dark eyes shone with a contentment Sora that rarely saw in the city, even inside the school. "Sora! We have not seen you in some time," Yelena exclaimed. "Have you come to fetch dinner for the old man?"

Sora laughed. "It had been some time since he had anything to eat, I suspect."

"I am not surprised," Sophie said disapprovingly. She was the youngest of the cooks, but she was the sourest. Her plain, pale face rarely smiled, and her light brown hair was always drawn back in a severe bun.

"Sit," Frida, the third cook ordered Sora, guiding her to the small table at which she'd once sat with Xen. Frida was small and dark and her tiny eyes looked mean, but she was the sweetest of the three. Few students or professors had ever bothered to discover this. "Have something yourself. You look positively famished."

Sora smiled. "I suppose I am quite hungry."

Yelena had already slid a plate of the evening's roasted fowl before her. "You could use some fattening up, girl. You should come see us more often."

They always said this, though she rarely skipped meals. She smiled nonetheless. "I will. Thank you." She ate quickly, for she did not know how long Zebulon's relenting attitude would last. She scooped up the bundle Frida placed beside her on the table. "Thank you all so much. I have to get back to work. I'll come back to see you soon."

She waved at their cheerful goodbyes and hurried back up to the tower as quickly as her legs would carry her. The door was closed once more. She sighed. Would she have to wait outside again for him to allow her in? Had he changed his mind? She tapped tentatively on the door. "Zebulon? I've brought dinner."

There was a long moment of silence.

Finally, he opened the door and peered out with narrow eyes. She held up the bundle. She was not certain he would step aside to allow her in. He did, however, and when she stepped into the room, she gasped. She had never seen it so cluttered. Books were strewn across the tables in disarray, and broken glass still littered the floor.

"You have been making quite a mess while I've been away," she told him gently.

"I have been working."

The door slammed, and she spun to him in surprise. He extended a long, thick finger to sketch a rune in the air. Something dark shimmered around them and spread across the door. She was trapped inside with him, and she had no magic to break the spell. She would have to soldier through it.

His face, his eyes were suddenly angry and dangerous. He glared into her face. "Have you come here to trick me, Sora? Do you think I will fall for this feeble peace offering?"

She opened and closed her mouth in shock. She had never seen him look so frightening. "No! I'm not here to trick you. I just--"

He moved so their faces were inches apart. She reared back slightly in surprise, but she held her ground. "Then what are you doing here?"

"I am your friend!"

"You were my friend until you turned on me," he hissed. "You went to those people. You're helping them destroy me!"

"No one is trying to destroy you, Zebulon! I swear."

"You're trying to stop me. You're trying to interrupt my great work. You don't even understand it! And you have joined with them!"

"No, Zebulon!" He sounded mad, but she knew he was not just paranoid. She gave him a large, innocent look. "I am not working with anyone. I just wanted

202

to go back to the way things were. I want to help you again. I was misguided. By him...by Xen. For a while. He convinced me what you were doing was wrong, and I know now how foolish I was to listen to him over you. I know you would never do anything like he is saying. He just doesn't understand!"

Zebulon did not relent. His eyes burned into hers.

"I want to work for you again! I've been working for you since long before he came along. It was just..." She turned her head in embarrassment. "I lost my head. I've never...Well, I just got caught up."

At this, the anger faded slightly from his eyes. His mouth turned up in a wry smile. "You fancy him?"

"I...yes. I fancy him." She blushed now, genuinely. "I've never liked anyone before. I didn't realise what I was feeling was clouding my judgment. I did not want to think he could be wrong, but I should have trusted you. I hardly know him at all. I should not have let him turn my head and put such a rift between us." She turned her innocent gaze back up to him. "I do trust you."

He narrowed his eyes. "Are you still seeing this man?"

"I have seen him. We are...there is much tension between us, but we are trying to agree to disagree and not discuss our differences." It wouldn't do to lie; he could find out easily enough. "I do like him, but I told him I could not see him if he came between me and my work with you."

"Has he spoken to you about me?"

She shook her head vehemently. "Only that which I have told you."

He didn't seem to believe her. "Are you sure about that? This isn't just a ploy you cooked up with him, Sora? You aren't helping him get to me? How can I know I can trust you?"

She gave him a hurt look. "You have known me all these years. I have never lied to you. I made a mistake, and I am so sorry. Don't let it come between us. We can be friends again."

He sighed, and she knew he loved her still as she loved him. He wanted to believe it. "It is true. You have never lied to me, and I have never doubted you before. I have...I have lost my head over a woman once or twice."

She smiled tentatively at this. "Will you let me come back? I can still help you with your spell."

He lifted an eyebrow. "You aren't afraid it will open a gate to a legendary dimension?"

Sora laughed, pressing her hands to her burning cheeks. "It is ridiculous, isn't it? I can't believe I...I can't believe I let myself get swept up in such nonsense. Can you forgive me?"

Zebulon considered her a long moment. Finally, he inclined his head. "All right. I will give you another chance. But you must promise to keep your head this time."

"Of course I promise." She laughed. "Thank you Zebulon. So, shall we get back to work, then? Have you discovered the seventh rune? Are you ready to try out your spell? Or are we back to the books?"

His eyes grew wary, but he did not say anything to this.

She strode to the bookshelf and began pulling books from it to stack on the table. "I have been doing some research on my own, and I have been thinking many of the runes seem to have origins in elemental magic."

He blinked. "Yes. They have, haven't they?" he mused.

"I thought we could look at the elemental runes first. At least it's somewhere to start that's a little less random than reading every text we can get our hands on."

He smiled. "Missed spending your nights pouring over old books, have you?"

"A little," she admitted, grinning. "I just want to be useful again. I am...well, I have nothing without you, Zebulon. I have no purpose at all. I'm just a substitute teacher without any–" She cut off and smiled sheepishly at him. He did not know about her magic, and she could not explain without revealing her deception. "Guidance," she finished. She realised suddenly how true this had been once. Now she had something else. She wasn't sure she wanted it, for it brought with it such horrible consequences.

Zebulon reached out to wrap her in a fatherly hug. She felt his fingers move behind her back. He leaned back, holding her at arm's length. For the first time since she'd entered the room, he smiled genuinely. "You are telling the truth."

"Yes." For the first time, she was glad for what Simon had done to her.

"You're really telling the truth." he laughed and hugged her again. This time, it felt warm and real. "I am so happy to have you back, my dear. I am sorry we rowed."

She smiled at him. "I am sorry, too. I never meant to doubt you. I am by your side, no matter what."

He grinned. "Even if I open a gate to an alternate dimension?"

She laughed. "Yes, even then because I know you won't have meant to do it, and I will be here to help you sort it out."

"That is why I took you on as my assistant, Sora. You are so very good at cleaning up my messes."

She rose up on her tiptoes to kiss him on the cheek, and then she sat down in her usual place at the table and opened the first book on the stack. "Shall we get to work, then?"

He grinned and nodded at her. She bent over the book and didn't notice when his smile faded to a frown.

\* \* \*

Sora tapped lightly on Oni's door. The hour was late, for she and Zebulon had worked into the deepest of night, but she knew they would be inside waiting for her. She wondered if any of them ever slept at all. They seemed to run on pure wicked energy. Well, Oni did, at least. The others just seemed to run on brooding bloody-mindedness and a general sense of resentment towards the world around them.

The door opened so abruptly, she reared back, but Oni reached out into the hall and yanked her inside. They all looked up at her anxiously. Xen was already on his feet, striding towards her with a look of glittering intensity. She held up her hands. "I'm okay. Nothing bad happened. He took me back."

Xen blinked in surprise. "He took you back?"

"Yes."

Sho frowned. "Just like that?"

"No. Not just like that. I had to do a lot of explaining and grovelling, but he came around eventually. For a moment..." She glanced up at Xen, whose brow furrowed. She held her tongue, for he would never let her return if she mentioned the moment in which she'd been afraid he'd gone mad. "For a moment I wasn't sure he would."

"Well done, Sora," Simon said heartily.

Xen and Sho did not look fully convinced. "Are you sure it's safe?" Xen demanded.

"I don't think he fully trusts me yet, and we need to be sure he does." She glanced at Oni. "I can't stay with you tonight."

Oni's face fell in disappointment. "Aw, but I was going to teach you to play Slam, Bomb or Knickers."

They all stared at her. "What in the hell is Slam, Bomb or Knickers?" Sho asked.

"It's a new game I just made up. It involves a lot of whiskey and a bomb hidden in lacy frilly things."

Sora ignored this. She never knew when the woman was serious. She turned back to Xen. "I am safe from Zebulon, but I need to appear as though I am not in league with you. Staying here would raise too many questions."

Xen sighed. "I don't like the idea of you being alone."

"This is bigger than that now, Xen." She had never sounded so cold, so resolute. "We have to do what's best."

"I could just stay with you!" Oni exclaimed. "You have a lot of lacy frilly things, don't you?"

"No, Oni. I'm still on shaky ground with Zebulon. He could change his mind and stop trusting me at any moment. I have to earn back his trust, which means I have to make every appearance of telling him the truth. He can't know about us working together. If he even suspects and shuts me out again, we'll never get inside in time to stop this thing."

No one could argue with her.

Her eyes met Xen's. "I think we should try to stay away from each other. For a while, at least."

"I don't like that," he growled.

"I don't like it, either, but it's the only way. If Zebulon gets it in his head I'm deceiving him, we'll lose our only chance."

"I won't be able to watch over you."

She rolled her eyes. "I haven't needed you to watch over me all these years. I will be all right."

He sighed. "But can I see you?"

"Oh! I can help you sneak around," Oni said helpfully. "I know all the places to have illicit encounters where no one will ever find you. Unless you want them

206

to."

They looked at her, appalled. "Oni!" Xen growled.

She looked completely unrepentant. "What?"

"I'm not trying to see her like that!"

"Well, why not? You fancy her, don't you?"

Xen scowled at Oni. Sora's cheeks flamed. "We can meet, Xen. I explained that I was still seeing you, though I would not want him to see me with all of you. In any case, he spends most of his days and nights in his workshop. But he can find out whatever it is he wants to know. He has always been able to do. I just can't be seen to be working with you."

Xen lifted an eyebrow. "But I can be seen to be courting you?"

Her mouth turned up in a shy smile. "Well, yes, if that is what you would like to call it."

He shrugged. "Whatever. As long as I can see you."

Sora looked at Sho. "So what do we do now?"

He leaned back in his chair. "You just keep doing what you are doing. Keep earning his trust and when the time comes, when you are close to completing the spell, report to us. We'll be ready."

"All right."

"And then you get out of there," Sho finished.

Oni looked at him strangely, but she looked at everyone strangely.

Sora frowned. "I'm not going to be allowed to be there when it happens?"

"Hell, no!" Xen replied vehemently. "It's far too dangerous."

"I am not a child! I am sorceress! I will not be treated like I do not know what I am doing."

"You're a sorceress who can't use magic anymore," he reminded her coldly.

She glared at him. This was deeply insulting. "Well, neither can you without going crazy."

"We like to call it the bad juju rage," Oni added.

"Oni!" Xen snapped. "Would you mind?"

"This is my room!"

"Oni!" He gestured at Sho and Simon, and they did not argue. Sho gripped Oni's arm and dragged her out of the room.

"We'll go to Simon's room."

"It's so boring there. All he has are books."

"Then we'll go to your classroom."

This seemed to perk Oni up. She didn't argue any further.

Sora turned back to Xen. He stepped towards her and gripped her arms. "I know the magic can't hurt you, Sora. I just...I couldn't stand it if something happened to you."

She stared up into his dark, intense eyes, and realisation struck her. She suddenly understood. Her stomach sank into her knees. She lifted a hand to touch his cheek. "I don't want anything to happen to you, either, Xen. Do you think it will be easy for me to just sit back while you go in? Potentially forever? And if you do come out—who knows what you will be?"

He wrapped an arm around her waist to draw her against him. He leaned down to kiss her. She rose up on her toes to deepen the kiss, clutching his neck so tightly, she might never let go. She understood. There was a terrible ache in her belly. It shouldn't have to be like this. Why did it have to be like this? She had only just met him, only just discovered how it felt to actually feel something for someone. It really wasn't fair at all.

She sighed, and he pulled away. "Sora..." His brow furrowed. He seemed not to know what to say.

She nodded. "I know. Me, too." His smile was sad, and she stared up into his eyes. She brushed his hair back from his face. "Xen, I have to...I have to go back to my room, but..." She took a deep breath. She'd never asked such a thing in her life. "Will you come with me?"

He blinked in surprise. For a moment, he studied her carefully, and then he leaned down to press his lips to hers. "Are you sure?" His voice was a husky whisper.

"Yes."

"What if Zebulon sees us?"

She shrugged. "I will tell him I lost my head. Besides, he is probably still locked away in his workshop."

Xen stared at her another moment. He nodded. "Okay."

She smiled and took his hand. They walked out of Oni's room together.

Oni was waiting outside the door. Sho and Simon had gone, leaving her behind. Sora didn't care if she'd been listening. She didn't care about anything at the moment. Oni grinned at them. "Good night, you two."

They ignored her. They didn't speak to each other as Sora led him to her room. They didn't need to say anything more.

\* \* \*

The air was so charged around the pair, he needed little imagination to guess what would come next. Zebulon's eyes narrowed and his jaw tightened as Sora pulled Xen into her chamber. "Oh, Sora," he murmured. "I knew you couldn't be trusted. I lost you a long time ago. The moment that man came here."

He turned from her door and hobbled up the stairs to his tower. His illusionary strength was failing him. The hour he had spent following his traitorous assistant had taken the last of it. He was gasping as he reached the door and pulled himself into the room. For a moment, he collapsed on the floor and lay there.

He caught his breath and shoved to his feet. He lurched towards the mirror hanging above the vanity in his sleeping chamber. He glared at his withered reflection. His eyes blazed back at him. Their colour was pale and dull, but they glittered with terrible, burning rage.

What is your game, Sora?

It didn't matter that she was a traitor, for the fact was he needed her. His mouth curved humourlessly in the mirror. And she had come right back to him. Like a perfect little lamb, she had appeared just as he'd understood that he could not do this without her.

Soon. It would all be over soon. He would miss her, but he had lost her the moment Xen had arrived. He had nothing left to lose now but the one thing he held dear. He smiled a brittle smile. Funny that the last thing he had already lost would be the only thing that could save it.

\* \* \*

Sora opened her eyes slowly, enjoying the intense warmth of the bed. Xen's body radiated extraordinary heat, and she wondered how he could live with it inside him without burning up. It was magic; she knew it was. She rolled over to look at him. His eyes were closed, and he looked so peaceful, she wondered that he was the same surly, brooding man she had come to know. She had only seen the charged, intense side of him. She had taken it for granted. She didn't know he had a side like this.

His flesh was taut over his lean muscles, tanned and scarred in so many places she wondered how he'd ever survived them. But he was beautiful, so painfully, heartbreakingly beautiful, and there was so much power in his body, she could feel it even now. She could feel where he'd touched her, inside and out, and she remembered the strength of him, the painstakingly careful tenderness of every touch, every movement.

She reached a hand to touch his bare chest, to sweep his long, black and white dreadlocks over his shoulder, but she could not wake him just yet. Her fingers fluttered a breath away from his skin. A sudden terrible, gasping pain surged through her. He hadn't hurt her, and she knew the pain was not so much physical. It felt like a yawning, black hole was opening in her chest.

A single tear slid down her nose. She didn't bother to wipe it away. She deserved to cry. If nothing else, she deserved that much.

She watched him sleep a moment longer, but the sun was just beginning to glitter through the curtains. She slipped carefully out of bed. It was a long-shot, and with nearly all of her being, she longed to fail.

She didn't fail, and the ache in her chest expanded.

She riffled swiftly through the pockets of Xen's black, brass-buttoned jacket. He always wore it, and she'd come to associate it so closely with him the sight of it pained her. It was there, in his breast pocket, as though he could not for a moment part with it. She did not know if they all had a copy, but she suspected they did. They seemed to have backup plan upon backup plan, and she knew Xen was the final resort.

He wouldn't have to be. She hurriedly copied the counter-spell on a scrap bit of parchment. Her heart thumped as she glanced over her shoulder at him, half of her praying he wouldn't awaken and the other desperately hoping he would.

He didn't. She refolded the parchment and tucked it back into the pocket.

"What are you doing?" His voice sounded sleepy.

She nearly jumped out of her skin, but when she turned to him, there was no suspicion in his eyes. She tucked the parchment she'd scribbled upon into a book on her desk with a careful, casual movement. She smiled at him. "Just going over some notes for class."

He sat up, and his long hair fell around his shoulders. He held out his arms to her, and though the pain only worsened, she moved into them instantly. He wrapped her up in his embrace, pulling her onto his lap. She curled into him, closing her eyes. He smelled of some sort of spice, perhaps, or he simply smelled like a man. She had not known what they smelled like, not up close, not up against their skin. She felt him kiss the top of her head, his lips lingering on her hair.

"Sora, I..."

She looked up at him and smiled. "I know, Xen."

He brushed her hair from her face and leaned down to press his mouth to hers. There was something sad in that kiss, and it was not just she that felt it, she knew. His lips moved against hers with such a strange, quiet emotion: a sort of desperation that sent chills along her spine and up her arms. She tangled her hands into his hair, holding him to her, and his hands clutched her against him urgently. Her body awakened once more in the memory of their night together, in the sensations that he sent now along her skin and within the very core of her being.

She couldn't. Not now. She pulled away from him, and she knew he knew that she must go. His dark eyes were intense and brooding once more, but there was a new emotion in them now that broke open her heart and made her wish so desperately that things could be different that she almost lost her nerve.

That wasn't going to happen. She smiled. "I have to get ready. I must bring Zebulon his breakfast."

Xen sighed. He did not release his hold upon her. "I am not comfortable with this."

"We both know it's the only way."

"When it's all over...when the spell is done, and we've stopped him..."

She pressed a hand to his lips. She smiled. She didn't want to hear what he had to say. She couldn't bear it. "Why don't we talk about it then?"

Sora had never guessed she could be so skilled at deception. He did not seem to notice the slight tremor in her voice. He smiled and kissed her fingertips. "I'll look forward to it."

She drew out of his arms with more difficulty than she had expected. "I have to go. I'm sorry."

"I would have liked to have had breakfast with you, at least." He sounded slightly sullen.

She leaned down and kissed him quickly on the mouth. "I have to keep up appearances. I'm sorry. I would have liked it, as well." She moved into the small washroom to clean up for classes as quickly as she could; she had lingered too long with him. She shouldn't have allowed herself.

He was only just rising from bed when she returned to the sleeping chamber, stretching languidly as he moved across the room. She stared at his nude, tanned body for several seconds without realising she was doing it. So beautiful. She had not realised a man's body could be beautiful, but it could, and his was, despite the scars that criss-crossed his muscular back, slightly paler than the tanned flesh there. Her eyes drifted lower, and she felt a shiver of naughty delight as she admired the sculpted shape of his bottom.

"See you something you like?"

He'd turned his head slightly to look at her, and she laughed, blushing. "Yes, I suppose I do."

He grinned at her. "I don't suppose you could skip breakfast this morning?" He started towards her, but she held up a hand. He lifted his shoulders in a shrug, and her eyes strayed down, shocked by the evidence of his fancy. She looked quickly away, heat spreading across her neck and cheeks. He laughed, but he did not tease her. Instead, he bent down to gather his clothes from the floor where they'd strewn them last night.

She could not help but watch him, slowly gathering her books without looking at them. She smiled as he pulled a button-down, black, long-sleeved shirt over a black undershirt. "You wear a lot of clothes."

He chuckled as he belted his trousers over his shirt and shouldered on the long jacket in one fluid motion. "And you don't?"

She looked down at her pale blue dress. Knickers, petticoats, lacy slip, vest, boots, spats. She shrugged. "I am a woman. I'm supposed to wear a lot of clothes."

He laughed, and she walked to the door. He sighed deeply as though he'd been putting off the moment. "Okay. Okay. I get it." He kissed her again, and it felt like the last time. Her face fell as she watched him stride away, down the corridor.

Xen turned back to her and waved, and the smile on his face was so unlike him, so innocent and boyish, her stomach clenched. She smiled and waved back, but as soon as he was out of sight, her smile faded. She pulled the door closed and leaned against it a moment. Then she pulled herself together and strode out into the corridor, the opposite way from which he'd gone.

\* \* \*

Zebulon smiled as he answered her light rap upon the workshop door. "Since when did you start knocking, Sora?" He seemed in cheerful spirits this morning.

She held out the small wrapped bundle of food she'd brought for his breakfast. "I just thought you would appreciate the courtesy."

He smiled at her. "Let us forget the past and forgive each other our trespasses, yes? All friends eventually find themselves in a disagreement."

She smiled back at him. "Yes. I would like that very much." She placed the bundle on the worktable. "I brought breakfast."

"I am grateful. I have been neglecting my good health these last few days."

She laughed, setting out plates of bacon, eggs, fried tomatoes and crispy potatoes. "I'm not surprised."

They ate in companionable silence. He had been neglecting his health, she knew, for he tucked in voraciously. She smiled as she watched him. He did need someone to look after him. He was lost without her.

"So have you had any success discovering the seventh rune?"

He sighed and shook his head. "I regret not. It has been tedious work, searching for the elements of our spell, hasn't it?"

"Well, I do not mind a little tedium. It is a refreshing change from the current atmosphere in the school." He lifted his eyebrows, and she continued, smiling a little wistfully. "It has been quite lively in classes lately, what with all the accidental nudity and gossip over the new professors. They seem to be exerting some sort of negative influence upon the students."

"How so?"

"They just...seem a bit more reckless than they once were. Why, just the other day one of our students attempted to perform a persuasion rune to get me to give her a better grade on her term paper."

Zebulon laughed. "And did it work?"

She grinned. "No, of course not. It was as poorly executed as her paper."

They smiled at each other, and a rush of contentment surged unexpectedly through her. She'd missed their companionable conversations and their close friendship. She'd missed his laughter and his carefree moods. Had it been so long? It seemed as though so much had happened. Sadness coursed through her then, and in the blink of an eye, the contentment was gone.

Zebulon, too, perhaps felt this loss as she did, for he smiled sadly at her across the table. "Zebulon?" she asked softly. "What's the matter?"

The sadness disappeared from his eyes as though it had never been there at all, and she wondered if she'd imagined it. Perhaps she had only seen her own feelings reflected in his eyes. "Nothing, nothing. You just seem so grown up these days. I feel like a father who looks at his child one day and realises she has suddenly become an adult."

She laughed, but she felt uneasy.

"You do seem different," he remarked. "Has something happened?"

Was it obvious? She fought the blush that threatened to steal across her cheeks and neck. Could he somehow see in her eyes what had happened last night? "No. Nothing's happened."

He stared at her a moment, and for the briefest instant, she almost thought he knew. But surely he could not know. "Have you seen Xen lately?"

Her stomach sank into her knees. She could not lie to him, not about this. "Yes," she admitted. "But it is not as it was between us."

"Whatever do you mean, dear?"

She sighed. She thought back to her estrangement with Xen before she'd come to understand the truth. "We have agreed to disagree on the matter of your work. He does not pester me about it, but it still remains between us, and it is creating a rift."

"Ah. Not torn apart yet, then, are you?"

"No, not torn apart. Just...not quite as we once were."

"Such is often the case with these things. Young people fall in love with chemistry and do not think about whether they share compatible values and beliefs. It is quite common."

"How does it end?"

He smiled. "It works, occasionally, when the two parties can come to a compromise."

"And the rest of the time?"

"Well, the two parties realise they are not right for each other and break apart.

214

Such is the way of love. It is a hit and miss sort of business."

She laughed. "You know a lot about these sorts of things?"

He feigned offence. "My dear, I'll have you know I have had my share of passionate relationships."

"Have you?"

"Of course. I am quite fit, in case you hadn't noticed. In my youth, I was quite widely admired."

She grinned. "I bet you had a new totty every week."

He guffawed. "That is not a very ladylike thing to say."

"I do beg your pardon." They were quiet a moment, and then she asked, "Zebulon, why did you never marry?"

He sighed deeply. "It is a sad tale, Sora."

"I would like to hear it, if it isn't too terribly hard to tell."

"No, it has long since passed." His eyes slid away in memory. "Her name was Amulya. We met when we were quite young; about your age. We were fresh out of Academy and full of ourselves and the opportunities ahead of us. She was a potions-maker, you see, and I was a runic sorcerer. We talked of hiring out our services, like magical mercenaries." He laughed. "It was Amulya's idea. She liked the idea of an exciting life, making custom spells and potions."

"What happened?"

His smile was very sad. "Well, we took posts with the school to gather enough capital to start up our own company. She was an assistant professor in the potions lab when there was a very bad accident. We never learned the nature of the accident, for there was nothing left of the lab to investigate. She was simply gone."

"Oh, Zebulon, I am so sorry!" She reached across the table to squeeze his hand. "I had no idea."

He lowered his head. "It was quite difficult. I remained at the school, but for many years I would see no one romantically, not for very long, and I buried myself in my work. I did fall in love again once or twice, but it never worked out in the end. I was always too wrapped up in my work."

She sighed. "I understand."

"If nothing else, take my advice upon this one thing, Sora: do not let it break you. If this—connection you have with Xen does not work out, do let allow it to close your heart to the possibility of something more."

She smiled. "I will take your advice. But Zebulon...have you not considered romance again? You are still fit, and there are many women who admire you. You need not be alone."

He laughed. "I am old and set in my ways. I do not think a romance at my age would be kind to me or the woman with whom I might become involved."

"Well, you never do know unless you try."

"Ah." He waved his hand dismissively. "But what will you do with your bloke?"

She lifted her shoulders. "I do not know. Perhaps there is nothing to do, as you say. Perhaps we do not share values and beliefs, and I nearly lost my life's work for him. Whatever I feel for him, it is not worth giving up what I have worked so hard for, not when there is such a chance it could fail. I would not give up everything for him."

Zebulon smiled. "My dear, sometimes giving up everything is the only way to know you really tried."

She laughed, but she thought perhaps he was more right than he knew.

# CHAPTER ELEVEN

His eyes narrowed as she slipped from the workshop late into the evening. He waited a beat, and then he muttered to himself, sketching runes in the air that swirled around his head like vapour. His hair and beard shortened, and his body expanded until he resembled a short, stout man with a bulbous nose. In this disguise, he was so innocuous as to be virtually invisible, for he rarely drew the notice of anyone he passed. He followed his traitorous assistant, but she did not veer towards Xen's or his friends' rooms this evening. Instead, she let herself into her chamber, alone.

Interesting. Where were the others? He paused in front of her door and sketched another rune in the air. A shimmering dash appeared in the air. Just one dash. She was, in fact, truly alone. Perhaps she was awaiting her gentleman caller. No matter. She was of little concern to him now. Alone, what was she against him?

Nothing.

He spun from her door and strode towards the Amulets and Talismans wing. He had spent little time there, but he had trailed Sho Sange's associates often enough to know where Xen resided. He listened for a moment at his door, but he heard nothing. Nevertheless, he sketched the same rune he had done upon Sora's door.

Nothing happened. There was no one inside.

A burning urgency surged in his chest. He sketched another rune, only half expecting it to work. It did, for Xen must have been confident enough that no one would dare attempt to enter his office uninvited. He turned he knob and slipped into the room, glancing out into the corridor to ensure he was unnoticed. No was seemed to be around at all.

He rushed to the desk, shuffling through the papers. Student essays, lesson plans, complicated spells for creating and charging talismans and runes, and—he snorted loudly—a love letter. It was not from Sora but from some student, who must have slipped it in with an essay. Well, wasn't he the popular one? Zebulon wondered if he'd noticed it yet. He thought for a moment of using it against him, but there was no name on the letter, and his connection with Sora was well known. It would do little good.

There was nothing at all about Zebulon Tan. Nothing. He had not even taken notes? How utterly insulting. Or perhaps the meddler was wise enough not to leave them strewn across his desk. He sat behind the desk, riffling through the drawers. They were a mess of amulets, bags of herbs, vials of potion and a bottle of very expensive liquor.

And then he saw it, tucked under a talisman as though it was nothing more than a scrap of paper.

**Heka: a rune to represent sickness, pain and suffering.**

**Hu: the force of will and determination.**

**Yaya: representing the spirit....**

He had seen enough. He knew what followed. He cursed angrily and returned the scrap of parchment where he'd found it. He didn't wonder that they had another copy. There were probably half a dozen of them by now.

"Sora," he hissed. "You miserable little traitor. I can't believe you've gone this far."

He spun away from the desk, hurrying to leave the room before its owner came back.

He sighed deeply as he reached his tower sanctuary. The disguise melted away into a withered old man once more. He glared around the room as though she were still in it. "Well. This will make things much more straightforward."

\* \* \*

*Meanwhile, amidst the outrageous and potentially lethal detritus of Oni's bedroom...*

Sho wondered that Oni could have amassed such a collection of wire, gears, clockworks, explosives, gadgets, tools, weapons and dirty knickers in such a short amount of time.

"So, she's really done it," Simon mused. "Tan has accepted her back."

"Yes," Xen said, and he felt a surge of pride. "I am not sure it is as it once was, but she will at least be able to keep us updated on his progress."

"But do you think he believes her?" Sho asked in a low voice. "Has he truly taken her back into his confidence?"

Xen shook his head. "We cannot be sure, but she believes he has done. They continue to search for the final rune."

"If he does not trust her, why would he take her back?" Oni asked carelessly. "Who wouldn't trust that sweet face?"

"It's not a joke, Oni," Sho told her. "If he doesn't trust her, he might have some other reason to have taken her back."

"He tested her," Xen said. "She told me he used a rune to determine her faith. It didn't work, obviously. He does not know what has been done to her. He will trust his own magic."

"That is a great risk to take," Simon mused.

Xen glared. "You don't have to tell me. I know that. I'm not happy about this. I'm just trying to stay positive so I don't—well, you know."

They knew. Bad juju rage.

Sho held up his hands. "We are going to have to take the risk. All we can do is wait and see. As long as she is with him every day, we are closer than we were to tracking his progress. It is the best we can hope for at the moment."

Oni fell back on the rumpled bed with an exaggerated sigh. "I hate waiting. It's the worst. Can't we just take another go at the door? Now that he's let Sora inside, it might be weaker."

"It wasn't weaker the last time she was inside," Xen reminded her, scowling.

"We can't risk it, Oni," Sho added. "He knows we're here, and he must know what we are up to. He's taken precautions. The plan remains the same. I am sorry if it bores you, but we wait and we go in when it's done."

They all sighed grimly. Oni sat up abruptly and gave the three men a stern look. "Are we going to talk about this or not?"

They didn't have to ask what she meant. "Oni has a point," Xen admitted. "We have the spell. Now how are we going to work it?"

Simon pushed his glasses up his nose with a miserable expression. "Well, there really is only one option--"

"No!" Xen snapped.

Simon looked highly offended by this interruption. "I was not going to suggest we use Sora. We're not going to sacrifice an innocent girl."

"Besides which," Oni put in. "She's not so innocent anymore, is she, Xen?" She leered at him.

"Oni!" Sho said warningly. "Not appropriate."

She rolled her eyes. "It doesn't matter how innocent she is anymore," Xen told her. "She is not going to be the sacrifice. Can we get some sort of animal?"

Sho sighed. "I'm not sure it will work, to be honest. It might not be powerful enough. You know what happens if we lose this one shot."

They all considered their options.

"So what are we going to do?" Xen sounded stressed. It wasn't good to stress Xen out. Sho laid a hand on his shoulder. A strange sort of calm coursed through him. He resented that he needed it at all, but he was grateful Sho knew when he was on edge.

"Oh, there are plenty of innocent souls out there who want to be sacrificed," Oni put in. "Can't we just find one? Someone we don't know, preferably. Or someone we don't like."

"And how do you suppose we do that?" Simon asked. "Put an advert in the newspaper?"

"Well, that's not a terrible idea. How soon do you think we could run it?"

Sho shook his head. "I think we need some help if we're going to do this without having to murder some innocent person. I think we need to...talk to Ptolemy."

They looked around at him in shock. "Ptolemy?"

"Well, he is the authority on pure and innocent souls, isn't he?"

"Do you think he will help us?" Simon asked doubtfully.

"He is the one who brought this to us to begin with," Sho reminded him.

"I thought Darius brought this," Oni said.

"At Ptolemy's bequest."

"I wondered why you said we'd be working for the good guys. I knew Darius wasn't good."

He ignored her. "It's time Ptolemy stepped in and helped." He rose to his feet with a determined expression.

"Where are you going?" Xen demanded.

"To find him." Sho did not wait to listen to their questions, and he did not invite them along. He strode through the corridors and out into the dark courtyard. It was late, though there were a few students and professors still hurrying from the main building to the library and laboratories and back,

220

carrying lanterns or balls of fire or glowing light in their hands. Sho ignored them all.

The moon was large and bright. Its light pooled across the thick, lush green lawn. Sho stood in the pool of moonlight and looked up at the sky. His chant was soft and low, for he knew Ptolemy would hear. He did not need to raise his voice. He kept chanting for a long time, the same words over and over, and he began to think Ptolemy would not come.

Then a light flashed briefly down from the heavens, and Ptolemy stood before him, scowling in annoyance. "What exactly do you think you're doing calling me here, Sho? Do you think I can just come flitting down whenever you need me? That is not exactly what we do. If my higher-ups--"

"Yeah, yeah. Don't talk to me about your higher-ups. I know the score as well as you. I don't need to hear it."

Ptolemy scowled at him. "You don't know everything, Darklord."

"Look, can we go somewhere else to talk?"

The angel rolled his eyes and clapped a hand on Sho's shoulder. In moments, they were sitting outside a little street cafe. A waiter passed them, blinking in surprise at their sudden arrival. Ptolemy gestured at the waiter, who hurried away. He turned back to Sho as though there had been no interruption.

"I know enough about what's going on," Sho said coldly, picking up where they had left off. "And I know you could have done something about this if you really wanted to. It is, in fact, within your particular wheelhouse. You could have talked your higher-ups into helping out."

Ptolemy's annoyance increased. "You know nothing about what happens up there, Sho."

"I know whatever side you're on seems to blur a little depending on the circumstances."

He sighed. "You know what I do, Sho. We all have a job. We all have a duty. You know all about that, don't you? I'm just doing my duty. You have to play the game on the side you're on. It's what you should be doing."

"If I was, you wouldn't have anyone to come in and clean up your messes."

The waiter returned with an elaborate tea service. Sho ignored it. Ptolemy, however, prepared his tea carefully. Then he looked over the lip of his cup with a scowl. "Is there a point to this audience? I do not have unlimited time to share tea with you."

221

"Yes, there is." Sho drew the slip of parchment from his breast pocket. "It's not going to be quite as easy to stop Tan as you had led us to believe. He clearly knows who I am, and he has found a way to stop me going near him."

Ptolemy looked up sharply from Ipwick's spell. "You can't stop him?"

"No."

"What's this for, then?"

"That spell is the counter to the combination. We have to let him open the gate first."

The angel scowled. "This is not what I had in mind when we gave you the job."

"You chose not to do it yourself. You will get what you paid for. When the gate is open, we will counter it. That spell will close the gate and hopefully seal it forever. If we're very lucky, no one will ever think of it again.

They shared a miserable sigh.

"So, what do you need me for?" Ptolemy demanded. "You seem to have things well in hand."

Sho frowned. "There's a problem."

"Well, what now?"

"In case you didn't actually read over the spell, it requires a sacrifice."

"Naturally. The best spells do. You can't get anything done without a sacrifice. Have a scone. They're lovely. What's the problem?"

Sho did not take a scone. He did not eat scones, not at street cafes in Aether City. He was a damned Darklord. "We don't have a sacrifice."

"What are you talking about? There are plenty of innocents running around the school."

"We can't just—we can't just pick one of them off to die."

"Why not? It's them or the entire world. You can't just make a decision?"

"It may be easy for you," Sho said coldly. "You are not cursed with human sentimentality or empathy. Even for the sake of the world, a sacrifice is murder."

Ptolemy sighed impatiently. "Humans. Such ideas. Well, what do you want me to do with it?"

"I need one."

"A sacrifice?"

"Yes."

"And you expect me to provide it?"

"That's what you do, isn't it? Maintain innocence?"

"We don't send humans out for slaughter, you know."

Sho passed a hand over his face. "You're the one who made it sound easy."

"Well, I don't know what you think I can do about it. It's not like we keep a list of ready and willing sacrifices. Besides, why do you need one from me? You have one."

"What do you mean, we have one?"

"The girl. The woman. Sora Bale."

Sho scowled. "She is not up for discussion."

"And why not? She's a perfectly good sacrifice. She helped bring the thing about to begin with. She's helped him with the spell. We would have had more time to come up with a better solution if not for her."

"No. I can't do it."

He paused with his teacup midway to his lips. "Is there any particular reason?"

"Yes."

Ptolemy raised his eyebrows. "Human sentimentality?"

"Something like that."

The angel sighed and sat back in his chair. He sipped his tea silently for a moment, appraising Sho with pale eyes that could see straight into his very soul. "This is why they shouldn't have given you all that. It would be a much simpler world." He considered this. "It would be much less interesting, though."

"Are you going to help me or not?"

"I don't think I can, Sho."

"Well, who can?"

Ptolemy's look was almost pitying. "You know what you have to do. Make the difficult decision. It's that woman or the world."

Sho scowled. Xen was not going to like it. In fact, if he suspected they were planning to do such a thing, he would sacrifice himself first before anyone had a chance to do anything about it.

Ptolemy rose. "Do what you have to do, Sho. And don't contact me again." He reached over the table and gave Sho's shoulder a forceful shove.

Sho landed back on his feet in the pool of moonlight. He turned back towards the school with a heavy step. He sighed. "I'm not sure how I'm going to explain this one. I rather think it will not go over well at all."

\* \* \*

*Meanwhile, it is another dark night in Penthos...*

Imogen surveyed the burning villages in the valleys below with a sense of deepest satisfaction. Her gruesome puppets shambled up the hill towards her, illuminated by the blaze in their wake. They looked even worse now than when she had set them upon the quiet villages. Their once beautiful burial shrouds were torn and bloody, and their flesh was scorched in the places the fire had touched them. Half of Mercy's once sweet, lovely face was melting.

Imogen clucked at them in disapproval. "Oh, your beautiful clothes. Well, you will be hard to hide in a crowd." She clapped her hands. "No matter. You will have other purposes to serve soon enough. These shells will hardly suit you."

They stared at her with their gaping, rotting mouths, but their eyes reflected the horror of what they had seen, of what they had done. The people: men, woman and children alike—especially the children—slaughtered in their beds or at their evening rest. Whole villages burned to the ground, people still screaming as their flesh heated and melted off. They had loved those people, Argus and Mercy, and the people had loved them.

"You have done very well, my dears," Imogen purred. "Very well indeed. "Why, there is hardly a village left in Penthos. Everyone who ever knew either of you, everyone who ever watched you spurn me for this woman and witnessed my humiliation is gone. If I chose, I could raise them as an army to march against all of Pandia."

She considered this, ignoring her puppets for the moment.

"Perhaps I will." Her mouth twisted up into a cold, humourless smile. "Perhaps it is my destiny. Yes. Yes, now that I have had my revenge on you and the people who laughed at me, it is all there is left to do. And you two, you will lead my army. You will march against the country and show them what I am capable of, what you can do. You will show them the horror you are and the madness and pain and suffering you are capable of inflicting."

Her laugh was low and cold, but then it grew louder and louder until it roared over the crackling flame and final, feeble screams in the valley below. "It is so poetic, is it not?"

Argus and Mercy turned their monstrous bodies to look at each other.

"What's this? Are you not enjoying your eternal life together? Are you not happy? Did I not give you what you said you wanted when you spurned me, Argus? Did you not wish for this when you stole him from me, Mercy?" She smiled. "It is only the beginning, my lovelies. Soon, all the world will know my name, and they will fear to speak it. And you will be there to witness it all. You will be integral. Can you not see it? Can you not picture it?"

They could picture it, in the very hearts of their maddened spirits, and it was horror such that they had not thought a human capable, of which Argus never knew his spurned lover was capable.

"Oh, it will be magnificent. It will be the sweetest revenge." She stopped laughing abruptly. She looked at them with narrow, appraising eyes. "I must prepare you. You can't march upon the country with all your bits falling off and your faces melting. I must preserve you yet. Come."

She snapped her fingers and trounced off, over the hills and away from Penthos. They resisted, but her pull was even stronger now, and their hesitation was brief. They trundled miserably after her.

\* \* \*

*Meanwhile, in the Darklands, things are beginning to look grim...*

Lady Blood looked up at her husband. He sat silently in his favourite chair in the study. He had long since forgotten the book he'd been reading, which now lay face down in his lap. He stared moodily into the depths of his blood red wine, swirling the contents around as though they might yield the answers to his darkest questions.

She quietly laid her own book in her lap. "Darling..."

He glanced up at her in surprise. She had rarely interrupted their nightly repose in the study, reading their respective books and enjoying each other's companionable silence. He raised his eyebrows expectantly.

"Did you notice anything odd at the ceremony?"

"Odd? What do you mean 'odd'?"

"Something..." She sighed. "I have been trying to forget it, to dismiss it as my imagination, but I felt as though...as though there was a spirit lingering in the air in the ballroom."

He laughed bitterly. "Well, dear..." His voice was sardonic, and she did not like it.

"No. Not the usual sort of spirit. I know it is his domain. Luca, it was something else. Something different."

"I am not sure what you are talking about, my dear. The spirits in his domain are peaceful. They move on as they are meant to do into the sea and beyond."

"This spirit lingered. It watched over the ceremony."

Lord Blood considered this. He sat back in his chair and took a pensive sip of the dark red wine. "But why would it be there?"

"Well, I'm sure I do not know, my darling. I was sure I was the only one who could sense him, but...but, well, I was sure Lord Sprit could, as well. As he was being sworn in, it lingered over him, and I was sure for a moment he felt it too. That he could see it as I did."

"But why would it be there?" As he repeated it, he did not sound quite so doubtful as before, for he knew his wife was not the sort of woman to imagine such things.

"Indeed, why?"

They met each other's gazes as they thought about this.

"Lord Spirit's death," the Lady began, "was quite mysterious, was it not? Even Malady could not determine its cause."

Her husband scowled. He did not wish to revisit this argument. "What are you suggesting? That Spirit murdered his own father?"

She laughed wryly. "No. No, but that is utterly ridiculous. You know the laws of our people. He would not even dream of such a thing, I am sure. Nevertheless, perhaps...perhaps there is a malignant spirit in Scathach. Perhaps something did kill him."

"But if so...if so, what was its motivation?" He frowned and surged to his feet. His wife, unlike his son, was a sensible woman. She did not alarm easily. "I must look into this at once."

"Darling, do, for if there is a mysterious malignant entity striking down the Darklords, we surely must stop it. But do...do be careful, please."

226

He sighed deeply and leaned down to kiss the crown of her long, dark hair. "I will, my dear. I would not wish the same fate upon our family."

\* \* \*

*Days pass, and nothing has happened...*

It wasn't until nearly a week later that Sora, sitting stiffly at a table in Zebulon's workshop late one evening, her eyes drooping and hope lost, discovered Nun, the final rune. She sat straight up in her chair with a sharp intake of breath. Zebulon looked up at her in surprise. "My dear? Are you all right?"

She laughed softly. "I believe I was nodding off. I awoke with a sudden start. I am so sorry, Zebulon."

He smiled at her. "It is getting quite late, and we have been at this for many days. You deserve a break. You should get some sleep. We can pick this back up in the morning."

She glanced down at the page upon which the final piece of this terrible puzzle was written. She smiled and turned a few pages idly, skimming them over, though she hardly saw the words upon them. She carefully placed the small engraved silver bookmark, a lovely gift from Zebulon upon her graduation, into the book and closed it. "You are right, Zebulon. I could use some rest. It is just that, I cannot help but think each time 'just one more page...'"

He laughed. "I understand the feeling quite well. And then 'just one more page' becomes another night."

She nodded. "It is so." She looked down at the closed book in front of her. "If it is all right, I would like to take my book. I just feel...I have a good feeling about it. I just want to look at it a bit more before bed."

He laughed. "Sora..." His tone was warning, and it was not the first time he had heard her say such a thing.

"I won't stay up too late. I promise."

"See that you don't."

She smiled and hugged the book close to her chest, afraid he would change his mind in the blink of an eye. She leaned over to lay a kiss on the top of his head. "I will see you in the morning, Zebulon. I will bring breakfast."

He waved her off good-naturedly. "I am capable of feeding and minding myself, you know."

"I know. But I think you do a lot better when someone is watching over you."

He grinned. "That is a true statement, my dear. All right, then. Off with you. I will see you in the morning."

He watched her slip from the room, clutching the book with a tired sort of smile. "Oh, Sora," he murmured as the door closed. "What are you up to now?" He rose and paced to his chamber mirror. The old man before him changed again into the short, fat and utterly forgettable man as whom he could freely wander.

He followed her, and this time Sora did not return immediately to her chamber, as she had done the last time. She veered into the Amulets and Talismans wing, her step swift. She rapped on Xen's door. As it opened, she stepped inside, carrying the book as though it might be taken from her at any moment. Zebulon's eyes narrowed.

"It won't be that easy to trick me, Sora," he murmured into the empty corridor. "I might need you, but I will not let you stop me."

\* \* \*

"Sora," Xen said in a rush of relief. His eyes burned down at her, glittering in that intense way that made her stomach swoop. She blushed slightly, though they knew each other well by now and modesty was hardly a concern with him, this beautiful, damaged man. He stepped aside to allow her to enter, and she felt his fingers brush down her arm with such lightness, the subtle caress was like a fire inside her.

She ignored the impulse to turn to him, for they were not alone. His team sat around the cluttered office, looking grim. They looked up at her with the same expressions with which they had looked at her each day: boredom, weariness, hopelessness. She did not hesitate to share this one victory.

"I have found it."

"What?" Sho sat straight up in his chair. The others received this information with ambivalence, for, though they wished for this miserable, cocked up assignment to finally be over, they were not entirely confident in the solution.

"I found the last rune," she said firmly, looking around at them.

"Oh, god," Xen muttered miserably.

"Does that mean it's time?" Oni asked, hopping up in excitement. "We get to finally be done with this awful job?"

Sora looked up as Xen strode towards her, laying his hands on her shoulders.

He squeezed gently, and she could feel the tension in his fingers. "We have them all," Sora confirmed. "When he sees it, it will be time."

"So what are we going to do?" Simon asked, squinting around the room. "You have not shown it to him yet?"

"No. No, he has not seen it. It is in this book." She displayed the book to them, but she drew it back as Simon reached out for it, as though he might snatch it away from her. "I kept it. I knew if…if I gave it to him tonight, it would be too late to stop him."

They sighed. "So you are going to give it to him? I don't suppose we could just…burn that book and have done with this?" Xen asked.

Simon shook his head. "There is always another book. He will find it eventually. We would only be putting off the inevitable. We want him to find the runes and finish the spell so we can close off Hao from our world forever. And the sooner the better."

"I still say we should just send Sora in with a bomb to just blow the whole workshop to bits with him inside," Oni said.

Sora looked at her, horrified. "I could never do that. Whatever he is, Zebulon does not deserve to die that way. I will not kill him."

"No one is killing anyone, Oni," Sho said through gritted teeth.

"Well, it would make all this a whole lot more straightforward," she muttered irritably.

"It would not ultimately solve the problem," Simon told them. "It is no longer so small as just one man. It has gone too far. The combination is out, and there are now several of us who know it. Though we might never use it, it could be found again and much more easily this time. We have to close it off forever or it will only happen again and likely again and again until the world is destroyed."

This was a rather grim outlook, but Simon was rarely wrong in matters such as these, for he had seen generations of humans making the same mistakes over and over again, regardless of the lessons of their forefathers.

"I could stall him for a while to give us a bit more time," Sora said. "But I do not think it will do much good. It is best to just…get it over with." Her voice was perfectly even, and her face did not bear any signs of the deep, aching sadness inside her chest that had in the last week spread throughout her entire body like a cancer. "I will behave as though I have just discovered the rune tomorrow. I will go right after class."

The tension in the room seemed palpable. "How will we know when to do the spell?" Oni asked.

"You must be ready at any moment."

"I think I will know," Xen said in a low voice. "I will feel it in my bones. I can feel everything in this place. I will know when the power spikes."

"But do you have to use dark magic?" Sora frowned.

"No. It is merely a side-effect of the artefact. I can feel it without doing anything. Do not worry, Sora." She sighed, but she nodded.

Sho glanced over at Simon. "Will your man be ready?"

Simon's lip curled slightly in distaste. "Yes, yes. He will be ready. I'll have him here." When he did not move, Sho lifted his eyebrows expectantly. Simon sighed. "All right, all right. I'm going. Oh, I hate that place."

"That's it, then," Sho said when Simon had gone from the room, and there was a grim tightness around his mouth that suggested he was not so unruffled as he sounded. "It happens tomorrow."

"But are we ready?" Xen's eyes glinted.

"I'm sure I don't know what you mean."

"Yes, you do. You know precisely what I mean. The sacrifice."

Sora looked up at him with a strange expression in her eyes. Since their first night together, he had seen her look at him every now and again with that same expression, but he still could not identify what it meant.

"It is taken care of." Sho's voice was deceptively casual. "We have found someone."

"Who?" Sora demanded, scowling. "You will let an innocent person die?"

Oni gave Sho an uncommonly shrewd look and then turned to Sora cheerfully. "There are plenty of people who would sacrifice themselves for a good cause."

Sora frowned. "That does not sound likely. Someone is just willing to walk into their death for someone else's cause?"

"It is actually quite a roaring trade in the city; what with all the sorcerers. They often need a blood sacrifice. Blood is the most powerful catalyst, you know."

Sora stared at her. Oni's expression was completely unreadable. She certainly could not be so positive at such an idea, but she could not tell if the idea horrified the woman as it did herself. "You mean people can buy sacrifices?"

"There are people who volunteer. People who wish to die for a cause. People with nothing to live for. They believe if they do, they will be reborn into a new, better life right away."

"And are they?"

"There is no statistical data, but it is the common belief."

Sora frowned at her. "It still sounds wrong."

"It is not up to us to decide what is right for those people." Her voice was almost gentle. "They make the choice, and we need them."

"All right." She sounded so cheerful, they all turned to look at her appraisingly. She did not say another word about it. "I had better get to bed. It has been a long day, and I will need to be ready for what is to happen in the morning." She smiled at Xen. "Will you walk me to my room?"

His dark eyes glittered down at her. He had walked her to her room every night for the past week, and he knew he would not be returning to his office until morning. He nodded to the others and laid a hand on Sora's back to lead her out.

As soon as the door closed behind them, Oni turned to Sho with a dangerous expression. "Why did I have to make up all that rubbish about willing sacrifices?"

"You're the one who went on and on about it," Sho told her.

"Well, I couldn't very well tell her the truth. You know perfectly well those people at those brokers are slaves. They are raised like cows to the slaughter."

He sighed. "I know."

"We don't use services like that. I am a maniac, but I am not a monster."

"I know that. I'm not the one who said all those things."

"Well, it's not like you were jumping in with any ideas. Have you come up with anything?"

"We aren't going to buy a sacrifice."

"Then what are we planning to do?" Her voice was soft, and there was a note of worry in it.

Sho sighed deeply. He was relieved to finally be alone with Oni, with whom he could speak freely. It had once been Xen to whom he could speak, but things had changed so quickly and so dramatically, Sho was uncertain who his friend was anymore.

"I talked to Ptolemy. He said..." He sighed miserably. "He said we have a perfectly good sacrifice here."

Oni narrowed her eyes. "Sora."

"Yes, Sora. Of course. Who else?"

"Xen will never allow it. We have all seen him with her. He's...well, he's all googly-eyed, and you know what that means."

"I know what it means."

"He will never forgive you, Sho. Never. Better you did buy one of those slaves. He will never ever forgive you."

"But he must understand."

"You can't do this!"

He surged to his feet and pushed his hands through his snow white hair. He looked at her with desperation in his eyes that made her stomach sink. "What else am I supposed to do, Oni? Do you have any other ideas?"

"Let's just grab one of the students!"

"We can't just murder an innocent person!"

"That's what you'll be doing to Sora. And she is your best friend's lady. You just can't."

"It's a hard choice, Oni. But I have to make it. It's the only way this will work. You know that. There's no getting around it. I have to do what I have to do." When she glared at him, he strode towards her, glaring right back. "Do you not comprehend the gravity of the situation?"

She rose to meet him, jabbing a finger into his chest. "Of course I do! I have never lost sight of it, despite appearances to the contrary. But this...Xen will never get over it. Who knows what he will do? He might tip back over to the dark side. When he realizes what you have planned, he will do everything in his power to stop you. He might even kill you."

"He won't be able to kill me. He could try, but it would do no good."

"But he could go back to the dark, and then he will be lost forever. He will use his powers to save her. We both know he will. And then all this will have been for nothing."

Sho sighed and looked up at her. His glare had slipped into an expression of deepest gloom. "It is a risk we will have to take. It is down to the wire, Oni. We have to be ready by tomorrow. Do you have any other suggestions?"

"I was counting on you having them! So you're going to just...what? You're going to just murder her in front of him?"

"I am going to try to keep him out of the room."

She looked scornful. "And how are you going to do that? He's never going to allow it. Not to mention, aside from you, he is the best at magic. If we need a backup plan, he's it."

Sho pinched the bridge of his nose. "I know. Oni...I just don't know what else to do."

She stepped towards him, running her hands up and down his arms. "We have to think about this. We just...we can't do it. We can't use her."

"But I can't see how there is any other way. Can you?"

She suddenly gripped his face in her hands and kissed him passionately, but when he tried to pull her closer, she stepped back, pressing a hand on his chest to ward him off. She held up a finger.

He lifted an eyebrow. "What was that for?"

"It helps me think."

"Did you come up with anything?"

She frowned. She was silent for a moment. "No."

"Well." He reached out and caught her around the waist, dragging her up against him. "Let's try it again then, shall we? I could use a little inspiration myself."

\* \* \*

Simon stared warily up at the faded wooden sign outside the Dirty Damastes. He didn't want to go back inside. Heavens, but did he hate the place. He sighed deeply and pinched the bridge of his nose. There wasn't time to waste now. Everything was drawing to an end. He'd made his choices, and he must follow through with them. If he'd simply kept out of it, hidden himself away in some conclave somewhere enjoying enjoy scholarly pursuits, this would all be someone else's problem.

But it wasn't someone else's problem. He stepped forward, pulling open the battered wooden door with a deep sigh. He did not notice the short, fat man who followed him inside. The man was so nondescript and forgettable that even when the fat man's belt snapped and his pants dropped to the floor, no one in the tavern looked up or noticed him at all.

Simon took only a moment to glance around the tavern then made a beeline for the three sleazy-looking men laughing together at a table and clinking their glasses. He recognised Holes' companions, and he heaved an even deeper sigh. A woman passed by the table as Simon reached it. She looked slightly peaky, and her face went suddenly stark white. Her eyes rolled up into the back of her head, and then she slid to the floor in a dead faint.

A man at the table beside her rushed forward to catch her. As he did, his clumsy fingers caught upon the buttons of her shirt. It popped open. He goggled down at her bare bosom.

"Hey!" A large man marched over to them, pushing his sleeves up over his elbows. "That's my girl! What the hell are you doing to her?"

"It was an accident!" the startled man exclaimed, lifting his hands in the air. The woman dropped to the dirty floor. "She fainted, and I just caught her!"

The larger man raised his fist. "I ought to pop you one."

Simon rolled his eyes. "Excuse me," he said primly, stepping between the two men without so much as a glance at either of them. It seemed to diffuse the tension in the air. The larger man bent down to scoop up his girlfriend, and the other scurried away. Simon sat down next to Holes.

"Hey, Nudie!"

"Don't call me that," Simon ordered through clenched teeth. "It's Simon."

"Right. Simon." Holes smirked.

"It's time for you to return my favour."

"Aw, man! Tonight? I was just getting into the swing of things here."

He glanced pointedly over at the large man, who wrapped his jacket around his girlfriend. She smiled hazily up at him as she slowly awoke and wrapped her arms tightly around his neck.

"You are disgusting," Simon told him.

"Well, get over it. They will have a beautiful life together. When the dust settles, anyway. Some people just need a little push in the right direction."

None of them noticed the short, fat man sit down in the seat the clumsy, startled man had just abandoned.

Simon glared at Holes, who waved his hand. "All right, all right. I am a man of my word. I promised you a hole, and I will give you a hole. What do you want me to do?"

"I need you at the Gwydion Academy tomorrow."

"Yeah, yeah. I'll be there." Holes grinned. "How about a drink?"

"I do not want a drink. I just want to get out of here."

"Why? You're so good for business. Stay a little longer."

"You can have just a little drink, can't you?" Fainting asked. He looked pale and shaky, but he grinned. He loved when Simon was around.

"All right, then. Just one drink." Simon hated this place, but he was already here, and he could use a drink.

"Tell us your troubles, old friend," Potentially Violent Scuffles said as Holes waved the waitress over for another round of drinks.

Simon sat back in his rickety wooden chair with a long-suffering sigh and sipped the cold, frothy beer the waitress brought with a speed that startled even him. There was one thing about this bar; the service was good. "It has been a dreadful two weeks."

"You mean the trouble at the Academy?" Fainting asked in a fading, breathless sort of voice.

"You know about that?"

"We all do," Potentially Violent Scuffles said grimly. "Word's been on the wind. No need to ask how you got involved in all of it."

"But everyone's right shocked that I'm the one you asked to help," Holes told him.

Simon laughed wryly. "Yes, well, you're the last person I expected I would ask for anything."

Holes lifted an eyebrow. "I will try not to take offence, since we are such good friends these days."

"We are not good friends," Simon told him petulantly. "We're just exchanging favours."

"Oh, don't be so shirty. You are no different than any of us."

"No," Simon agreed. "I would just like to be."

The other three looked slightly offended, but it was difficult to fault him. He was no different. "So what's the deal, eh?" Fainting asked, dissolving the tension.

"Some mad wizard's gone and found himself the combination to open a gate to Hao," Potentially Violent Scuffled answered for him.

"Hao? I thought that place was closed off centuries ago."

"Well, you know how it is," Holes put in.

"How'd he find out how to do it?"

"Lucian," they all said at the same time.

"That sleazy bastard," Simon added.

Holes shrugged. "He does a good trade. I heard he's done quite well for himself with that little business of his."

"In any case, he's usually causing some kind of trouble."

"But why did they ask you to step in and help?" Fainting demanded. "I thought you were out."

"You haven't heard?" Potentially Violent Scuffles asked, grinning over the top of his mug. "Simon's working for a Darklord these days."

"A Darklord? That's a little risky, isn't it? They're practically...well, gods."

Simon rolled his eyes. "They aren't. They are far more breakable. In any case, it's not a bad job. I stay very busy, and it's often pleasurable; that is, when I'm not cleaning up the messes of my mostly insane colleagues."

The short, fat man leaned closer, narrowing his small, beady eyes. No one even glanced his way.

"So what are you going to do about this one, then?" Potentially Violent Scuffles asked. "You'd better have something good. If you don't manage to stop your wizard, all of this will be over." He considered and then waved his hand. "Well, the infernal and angelic will be fine. They'll just be sent into the aether, but us...well, I'm not sure what will happen to us. With the humans...if they all die, what we embody will die."

"It's a rather cruel joke, isn't it, our existence?" Holes didn't sound too upset about this.

"It is, indeed."

They sipped their beers silently. "So do you have a plan?" Fainting asked breathlessly.

Simon dropped his forehead in his hands. "Not a very good one. Holes will get us in…and I believe we'll be winging it from there. We have a counter-spell, but…well; we can only hope the mad elemental wizard who created it isn't just trying to kill us all. We've really no guarantee it will work. It's not as if we can test it out prior to launch time."

The fat man frowned at this. The Darklord already had a counter-spell and a man who made holes, and, if the fat man had not grossly misinterpreted the conversation, that man and his companions were rather more than mere men.

"Well, I wish you luck, for the sake of us all," Potentially Violent Scuffles told him, raising his glass in salute. "It might not be a rewarding existence, but it is better than no existence at all."

"Yes, true." Simon peered gloomily into his empty mug.

"Another?" Holes asked hopefully.

Simon shrugged. "I might as well. If it's going to be my last night on terra firma, I might as well squander it. It's not as if I have anything better to be doing."

Holes gestured again, and the waitress returned with another round. Fainting held up his mug. "To the last night of our pitiful lives!"

"Here here!"

They did not even notice when the fat man rose from his seat and slipped out of the Dirty Damastes with a small smile.

# CHAPTER TWELVE

A pale, grey dawn was just lightening Sora's bedchamber. She had not slept the night, for she had felt utterly, completely awake. She did not want to miss a single moment of her last night with him. She lay on her side, watching him sleep with such a terrible, heart-breaking tenderness that she felt an ache in her stomach. It was painful to look at him. Nothing had ever hurt so badly, not any physical pain she'd ever experienced.

She sighed deeply. If she had never met him, it would be much easier. If she had never met him, perhaps she would not be where she was now, watching her last night disappear as the sun slowly rose on her last day. She did not let herself regret this. She would rather have spent her last night with him, loving him and being loved by him, than live on for another hundred years without ever having met him at all.

It was foolish to think such things, but if she was going to think them, now was the time. She would not have another chance.

She pushed aside the pain and the sadness, and she reached to brush his long hair from his face. He sighed in his sleep, pulling her closer against him, and she felt suddenly warmly content. His body was so hot, but she was used to it now, and she was cold without him beside her. She looked at him, and she was surprised to discover that she was not afraid.

She did not know what would happen or how it would happen, but it would happen, and there was no sense in being afraid. She knew the end of the story, and there was a strange, unexpected peace in knowing and choosing her own fate. She smiled and leaned forward to press a kiss to Xen's temple.

He stirred slightly, and she felt his arms tighten around her. When he opened his eyes and smiled up at her, her stomach lurched.

"Hey," she whispered.

"Good morning. You're up early."

"Yes. I couldn't sleep."

His brow furrowed slightly. Without thinking, she reached up to smooth it once more. He caught her hand and kissed her fingertips. "Are you worried?"

"No. I'm not worried." She was telling the truth. "I'm just...anxious to get it over with."

He pulled her down to kiss her. "There is nothing you need to worry about, Sora. You're going to be safe. It will all be over soon."

She knew he meant to keep this promise. "I don't want anything bad to happen to you."

He smiled. "Me, neither."

"And I don't want you to do anything bad."

"I will do my best not to. We have it all figured out. When Tan finishes the spell, we will get through and Sho will perform the counter-spell. There is nothing else to it."

"You make it sound so easy."

"It will be."

There was sadness in her quiet laugh. "I hope you're right." She closed her eyes briefly as he ran a hand through her long, blonde hair. "I just want you to be safe."

He chuckled. "I'll be fine. I've dealt with much, much worse."

She lifted a sceptical eyebrow.

He grinned. "Well, perhaps not much *much* worse."

"Worse than the unmaking of the entire world?"

Xen waved a dismissive hand. "Oh, this sort of thing is happening all the time. It's usually just being perpetrated by much more foolish people, not someone as clever and formidable as Zebulon Tan."

She sighed. "That makes it so much worse for me. He was my closest friend. But I do not even know him anymore. He's become someone else entirely."

"Perhaps he was never as you thought him to be."

She frowned. "I think I am a better judge of character than that."

"I am sorry. I did not mean to suggest you were fooled. Just...perhaps his relationship with you was genuine and masked some darker side of himself."

"I still believe he is not intending such an outcome. He does not understand the consequences. You won't...you won't kill him, will you?"

"I will endeavour to preserve his life."

"Thank you, Xen."

"I cannot ensure there will not be some grave consequence for his action, Sora. I do not know what will be done to him if he is presented before a tribunal."

She frowned. "Must he be?"

"Of course he must. He has been warned of the consequences, and he has chosen to ignore them. He will have to face judgment for his actions. He should have to pay for the trouble he has caused."

Sora sighed. "I understand. I wish he had not done this. Everything has changed."

"I'm sorry for that."

"It's not all bad." She smiled. "I suppose if he had not done it, I would not have met you."

"I am also not complaining about that part of this whole mess." He pulled her down for another kiss. "What will we do when all this is over, Sora?"

Her smile wavered. "I don't know." Her voice was light, but her heart weighed heavy in her chest. "What do you want to do?"

"I'll go back to work."

"Of course."

"But I still want to see you. Every day if I can."

It wouldn't hurt to indulge the fantasy, for a little while. No, it would hurt, but if one deserved to lie to themselves, it was surely on their last day. "Yeah?"

"Of course. Do you think I was just using you to get close to Zebulon?"

"Well, you were."

He laughed. "In the beginning, anyway. It's not like that, Sora. You know that, don't you?"

"Yes. I know." She had known almost from the beginning. His dark eyes were so expressive they could not lie even when his face was as cold as ice. She had never loved or been loved before she'd met him, but she had no doubts about his feelings or hers. It made it harder, but it made it so very much sweeter.

"When this is over, I will show you."

She leaned forward to kiss him. She did not want to make promises she could not keep, but she could not resist the fantasy he was weaving around her. "I would like that."

"I can show you more of the city. There's a lot to see." His eyes glittered. "I can show you all of Pandia."

She smiled. "I would like to go to Komodia and see the circus."

"I will take you. I will take you everywhere. I will show you things you never knew existed."

"I would like that very much." A tear escaped from the corner of her eye, despite her smile.

Xen wiped it away with the pad of his thumb. His voice was gentle. "What's wrong?"

"It just...sounds really nice."

"Sora...you are worried, aren't you?"

"I just...hope you make it out of there. You know, without the juju rage."

He laughed. "I'm not going to have to do that. We have a plan. We'll fix it, and I'll come back to you. Besides, maybe...maybe you'll be able to draw me out. You know; if I ever go back under."

She looked at him silently for a long moment. "Do you think I could?"

"I think if anything could, it would be you."

"I don't want to have to test that theory."

"Neither do I."

The sun was golden now, glittering behind the thin curtains. She knew the time was coming. She didn't want it to be over, not yet. When the small, glowing orb on her nightstand chimed an alarm, she sighed deeply. She didn't want to get up, not in that moment. The desperation to stay there beside him, in his arms, was so intense, she nearly lost her nerve.

But there was no choice.

"I have to get ready for class," she whispered, and it was as though the words tore a hole in her chest. She rose slowly, and every movement that took her from him was painful. He followed her and pulled her into his arms. She leaned into his chest.

"Sora, we will sort this out," he promised in a low voice. "I know it will be hard, but Sho is the best. And we are the best. We've sorted out worse problems. This will all be over soon. I don't want you to worry."

She nodded, but she knew he felt the moisture on his naked chest. "I won't. "

"Promise."

She thought she could keep this one. She was relieved she would not have to lie to him. He knew nothing of her plans. "I promise."

He leaned down to kiss her again. When he pulled away, she stared up at him for several long moments. She memorised his face, for she wanted it so clear in her mind, and when she saw it again, it would be the last time. But there would be one more time.

She reached up to touch his cheek. "Xen," she whispered. "I love you, you know."

He blinked at her in surprise for several seconds. Then he smiled. "You do?"

"Yes. I'm sorry if...I might not know much, but I know you aren't supposed to say that so soon. But just...just in case."

"There is no just in case."

She smiled sadly. "All the same. Just in case...I want you to know. I want you to remember." She took a hitching breath and blinked back the tears that threatened to spill from her eyes. "You don't have to say anything. I just wanted to tell you."

He pressed his mouth to hers, and he did not need to speak. He said nothing.

She stepped away from him. "I have to get ready. It's going to be...it's going to be a very short day."

He lifted his eyebrows as she turned towards the bathroom. "Sora..."

She did not want him to see the tears welling in her eyes now, but she could not stop herself from looking back at him one more time. "You'd better go."

"Sora." He caught her arm and spun her back to him. "I will be waiting right outside. Tonight, when the spell is done, I will be there. You will be safe. I'll pull you out of there."

"Just...just promise you won't hurt Zebulon. If you can help it."

He chuckled wryly. "I promise. I will do my best. I know how much he means to you." He kissed her on the forehead. "I will see you soon."

"Okay." She watched him go, and as soon as the door closed, she let the tears spill over her eyes. She did not bother to swipe them away. "Goodbye, Xen."

\* \* \*

242

Sho lifted an eyebrow. "Don't you guys work here? Shouldn't you be in class?"

Xen hadn't bothered to attend his own classes that morning. There wasn't much point, and he'd heard that Professor Omari had finally returned from hospital. If they needed him to return, no one had hunted him down. He wondered if even Whip and the administrators suspected something was happening, something was wrong, and it was best to let the people whose problem it actually was get on with taking care of it.

"Oh, no. We don't work here for real," Oni replied.

"I'm sure it's covered," Xen replied unconcernedly. "There's not a lot of point in keeping up the charade, is there?" He narrowed his eyes. "Have you determined what to do about this sacrifice business?"

Sho and Oni exchanged a glance, but it was so quick and unreadable, no one else seemed to have caught it. "Ptolemy is taking care of it."

Xen frowned. "The angel is going to find us a human sacrifice?"

"He has little choice in the matter. It is his job."

"It is terrible, though," Simon murmured. "Having to murder an innocent person. It isn't exactly how I enjoy spending my day."

Oni glared furiously at Sho, but he would not meet her gaze.

"What the matter, Oni?" Xen demanded. He'd seen her angry at Sho before, but he'd never seen her look at him with such reproach. Oni rarely condemned anyone for anything, even the foulest of acts, and least of all did she judge Sho. Something about it set Xen's sensitive nerves ablaze with anxiety.

Oni lifted her chin. The heat of her gaze did not cool. "Nothing." She looked more serious than he had ever seen her. "This is going to be fine. We're going to sort it out."

"Simon, you're certain your man will be here?"

Simon nodded. "He is on his way. He'll be here. He might be a right sleazy bastard, but he is a man of his word."

"What is Sora doing?" Sho asked. His voice was deceptively casual. "When will she give him the final rune?"

"She is in class," Xen replied. "It will happen this evening."

"You're sure he'll perform the spell right away?" Simon asked.

"No, but he seems desperate enough. He likely will wish to do it as soon as possible. I think we can count on tonight."

The delicate rap on the door startled them all. They looked at each other warily. Sho put up a hand to quiet them and stalked towards the door. "Who is it?"

"It's me. Open the damn door."

Sho recognised the clipped, arrogant voice instantly. He hurried to pull open the door. The dark man in the dark suit stood in the doorway with an arch expression. "Darius, what are you doing here?"

Darius strode past him into the room. "I just want to talk. I can't visit these days?"

Sho narrowed his eyes. "You just want to talk?"

"Well, I wanted to congratulate you. It sounds as though you've got this little problem just about wrapped up."

"We do."

"I am most delighted." He smiled pleasantly at them. "However..."

"Just spit it out, Darius," Sho snapped.

Darius arched an elegant eyebrow. "Ptolemy seems to think you are having a little trouble chasing up an appropriate sacrifice."

Oni and Sho exchanged a glance. Xen furrowed his brow. "I thought you had that sorted."

Darius grinned around at them. It was worrying. They all eyed him warily.

"What's got you so smug?" Simon asked.

The grin stretched until the fallen angel looked as though he might unhinge his jaw and swallow one of them whole. "Ptolemy can't really help with that little bit of the spell, but I think I can."

Sho gestured him to get on with it. "How?"

"Well, you know why Ptolemy sent me to take care of this particular problem."

"No. Not really. I assumed he didn't want to get his hands dirty if things went awry."

"Well, there is that, but that's not exactly it. You see, he could not actually

244

intervene in this particular affair. The subject is one of his people."

They stared at him blankly.

"Think about it, people." He rolled his eyes as they continued to stare at him, uncomprehending.

Oni snapped her fingers. "Zebulon Tan is one of Ptolemy's."

"Yes." Darius smiled as Sho's face lit up in understanding. "He hasn't actually done anything wrong, you see. His intentions are pure. His soul is pure. Had he not begun this quest, he might have been highly favoured up there. As long as he remains pure..."

"He is the sacrifice," Sho finished.

"Yay!" Oni burst out. "Now we won't have to use Sora!"

Sho glared angrily at her. Xen's head snapped around to her so quickly, his black and white dreadlocks lashed Simon in the face. "You were going to use Sora?" His voice was deadly quiet.

Sho's face set rigidly. "It was the only way."

"You lied to me? And to her?"

"She was the only one who made sense. She, at least, was the one who helped him."

"I can't believe this!" Xen's dark eyes glinted with such cold anger he seemed to chill the air around him. "I thought you were my friend."

"Do you think it was an easy decision to make? You think I wanted anything to happen to her? We had no one else! Could you have just picked an innocent child out of a classroom to be slaughtered?"

"You said it couldn't be her. She is immune to magic." Xen looked at Simon as if he might offer some confirmation of this.

Simon shook his head sadly. "We couldn't separate her soul, but...her body still possesses a pure, innocent soul. She does not need to have magic to be useful."

Xen glared at Sho. "I can't believe you would go behind my back like this."

Sho stepped towards him, but Xen's eyes almost glowed with rage. Sho stopped. "You know I would not have done if I could see any other option."

"Boys," Oni put in reasonably. "You are forgetting the obvious."

They both turned flaming, angry eyes on her. "What?" Xen snapped.

"It is a moot point. We don't need her now. It's poetic, isn't it? The one who started this all is the one who we will use to stop it all."

Xen stared at her, but the chill around him warmed slightly. He took several deep breathes. It wouldn't do to lose it, not yet. He still needed to be coherent for a little while longer. If Darius was right, he might be able to remain coherent through it all.

"Well," Darius said, smiling pleasantly as though the argument had never occurred. "I think my work here is done. I trust you all will have it sorted out by morning. So, if that's all, I have a date. See you on the other side."

He gave them a little wave of farewell and snapped his fingers. In the next instant, he was gone. The puff of smoke he left behind smelled faintly of brimstone.

Oni smiled happily, but Xen did not look as though he had forgiven Sho's betrayal. He spun towards the door. "Where are you going?" Sho demanded.

Xen paused, but he did not turn back to look at him. "Out. I have to think about this."

"Xen, you need to stay close," Sho said sternly. "It could happen any time."

Now he turned to glare at him. "You don't get to tell me what to do anymore. I'm not sure I work for you anymore. I will stay here and help you get this job done, but after that..." He didn't finish. Instead, he gripped the doorknob and stepped out into the hall.

"Xen!" Oni jumped up to chase after him, but Sho caught her arm in an unyielding grip.

"He will get over it," he told her in a low voice, though his dark eyes did not seem to believe the sentiment. "He will see when he is no longer wrapped up in his emotions that it was the only reasonable choice."

Oni frowned. "I'm really not sure, Sho. This time, I think you went too far."

\* \* \*

Sora's step faltered on the stairs leading up to Zebulon's workshop. It was as though she was walking to her execution. She knew now how prisoners felt as they walked the gallows. At least in her case, she was not to be executed for her crimes but in order to stop the unmaking of the world. It was some comfort. It was only right and appropriate. No one else would have to pay for her mistakes.

Perhaps she was, after all, paying for her crimes, however innocently and inadvertently she'd committed them.

Xen's face flashed in her mind, beautiful as he slept in the grey dawn light. It hurt to think of him, and she swiped at the tear that slid from her eye. She didn't try to push the image away, not for a single moment. If she must die, it would not be for nothing. She would not die with nothing. It would hurt him, surely, for she knew he had come to love her. She knew it as surely as she knew she would be able to do as she must, for she would be saving him.

She smiled, but a terrible pang of sadness seized her chest. It was as it should be.

Sora lifted her chin and steeled her resolve. She could see Zebulon's door, and she could not put it off any longer. She climbed the stairs more swiftly until she was running, taking them two at a time. When she reached the door, she did not hesitate. She banged upon it. "Zebulon! Zebulon!"

He looked startled as he opened the door to her. "What is it? What's the matter, Sora?"

She gasped for breath, and he pulled her into the room. She held up the ancient tome she had taken with her the previous night. "I found it. I found the final rune."

"What?" His voice was almost hushed.

"It's here. In this book." She opened the page she'd marked with her silver bookmark.

"You found it?" His face lit up, and, for a moment, he looked so young, so vital she was sure they must all be mistaken. He could not be sick. He could not be dying.

But his delight was such that she knew it was true. No matter how badly she wanted it all to go away, she knew he would stop at nothing.

"It's here," she repeated, and she did not have to fake her breathlessness.

He pulled her into a hug and spun her around. "Sora, you found it! When did you find it?"

"I was just going through the book during a break between classes. I could hardly wait to show you."

His laugh was loud and jubilant. "This is wonderful." He snatched the book from her hands and spun towards the podium to copy the rune in his grimoire beneath the others. He spun away from the book, and Sora noticed for the first time that he had torn down a section of the bookshelf, leaving a blank space on the wall behind his podium.

His eyes glittered feverishly. Even without her magic, she could sense the power building around him. She felt a sudden surge of fear. Her heart thumped wildly.

"Are you going to do the spell now?" Her voice sounded slightly choked.

He did not notice. He spun sharply towards her. "Well, why not, my dear?" His voice sounded strange, deep and almost garbled. It echoed in the chamber around him. "What need have we to wait?"

"I can stay?"

He smiled. His brilliant blue eyes had started to glow. "Oh, I think so." There was a frightening edge to his smile, as though he were intending to leapt at her and tear her throat out with his teeth.

He didn't frighten her, for what more could frighten her than that which she planned for herself? She felt the pretence between them slipping away. She breathed a sigh of relief; she had expected him to attempt to eject her from the room when the spell began. She had constructed a number of very complicated arguments to convince him otherwise. She would not need them now.

She had studied the spell again and again. It would not require her to possess her runic magic. It would only require a series of incantations any beginning incanter could speak with ease. The power would come from her, not from magic but from the only thing she had left to give.

She intended to finish this before Xen and the others ever realised it was happening.

"Oh, yes," Zebulon said. "You simply must stay, Sora. You have earned it, after all."

\* \* \*

*Meanwhile, things are tense between Sho Sange & Associates...*

Oni glared at Sho across Xen's cluttered desk. "You shouldn't have done that."

Sho scowled back at her. "I know, Oni!"

"He's your best friend."

"Since when did you become the voice of reason and compassion, anyway?"

"Well, someone had to be. This job has everything turned upside down. It might as well be me."

Sho sighed. "I didn't want to hurt anyone, Oni. You know that."

"Yes, I do know that." Now she smiled. "But now you don't have to. Buck up. It will all sort itself out."

Simon did not bother to knock as he entered the room. A shifty, rat-faced man in a cheap suit strode in behind him, looking rather unimpressive. The rat-faced man wiggled his eyebrows at Oni when he caught sight of her. She returned his leer with a dangerous glare.

The man in the cheap suit quelled under her gaze. "So, is it time, then?" he asked.

"About," Sho replied. He did not have to ask who the man was; Simon's discomfort in his presence was enough to recommend him. "We are waiting for the signal."

"What signal?" Simon demanded.

"Xen. That is, if he hasn't take off by now."

Oni shook her head. "No. He wouldn't just give up, not with Sora up there with Tan. As long as she is still in danger, he will stay with us until he's sure she is safe."

Simon sighed. "At least we have that to count on."

Hole sat in the scuffed leather wing-backed chair and kicked his feet up on Xen's desk, unsettling a stack of term papers. "So, if I'm not needed at the moment, where can I find some business around here?"

Simon scowled. "Can you focus, please? We have one job to do. You can go ruin people's lives when this is all done."

Holes held up his hands in surrender. "Okay, okay." He lifted his eyebrows at them. "I don't suppose any of you have a need? Young lady?"

Oni sneered at him. "No, thank you."

He shook his head in disappointment. "Well, you are a cheerful bunch, aren't you?"

\* \* \*

*Meanwhile, where all the action is...*

249

There was a quality to Zebulon's voice that Sora had never heard before. It unnerved her so thoroughly she felt a sudden rush of fear surge through her belly. There was something she didn't know; something she didn't understand. The sixth rune. What is the sixth rune? Suddenly, it seemed the only thing in the world of any importance at all.

But it didn't really matter, did it? What could possibly matter now?

She watched as her mentor picked up the long, thin-bladed dagger on the podium before him. For a moment, she thought he would set upon her with it, but instead he spun towards the blank spot on the wall, where he began to carve the seven runes. They were large and jagged, and the formations were crude, but she could feel magic building up in the room. The air was thickening until it was difficult to breathe.

She went over the spell in her mind. Seven incantations. That was all. She knew them all by heart. It had to happen when the seventh rune was charged. Not a moment sooner. Not a moment later. She did not know what would happen when the runes were cast, but she knew she had to keep her head.

Zebulon held up his hand, angling his palm towards the first rune. Heka. The formation glowed and undulated. Hu. It sparked to life as the one before it. The energy danced in the air around it. Yaya. The formation glittered. Thrall. There was darkness around this rune, and it seemed to be straining, trying to escape the prison of the wall upon which it was etched.

\* \* \*

*Meanwhile, there is a disturbance in the air...*

Xen prowled the courtyard like a large jungle cat confined to a cage. Something rippled in the air, and he drew to an abrupt stop. One ripple.

Two ripples.

"It's happening."

He was already racing across the courtyard towards the office when he felt the third disturbance in the magic around the Academy. He burst inside, his eyes burning.

Sho, Oni and Simon looked up at him in alarm. The other man, the one with the rat face just lifted an eyebrow.

"It's happening." Xen was slightly out of breath.

"What? Now?" Sho said, shooting to his feet.

"Yes. Now."

"Well, there might have been some warning," Simon complained.

Xen glared at him. "Sora would have warned us if she could. She must not have had the time."

"Well, he's keen, isn't he?" Holes asked the room at large.

"There is no time to sit around here cheeking about it," Xen snapped. "Go!"

They did not need told twice. They did not pause until they stood on the steps leading to Zebulon Tan's tower. Sho closed his eyes, extending his senses but though he could feel the disturbance in the skeins of energy around them, he could not determine anything else.

"Is it finished?" Sho demanded.

Xen shook his head. "No. I can feel it building. I felt three ripples." His face contorted. "Oh, there's another one."

"It's really weird how you can do that," Oni remarked.

"It's one of the perks of being a dark wizard," he told her wryly.

"Sho?" Oni looked up him, but he looked uncertain what to do next.

"We have to wait for the right moment. We have to seal the gate forever. We need to let him finish the spell."

"But what about when we get inside? You think he'll just let us perform the counter-spell?"

Sho's expression was grim. "No. I don't think he will. But he won't have time to do anything. We need to time the spell just right, so all that's left to do when we get inside is shove him into the gate."

"I like it," Oni told him cheerfully. "Burst inside, take him by surprise and send him to Hao. It just feels right."

"Sora is going to kill me," Xen said, scowling. "I promised I wouldn't kill him if I could help it."

"Well, we you can't help it," Sho snapped. "It's the only way to stop this. It's him or her."

"I know that," Xen replied coldly. For a long moment, they glared at each other.

"You just pay attention to what's going on in there," Sho ordered finally. "I'll worry about the spell."

Xen curled his lip, but he turned back to Zebulon's door.

\* \* \*

*Meanwhile, behind the door...*

Sora's heart raced. Thrall still glowed brightly, but Zebulon faltered on the next rune. The effort to charge the runes seemed to be sapping Zebulon's energy much more quickly than it ever had done. His face was drawn and pale, and there was weariness around his eyes. He wiped sweat from his brow.

"Can I help?" Her voice was almost inaudible in the quiet room. The energy around them filled their ears like a gales of howling wind.

Zebulon half turned towards her, and she was struck by the transformation he had undergone in those few short moments. He looked ancient and withered, frail and grizzled. He looked nothing like himself, and she understood finally that this was his true face. This was the true Zebulon, as he was when he was not disguised as the man she had known. Had he always been this way, or had it happened slowly, over time? Perhaps he was truly quite ill.

If he was only trying to save his life, could she stop him?

He turned fully upon her, and she recoiled from him. His eyes burned with feverish intensity. "You will, my dear." His voice was a feeble rasp. "You will be integral." Despite the fading quality of his voice, there was something terrifying in it.

She wanted to turn and race from the room, as Xen had wanted her to do, but she knew she could not. It was too late. There was nothing else to be done. She would see it through.

Zebulon took a deep, shallow breath. He lifted his hand to the fifth formation. It glowed only briefly before it seemed to sputter and the faint light died out.

He cursed vehemently. "No! No! I was so sure...I was sure I would be able..."

He took a step back from the wall. He closed his eyes and took several deep breaths, as though he were gathering his strength.

"Just three more," he muttered to himself. "Three more!"

Sora watched him. He sounded like a mad man, and she finally understood that he was just that.

# Chapter Thirteen

*Meanwhile, in Aether City...*

Two men sat across from each other in a dark street cafe. The hour was late, but the cafe was still bustling, though its fare had shifted from the daytime teas to the evening spirits. The two men did not speak to each other. There was little to say, for nothing would matter in a few more moments. They peered silently into each other's eyes; one pair Stygian dark, the other as pale blue as the sea.

Finally, the pale-eyed man spoke. "Are you sure about this?" His voice was subdued. There was no anger, no irritation or even austerity in it now.

"As sure as I can be in this situation, I suppose," Darius replied. "We don't have a lot of choice, do we? We have to let it play out."

"Shouldn't we be with our friends and family at a time like this?"

Darius lifted an elegantly arched eyebrow. "Do you have any of that?"

Ptolemy sighed. "No. You?"

"I have a wonderful masseuse named Enid, but she was otherwise engaged for the evening. It's just you and me. So, what do you want to do with your last moments on earth?"

The angel scowled. "Not spend them with you."

Darius looked offended. "Yes, well, it's not my ideal scenario, either."

Ptolemy sighed once more. "It was nice knowing you, Darius."

The fallen angel inclined his head. His mouth tightened in a grim line. "And you, Ptolemy. Perhaps next time..."

"Perhaps next time we'll end up on the same side, and we can actually be friends."

"Do you think there will be a next time?"

Ptolemy lifted his shoulders, but there was no hope upon his face.

\* \* \*

*And meanwhile, at a dodgy bar...*

Everyone in the Dirty Damastes looked grim. Tricks riffled his cards nervously. Unrequited Love reached over to still his hands. He looked up at her and sighed. "So this is the end? It's quite disappointing, isn't it?"

Minor Inconveniences lifted his shoulders. "Oh, it's not so bad. It might all pan out."

"You think so?" Tricks sounded overly eager, even to his own ears.

"Perhaps."

For a long moment, there was silence. Around them, the humans went about their business none the wiser, as though nothing at all had changed, but the others—the gods—they could feel the grimness in the air. They could feel that even their powers seemed to have weakened, for none of the humans were scuffling or being attacked by animals.

It really was the beginning of the end.

"Where's DC tonight?" Tricks asked, looking around the bar.

Unrequited Love shrugged. "Not here. I'm grateful for that. At least we won't have to spend our last hours with our powers directly correlating to the humans' behaviour."

Tricks sighed deeply. "Do you think...perhaps next time I will be reborn as a better god?"

"Could be," the hirsute man told him. "There's no way to know."

"We don't even know if we'll survive this thing," Severe Errors in Judgment added. "If the Shadow Council—"

"Shhh!" everyone but Tricks hissed at her. Tricks blinked at them all in surprise.

"Shadow Council?" he repeated.

"What?" Severe Errors in Judgment asked the others, looking around at them. "We're not supposed to know about that? I thought everyone knew about that."

"Not everyone knows about it," Unrequited Love snapped. "And I don't know how you learned, but since you did, you can be sure it's something you ought not to know."

"I don't understand," Tricks said.

The heartbreakingly beautiful woman tossed her dark hair. "It's nothing. Just...a bedtime story. Like a bogeyman for the gods. It's nothing to worry about, especially not tonight."

Tricks sighed. "There is so much I never learned." He leaned back in the stiff wooden seat, sipping his beer. "So this Shadow Council--"

"Do not say the name," the hirsute man ordered him sternly.

He ignored this. "It's the end of the world. What does it matter? Are they the ones handing out the powers?"

"No," Minor Inconveniences said in a low voice. "They don't hand out powers. They don't deal in power. They deal in balance."

Tricks frowned. "So, if the world is throw out of balance, maybe...maybe we'll be thrown out of balance. We could end up...the opposite of ourselves?"

"I don't see why that would be the case," the hirsute man replied grimly.

"But it could happen, yeah? We could...come back as something better? Someone who's good at something?"

"You really need to make peace with yourself, man," Minor Inconveniences told him. "This is the unmaking of everything. Are you going to let yourself die feeling so bitter?"

"That seems appropriate. My followers do often enough." Tricks considered. "Should I be drowning myself in a tank of water or something?"

"It wouldn't work," Unrequited Love told him. "You're just going to have to sit it out with the rest of us."

He sighed again. "This has been a very disappointing existence."

"Will you please shut your mouth?" the hirsute man snapped. "If we're going to die, I would like to do it in peace."

"I'm sorry. It's just...I just really hope I come back as the patron god of Superbly Successful Magic Tricks or something. Maybe something that doesn't even have to do with magic tricks. I would like to be...Good Taste or Serenity or something instead. Something cool. Something people like."

They were all quiet a moment. "I wouldn't mind coming back as Love Triangles," Unrequited Love piped in. "That sounds fun."

"What about you, Minor Inconveniences?" Tricks asked.

He didn't even have to think about it. "I'd like to be Defenestration."

They all looked at him, perplexed.

"What?" Unrequited Love asked.

"You know, throwing things out windows."

They stared at him in silence.

"What? I like throwing things out windows."

"Oh!" Severe Errors in Judgment exclaimed keenly. "I could be Conks on the Head, and we can still be friends."

They all turned to the hirsute man, who looked deeply contemplative.

"I think I would like to be…" He shook his head. "No. I would still like to be Animal Attacks."

They stared at him incredulously.

"What? Animal Attacks are awesome."

"See?" Severe Errors in Judgment said. "Maybe the unmaking of everything isn't the end of the world, after all."

"Oh, no," Unrequited Love replied grimly. "It is. It is the end of the world. That is exactly what it is."

They looked around at each other.

Animal Attacks lifted his glass to them. "Drink up."

\* \* \*

*Meanwhile, the night has never been so dark…*

Imogen halted abruptly. "Stop!"

The re-animated horrors that had been Argus Moon and Mercy Song jerked to a violent stop. Their bones rattled.

Imogen lifted her head, peering out over the dark hills upon which they travelled. The air rippled all around them. The universe was coming apart. She could feel it.

"It's happening already, my darlings." Her voice was a low, satisfied purr. "Someone has already begun my great work."

She began to laugh, softly at first and then louder and louder. Her laugh bounded over the hills and valleys, and no one left alive in Penthos could doubt that something very, very bad was about to happen.

\* \* \*

*Meanwhile, in the eye of the storm...*

"Zebulon?"

He looked back at her with burning eyes. "I am fine! Leave me be. Just wait for your part."

Something very bad was about to happen. She could feel it in her bones. Her heart raced.

He gritted his teeth. Janus. A flare of energy lit the fifth formation. The air shifted. The glow from the runes spread until it swirled around them, throwing them backward, away from the wall where a vortex was forming.

Sora blinked uncomprehending at the maelstrom. There was no rhyme, no reason or colour to the energy forming around them. She could make no sense of it at all. If she looked directly into the vortex, her eyes seemed to bounce off it, as though it was constantly moving.

Zebulon threw his head back and laughed. "Yes. Yes!"

Something shimmered in the swirling maelstrom. It was difficult to focus upon the spectre, as though its shape and features were constantly shifting and changing. Sora's head ached with the effort to understand the thing. She could not look at it directly, for it sent her mind spinning in confusion. Her thoughts raced uselessly around her brain, as difficult to grasp as the spectre's form.

Oh, god. It's already happening.

\* \* \*

*Meanwhile, in the corridor outside, things are much less exciting...*

"This is it," Xen said, gritting his teeth against the surge of energy that jolted his entire body. "He's done it."

"Are you sure?" Sho's voice was tight. "It was only the fifth rune."

"I'm sure! Go!"

The rat-faced man stepped forward. "I got this." He rubbed his hands together and blew on his fingers. "Step aside, dark man."

Xen backed away from the door, but he looked as though he was prepared to bolt into the room the moment it opened. Holes lifted his hands and grinned over his shoulder at them all.

Simon rolled his eyes. "Stop showing off and just get on with it."

Holes looked sulky. "Okay, okay." He lifted his hands and touched the door.

They waited.

"Um...okay." He lifted his hands again.

Nothing happened.

"Uh, guys..."

"What is it?" Sho demanded.

"Uh...well..."

"Why aren't we inside?" Oni snapped, holding up a threatening fist. "I thought you were good at this."

He looked sheepish. "Well...it rather seems as though there is something keeping me out."

"What do you mean something is keeping you out? You're a god!"

"Well...you know, there is always something that can negate my powers. It seems as though maybe...well, as though Last Minute Precautions has been here."

"Last Minute Precautions?" Simon growled.

"Oh, that cheeky, arrogant bastard. He loves messing with my mojo!"

"So you're telling us you can't get us in?" Sho asked.

"That's unfortunately exactly what I'm telling you."

Simon pinched the bridge of his nose. "Oh, god. I did that...I did it for nothing?"

Sho scowled. "Isn't there something you can do?"

Holes lifted his shoulders. "My being here negates his powers, but it negates mine too. I am, as they say, shooting blanks. Pardon the pun."

They all stared at him.

"There is not time for this," Xen said. "We have to get inside now."

"Sho?" Oni looked at him urgently, as though he might have some new answer to their dilemma.

Sho drew a finger across his palm in a slashing gesture. His blood spilled across the marble floor. Xen caught his arm and drew him away from the door.

"Don't bother." Xen's voice was low. His body vibrated with pent-up energy. "We knew it would come to this in the end."

Holes looked around at them, uncomprehending. They ignored him. "Xen, no!" Oni said, striding forward to catch his arm.

She rebounded off the swirl of black energy surging up around him. Sho caught her shoulders and drew her away from Xen. The dark magic surrounded him, obscuring him from their view and filling the air. It sent the others reeling back as it touched them.

The door blasted off its hinges. They did not waste time lamenting the inevitable loss of Xen's mind. They rushed into the room.

\* \* \*

*Meanwhile, trouble meets more trouble...*

Sora spun to them in shock. Xen stormed into the room, but he was not the man she had left this morning, in the afterglow of their night together. He looked so frightening, she recoiled from him. His eyes were pure, bottomless black. Tendrils of dark magic licked around his body, flying from his fingertips and issuing from his mouth as he bared his teeth like a wild dog.

"Xen, no." Her whisper was lost in the rush of deafening white noise from the maelstrom.

The creature shimmered in the vortex, coming closer and closer, but it still hovered behind the glimmering veil that separated their worlds, had separated them for centuries until Zebulon Tan had foolishly broken open the gate.

Zebulon stepped towards the creature, lifting a gnarled hand to it. He could not touch it, for his fingers could not breech the invisible barrier.

It wasn't finished. The spell wasn't done yet. They were too soon.

The old wizard did not even notice they were there. Xen rushed forward, though by now he seemed not to have any particular motivation for doing so. He was mindless, furious and determined to reach the old wizard.

He could not reach him; none of them could. The energy around the vortex caught them, sending their minds spinning and their feet walking in endless, futile circles. They called to each other, each lost in a blind and silent void.

Sora watched Xen and his friends as they spun round and round in confusion, bumping and rebounding off each other without realising the others were there. "Oh, thank god," she breathed.

She spun back to Zebulon, but he was rapt and silent. He made no sound, but he appeared to be speaking to the spectre. His mouth moved, but she could not hear the words if he spoke them aloud.

It was nearly time.

\* \* \*

The Haosul Cel had no features, no face or shape. Zebulon understood it now. The creature was pure chaos. The void beyond the creature yawned barren and senseless. Deep terror seized his chest.

What have I done?

Another voice invaded his thoughts. It was not a voice he knew, and it did not form words as he knew them, even the most ancient of languages, for if it had a tongue at all, it could not speak as a human tongue. It spoke in silent images and ideas in his mind, but he understood them all the same.

Why have you called me?

It took a moment to puzzle out, but Zebulon understood. "I need you. I need your gifts."

The Haosul Cel shimmered and shifted, and Zebulon did not know if it understood him, as well. Want out.

"I need you to make me whole again. Make me well."

ᴏᴜᴛ! ᴏᴜᴛ ᴏᴜᴛ ᴏᴜᴛ! The senseless words were like a scream bouncing off the walls of his mind.

"I will let you out. You have to give me what I want!"

The creature battered itself agitatedly against the barrier between their worlds. Then it seemed to stop, pressed against the veil like a punished child pressed against his window pane, peering down at the other children playing in the courtyard below. It lifted a tendril of its shapeless form, seeming to point at him through the barrier. Want. Want out!

"Make me well again!"

A desperate, impotent anger rippled through the barrier as the creature fought against the restraints separating their world. The spell was not yet complete. Open gate.

"You will give me what I want."

ʏᴇssssssss. ᴏᴜᴛ. ʟᴇᴛ ᴍᴇ ᴏᴜᴛ!

Zebulon glanced over his shoulder at his young assistant in the maelstrom beside him. Her heart-shaped face was pale with alarm, but she could not hear his words or make any more sense of the creature. His useless, defeated enemies flailed helplessly, caught up in the vortex in his periphery. He did not bother with them; they could do nothing now. It was too late. Far, far too late.

He lifted his hand to Sora. She looked back at him with large, innocent blue eyes. "It is time, Sora. I need you now."

\* \* \*

Sho yanked Oni back out of the vortex. She shrugged off his hand and raced headlong into the swirling energy around them. This time, she bounced off the wall Sho had thrown up around her and flew backward, landing on her bottom at his feet, dazed. Sho thought he could see stars hovering above her head, but when he blinked, they were gone. There was enough magic in the room to turn anyone utterly mad.

He cursed. "Sora, get out of there!" he shouted.

"No."

Sho looked around at Simon in surprise. "What do you mean no?"

Simon's mouth set in a grim line. "No!"

"What's wrong? What's happening?"

"This is very, very bad." He pinched the bridge of his nose. "Sho, start the spell."

"But we can't get in there! We can't get close enough!"

"You have to do it now!"

Sho had never heard Simon sound so alarmed. "What is happening?"

"It's the sixth rune. I know what it is now."

"What does it matter?"

"It matters! It's sacrifice."

Simon did not have to explain; Sho understood perfectly well. "Oh, no." His head snapped around to Xen, but even in his super-charged state, the dark wizard was useless in the maelstrom. Xen ploughed forward, growling in fury, but he could get no further than the periphery of the vortex. He seemed not to even realise it. His nostrils flared and his eyes burned black as cinder.

He was not completely lost. Not yet. Oni leapt to her feet, shaking her head as though to clear it. "Xen! Xen, you have to get in there! Save Sora! He's going to kill her!"

He seemed not to even notice she was there. She tried to reach for him, but Sho caught her arm to keep her from being caught back up in the mindless maelstrom.

"Sho, the spell!" Simon snapped.

Sho shoved Oni towards Simon and drew the spell from his pocket. He read the incantations quickly, but the vortex seemed to suck the ancient words from his throat. He could not know for sure they had been spoken aloud at all. He tried again.

Oni shoved Simon away. "But Tan's not done yet! You said he had to finish it."

"The sixth rune is sacrifice," Simon repeated. "And it appears as though he is about to charge it. I think we both know who he intends to use."

Oni paled alarmingly. "If he does this, if he sacrifices someone for his own gain..."

"You are smarter than I give you credit for. Yes. He will no longer be a pure, innocent soul."

Oni cupped her hands over her mouth to shout into the vortex. "Sora, get out of there!"

\* \* \*

Sora could not hear Oni and the others shouting at her from outside the vortex. She ignored them. They were of nothing now. They could do no good, be of no help. She was alone inside the maelstrom. She looked up at the Haosul Cel, rapt. She could not make sense of the thing, but she could feel the desire and the need pouring from it in terrible waves.

It was all directed at her.

She shuddered. It wanted her. She suddenly understood perfectly. She knew why Zebulon had taken her back so easily after their row. How foolish she had been. He'd never believed she'd come back to him. He'd never trusted her. She should have known from the beginning. It was as Sho had said. All powerful magic required blood. He needed her.

Zebulon was going to give the creature her blood.

She turned slowly away from the creature to look at her mentor. He was looking back at her, but he looked nothing like himself anymore. He was old and frail, but his eyes burned feverishly out of his wrinkled face. "I need you, Sora," he told her. "I have always needed you for this very moment."

Sora did not try to stop him. She watched him lift a hand to charge the last two runes. She could almost hear the creature speaking to him. Finish. Charge the runes and give her to me. Perhaps it was only Zebulon's intentions that she heard now. It did not matter.

It was time. Now, it was time. She spun towards the others. She did not know if they could hear her through the vortex, though she could see them quite clearly. Simon shifted uneasily from foot to foot. Oni shouted helplessly at her, frantically waving her arms, but it did not matter now what she meant to say. Sho seemed lost in a trance or perhaps he was performing the spell. Sora doubted his words could be of much good now, lost in the maelstrom. There was no other choice.

She turned to Xen. He marched determinedly in place, seeming not to even notice that he had not moved a single inch. His lips peeled back to reveal his startlingly white teeth. She could not touch him now, for she could not reach him through the maelstrom. Her heart sank as she realised it had all been for nothing. He had still gone over. He was still lost, and it had not saved anyone.

It didn't matter now. She was all that was left.

"Xen!" She did not care if Zebulon and the creature were waiting for her, waiting to lay open her belly and spill her blood. "Xen, I love you!"

She did not wait to see if he responded to these words, for it did not matter anymore than anything else. She said them because if they were to be her last coherent words, she would want nothing less. She spun back to Zebulon and the waiting creature. She knew the seven incantations by heart. She had been practising them in her mind since the moment she'd walked into the workroom.

The ancient words were little more than a whisper.

Zebulon's head snapped towards her. "What are you doing? What are you doing!"

He rushed towards her, but she spit out the last incantation, throwing her hands up towards the creature.

\* \* \*

"Oh, no!" Oni moaned.

"Another 'oh, no'?" Simon demanded irritably. "What could possibly be wrong now?"

"She's got the spell! She's doing the spell!"

"What?"

Oni rushed towards the vortex, and this time, Sho did not stop her. He shook his head from side to side, as though the Haosul Cel's chaos was creeping into his brain once more. "Xen! Xen, you have to get in there! You have to stop her!"

Simon grabbed Oni's arm and drew her back. "No, Oni." His voice was low and defeated. "I'm sorry. There is no other way. You know there isn't. It has to be like this."

"No! We can't let her! Xen!" She reached into the vortex now, fighting the senselessness that seemed to creep up into her mind from the place she touched the swirling energy. She caught Xen's hand, but he threw her off so violently, she flew back into Simon.

Oni didn't let this stop her. She screamed at him. "She is going to sacrifice herself! Sora is going to die!"

Something seemed to flicker in Xen's black eyes. For a moment, they looked almost as if they would return to normal. He stopped moving. He blinked several times, as though trying to make sense of his surroundings.

It was little good. Even if he threw off the black magic and returned to himself, the chaos still swirled around him.

Inside the circle, Sora chanted relentlessly.

"Stop!" Zebulon screamed. "What are you doing? Stop it!"

It was too late. She threw out her arms towards the centre of the maelstrom. The shimmering creature did not make a sound, but it seemed to scream in their minds, a long, maddening vibration that set their teeth rattling in their heads. Everyone but Sora covered their ears, but it did nothing to block out the noise in their head.

Sora ran straight into the centre of the vortex, into the arms of the Haosul Cel.

Energy exploded around them, throwing them back onto their bottoms on the marble floor. Xen rebounded against the wooden door, and through the haze of black magic he blinked, and then he finally saw.

"No!" Zebulon screamed, clawing at the barrier as though he could reach in and draw the Haosul Cel back into their world.

The vortex was shrinking smaller and smaller, drawing in on itself towards its centre, bringing Sora, Zebulon and the Haosul Cel along with it.

Xen shot to his feet. He raced towards Sora as though he intended to throw himself into the vortex with her. "No!"

Sho leapt up to stop him, but he flew backwards, blasted off his feet by a burst of Xen's black magic.

"Sora!"

She was receding before his eyes.

He leapt for her, but he slammed into the blank, barren wall. The vortex had disappeared without so much as a pop of noise.

There was silence around them. Sora was gone.

"No!" Xen pounded the wall with his fist, as though he might be able to break it open and yank her back out. "No! Sora!" His fingernails scraped the plaster, but nothing happened.

He stepped back and threw out his hand. A burst of black energy shot from his palm and blasted a hole in the tower wall. The night air swirled into the room, chilly and crisp.

There was no gate. No Haosul Cel. No Sora. No Zebulon Tan.

She was gone. Truly gone.

The energy drained from Xen's body. His eyes turned to normal, and he sunk to his knees. His voice was nothing more than a ragged whisper. "Sora."

# CHAPTER FOURTEEN

*M*eanwhile, the night has gotten a little bit brighter...

Imogen paused. She frowned. Whatever had been in the air, whatever had disrupted the delicate fabric of Pandia's magic was done. It had stopped.

She sighed deeply. "What a disappointment."

Then she turned to smile at her gruesome meat puppets. "Oh, well. Not to worry, my dears. At least this way I'll get to be the one to take credit for it."

\* \* \*

*Meanwhile, meanwhile, on a crimson beach in Scathach...*

Darklord Blood and his wife strolled hand and hand along the sandy scarlet shore in the Blood Domain. Blood paused abruptly, looking out at the frothy red water. "Did you hear something?"

Lady Blood lifted an eyebrow. "The spirit?"

"No. Something else. Something...I don't know." His still handsome face screwed up in concentration. "It seems as though something rather important has just occurred, and then it just...stopped."

His wife laughed. "Don't be ridiculous, darling. What sort of important thing could possibly have happened?"

His elegant dark eyebrows rose archly.

Lady Blood smiled. "Ah. Well. I see."

He tugged gently on her hand, guiding her to continue their leisurely stroll. He was silent a long moment. "I suppose perhaps that son of ours is not so worthless after all."

She nudged him playfully. "You know he isn't. He's your son, after all."

"Do you suppose he really did just stop the unmaking of the world?"

"Well, if he did, I don't suppose that will compel you to give him a pass just this once?"

Lord Blood snorted inelegantly. "Not likely."

"Well, a mother does have to try."

* * *

*Meanwhile in the Dirty Damastes...*

Everyone in the bar gave a little jolt. Tricks looked around bemusedly. Suddenly, everything was back to normal, as though a dark cloud had lifted from the mood in the room. Nothing had actually happened, so far as he could tell, but the sense of utter relief all around him was almost palpable. A man at the bar motioned the publican and bought everyone in the tavern a round of drinks.

Tricks blinked around at his friends. "Is it over, then?"

"It seems to be." Unrequited Love's voice was subdued.

"We're all still here," Animal Attacks said, patting his hirsute chest and beard as though to ensure every hair was still firmly in place.

"Nothing's changed," Minor Inconveniences added in a falsely cheerful voice.

They all looked at each other silently. Then they sighed in disappointment.

"Obviously not," Unrequited Love said stiffly.

Tricks sighed deeply. "Well. This has been a really dissatisfying day."

Severe Errors in Judgment pushed a beer across the table to him. "Drink up."

* * *

*In the meantime, at Sho Sange and Associates...*

Hyde leaned over Panya's shoulder. "I think that piece goes there. Here. Give me the screwdriver."

Panya's cheeks heated. She clutched the screwdriver as though she would never let it go.

"Panya." Even his voice was like velvet. How did he change his voice like that, too? He wrapped his long, slender fingers around hers and gently pried the screwdriver from them. He rested a hand on her shoulder to brace himself as he bent over the busted open brass ball in front of her. Its clockwork innards ground and sputtered in jerky, awkward motions.

She snatched the screwdriver back from him. "I know where it goes!" she snapped.

The tall, dark handsome man rounded the table and lifted an arch eyebrow at her. Her cheeks blazed. She turned her head sharply away from him.

"I wonder how the team is doing." His tone was deceptively casual, and she glanced back to him. He smiled, which only made matters worse. It was such a gorgeous smile...

She clutched at this new topic keenly. "Oh, they're probably mucking everything up by now. I wonder if we're all going to die."

The handsome Hyde considered this. "Do you think we'll notice when it happens?"

"Probably. I think we'll definitely know."

He eyed her contemplatively.

"What?" she demanded.

He lifted his broad shoulders. "Nothing. If you say so. I'm sure you're right."

"I am right! I have a very keen sense of what is happening in the aether."

He looked amused, and she couldn't hold his dark, glittering gaze. This form was very unnerving.

She bent back over the twisted clockwork. "Hand me that wrench, will you?"

\* \* \*

*Additionally meanwhile, at a street cafe in Aether City...*

Darius opened his eyes and blinked around at the cafe. It was still there. He was still there. Ptolemy was still there, and Darius was gripping his hand and huddling beside the angel as though they might brace each other against the onslaught of the unmaking of everything. The unmaking of everything that hadn't come.

The two angels, one heavenly and the other infernal, gasped and dropped each other's hands as though they might burn them.

They avoided each other's eyes awkwardly.

"Well," Darius said flatly.

"Yes, well..."

"So. The world's..."

"It's still here."

"Right."

"So your people managed it after all."

Darius drew himself up indignantly. "Well, I did tell you they were the best."

Ptolemy's smooth, pale face looked unusually pink. "Right, well…"

"Yes, well."

"If that's it, then."

"Yes, that's it."

Without awaiting a reply or bidding Darius farewell, Ptolemy suddenly lifted up into the sky and was gone in a flash of heavenly light. At the same moment, Darius snapped his fingers and disappeared in a puff of smoke.

A young waiter in a very crispy white uniform stopped at their table, carrying two drinks. He blinked in surprise when he found his two customers had disappeared with hardly a trace. "I thought they wanted another round."

Five banknotes lay in the centre of the table. Three of them seemed to have holes burnt into them. His nose wrinkled. The notes would barely cover the drinks they'd had, and so much for a tip.

There was a distinct smell of sulphur in the air.

The waiter sighed deeply. "Not again. I will be happy when this nightmare shift is over."

\* \* \*

*Meanwhile, where it has all happened…*

"Is it over?" Holes poked his rat-face into the workroom from the corridor, where he had been cowering through the entire affair. Not that Simon minded; he could have been of little help. None of them had been of any help, when it came down to it.

They all looked around. The room was quiet. The swirling, chaotic maelstrom was gone. The runes Zebulon Tan had etched upon the blank wall were gone, lost when the wall had blown apart. A soft, gentle breeze swirled the loose papers around the workshop.

There was no sign of the misguided wizard or his assistant.

Xen knelt in front of the gaping hole in the wall, his head in his hands. He muttered to himself, his voice low and desperate. He only spoke one word. Sora.

Oni pushed herself to her feet and stumbled over to him. She reached for his shoulder. "Xen? It's…it's over. Xen, we should go--"

"No!" His voice was a roar, and his eyes burned furiously as he glanced over his shoulder at her. She recoiled from him. "No. I have to get back in. I have to go get her!"

Sho rose to his feet. His expression was cold, but there was a horrible sadness in his eyes. "Xen, I am sorry. There is no way. The gate...it's closed. Forever."

"No!" Xen surged to his feet and advanced angrily upon his old friend. "I'm not going to let her go. I'm not going to leave her there!"

"I am sorry, Xen." Simon sounded hoarse. "But...but she is probably already dead. Humans cannot live in Hao. It is pure chaos. She would be torn apart. She's gone."

This did not soothe Xen. His eyes gleamed, and his body vibrated with the pent-up black magic inside him. They braced themselves, for it was only a matter of time before the dam broke again, when his rage overwhelmed his confusion and grief. "No! How can this—how can she—"

"She chose this, Xen," Oni told him gently. "There was no other way. Without her—"

"You said we could use Tan! You said she wouldn't have to be the one. You said it was sorted out!"

Simon shook his head sadly. "Tan was going to sacrifice her to save himself. He was no longer pure and innocent. He was a killer. She was the only one."

"Besides that, we couldn't reach her," Oni said. "I tried. We couldn't do anything once she was inside that vortex."

Xen turned his burning glare on Sho. "You could have stopped her. You should have stopped her! Why didn't you stop her?"

"Xen..." Sho took a deep breath. "You know there was nothing I could do. None of us could get through that, and I couldn't even perform the spell. If not for Sora—she was the only one who kept her head. She is the one who stopped this. She chose her own path."

Xen's eyes darkened alarmingly. Tendrils of black magic swirled around him.

"Xen, no!" Oni cried.

Sho reached forward and gripped Xen's shoulder. A painful shock shot up Sho's arm, but he ignored it. He gritted his teeth and held on. "Xen, you cannot go down that path. You know what will happen if you do."

Xen's voice was a low, guttural growl. "I don't care. I don't care! Nothing matters now. She's gone." He threw up his hand, and the others flew backward from the force of the blast, crashing against tables and cabinets, shattering glass and scattering books.

He spun and raced full speed towards the hole in the tower.

Sho scrambled to his feet, but he was not quick enough to catch his friend. "Xen, no!"

Xen leapt out of the tower, into the night.

They rushed to the blown open wall. Oni didn't stop herself in time, and teetered dangerously near the edge. Sho pulled her back, rolling his eyes.

Below, Xen's dark figure landed on his feet, bending at the knees to brace himself. He should not have survived the jump, but it seemed not to even have fazed him. He did not look back up at his friends. He streaked across the courtyard with superhuman speed, into the darkness, and then he was simply gone.

"Well," Simon said grimly.

They looked around at each other.

"Well," Holes added from the doorway. "This has become rather awkward. I think I'll just head back to the bar now and see what kind of business I can stir up."

No one paid him any attention, and he backed slowly and quietly away.

"Do you think he'll be back?" Oni asked in a hushed voice.

"No, and I expect he'll steer clear of me the next time I go looking for a favour round the Dirty Damastes," Simon said.

She scoffed. "Not him! Xen!"

Sho sighed. "It's hard to say."

"We'll have to hunt him down, won't we?"

"It's us or the Lumina."

"Oh, this is just great," Simon snapped. "Honestly, could we possibly have mucked this up any worse?"

Sho and Oni turned to him in a single movement. "Yes," Sho said positively. "Yes, we could have. The world could be unmade."

They stared at each other silently a moment.

"Right," Simon said. "So, success."

"Anyone feel like celebrating?" Oni asked half-heartedly.

"No."

\* \* \*

*Finally, outside a dodgy bar...*

Simon peered up at the battered wooden sign. The Dirty Damastes. He sighed, wondering what he was even doing there, but it seemed an appropriate place the end the entire terrible debacle. He squared his shoulders and stepped inside the old, dusty tavern. He passed the beautiful, dark-haired woman on her way to the bar. Unrequited Love did not bother to sneer at him. She simply stared wearily at him.

He inclined his head and hurried by. He did not stop at the table where a hirsute man sat with a nondescript man, a blue-haired woman and a wild-haired clown inexpertly riffling a deck of cards. An air of dejection hung over them. They gazed up at him with resentful eyes.

He frowned at them. It wasn't as though it was his fault things had not gone according to plan. At least they'd stopped it before the entire world was unmade.

The rat-faced man lifted an eyebrow as Simon approached the table at which he sat with his ubiquitous drinking companions, Potentially Violent Scuffles and Fainting. "Well!" Holes said, rising to slap him on the back. "Simon! I didn't expect to see you here again. Do you need another favour already?"

Simon sighed. "No. I just...wanted a drink."

"Sit, sit." Fainting kicked out a chair for him. Simon eyed it warily for a moment, but he'd come all this way, and for a purpose. He dropped into the chair with a long-suffering sigh.

Holes waved at the waitress for another round of the frothy beer. When she returned to the table, Simon's three companions leaned forward with eager, leering expressions.

Nothing happened.

Simon smiled at her. "Thank you, miss."

She gave him a sweet smile and spun away. His companions leaned back in their seats and sipped their beers in disappointment.

A sudden breeze swirled through the bar, lifting the pretty waitress's skirt. Simon's companions leaned forward again in excitement.

She wore frilly pink bloomers underneath her short skirt. She slapped a hand over her bottom to cover them, but there was no real urgency in her movement. She glanced over her shoulder at them and fluttered her eyelashes. She pressed a coy finger to her lips. "Whoops."

Holes and his friends sighed in disappointment, turned back to their beers as she trounced away, giggling. "So, Simon...how are things with you?"

Simon shrugged.

"I heard you all saved the world and such," Potentially Violent Scuffles said.

"No, not us. A sweet young girl." Simon's mouth turned down sadly. "She gave her life for all of us."

They were quiet as they sipped their beers, pondering this bit of human grace. They watched a young man sidle up to the bar to chat up two pretty young ladies. As he turned to the publican to order them all a drink, his belt buckle snapped. He caught the waistband as they fell, but not before the ladies caught a glimpse of his bottom, which was clad in boxers with little pink kittens batting around a ball of yarn.

He turned back to the ladies with a leer. "Whoops." He thrust out his hips to display his kitten boxers as he re-fastened his belt. "I must have lost control of my mojo."

The ladies giggled to each other. "Kittens. Little pink kittens."

The man looked bemused. "Can I buy any of you ladies a drink?"

They did not reply to this. They fell upon each other, overwhelmed with laughter.

Simon smiled pleasantly at his companions.

"Uh...so, how is the rest of the team?" Holes asked distractedly. "Are they coping?"

Simon's expression grew grave. His voice was low. "I would not say they're coping. Xen is still AWOL. We haven't heard of him razing any cities yet, but it's only a matter of time. Sho and Oni are still out hunting for him."

"He'll be sorry if the Lumina catches him first," Fainting put in breathlessly.

"Yes. He will." Simon sighed, and silence resumed.

Across the bar, a homely woman with thick scarlet lipstick cornered a long-suffering man against the bar, pressing her hand to his chest as she giggled coyly up at him. She pressed closer to him, and the buttons of her shirt caught the long, gold chain around his neck. Simon's companions watched eagerly. Her collar popped open, revealing a grimy, yellowing camisole underneath. The man looked away in disgust. The woman tittered, half-heartedly covering her exposed underthings.

Holes frowned. "What the hell is going on, Simon? It's usually so much fun having you around."

To his astonishment, Simon grinned. He did not reply to this. He sipped his beer contentedly. Then he sighed. "I do hope they find Xen before something dreadful happens."

They all looked at him incredulously.

"What? Well, he is hopped up on black magic. He shouldn't be allowed to be loose in the world. We need to bring him back to himself." He considered this. "I'm not sure he'll make it out this time. Truth to tell, I'm not sure he wants to. Perhaps the darkness is better than coming back to what he's lost." He glanced sadly down at his beer.

They stared at him.

A young, muscular man slowed as he passed a table of young, pretty women. Somehow, his white tee-shirt snagged on a red-head's barrette and ripped down the middle. He paused, trying to look embarrassed. Then he flexed his rippling muscles and wiggled his eyebrows at them.

They women stared at him for several seconds, and then they burst into laughter. He looked down, confused, and discovered he was wearing a lacy red corset beneath the tee-shirt. His cheeks flamed, and he clutched the tee-shirt around him, hurrying out of the tavern without a single glance back at the giggling women.

Simon's three companions turned to look at him.

He looked innocent. It had been a long time since he'd simply enjoyed a drink, especially in the Dirty Damastes. He smiled at his friends. "It's nice to be able to talk about this. Panya and Hyde are too busy pretending not to flirt with each other to bend a sympathetic ear, and there's nothing much else to do with everyone else running off across Pandia trying to rein in the rogue black wizard." He sighed. "It would have been nice if I could have kept my job at the Academy, though, but, well...well, they said there was just too much...embarrassment when I was around."

Holes lifted his eyebrows. "Speaking of that."
274

Simon ignored him. His face lit up. "Oh! Here's my friend now."

They turned to look at the woman who approached their table. She was tall and curvy. Her long, gauzy, shapeless dress was unexpectedly revealing, as bits of her anatomy seemed to be scarcely covered by the thin, sheer material. Her hips swayed as she moved closer to them. She smiled at them as they gaped at her, but her blush was rather coy. She swept aside her skirt to sit beside Simon, treating the men to a view of one pale, smooth thigh.

"Hello, boys." Her voice was a demure purr.

"I was wondering when you were going to stop playing around over there," Simon told her. He looked positively delighted to see her.

She tittered, waving her hand at him. "I had to have a little fun since you dragged me away from that beauty pageant in Aether City." She rolled her eyes and turned to Simon's companions conspiratorially. "Simon simply loathes going anywhere without me."

They goggled at her.

She smiled radiantly. "The trouble is, I am a very busy woman." She held out her hand to Holes. "It is a pleasure to meet you all. I'm False Modesty." She winked. "But you can call me Claire."


THE END

# ABOUT THE AUTHOR

Stella Drexler is the author of several science fiction and fantasy novels, instruction manuals, essays, articles, and shopping lists. She lives in Dallas, Texas and enjoys doing things that are fun. For more about Stella and her ill-advised adventures, visit her blog Books, Monkeys and Cheeky Dreams at

www.stelladrexler.wordpress.com

**More books by Stella:**

Nightmare Island Book One: False Awakening

Nightmare Island Book Two: Dream Walker

Rebel Grey

Angel of the Abyss

Hex Breaker

CHANT

Little Agnes and the Ghosts of Kelpie Wharf

And the newly released: Wandering Star

www.ingramcontent.com/pod-product-compliance
Lightning Source LLC
Chambersburg PA
CBHW020247180626
46810CB00006B/2405